Henry James

Transatlantic Sketches

Anatiposi

Henry James

Transatlantic Sketches

Reprint of the original, first published in 1875.

1st Edition 2024　|　ISBN: 978-3-38282-951-3

Anatiposi Verlag is an imprint of Outlook Verlagsgesellschaft mbH.

Verlag (Publisher): Outlook Verlag GmbH, Zeilweg 44, 60439 Frankfurt, Deutschland
Vertretungsberechtigt (Authorized to represent): E. Roepke, Zeilweg 44, 60439 Frankfurt, Deutschland
Druck (Print): Books on Demand GmbH, In de Tarpen 42, 22848 Norderstedt, Deutschland

TRANSATLANTIC SKETCHES.

BY

HENRY JAMES, Jr.

BOSTON:
JAMES R. OSGOOD AND COMPANY,
LATE TICKNOR & FIELDS, AND FIELDS, OSGOOD, & CO.
1875

CONTENTS.

vi

Transatlantic Sketches.

CHESTER.

Chester, May, 1872.

IF the Atlantic voyage is counted, as it certainly may be, even with the ocean in a fairly good humor, an emphatic zero in the sum of one's better experience, the American traveller arriving at this venerable town finds himself transposed, without a sensible gradation, from the edge of the New World to the very heart of the Old. It is almost a misfortune, perhaps, that Chester lies so close to the threshold of England; for it is so rare and complete a specimen of an antique town, that the later-coming wonders of its sisters in renown — of Shrewsbury, Coventry, and York — suffer a trifle by comparison, and the tourist's appetite for the picturesque just loses its finer edge. Yet the first impressions of an observant American in England — of our old friend the sentimental tourist — stir up within him such a cloud of sensibility that while the charm is still unbroken, he may perhaps as well dispose, mentally, of the greater as of the less. I have been playing at first impressions for the second time, and have won the game against a cynical adversary. I have been strolling and restrolling along the ancient

wall — so perfect in its antiquity — which locks this
dense little city in its stony circle, with a certain friend
who has been treating me to a bitter lament on the
decay of his relish for the picturesque. " I have turned
the corner of youth," is his ceaseless plaint; " I suspected it, but now I know it, — now that my heart
beats but once where it beat a dozen times before, and
that where I found sermons in stones and pictures in
meadows, delicious revelations and intimations ineffable, I find nothing but the stern, dark prose of British
civilization." But little by little I have grown used to
my friend's sad monody, and indeed feel half indebted
to it as a warning against cheap infatuations.

I defied him, at any rate, to spoil the walls of Chester
for me. There could be no better example of that
phenomenon so delightfully frequent in England, — an
ancient monument or institution, lovingly readopted
and consecrated to some modern amenity. The good
Cestrians may boast of their walls, without a shadow
of that mental reservation on grounds of modern ease,
which is so often the tax paid by the picturesque; and
I can easily imagine, that though most modern towns
contrive to get on comfortably without this stony girdle, these people should have come to regard theirs as
à prime necessity. For through it, surely, they may
know their city more intimately than their uncinctured
neighbors, — survey it, feel it, rejoice in it as many
times a day as they please. The civic consciousness,
sunning itself thus on the city's rim, and glancing at
the little, swarming, towered, and gabled town within,
and then at the blue undulations of the near Welsh

border, may easily deepen to delicious complacency.
The wall encloses the town in a continuous ring, which,
passing through innumerable picturesque vicissitudes,
often threatens to snap, but never fairly breaks the
link; so that starting at any point, an hour's easy stroll
will bring you back to your station. I have quite lost
my heart to this charming wall, and there are so many
things to be said about it that I hardly know where to
begin. The great fact, I suppose, is that it contains a
Roman substructure, and rests for much of its course
on foundations laid by that race of master-builders.
But in spite of this sturdy origin, much of which is
buried in the well-trodden soil of the ages, it is the
gentlest and least offensive of ramparts, and completes
its long irregular curve without a frown or menace in
all its disembattled stretch. The earthy deposit of
time has, indeed, in some places climbed so high about
its base, that it amounts to no more than a terrace of
modest proportions. It has everywhere, however, a
rugged outer parapet and a broad hollow flagging, wide
enough for two strollers abreast. Thus equipped, it
wanders through its adventurous circuit; now sloping,
now bending, now broadening into a terrace, now narrowing into an alley, now swelling into an arch, now
dipping into steps, now passing some thorn-screened
garden, and now reminding you that it was once a
more serious matter than all this, by the occurrence of
a rugged, ivy-smothered tower. Its present mild innocence is increased, to your mind, by the facility with
which you can approach it from any point in the town.
Every few steps as you go you see some little court or

1 *

alley boring toward it through the close-pressed houses.
It is full of that delightful element of the crooked, the
accidental, the unforeseen, which, to American eyes, accustomed to our eternal straight lines and right angles,
is the striking feature of European street scenery. An
American strolling in the Chester streets finds a perfect
feast of crookedness, — of those random corners, projec-
tions, and recesses, odd domestic interspaces charmingly saved or lost, those innumerable architectural
surprises and caprices and fantasies which offer such a
delicious holiday to a vision nourished upon brown-stone
fronts. An American is born to the idea that on his
walks abroad it is perpetual level wall ahead of him, and
such a revelation as he finds here of infinite accident
and infinite effect gives a wholly novel zest to the use of
his eyes. It produces, too, the reflection — a superficial and fallacious one, perhaps — that amid all this
cunning chiaroscuro of its *mise en scène*, life must have
more of a certain homely entertainment. It is at least
no fallacy to say that childhood — or the later memory
of childhood — must borrow from such a background
a kind of anecdotical wealth. We all know how in
the retrospect of later moods the incidents of early
youth "compose," visibly, each as an individual picture,
with a magic for which the greatest painters have no
corresponding art. There is a vivid reflection of this
magic in some of the early pages of Dickens's "Cop-
perfield" and of George Eliot's "Mill on the Floss,"
the writers having had the happiness of growing up
among old, old things. Two or three of the phases of
this rambling wall belong especially to the class of

things fondly remembered. In one place it skirts the edge of the cathedral graveyard, and sweeps beneath the great square tower and behind the sacred east window of the choir. Of the cathedral there is more to say; but just the spot I speak of is the best standpoint for feeling how fine an influence in the architectural line — where theoretically, at least, influences are great — is the massive tower of an English abbey, dominating the homes of men; and for watching the eddying flight of swallows make vaster still to the eye the large calm fields of stonework. At another point, two battered and crumbling towers, decaying in their winding-sheets of ivy, make a prodigiously picturesque diversion. One inserted in the body of the wall and the other connected with it by a short, crumbling ridge of masonry, they contribute to a positive jumble of local color. A shaded mall wanders at the foot of the rampart; beside this passes a narrow canal, with locks and barges and burly watermen in smocks and breeches; while the venerable pair of towers, with their old red sandstone sides peeping through the gaps in their green mantles, rest on the soft grass of one of those odd fragments of public garden, a crooked strip of ground turned to social account, which one meets at every turn, apparently, in England, — a tribute to the needs of the "masses." *Stat magni nominis umbra.* The quotation is doubly pertinent here, for this little garden-strip is adorned with mossy fragments of Roman stonework, bits of pavement, altars, and baths, disinterred in the local soil. England is the land of small economies, and the present rarely fails to find good use for the odds and ends of the past. These two hoary shells of masonry are therefore converted into "museums," receptacles for the dustiest and shabbiest of tawdry back-parlor curiosities. Here preside a couple of those grotesque creatures, à la Dickens, whom one finds squeezed into every cranny of English civilization, scraping a thin subsistence, like mites in a mouldy cheese.

Next after its wall — possibly even before it — Chester values its Rows, — an architectural idiosyncrasy which must be seen to be appreciated. They are a sort of Gothic edition of the blessed arcades of Italy, and consist, roughly speaking, of a running public passage, tunnelled through the second story of the houses. The low basement is thus directly on the drive-way, to which a flight of steps descends, at frequent intervals, from this superincumbent veranda. The upper portion of the houses projects to the outer line of the arcade, where they are propped with pillars and posts and parapets. The shop-fronts face along the arcade, and admit you to little caverns of traffic, more or less dusky according to their opportunities for illumination in the rear. If the picturesque is measured by its hostility to our modern notions of convenience, Chester is probably the most picturesque city in the world. This arrangement is endlessly rich in opportunities for effect. But the full charm of the architecture of which it is so essential a part must be observed from the street below. Chester is still an antique city, and mediæval England sits bravely under her gables. Every third house is a " specimen," — gabled and latticed, timbered and carved, and wearing its years more or less lightly. These ancient dwellings present every shade and degree of historical color and expression. Some are dark with neglect and deformity, and the horizontal slit admitting light into the lurking Row seems to collapse on its dislocated props like a pair of toothless old jaws. Others stand there square-shouldered and sturdy, with their beams painted and straightened, their plaster whitewashed, their carvings polished, and the low casement covering the breadth of the frontage adorned with curtains and flower-pots. It is noticeable that the actual townsfolk have bravely accepted the situation bequeathed by the past, and the large number of rich and intelligent restorations of the old façades speaks well both for their tastes and their means. These elaborate and ingenious repairs attest a pious reverence for the peculiar stamp of the city. I indeed suspect many of these fresh antiques of being better royalists than the king, and of having been restored with interest. About the genuine antiques there would be properly a great deal to say, for they are really a theme for the philosopher ; but the theme is too heavy for my pen, and I can give them but the passing tribute of a sigh. They are fatally picturesque. — horribly eloquent. Fix one of them with your gaze, and it seems fairly to reek with mortality. Every stain and crevice seems to syllable some human record, — a record of unillumined lives. I have been trying hard to fancy them animated by the children of "Merry England," but I am quite unable to think of them save as peopled by the victims of dismal old-world pains and fears. Human life, surely, packed away behind those impenetrable lattices of lead and bottle-glass, just above which the black outer beam marks the suffocating nearness of the ceiling, can have expanded into but scanty freedom and bloomed into little sweetness.

. Nothing has struck me more in my strolls along the Rows than the fact that the most zealous observation can keep but uneven pace with the fine differences in national manners. Some of the most sensible of these differences are yet so subtle and indefinable that one must give up the attempt to express them, though the omission leaves but a rough sketch. As you pass with the bustling current from shop to shop, you feel local custom and tradition — the foreign tone of things — pressing on you from every side. The tone of things is, somehow, heavier than with us; manners and modes are more absolute and positive; they seem to swarm and to thicken the atmosphere about you. Morally and physically it is a denser air than ours. We seem loosely hung together at home as compared with the English, every man of whom is a tight fit in his place. It is not an inferential, but a palpable fact, that England is a crowded country. There is stillness and space — grassy, oak-studded space — at Eaton Hall, where the Marquis of Westminster dwells (or I believe can afford to humor his notion of *not* dwelling), but there is a crowd and a hubbub in Chester. Wherever you go, the population has overflowed. You stroll on the walls at eventide, and you hardly find elbow-room. You haunt the cathedral shades, and a dozen sauntering mortals temper your solitude. You glance up an alley or side street, and discover populous windows and doorsteps. You roll along country roads, and find countless humble pedestrians dotting the green waysides. The English landscape is always a "landscape with figures." And everywhere you go, you are accompanied by a vague consciousness of the British child hovering about your knees and coat-skirts, naked, grimy, and portentous. You reflect, with a sort of physical relief, on Australia, Canada, and India. Where there are many men, of course there are many needs; which helps to justify to the philosophic stranger the vast number and the irresistible coquetry of the little shops which adorn these low-browed Rows. The shop-fronts have always seemed to me the most æsthetic things in England; and I waste more time than I should care to confess to in covetous contemplation of those vast, clear panes, behind which the nether integuments of gentlemen are daintily suspended from glittering brass rods. The manners of the dealers in these comfortable wares seldom fail to confirm your agreeable impressions. You are thanked with effusion for expending twopence, — a fact of deep significance to the truly analytic mind, and which always seems to me a vague reverberation from certain of Miss Edgeworth's novels, perused in childhood. When you think of the small profits, the small jealousies, the long waiting, and the narrow margin for evil days implied by this redundancy of shops and shopmen, you hear afresh the steady rumble of that deep key-note of English manners, overscored so often, and with such sweet beguilement, by finer harmonies, but never extinguished, — the " struggle for existence."

The Rows are picturesque and entertaining, and it is a pity that, thirty years ago, when they must have been more so, there was no English Balzac to introduce them into realistic romance, with a psychological commentary. But the cathedral is better, modestly as it stands on the roll of English abbeys. It is of moderate dimensions, and rather meagre in form and ornament; but to an American it is a genuine cathedral, and awakens all the proper emotions. Among these is a certain irresistible regret that so much of its hoary substance should give place to the fine, fresh-colored masonry with which Mr. Gilbert Scott — that man of many labors — is so intelligently investing it. The red sandstone of the primitive structure, darkened and devoured by time, survives in many places, in frowning mockery of all of this modern repair. The great tower, however, — completely restored, — rises high enough to seem to belong, as cathedral towers should, to the far-off air that vibrates with the chimes and the swallows, and to square serenely, east and west and south and north, its embossed and fluted sides. English cathedrals, within, are apt at first to look pale and naked; but after a while, if the proportions are fair and the spaces largely distributed, when you perceive the light beating softly down from the cold clerestory and your eye measures caressingly the tallness of columns and the hollowness of arches, and lingers on the old genteel inscriptions of mural marbles and brasses; and, above all, when you become conscious of that sweet, cool mustiness in the air which seems to haunt these places, like the very climate of Episcopacy, you may grow to feel that they are less the empty shells of a departed faith than the abodes of a faith which is still a solid institution and "establishment." Catholicism has gone, but the massive respectability of Anglicanism is a rich enough substitute. So at least it seemed to me, a Sunday or two since, as I sat in the choir at Chester, awaiting a discourse from Canon Kingsley. The Anglican service had never seemed to my profane sense so much an affair of magnificent intonations and cadences, — of pompous effects of resonance and melody. The vast oaken architecture of the stalls among which we nestled, — somewhat stiffly, and with a due apprehension of wounded ribs and knees, — climbing vainly against the dizzier reach of the columns, — the beautiful English voices of certain officiating canons, — the little rosy " king's scholars " sitting ranged beneath the pulpit, in white-winged surplices, which made their heads, above the pew-edges, look like rows of sleepy cherubs, — every element in the scene gave it a great spectacular beauty. They suggested, too, what is suggested in England at every turn, that conservatism here has all the charm, and leaves dissent and democracy and other vulgar variations nothing but their bald logic. Conservatism has the cathedrals, the colleges, the castles, the gardens, the traditions, the associations, the fine names, the better manners, the poetry; Dissent has the dusky brick chapels in provincial by-streets, the names out of Dickens, the uncertain tenure of the *h*, and the poor *mens sibi conscia recti*. Differences which in other countries are slight and varying, almost metaphysical, as one may say, are marked in England by a gulf. Nowhere else does the degree of one's respectability involve such solid consequences, and I am sure I don't wonder that the sacramental word which with us (and in such correlatives as they possess, more or less among the continental races) is pronounced lightly and facetiously, and as a quotation from the Philistines, is uttered here with a perfectly grave face. To have the courage of one's opinions is in short to have a prodigious deal of courage, and I think one must need as much to be a Dissenter as one needs patience not to be a duke. Perhaps the Dissenters (to limit the question to them) manage to stay out of the church by thinking exclusively of the sermon. Canon Kingsley's discourse was one more example of the familiar truth, — not without its significance to minds zealous for the good old fashion of "making an effort," — that there is a mysterious affinity between large accessories and slender essentials. The sermon, beneath that triply consecrated vault, should have been of as fine a quality as the church. It was not; and I confess that a tender memory of ancient obligations to the author of "Westward Ho!" and "Hypatia" forbids me saying more of it. An American, I think, is not incapable of taking a secret satisfaction in an incongruity of this kind. He finds with relief that mortals reared amid all this rich æsthetic privilege are after all but mortals. His constant sense of the beautiful scenic properties of English life is apt to beget a habit of melancholy reference to the dead-blank wall which forms the background of our own life-drama; and from doubting in this fantastic humor whether we have even that modest value in the picturesque scale that he has sometimes fondly hoped, he lapses into a moody scepticism as to our value in the intellectual, and finds himself wondering vaguely whether this is not a mightier race as well as a lovelier land. This of course will never do; so that when after being escorted down the beautiful choir, in what, from the American point of view, is an almost gorgeous ecclesiastical march, by the Dean in a white robe trimmed with scarlet, and black-robed sacristans carrying silver wands, the officiating canon mounts into a splendid canopied and pinnacled pulpit of Gothic stonework and proves — not a Jeremy Taylor in ordinary, our poor sentimental tourist begins to hold up his head again, and to reflect with complacency that opportunity wasted is not our national reproach. I am not sure, indeed, that in the excess of his elation he is not tempted to accuse his English neighbors of being indifferent, unperceptive, uninspired, and to affirm that they do not half discern their good fortune, and that it takes a poor disinherited Yankee to appreciate the " points " of this admirable country.

LICHFIELD AND WARWICK.

Oxford, June 11, 1872.

TO write at Oxford of anything but Oxford requires, on the part of the sentimental tourist,
no small power of mental abstraction. Yet I have
it at heart to pay to three or four other scenes recently visited the debt of an enjoyment hardly less
profound than my relish for this scholastic paradise.
First among these is the cathedral city of Lichfield.
I say the city, because Lichfield had a character of
its own apart from its great ecclesiastical feature.
In the centre of its little market-place — dullest and
sleepiest of provincial market-places — rises a huge
effigy of Dr. Johnson, the *genius loci*, who was constructed, humanly, with very nearly as large an architecture as the great abbey. The Doctor's statue,
which is of some inexpensive composite, painted a
shiny brown, and of no great merit of design, fills
out the vacant dulness of the little square in much
the same way as his massive personality occupies —
with just a margin for Garrick — the record of his
native town. In one of the volumes of Croker's
" Boswell " is a steel plate of the old Johnsonian
birth-house, by the aid of a vague recollection of

which I detected the dwelling beneath its modernized frontage. It bears no mural inscription, and,
save for a hint of antiquity in the receding basement,
with pillars supporting the floor above, seems in no
especial harmony with Johnson's time or fame. Lichfield in general appeared to me, indeed, to have little
to say about her great son, beyond the fact that the
dreary provincial quality of the local atmosphere, in
which it is so easy to fancy a great intellectual appetite turning sick with inanition, may help to explain
the Doctor's subsequent, almost ferocious, fondness for
London. I walked about the silent streets, trying to
repeople them with wigs and short-clothes, and, while
I lingered near the cathedral, endeavored to guess the
message of its Gothic graces to Johnson's ponderous
classicism. But I achieved but a colorless picture at
the best, and the most vivid image in my mind's eye
was that of the London coach facing towards Temple
Bar, with the young author of "Rasselas" scowling
near-sightedly from the cheapest seat. With him goes
the interest of Lichfield town. The place is stale,
without being really antique. It is as if that prodigious temperament had absorbed and appropriated its
original vitality.

If every dull provincial town, however, formed but
a girdle of quietude to a cathedral as rich as that of
Lichfield, one would thank it for its unimportunate
vacancy. Lichfield Cathedral is great among churches,
and bravely performs the prime duty of a cathedral,
— that of seeming for the time (to minds unsophisticated by architectural culture) the finest, on the

whole, of all cathedrals. This one is rather oddly
placed, on the slope of a hill, the particular spot
having been chosen, I believe, because sanctified by
the sufferings of certain primitive martyrs; but it is
fine to see how its upper portions surmount any crookedness of posture, and its great towers overtake in
mid-air the conditions of perfect symmetry.

The close is a singularly pleasant one. A long
sheet of water expands behind it, and, besides leading the eye off into a sweet green landscape, renders
the inestimable service of reflecting the three spires
as they rise above the great trees which mask the
Palace and the Deanery. These august abodes edge
the northern side of the slope, and behind their
huge gate-posts and close-wrought gates the atmosphere of the Georgian era seems to abide. Before
them stretches a row of huge elms, which must have
been old when Johnson was young; and between
these and the long-buttressed wall of the cathedral,
you may stroll to and fro among as pleasant a mixture of influences (I imagine) as any in England.
You can stand back here, too, from the west front
farther than in many cases, and examine at your
ease its lavish decoration. You are, perhaps, a trifle
too much at your ease; for you soon discover what
a more cursory glance might not betray, that the
immense façade has been covered with stucco and
paint, that an effigy of Charles II., in wig and plumes
and trunk-hose, of almost Gothic grotesqueness, sur-
mounts the middle window; that the various other
statues of saints and kings have but recently climbed

into their niches; and that the whole expanse, in short, is an imposture. All this was done some fifty years ago, in the taste of that day as to restoration, and yet it but partially mitigates the impressiveness of the high façade, with its brace of spires, and the great embossed and image-fretted surface, to which the lowness of the portals (the too frequent reproach of English abbeys) seems to give a loftier reach. Passing beneath one of these low portals, however, I found myself gazing down as noble a church vista as any I remember. The cathedral is of magnificent length, and the screen between nave and choir has been removed, so that from stem to stern, as one may say, of the great vessel of the church, it is all a mighty avenue of multitudinous slender columns, terminating in what seems a great screen of ruby and sapphire and topaz, — one of the finest east windows in England. The cathedral is narrow in proportion to its length; it is the long-drawn aisle of the poet in perfection, and there is something grandly elegant in the unity of effect produced by this unobstructed perspective. The charm is increased by a singular architectural fantasy. Standing in the centre of the doorway, you perceive that the eastern wall does not directly face you, and that from the beginning of the choir the receding aisle deflects slightly to the left, in suggestion of the droop of the Saviour's on the cross. Here, as elsewhere, Mr. Gilbert Scott has recently been at work; to excellent purpose, from what the sacristan related of the barbarous encroachments of the last century. This extraor-

dinary period expended an incalculable amount of
imagination in proving that it had none. Universal
whitewash was the least of its offences. But this
has been scraped away, and the solid stonework left
to speak for itself, the delicate capitals and cornices
disencrusted and discreetly rechiselled, and the whole
temple æsthetically rededicated. Its most beautiful
feature, happily, has needed no repair, for its perfect
beauty has been its safeguard. The great choir window of Lichfield is the noblest glass-work I remember to have seen. I have met nowhere colors so
chaste and grave, and yet so rich and true, or a cluster of designs so piously decorative, and yet so pictorial. Such a window as this seems to me the most
sacred ornament of a great church; to be, not like
vault and screen and altar, the dim contingent promise of heaven, but the very assurance and presence
of it. This Lichfield glass is not the less interesting
for being visibly of foreign origin. Exceeding so obviously as it does the range of English genius in this
line, it indicates at least the heavenly treasure stored
up in continental churches. It dates from the early
sixteenth century, and was transferred hither sixty
years ago from a decayed Belgian abbey. This, however, is not all of Lichfield. You have not seen it
till you have strolled and restrolled along the close
on every side, and watched the three spires constantly
change their relation as you move and pause. Nothing can well be finer than the combination of the
two lesser ones soaring equally in front, and the third
riding tremendously the magnificently sustained line

of the roof. At a certain distance against the sky, this long ridge seems something infinite, and the great spire to sit astride of it like a giant mounted on a mastodon. Your sense of the huge mass of the building is deepened by the fact that though the central steeple is of double the elevation of the others, you see it, from some points, borne back in a perspective which drops it to half their stature, and lifts them into immensity. But it would take long to tell all that one sees and fancies and thinks in a lingering walk about so great a church as this.

To walk in quest of any object that one has more or less tenderly dreamed of, to find your way, to steal upon it softly, to see at last if it is church or castle, the tower-tops peeping above elms or beeches, — to push forward with a rush, and emerge, and pause, and draw that first long breath which is the compromise between so many sensations, — this is a pleasure left to the tourist even after the broad glare of photography has dissipated so many of the sweet mysteries of travel, — even in a season when he is fatally apt to meet a dozen fellow-pilgrims returning from the shrine, each *gros Jean comme devant,* or to overtake a dozen more, telegraphing their impressions down the line as they arrive. Such a pleasure I lately enjoyed, quite in its perfection, in a walk to Haddon Hall, along a meadow-path by the Wye, in this interminable English twilight, which I am never weary of admiring, watch in hand. Haddon Hall lies among Derbyshire hills, in a region infested, I was about to write, by Americans. But I achieved my own sly pilgrimage in perfect soli-

2

tude; and as I descried the gray walls among the rook-
haunted elms, I felt, not like a tourist, but like an
adventurer. I have certainly had, as a tourist, few
more charming moments than some — such as any one,
I suppose, is free to have — that I passed on a little
ruined gray bridge which spans, with its single narrow
arch, a trickling stream at the base of the eminence
from which those walls and trees look down. The twilight deepened, the ragged battlements and the low,
broad oriels glanced duskily from the foliage, the rooks
wheeled and clamored in the glowing sky; and if there
had been a ghost on the premises, I certainly ought to
have seen it. In fact, I did see it, as we see ghosts
nowadays. I felt the incommunicable spirit of the
scene with almost painful intensity. The old life, the
old manners, the old figures seemed present again. The
great *coup de théâtre* of the young woman who shows
you the Hall — it is rather languidly done on her
part — is to point out a little dusky door opening from
a turret to a back terrace, as the aperture through
which Dorothy Vernon eloped with Lord John Manners. I was ignorant of this episode, for I was not to
enter the Hall till the morrow; and I am still unversed
in the history of the actors. But as I stood in the
luminous dusk weaving the romance of the spot, I
divined a Dorothy Vernon, and felt very much like a
Lord John. It was, of course, on just such an evening
that the delicious event came off, and, by listening with
the proper credulity, I might surely hear on the flags
of the castle-court the ghostly footfall of a daughter
of the race. The only footfall I can conscientiously

swear to, however, is the by no means ghostly tread of the damsel who led me - through the mansion in the prosier light of the next morning. Haddon Hall, I believe, is one of the places in which it is the fashion to be " disappointed "; a fact explained in a great measure by the absence of a formal approach to the house, which shows its low, gray front to every trudger on the high-road. But the charm of the place is so much less that of grandeur than that of melancholy, that it is rather deepened than diminished by this atti- tude of obvious survival and decay. And for that matter, when you have entered the steep little outer court through the huge thickness of the low gateway, the present seems effectually walled out, and the past walled in, — like a dead man in a sepulchre. It is very dead, of a fine June morning, the genius of Haddon Hall; and the silent courts and chambers, with their hues of ashen gray and faded brown, seem as time- bleached as the dry bones of any mouldering organism. The comparison is odd; but Haddon Hall reminded me perversely of some of the larger houses at Pompeii. The private life of the past is revealed in each case with very much the same distinctness and on a small enough scale not to stagger the imagination. This old dwelling, indeed, has so little of the mass and expanse of the classic feudal castle that it almost suggests one of those miniature models of great buildings which lurk in dusty corners of museums. But it is large enough to be deliciously complete and to contain an infinite store of the poetry of grass-grown courts, looked into by long, low oriel casements, and climbed out of by crooked stone stairways, mounting against the walls to little high-placed doors. The "tone" of Haddon Hall, of all its walls and towers and stonework, is the gray of unpolished silver, and the reader who has been in England need hardly be reminded of the sweet accord — to eye and mind alike — existing between all stony surfaces covered with the pale corrosions of time and the deep living green of the strong ivy which seems to feed on their slow decay. Of this effect and of a hundred others, — from those that belong to low-browed, stone-paved empty rooms, where countesses used to trail their cloth-of-gold over rushes, to those one may note where the dark tower stairway emerges at last, on a level with the highest beech-tops, against the cracked and sun-baked parapet which flaunted the castle standard over the castle woods, — of every form of sad desuetude and picturesque decay Haddon Hall contains some delightful example. Its finest point is undoubtedly a certain court from which a stately flight of steps ascends to the terrace where that daughter of the Vernons whom I have mentioned proved that it was useless to have baptized her so primly. These steps, with the terrace, its balustrade topped with great ivy-muffled knobs of stone, and its vast background of lordly beeches, form the ideal *mise en scène* for portions of Shakespeare's comedies. "It's Elizabethan," said my companion. Here the Countess Olivia may have listened to the fantastic Malvolio, or Beatrix, superbest of flirts, have come to summon Benedick to dinner.

The glories of Chatsworth, which lies but a few

miles from Haddon, serve as a fine *repoussoir* to its
more delicate merits, just as they are supposed to gain,
I believe, in the tourist's eyes, by contrast with its
charming, its almost Italian shabbiness. But the glories of Chatsworth, incontestable as they are, were so
effectually eclipsed to my mind, a couple of days later,
that in future, when I think of an English mansion, I
shall think only of Warwick, and when I think of an
English park, only of Blenheim. Your run by train
through the gentle Warwickshire landscape does much
to prepare you for the great spectacle of the castle,
which seems hardly more than a sort of massive symbol and synthesis of the broad prosperity and peace
and leisure diffused over this great pastoral expanse.
The Warwickshire meadows are to common English
scenery what this is to that of the rest of the world.
For mile upon mile you can see nothing but broad
sloping pastures of velvet turf, overbrowsed by sheep
of the most fantastic shagginess, and garnished with
hedges out of the trailing luxury of whose verdure
great ivy-tangled oaks and elms arise with a kind of
architectural regularity. The landscape, indeed, sins
by excess of nutritive suggestion; it savors of larder
and manger; it is too ovine, too bovine, it is almost
asinine; and if you were to believe what you see before
you, this rugged globe would be a sort of boneless ball,
neatly covered with some such plush-like integument
as might be figured by the down on the cheek of a
peach. But a great thought keeps you company as
you go and gives character to the scenery. Warwickshire was Shakespeare's country. Those who think

that a great genius is something supremely ripe and healthy and human may find comfort in the fact. It helps greatly to enliven my own vague conception of Shakespeare's temperament, with which I find it no great shock to be obliged to associate ideas of mutton and beef. There is something as final, as disillusioned of the romantic horrors of rock and forest, as deeply attuned to human needs, in the Warwickshire pastures, as there is in the underlying morality of the poet.

With human needs in general Warwick Castle may be in no great accord, but few places are more gratifying to the sentimental tourist. It is the only great residence that I ever cóveted as a home. The fire that we heard so much of last winter in America appears to have consumed but an inconsiderable and easily spared portion of the house, and the great towers rise over the great trees and the town with the same grand air as before. Picturesquely, Warwick gains from not being sequestered, after the common fashion, in acres of park. The village street winds about the garden walls, though its hum expires before it has had time to scale them. There can be no better example of the way in which stone-walls, if they do not of necessity make a prison, may on occasions make a palace, than the tremendous privacy maintained thus about a mansion whose windows and towers form the main feature of a bustling town. At Warwick the past join hands so stoutly with the present that you can hardly say where one begins and the other ends, and you rather miss the various crannies and gaps of what I just now called the Italian shabbiness of Haddon. There is a Cæsar's

tower and a Guy's tower and half a dozen more, but
they are so well-conditioned in their ponderous antiquity that you are at loss whether to consider them
parts of an old house revived or of a new house picturesquely superannuated. Such as they are, however,
plunging into the grassed and gravelled courts from
which their battlements look really feudal, and into
gardens large enough for all delight and too small, as
they should be, to be amazing; and with ranges between them of great apartments at whose hugely
recessed windows you may turn from Vandyck and
Rembrandt, to glance down the cliff-like pile into the
Avon, washing the base like a lordly moat, with its
bridge, and its trees, and its memories, — they mark the
very model of a great hereditary dwelling, — one which
amply satisfies the imagination without irritating the
democratic conscience. The pictures at Warwick reminded me afresh of an old conclusion on this matter;
that the best fortune for good pictures is not to be
crowded into public collections, — not even into the
relative privacy of Salons Carrés and Tribunes, — but to
hang in largely spaced half-dozens on the walls of fine
houses. Here the historical atmosphere, as one may
call it, is almost a compensation for the often imperfect
light. If this is true of most pictures, it is especially
so of the works of Vandyck, whom you think of, wherever you may find him, as having, with that immense
good-breeding which is the stamp of his manner, taken
account in his painting of the local conditions, and predestined his picture to just the spot where it hangs.
This is, in fact, an illusion as regards the Vandycks at

Warwick, for none of them represent members of the house. The very finest, perhaps, after the great melancholy, picturesque Charles I., — death, or at least the presentiment of death on the pale horse, — is a portrait from the Brignole palace at Genoa ; a beautiful noble matron in black, with her little son and heir. The last Vandycks I had seen were the noble company this lady had left behind her in the Genoese palace, and as I looked at her, I thought of her mighty change of circumstance. Here she sits in the mild light of midmost England ; there you could almost fancy her blinking in the great glare sent up from the Mediterranean. Picturesque for picturesque, I hardly know which to choose.

NORTH DEVON.

FOR those fanciful observers to whom broad England means chiefly the perfection of the rural picturesque, Devonshire means the perfection of England. I, at least, had so complacently taken it for granted that all the characteristic graces of English scenery are here to be found in especial exuberance, that before we fairly crossed the border I had begun to look impatiently from the carriage window for the veritable landscape in water-colors. Devonshire meets you promptly in all its purity. In the course of ten minutes you have been able to glance down the green vista of a dozen Devonshire lanes. On huge embankments of moss and turf, smothered in wild flowers and embroidered with the finest lace-work of trailing ground-ivy, rise solid walls of flowering thorn and glistening holly and golden broom, and more strong, homely shrubs than I can name, and toss their blooming tangle to a sky which seems to look down between them, in places, from but a dozen inches of blue. They are overstrewn with lovely little flowers with names as delicate as their petals of gold and silver and azure, — bird's-eye and king's-finger and wandering-sailor, — and

2 *   c

their soil, a superb dark red, turns in spots so nearly to
crimson that you almost fancy it some fantastic compound purchased at the chemist's and scattered there
for ornament. The mingled reflection of this rich-hued
earth and the dim green light which filters through
the hedge is a masterpiece of local color. A Devonshire cottage is no less striking a local "institution."
Crushed beneath its burden of thatch, coated with a
rough white stucco of a tone to delight a painter, nestling in deep foliage, and garnished at doorstep and
wayside with various forms of chubby infancy, it seems
to have been stationed there for no more obvious purpose than to keep a promise to your fancy, though it
covers, I suppose, not a little of the sordid misery
which the fancy loves to forget.

I rolled past lanes and cottages to Exeter, where I
found a cathedral. When one has fairly tasted of the
pleasure of cathedral-hunting, the approach to each new
shrine gives a peculiarly agreeable zest to one's curiosity. You are making a collection of great impressions,
and I think the process is in no case so delightful as
applied to cathedrals. Going from one fine picture to
another is certainly good; but the fine pictures of the
world are terribly numerous, and they have a trouble-
some way of crowding and jostling each other in the
memory. The number of cathedrals is small, and the
mass and presence of each specimen is great, so that, as
they rise in the mind in individual majesty, they dwarf
all common impressions. They form, indeed, but a
gallery of vaster pictures; for, when time has dulled
the recollection of details, you retain a single broad

image of the vast gray edifice, with its towers, its tone
of color, and its still, green precinct. All this is
especially true, perhaps, of one's memory of English
cathedrals, which are almost alone in possessing, as
pictures, the setting of a spacious and harmonious close.
The cathedral stands supreme, but the close makes
the *scene*. Exeter is not one of the grandest, but, in
common with great and small, it has certain points
on which local science expatiates with peculiar pride.
Exeter, indeed, does itself injustice by a low, dark
front, which not only diminishes the apparent altitude
of the nave, but conceals, as you look eastward, two
noble Norman towers. The front, however, which has
a gloomy picturesqueness, is redeemed by two fine features: a magnificent rose-window, whose vast stone
ribs (inclosing some very pallid last-century glass) are
disposed with the most charming intricacy; and a long
sculptured screen, — a sort of stony band of images, —
which traverses the façade from side to side. The
little broken-visaged effigies of saints and kings and
bishops, niched in tiers along this hoary wall, are prodigiously black and quaint and primitive in expression;
and as you look at them with whatever contemplative
tenderness your trade of hard-working tourist may
have left at your disposal, you fancy that somehow
they are consciously historical, — sensitive victims of
time; that they feel the loss of their noses, their toes,
and their crowns; and that, when the long June twilight turns at last to a deeper gray and the quiet of the
close to a deeper stillness, they begin to peer sidewise
out of their narrow recesses, and to converse in some

strange form of early English, as rigid, yet as candid, as their features and postures, moaning, like a company of ancient paupers round a hospital fire, over their aches and infirmities and losses, and the sadness of being so terribly old. The vast square transeptal towers of the church seem to me to have the same sort of *personal* melancholy. Nothing in all architecture expresses better, to my imagination, the sadness of survival, the resignation of dogged material continuance, than a broad expanse of Norman stonework, roughly adorned with its low relief of short columns, and round arches, and almost barbarous hatchet-work, and lifted high into that mild English light which accords so well with its dull-gray surface. The especial secret of the impressiveness of such a Norman tower I cannot pretend to have discovered. It lies largely in the look of having been proudly and sturdily built, — as if the masons had been urged by a trumpet-blast, and the stones squared by a battle-axe, — contrasted with this mere idleness of antiquity and passive lapse into quaintness. A Greek temple preserves a kind of fresh immortality in its concentrated refinement, and a Gothic cathedral in its adventurous exuberance; but a Norman tower stands up like some simple strong man in his might, bending a melancholy brow upon an age which demands that strength shall be cunning.

The North Devon coast, whither it was my design on coming to Exeter to proceed, has the primary merit of being, as yet, virgin soil as to railways. I went accordingly from Barnstaple to Ilfracombe on the top of a coach, in the fashion of elder days;

to my position, I managed to enjoy the landscape in
spite of the two worthy Englishmen before me who
were reading aloud together, with a natural glee which
might have passed for fiendish malice, the Daily Tel-
egraph's painfully vivid account of the defeat of the
Atalanta crew. It seemed to me, I remember, a sort
of pledge and token of the invincibility of English
muscle that a newspaper record of its prowess should
have power to divert my companions' eyes from the
bosky flanks of Devonshire combes. The little watering-place of Ilfracombe is seated at the lower verge
of one of these seaward-plunging valleys, between a
couple of magnificent headlands which hold it in a
hollow slope and offer it securely to the caress of the
Bristol Channel. It is a very finished little specimen
of its genus, and I think that during my short stay
there I expended as much attention on its manners
and customs and its social physiognomy as on its cliffs
and beach and great coast-view. My chief conclusion,
perhaps, from all these things, was that the terrible
summer question which works annual anguish in so
many American households would be vastly simplified
if we had a few Ilfracombes scattered along our Atlantic coast; and furthermore, that the English are masters
of the art of uniting the picturesque with the comfortable, — in such proportions, at least, as may claim the
applause of a race whose success has as yet been confined to an ingenious combination of their opposites.
It is just possible that at Ilfracombe the comfortable
weighs down the scale ; so very substantial is it, so
very officious and business-like. On the left of the

town (to give an example), one of the great cliffs I have mentioned rises in a couple of massive peaks, and presents to the sea an almost vertical face, all muffled in tufts of golden broom and mighty fern. You have not walked fifty yards away from the hotel before you encounter half a dozen little sign-boards, directing your steps to a path up the cliff. You follow their indications, and you arrive at a little gate-house, with photographs and various local gimcracks exposed for sale. A most respectable person appears, demands a penny, and, on receiving it, admits you with great civility to commune with nature. You detect, however, various little influences hostile to perfect communion. You are greeted by another sign-board threatening legal pursuit if you attempt to evade the payment of the sacramental penny. The path, winding in a hundred ramifications over the cliff, is fastidiously solid and neat, and furnished at intervals of a dozen yards with excellent benches, inscribed by knife and pencil with the names of such visitors as do not happen to have been the elderly maiden ladies who now chiefly occupy them. All this is prosaic, and you have to subtract it in a lump from the total impression before the sense of pure nature becomes distinct. Your subtraction made, a great deal assuredly remains; quite enough, I found, to give me an ample day's entertainment: for English scenery, like everything else that England produces, is of a quality that wears well. The cliffs are superb, the play of light and shade upon them is a perpetual study, and the air a delicious mixture of the mountain-breeze and the sea-breeze. I was very glad, at the end of my

climb, to have a good bench to sit upon, — as one must
think twice in England before measuring one's length
on the grassy earth ; and to be able, thanks to the
smooth foot-path, to get back to the hotel in a quarter
of an hour. But it occurred to me that if I were an
Englishman of the period, and, after ten months of a
busy London life, my fancy were turning to a holiday,
to rest, and change, and oblivion of the ponderous
social burden, it might find rather less inspiration than
needful in a vision of the little paths of Ilfracombe, of
the sign-boards and the penny fee and the solitude
tempered by old ladies and sheep. I wondered whether
change perfect enough to be salutary does not imply
something more pathless, more idle, more unreclaimed
from that deep-bosomed Nature to which the overwrought mind reverts with passionate longing ; something, in short, which is attainable at a moderate distance from New York and Boston. I must add that I
cannot find in my heart to object, even on grounds the
most æsthetic, to the very beautiful and excellent hotel
at Ilfracombe, where such of my readers as are perchance actually wrestling with the summer question
may be interested to learn that one may live *en pension*,
very well indeed, at a cost of ten shillings a day. I
have paid very much more at some of our more modest
summer resorts for very much less. I made the acquaintance at this establishment of that somewhat
anomalous institution, the British table d'hôte, but I
confess that, faithful to the duty of a sentimental tourist, I have retained a more vivid impression of the talk
and the faces than of our *entrées* and *relevés*. I noticed

here what I have often noticed before (the fact perhaps
has never been duly recognized), that no people profit
so eagerly as the English by the suspension of a common social law. A table d'hôte, being something ab-
normal and experimental, as it were, it produced, apparently, a complete reversal of the national characteris-
tics. Conversation was universal, — uproarious, almost ;
and I have met no vivacious Latin more confidential
than a certain neighbor of mine, no speculative Yankee
more inquisitive.

These are meagre memories, however, compared with
those which cluster about that enchanting spot which
is known in vulgar prose as Lynton. I am afraid I
should seem an even more sentimental tourist than I
pretend to be if I were to declare how vulgar all prose
appears to me applied to Lynton with descriptive intent. The little village is perched on the side of one
of the great mountain cliffs with which this whole
coast is adorned, and on the edge of a lovely gorge
through which a broad hill-torrent foams and tumbles
from the great moors whose heather-crested waves rise
purple along the inland sky. Below it, close beside the
beach, where the little torrent meets the sea, is the
sister village of Lynmouth. Here — as I stood on the
bridge that spans the stream and looked at the stony
backs and foundations and overclambering garden verdure of certain little gray old houses which plunge their
feet into it, and then up at the tender green of scrub-
oak and ferns and the flaming yellow of golden broom
climbing the sides of the hills, and leaving them bare-
crowned to the sun, like miniature mountains — I could

have fancied the British Channel as blue as the Mediterranean and the village about me one of the hundred hamlets of the Riviera. The little Castle Hotel at Lynton is a spot so consecrated to delicious repose,—to sitting with a book in the terrace-garden among blooming plants of aristocratic magnitude and rarity, and watching the finest piece of color in all nature, — the glowing red and green of the great cliffs beyond the little harbor-mouth, as they shift and change and melt the livelong day, from shade to shade and ineffable tone to tone, — that I feel as if in helping it to publicity I were doing it rather a disfavor than a service. It is in fact a very charming little abiding-place, and I have never known one where purchased hospitality wore a more disinterested smile. Lynton is of course a capital centre for excursions, but two or three of which I had time to make. None is more beautiful than a simple walk along the running face of the cliffs to a singular rocky eminence whose curious abutments and pinnacles of stone have caused it to be named the " Castle." It has a fantastic resemblance to some hoary feudal ruin, with crumbling towers and gaping chambers, tenanted by wild sea-birds. The late afternoon light had a way, while I was at Lynton, of lingering on until within a couple of hours of midnight; and I remember among the charmed moments of English travel none of a more vividly poetical tinge than a couple of evenings spent on the summit of this all but legendary pile, in company with the slow-coming darkness, and the short, sharp cry of the sea-mews. There are places whose very aspect is a story. This jagged and pinnacled coast-wall,

with the rock-strewn valley behind it, into the shadow
of one of whose bowlders, in the foreground, the glance
wandered in search of the lurking signature of Gustave
Doré, belonged certainly, if not to history, to legend.
As I sat watching the sullen calmness of the unbroken
tide at the dreadful base of the cliffs (where they divide
into low sea-caves, making pillars and pedestals for the
fantastic imagery of their summits), I kept forever repeating, as if they contained a spell, half a dozen words
from Tennyson's "Idyls of the King," —

> "On wild Tintagil, by the Cornish sea."

False as they were to the scene geographically, they
seemed somehow to express its essence ; and, at any
rate, I leave it to any one who has lingered there with
the lingering twilight to say whether you can respond
to the almost mystical picturesqueness of the place
better than by spouting some sonorous line from an
English poet.

The last stage in my visit to North Devon was the
long drive along the beautiful remnant of coast and
through the rich pastoral scenery of Somerset. The
whole broad spectacle that one dreams of viewing in a
foreign land to the homely music of a postboy's whip,
I beheld on this admirable drive, — breezy highlands
clad in the warm blue-brown of heather-tufts, as if in
mantles of rusty velvet, little bays and coves curving
gently to the doors of clustered fishing-huts, deep pastures and broad forests, villages thatched and trellised as
if to take a prize for local color, manor-tops peeping over
rook-haunted avenues. I ought to make especial note

of an hour I spent at midday at the little village of Porlock, in Somerset. Here the thatch seemed steeper and heavier, the yellow roses on the cottage walls more cunningly mated with the crumbling stucco, the dark interiors within the open doors more quaintly pictorial, than elsewhere; and as I loitered, while the horses rested, in the little cool old timber-steepled, yew-shaded church, betwixt the high-backed manorial pew and the battered tomb of a crusading knight and his lady, and listened to the simple prattle of a blue-eyed old sexton, who showed me where, as a boy, in scantier corduroys, he had scratched his name on the recumbent lady's breast, it seemed to me that this at last was old England indeed, and that in a moment more I should see Sir Roger de Coverley marching up the aisle; for certainly, to give a proper account of it all, I should need nothing less than the pen of Mr. Addison.

WELLS AND SALISBURY.

THE pleasantest things in life, and perhaps the rarest, are its agreeable surprises. Things are often worse than we expect to find them; and when they are better, we may mark the day with a white stone. These reflections are as pertinent to man as a tourist as to any other phase of his destiny, and I recently had occasion to make them in the ancient city of Wells. I knew in a general way that it had a great cathedral to show, but I was far from suspecting the precious picturesqueness of the little town. The immense predominance of the Minster towers, as you see them from the approaching train over the clustered houses at their feet, gives you indeed an intimation of it, and suggests that the city is nothing if not ecclesiastical; but I can wish the traveller no better fortune than to stroll forth in the early evening with as large a reserve of ignorance as my own, and treat himself to an hour of discoveries. I was lodged on the edge of Cathedral Green, and I had only to pass beneath one of the three crumbling Priory gates which enclose it, and cross the vast grassy oval, to stand before a minster-front which ranks among the first three or four in England. Wells Cathedral is extremely fortunate in being approached by this wide green level, on which the spectator may loiter and stroll to and fro, and shift his stand-point to his heart's content. The spectator who does not hesitate to avail himself of his privilege of unlimited fastidiousness might indeed pronounce it too isolated for perfect picturesqueness, — too uncontrasted with the profane architecture of the human homes for which it pleads to the skies. But, in fact, Wells is not a city with a cathedral for a central feature; but a cathedral with a little city gathered at its base, and forming hardly more than an extension of its spacious close. You feel everywhere the presence of the beautiful church ; the place seems always to savor of a Sunday afternoon ; and you fancy that every house is tenanted by a canon, a prebendary, or a precentor.

The great façade is remarkable not so much for its expanse as for its elaborate elegance. It consists of two great truncated towers, divided by a broad centre, bearing beside its rich fretwork of statues three narrow lancet windows. The statues on this vast front are the great boast of the cathedral. They number, with the lateral figures of the towers, no less than three hundred ; it seems densely embroidered by the chisel. They are disposed in successive niches, along six main vertical shafts ; the central windows are framed and divided by narrower shafts, and the wall above them rises into a pinnacled screen, traversed by two superb horizontal rows. Add to these a close-running cornice of images along the line corresponding with the summit of the aisles, and the tiers which complete the decoration of the towers on either side, and you have an immense system of images, governed by a quaint theological order and most impressive in its completeness. Many of the little high-lodged effigies are mutilated, and not a few of the niches are empty, but the injury of time is not sufficient to diminish the noble serenity of the building. The injury of time is indeed being handsomely repaired, for the front is partly masked by a slender scaffolding. The props and platforms are of the most delicate structure, and look, in fact, as if they were meant to facilitate no more ponderous labor than a fitting-on of noses to disfeatured bishops, and a rearrangement of the mantle-folds of straitlaced queens, discomposed by the centuries. The main beauty of Wells Cathedral, to my mind, is not its more or less visible wealth of detail, but its singularly charming tone of color. An even, sober, mouse-colored gray covers it from summit to base, deepening nowhere to the melancholy black of your truly romantic Gothic, but showing, as yet, none of the spotty brightness of "restoration." It was a wonderful fact, that the great towers, from their lofty outlook, see never a factory chimney, — those cloud-compelling spires which so often break the charm of the softest English horizons ; and the general atmosphere of Wells seemed to me, for some reason, peculiarly luminous and sweet. The cathedral has never been discolored by the moral malaria of a city with an independent secular life. As you turn back from its portal and glance at the open lawn before it, edged by the mild gray Elizabethan deanery, and the other dwellings, hardly less stately, which seem

to reflect in their comfortable fronts the rich respectability of the church, and then up again at the beautiful clear-hued pile, you may fancy it less a temple for
man's needs than a monument of his pride, — less a
fold for the flock than for the shepherds, — a visible
sign that, besides the actual assortment of heavenly
thrones, there is constantly on hand a choice lot of
cushioned cathedral stalls. Within the cathedral this
impression is not diminished. The interior is vast and
massive, but it lacks incident, — the incident of monuments, sepulchres, and chapels, — and it is too brilliantly lighted for picturesque, as distinguished from strictly
architectural, interest. Under this latter head it has, I
believe, great importance. For myself, I can think of
it only as I saw it from my place in the choir during
afternoon service of a hot Sunday. The Bishop sat
facing me, enthroned in a stately Gothic alcove, and
clad in his crimson band, his lawn sleeves, and his
lavender gloves ; the canons, in their degree, with the
archdeacons, as I suppose, reclined comfortably in the
carven stalls, and the scanty congregation fringed the
broad-aisle. But though scanty, the congregation was
select ; it was unexceptionably black-coated, bonneted,
and gloved. It savored intensely, in short, of that inexorable gentility which the English put on with their
Sunday bonnets and beavers, and which fills me — as a
purely sentimental tourist — with a sort of fond re-
actionary remembrance of those animated bundles of
rags which one sees kneeling in the churches of Italy.
But even here, as a purely sentimental tourist, I found
my account : one always does in some little corner in

England. Before me and beside me sat a row of the
comeliest young men, clad in black gowns, and wearing
on their shoulders long hoods trimmed with white fur.
Who and what they were I know not, for I preferred
not to learn, lest by chance they should not be so
mediæval as they looked.

My fancy found its account even better in the singular quaintness of the little precinct known as the
Vicars' Close. It directly adjoins the Cathedral Green,
and you enter it beneath one of the solid old gate-
houses which form so striking an element in the ecclesiastical furniture of Wells. It consists of a narrow,
oblong court, bordered on each side with thirteen small
dwellings, and terminating in a ruinous little chapel.
Here formerly dwelt a congregation of vicars, estab-
lished in the thirteenth century to do curates' work
for the canons. The little houses are very much modernized; but they retain their tall chimneys, with
carven tablets in the face, their antique compactness
and neatness, and a certain little sanctified air, as of
cells in a cloister. The place is deliciously picturesque;
and, approaching it as I did in the first dimness of
twilight, it looked to me, in its exaggerated perspective,
like one of those "streets" represented on the stage,
down whose impossible vista the heroes and confidants
of romantic comedies come swaggering arm-in-arm, and
hold amorous converse with the heroines at second-story
windows. But though the Vicars' Close is a curious
affair enough, the great boast of Wells is its episcopal
Palace. The Palace loses nothing from being seen for
the first time in the kindly twilight, and from being

approached with an unexpectant mind. To reach it (unless you go from within the cathedral by the cloisters), you pass out of the Green by another ancient gateway into the market-place, and thence back again through its own peculiar portal. My own first glimpse of it had all the felicity of a *coup de théâtre*. I saw within the dark archway an enclosure bedimmed at once with the shadows of trees and heightened with the glitter of water. The picture was worthy of this agreeable promise. Its main feature is the little gray-walled island on which the Palace stands, rising in feudal fashion out of a broad, clear moat, flanked with round towers, and approached by a proper drawbridge. Along the outer side of the moat is a short walk beneath a row of picturesquely stunted elms; swans and ducks disport themselves in the current and ripple the bright shadows of the overclambering plants from the episcopal gardens and masses of purple valerian lodged on the hoary battlements. On the evening of my visit the haymakers were at work on a great sloping field in the rear of the Palace, and the sweet perfume of the tumbled grass in the dusky air seemed all that was wanting to fix the scene forever in the memory. Beyond the moat, and within the gray walls, dwells my lord Bishop, in the finest palace in England. The mansion dates from the thirteenth century; but, stately dwelling though it is, it occupies but a subordinate place in its own grounds. Their great ornament, picturesquely speaking, is the massive ruin of a banqueting-hall, erected by a free-living mediæval bishop, and more or less demolished at the Reformation. With its

3   D

still perfect towers and beautiful shapely windows, hung
with those green tapestries so stoutly woven by the
English climate, it is a relic worthy of being locked
away behind an embattled wall. I have among my
impressions of Wells, besides this picture of the moated
Palace, half a dozen memories of the pictorial sort,
which I lack space to transcribe. The clearest impression, perhaps, is that of the beautiful church of
St. Cuthbert, of the same date as the cathedral, and in
very much the same style of elegant, temperate Early
English. It wears one of the high-soaring towers for
which Somersetshire is justly celebrated, as you may
see from the window of the train as you roll past its
almost top-heavy hamlets. The beautiful old church,
surrounded with its green graveyard, and large enough
to be impressive, without being too large (a great merit,
to my sense) to be easily compassed by a deplorably
unarchitectural eye, wore a native English expression
to which certain humble figures in the foreground gave
additional point. On the edge of the churchyard was
a low-gabled house, before which four old men were
gossiping in the eventide. Into the front of the house
was inserted an antique alcove in stone, divided into
three shallow little seats, two of which were occupied
by extraordinary specimens of decrepitude. One of
these ancient paupers had a huge protuberant forehead,
and sat with a pensive air, his head gathered painfully
upon his twisted shoulders, and his legs resting across
his crutch. The other was rubicund, blear-eyed, and
frightfully besmeared with snuff. Their voices were
so feeble and senile that I could scarcely understand

them, and only just managed to make out the answer to my inquiry of who and what they were, — " We 're Still's Almshouse, sir."

One of the lions, almost, of Wells (whence it is but five miles distant) is the ruin of the famous Abbey of Glastonbury, on which Henry VIII., in the language of our day, came down so heavily. The ancient splendor of the architecture survives, but in scattered and scanty fragments, among influences of a rather inharmonious sort. It was cattle-market in the little town as I passed up the main street, and a savor of hoofs and hide seemed to accompany me through the easy labyrinth of the old arches and piers. These occupy a large back yard, close behind the street, to which you are most prosaically admitted by a young woman who keeps a wicket and sells tickets. The continuity of tradition is not altogether broken, however, for the little street of Glastonbury has rather an old-time aspect, and one of the houses at least must have seen the last of the abbots ride abroad on his mule. The little inn is a capital bit of picturesqueness, and as I waited for the 'bus under its low dark archway (in something of the mood, possibly, in which a train was once waited for at Coventry), and watched the barmaid flirting her way to and fro out of the heavy-browed kitchen and among the lounging young appraisers of colts and steers and barmaids, I might have imagined that the merry England of the Tudors was not utterly dead. A beautiful England this must have been as well, if it contained many such abbeys as Glastonbury. Such of the ruined columns and portals and windows

as still remain are of admirable design and finish. The
doorways are rich in marginal ornament, — ornament
within ornament, as it often is; for the dainty weeds
and wild-flowers overlace the antique tracery with their
bright arabesques, and deepen the gray of the stonework, as it brightens their bloom. The thousand flowers which grow among English ruins deserve a chapter
to themselves. I owe them, as an observer, a heavy
debt of satisfaction, but I am too little of a botanist to
pay them in their own coin. It has often seemed to
me in England that the purest enjoyment of architecture was to be had among the ruins of great buildings. In the perfect building one is rarely sure that
the impression is simply architectural: it is more or
less pictorial and sentimental; it depends partly upon
association and partly upon various accessories and details which, however they may be wrought into harmony with the architectural idea, are not part of its
essence and spirit. But in so far as beauty of structure
is beauty of line and curve, balance and harmony of
masses and dimensions, I have seldom relished it as
deeply as on the grassy nave of some crumbling church,
before lonely columns and empty windows, where the
wild-flowers were a cornice and the sailing clouds a
roof. The arts certainly have a common element.
These hoary relics of Glastonbury reminded me in
their broken eloquence of one of the other great ruins
of the world, — the Last Supper of Leonardo. A beautiful shadow, in each case, is all that remains; but that
shadow is the artist's thought.

Salisbury Cathedral, to which I made a pilgrimage

on leaving Wells, is the very reverse of a ruin, and you take your pleasure there on very different grounds from those I have just attempted to define. It is perhaps the best known cathedral in the world, thanks to its shapely spire; but the spire is so simply and obviously fair, that when you have respectfully made a note of it you have anticipated æsthetic analysis. I had seen it before and admired it heartily, and perhaps I should have done as well to let my admiration rest. I confess that on repeated inspection it grew to seem to me the least bit *banal*, as the French say, and I began to consider whether it does not belong to the same range of art as the Apollo Belvedere or the Venus de' Medici. I am inclined to think that if I had to live within sight of a cathedral, and encounter it in my daily comings and goings, I should grow less weary of the rugged black front of Exeter than of the sweet perfection of Salisbury. There are people who become easily satiated with blond beauties, and Salisbury Cathedral belongs, if I may say so, to the order of blondes. The other lions of Salisbury, Stonehenge and Wilton House, I revisited with undiminished interest. Stonehenge is rather a hackneyed shrine of pilgrimage. At the time of my former visit a picnic-party was making libations of beer on the dreadful altar-sites. But the mighty mystery of the place has not yet been stared out of countenance; and as on this occasion there were no picnickers, we were left to drink deep of the harmony of its solemn isolation and its unrecorded past. It stands as lonely in history as it does on the great plain, whose many-tinted green waves, as they roll

away from it, seem to symbolize the ebb of the long
centuries which have left it so portentously unex-
plained. You may put a hundred questions to these
rough-hewn giants as they bend in grim contemplation
of their fallen companions; but your curiosity falls
dead in the vast sunny stillness that enshrouds them,
and the strange monument, with all its unspoken memories, becomes simply a heart-stirring picture in a land
of pictures. It is indeed immensely picturesque. At
a distance, you see it standing in a shallow dell of the
plain, looking hardly larger than a group of ten-pins
on a bowling-green. I can fancy sitting all a summer's
day watching its shadows shorten and lengthen again,
and drawing a delicious contrast between the world's
duration and the feeble span of individual experience.
There is something in Stonehenge almost reassuring;
and if you are disposed to feel that life is rather a superficial matter, and that we soon get to the bottom of
things, the immemorial gray pillars may serve to remind you of the enormous background of Time. Salisbury is indeed rich in antiquities. Wilton House, a
delightful old residence of the Earls of Pembroke,
contains a noble collection of Greek and Roman marbles. These are ranged round a charming cloister,
occupying the centre of the house, which is exhibited
in the most liberal fashion. Out of the cloister opens
a series of drawing-rooms hung with family portraits,
chiefly by Vandyck, all of superlative merit. Among
them hangs supreme, as the Vandyck *par excellence*,
the famous and magnificent group of the whole Pembroke family of James I.'s time. This splendid work

has every pictorial merit, — design, color, elegance, force, and finish, and I have been vainly wondering to this hour what it needs to be the finest piece of portraiture, as it surely is one of the most ambitious, in the world. 'What it lacks, characteristically, in a certain uncompromising solidity it recovers in the beautiful dignity of its position — unmoved from the stately house in which its author sojourned and wrought, familiar to the descendants of its noble originals.

SWISS NOTES.

Thusis, August, 1872.

I HAVE often thought it, intellectually speaking,
indifferent economy for the American tourist to devote many of his precious summer days to Switzerland.
Switzerland represents, generally, nature in the rough,
and the American traveller in search of novelty enter-
tains a rational preference for nature in the refined
state. If he has his European opportunities very much
at heart, he will be apt to chafe a little on lake-side
and mountain-side with a sense of the beckoning, un-
visited cities of Germany, France, and Italy. As to
the average American tourist, however, as one actually
meets him, it is hard to say whether he most neglects
or abuses opportunity. It is beside the mark, at any
rate, to talk to him about economy. He spends as he
listeth, and if he overfees the waiters he is frugal of his
hours. He has long since discovered the art of compre-
hensive travel, and if you think he had better not be
in Switzerland — *rassurez-vous* — he will not be there
long. I am, perhaps, unduly solicitous for him from a
vague sense of having treated myself to an overdose of
Switzerland. I relish a human flavor in my pleasures,
and I fancy that it is a more equal intercourse between

man and man than between man and mountain. I
have found myself grumbling at moments because the
large-hewn snow-peaks of the Oberland are not the
marble pinnacles of a cathederal, and the liquid sapphire and emerald of Leman and Lucerne are not firm
palace-floors of lapis and verd-antique. But, after all,
there is a foreground in Switzerland as well as a background, and more than once, when a mountain has
stared me out of countenance, I have recovered my
self-respect in a sympathetic gaze at the object which
here corresponds to the Yankee town-pump. Swiss
village fountains are delightful; the homely village life
centres about the great stone basin (roughly inscribed,
generally, with an antique date), where the tinkling
cattle drink, where the lettuce and the linen are
washed, where dusty pedestrians, with their lips at
the spout, need scarcely devote their draught to the
" health " of the brawny beauties who lean, brown-
armed, over the trough, and the plash of the cool, hard
water is heard at either end of the village street. But
I am surely not singular in my impulse thus occasionally to weigh detail against mass in Switzerland ; and
İ apprehend that, unless you are a regular climber, or
an æsthetic Buddhist, as it were, content with a purely
contemplative enjoyment of natural beauty, you are
obliged eventually in self-defence to lower, by an imaginative effort, the sky-line of your horizon. You
may sit for days before the hotel at Grindelwald, looking at the superb snow-crested granite of the Wetter-
horn, if you have a slowly ripening design of measuring
your legs, your head, and your wind against it ; and

3 *

a fortiori, the deed being done, you may spend another
week in the same position, sending up patronizing
looks at those acres of ice which the foolish cockneys
at your side take to be inches. But there is a limit to
the satisfaction with which you can sit staring at a
mountain — even the most beautiful — which you have
neither ascended nor are likely to ascend; and I know
of nothing to which I can better compare the effect on
your nerves of what comes to seem to you, at last, its
inhuman want of condescension than that of the expression of back of certain persons whom you come as
near detesting as your characteristic amiability per-
mits. I appeal on this point to all poor mountaineers.
They might reply, however, that one should be either
a good climber or a good idler.

If there is truth in this retort, it may help to explain
an old-time kindness of mine for Geneva, to which I
was introduced years ago, in my school-days, when I
was as good an idler as the best. And I ought in justice to say that, with Geneva for its metropolis, Switzerland may fairly pretend to possess something more
than nature in the rough. A Swiss novelist of incomparable talent has indeed written a tale expressly to
prove that frank nature is wofully out of favor there,
and his heroine dies of a broken heart because her
spontaneity passes for impropriety. I don't know
whether M. Cherbuliez's novel is as veracious as it is
clever; but the susceptible stranger certainly feels that
the Swiss metropolis is a highly artificial compound.
It makes little difference that the individuality of the
place is a moral rather than an architectural one; for

the streets and houses express it as clearly as if it were syllabled in their stones. The moral tone of Geneva, as I imagine it, is epigrammatically, but on the whole justly, indicated by the fact, recently related to me by a discriminating friend, that, meeting one day in the street a placard of the theatre, superscribed *Bouffes-Genevois*, he burst into irrepressible laughter. To appreciate the irony of the phrase, one must have lived long enough in Geneva to suffer from the want of humor in the local atmosphere, and the absence, as well, of that æsthetic character begotten of a generous view of life. There is no Genevese architecture, nor museum, nor theatre, nor music, not even a worthy promenade, — all prime requisites of a well-appointed foreign capital; and yet somehow Geneva manages to assert herself powerfully without them, and to leave the impression of a strongly featured little city, which, if you do not enjoy, you may at least grudgingly respect. It was, perhaps, the absence of these frivolous attributes which caused it to be thought a proper place for the settlement of our solemn wrangle with England, — though surely a community which could make a joke would have afforded worthier spectators to certain phases of the affair. But there is such a thing, after all, as drawing too sober-colored a picture of the Presbyterian mother-city, and I suddenly find myself wondering whether, if it were not the most respectable of capitals, it would not still be the prettiest; whether its main interest is not, possibly, the picturesque one, — the admirable contrast of the dark, homely-featured mass of the town, relieved now, indeed, at the water's edge by a shining rim of white-walled hotels, — and the incomparable vivacity of color of the blue lake and Rhone. This divinely cool-hued gush of the Rhone beneath the two elder bridges is one of the loveliest things in Switzerland, and ought itself to make the fortune of unnumbered generations of inn-keepers. As you linger and watch the shining tide, you make a rather vain effort to connect it with the two great human figures in the Genevese picture, — Calvin and Rousseau. It seems to have no great affinity with either genius, — one of which it might have brightened and the other have cleansed. There is indeed in Rousseau a strong limpidity of style which, if we choose, we may fancy an influence from the rushing stream he must so often have tarried in his boyish breeches to peep at between the bridge-rails ; but I doubt whether we can twist the Rhone into a channel for even the most diluted Calvinism. It must have seemed to the grim Doctor as one of the streams of the paradise he was making it so hard to enter. For ourselves, as it hurries undarkened past the gray theological city, we may liken it to the impetus of faith shooting in deep indifference past the doctrine of election. The genius that contains the clearest strain of this anti-Calvinistic azure is decidedly that of Byron. He has versified the lake in the finest Byronic manner, and I have seen its color, of a bright day, as beautiful, as unreal, as romantic as the most classical passages of "Childe Harold." Its shores have not yet lost the echo of three other eminent names, — those of Voltaire, of Gibbon, and of Madame de Staël. These great writers,

however, were all such sturdy non-conductors of the
modern tendency of landscape to make its way into
literature, that the tourist hardly feels himself indebted to their works for a deeper relish of the lake
— though, indeed, they have bequeathed him the opportunity for a charming threefold pilgrimage. About
Ferney and Coppet I might say a dozen things which
the want of space forbids. As for the author of that
great chronicle which never is but always to be read,
you may take your coffee of a morning in the little
garden in which he wrote *finis* to his immortal work,
— and if the coffee is good enough to administer a
fillip to your fancy, perhaps you may yet hear the
faint reverberation among the trees of the long, long
breath with which he must have laid down his pen.
It is, to my taste, quite the reverse of a profanation to
commemorate a classic site by a good inn; and the
excellent Hôtel Gibbon at Lausanne, ministering to
that larger perception which is almost identical with
the aftertaste of a good *cuisine*, may fairly pretend to
propagate the exemplary force of a great human effort. There is a charming Hôtel Byron at Villeneuve,
the eastern end of the lake, of which I have retained
a kindlier memory than of any of my Swiss resting-
places. It has about it a kind of mellow gentility
which is equally rare and delightful, and which perhaps rests partly on the fact that — owing, I suppose,
to the absence just thereabouts of what is technically
termed a "feature" — it is generally just thinly enough
populated to make you wonder how it can pay, and
whether the landlord is not possibly entertaining you at

a sacrifice. It has none of that look of heated prosperity which has come of late years to intermingle so
sordid an element with the pure grandeur of Swiss
scenery.

The crowd in Switzerland demands a chapter by
itself, and when I pause in the anxious struggle for
bed and board to take its prodigious measure, — and,
in especial, to comprehend its huge main factor, the
terrible German element, — mountains and men seem
to resolve themselves into a single monstrous mass,
darkening the clear heaven of rest and leisure. Crossing lately the lovely Scheideck pass, from Grindelwald
to Meyringen, I needed to remember well that this is
the great thoroughfare of Swiss travel, and that I might
elsewhere find some lurking fragment of landscape
without figures, — or with fewer, — not to be dismayed
by its really grotesque appearance. It is hardly an
exaggeration to say that the road was black with way-
farers. They darkened the slopes like the serried pine
forests, they dotted the crags and fretted the sky-line
like far-browsing goats, and their great collective hum
rose up to heaven like the uproar of a dozen torrents.
More recently, I strolled down from Andermatt on the
St. Gothard to look at that masterpiece of sternly romantic landscape, the Devil's Bridge. Huge walls of
black granite inclose the scene, the road spans a tremendous yellow cataract which flings an icy mist all
abroad, and a savage melancholy, in fine, marks the
spot for her own. But half a dozen carriages, jingling
cheerily up the ascent, had done their best to dispos-
sess her. The parapet of the bridge was adorned with

as many gazers as that of the Pont Neuf when one of its classic anglers has proclaimed a bite, and I was obliged to confess that I had missed the full force of a sensation. If the reader's sympathies are touched by my discomfiture, I may remind him that though, as a fastidious few, we laugh at Mr. Cook, the great *entrepreneur* of travel, with his coupons and his caravans of "personally-conducted" sight-seers, we have all pretty well come to belong to his party in one way or another. We complain of a hackneyed and cocknified Europe; but wherever, in desperate quest of the untrodden, we carry our much-labelled luggage, our bad French, our demand for a sitz-bath and pale ale, we rub off the precious primal bloom of the picturesque, and establish a precedent for unlimited intrusion. I have even fancied that it is a sadly ineffectual pride that prevents us from buying one of Mr. Cook's little bundles of tickets, and saving our percentage, whatever it is, of money and trouble; for I am sure that the poor bewildered and superannuated genius of the old Grand Tour, as it was taken forty years ago, wherever she may have buried her classic head, beyond hearing of the eternal telegraphic click bespeaking "rooms" on mountain-tops, confounds us all alike in one sweeping reprobation.

I might, perhaps, have purchased exemption from her curse by idling the summer away in the garden of the Hôtel Byron, or by contenting myself with such wanderings as you may enjoy on the neighboring hillsides. The great beauty of detail in this region seems to me to have been insufficiently noted. People come

hither, indeed, in swarms, but they talk more of places
that are not half so lovely; and when, returning from a
walk over the slopes above Montreux, I have ventured
to hint at a few of the fine things I have seen, I have
been treated as if I were jealous, forsooth, of a projected tour to Chamouni. These slopes climb the
great hills in almost park-like stretches of verdure,
studded with generous trees, among which the walnut
abounds, and into which, as you look down, the lake
seems to fling up a blue reflection which, by contrast,
turns their green leaves to yellow. Here you may
wander through wood and dell, by stream and meadow,
— streams that narrow as they wind ever upward, and
meadows often so steep that the mowers, as they swing
their scythes over them, remind you of insects on a
wall brandishing long *antennæ*, — and range through
every possible phase of sweet sub-Alpine scenery.
Nowhere, I imagine, can you better taste the charm, as
distinguished from the grandeur, of Swiss landscape;
and as in Switzerland the grandeur and the charm are
constantly interfused and harmonized, you have only to
ramble far enough and high enough to get a hint of
real mountain sternness, — to overtake the topmost
edge of the woods and emerge upon the cool, sunny
places where the stillness is broken only by cattle-bells
and the plash of streams, and the snow-patches, in the
darker nooks, linger till midsummer. If this does not
satisfy you, you may do a little mild mountaineering
by climbing the Rochers de Noye or the Dent de
Jaman, — a miniature Matterhorn. But the most
profitable paths, to my taste, are certain broad-flagged,

grass-grown footways, which lead you through densely fruited orchards to villages of a charming quaintness, nestling often in so close a verdure that from the road by the lake you hardly suspect them. The pictu-resqueness of Vaudois village life ought surely to have produced more sketchers and lyrists. The bit of coun-try between Montreux and Vevay, though disfigured with an ugly fringe of vineyards near the lake, is a perfect nest of these fantastic hamlets. The houses are, for the most part, a delightfully irregular combina-tion of the chalet and the rustic *maison bourgeoise;* and — with their rugged stony foundations, pierced with a dusky stable-arch and topped with a random superstructure of balconies, outer stairways, and gables, weather-browned beams and sun-cracked stucco, their steep red roofs with knob-crowned turrets, their little cobble-paved courts, with the great stone fountain and its eternal plash — they are at once so pleasantly gro-tesque and yet so sturdily well-conditioned, that their aspect seems a sort of influence from the blue glitter of the lake as it plays through the trees with genial *invraisemblance.* The little village of Veytaux, above Chillon, where it lurks unperceived among its foliage, is an admirable bit of this Vaudois picturesqueness. The little grassy main street of the village enters and passes bodily through a house, — converting it into a vast dim, creaking, homely archway, — with an au-dacity, a frank self-abandonment to local color, which is one of the finest strokes of the sort I ever encoun-tered. And yet three English sisters whom I used to meet thereabouts had preferred one morning to station

E

themselves at the parapet of the road by the lake, and, spreading their sketch-books there, to expend their precious little tablets of Winsor & Newton on those too, too familiar walls and towers where Byron's Boninvard languished.   Even as I passed, the railway train whizzed by beneath their noses, and the *genius loci* seemed to flee howling in the shriek of its signal. Temple Bar itself witnesses a scarcely busier coming and going than, in these days, those hoary portals of Chillon.   My own imagination, on experiment, proved too poor an alchemist, and such enjoyment as I got of the castle was mainly my distant daily view of it from the garden of the Hôtel Byron, — a little, many-pinnacled white promontory, shining against the blue lake. When I went, Bädeker in hand, to "do" the place, I found a huge concourse of visitors awaiting the reflux of an earlier wave.   "Let us at least wait till there is no one else," I said to my companion.   She smiled in compassion of my naïveté, " *There is never no one else*," she answered.   "We must treat it as a crush or leave it alone."

Any truly graceful picturesqueness here is the more carefully to be noted that the graceful in Switzerland — especially in the German cantons — is a very rare commodity, and that everything that is not rigorously a mountain or a valley is distinctly tainted with ugliness. The Swiss have, apparently, an insensibility to comeliness or purity of form, — a partiality to the clumsy, coarse, and prosaic which one might almost interpret as a calculated offset to their great treasure of natural beauty, or at least as an instinctive protest of the na-

tional genius for frugality. Monte Rosa and the Jungfrau fill their pockets ; why should they give double
measure when single will serve ? Even so solidly picturesque a town as Berne — a town full of massive
Teutonic quaintness and sturdy individuality of feature
— nowhere by a single happy accident of architecture
even grazes the line of beauty. The place is so full of
entertaining detail that the fancy warms to it, and you
good-naturedly pronounce it charming. But when the
sense of novelty subsides, and you notice the prosaic
scoop of its arcades, the wanton angularity of its grotesque, umbrella - shaped roofs, the general plebeian
stride and straddle of its architecture, you half take
back your kindness, and declare that nature in Switzerland might surely afford to be a trifle less jealous of art.
But wherever the German tone of things prevails, a
certain rich and delectable homeliness goes with it, and
I have of Berne this pleasant recollection : the vision
of a long main street, looking dark, somehow, in spite
of its breadth, and bordered with houses supported on
deep arcades, whereof the short, thick pillars resemble
queerly a succession of bandy legs, and overshaded by
high-piled pagoda roofs. The dusky arcades are lined
with duskier shops and bustling with traffic ; the windows of the houses are open, and filled with charming
flowers. They are invariably adorned, furthermore,
with a bright red window-cushion, which in its turn
sustains a fair Bernese, — a Bernese fair enough, at least,
to complete the not especially delicate harmony of the
turkey-red cushion and the vividly blooming plants.
These deep color-spots, scattered along the gray stretch

of the houses, help to make the scene a picture ; yet if
it remains, somehow, at once so pleasant and so plain,
you may almost find the explanation in the row of
ancient fountains along the middle of the street, — the
peculiar glory of Berne, — each a great stone basin
with a pillar rising from the centre and supporting a
sculptured figure more or less heraldic and legendary.
This richly wrought chain of fountains is a precious
civic possession, and has an admirably picturesque effect ; but each of the images which presides at these
sounding springs — sources of sylvan music in the ancient street — appears, when you examine it, a mon-
ster of awkwardness and ugliness.

I ought to add that I write these lines in a place so
charming that it seems pure perversity to remember
here anything but the perfect beauty of Switzerland.
From my window I look straight through the gray-blue
portals of the Via Mala. Gray-blue they are with an
element of melancholy red — like the rust on an ancient sword ; and they rise in magnificent rocky crags
on either side of this old-time evil way, in which the
waning afternoon is deepening the shadows against a
splendid background of sheer gray rock, muffled here
and there in clinging acres of pine forest. The car-
riage-road winds into it with an air of solemnity which
suggests some almost metaphysical simile, — the advance of a simple, credulous reader, say, into some
darksome romance. If you think me fantastic, come
and feel the influence of this lovely little town of Thusis. I may well be fantastic, however, for I have fresh
in my memory a journey in which the fancy finds as

good an account as in any you may treat it to in Switzerland, — a long two-days' drive through the western Grisons and the beautiful valley of the Vorder-Rhein. The scenery is, perhaps, less characteristically Swiss than that of many other regions, but it can hardly fail to deepen your admiration for a country which is able so liberally to overheap the measure of great impressions. It is a landscape rather of ruin-crowned cliff and crag, than of more or less virginal snow-peaks, but in its own gentler fashion it is as vast and bold and free as the Oberland. Coming down from the Oberalp which divides this valley from that of the St. Gothard, we entered a wondrous vista of graduated blue distances, along which the interlapping mountain-spurs grew to seem like the pillars — if one can imagine reclining pillars — of a mighty avenue. The landscape was more than picturesque, it was consummately pictorial. I fancied that I had never seen in nature such a wealth of blue, — deep and rich in the large foreground, and splendidly contrasted with the slopes of ripening grain, blocked out without hedge or fence in yellow parallelograms, and playing thence through shades of color, which were clear even in the vague distances. Foreground and distance here have alike a strong historic tinge. The little towns which yet subsist as almost formless agglomerations of rugged stone were members of the great Gray League of resistance to the baronial brigands whose crumbling towers and keeps still make the mountain-sides romantic. These little towns, Ilanz in especial, and Dissentis, overstared by the great blank façade of its useless monastery, are hardly more than rather putrid masses of mouldy masonry ; but with their desolate air of having been and ceased to be, their rugged solidity of structure, their low black archways, surmounted with stiffly hewn armorial shields, their lingering treasures in window-screen and gate of fantastically wrought-iron, they are among the things which make the sentimental tourist lean forth eagerly from his carriage with an impulse which may be called the prevision of retrospect.

FROM CHAMBÉRY TO MILAN.

YOUR truly sentimental tourist can never *bouder*
long, and it was at Chambéry — but four hours
from Geneva — that I accepted the situation, and decided that there might be mysterious delights in entering Italy whizzing through an eight-mile tunnel, like
some highly improved projectile of the period. I found
my reward in the Savoyard landscape, which greets
you betimes with something of a southern smile. If
it is not as Italian as Italy, it is at least more Italian than Switzerland, — more Italian, too, I should
think, than can seem natural and proper to the swarming red-legged soldiery who so ostentatiously assign it
to the dominion of M. Thiers. The light and coloring
had, to my eyes, not a little of that mollified depth
which they had last observed in Italy. It was simply,
perhaps, that the weather was hot and that the mountains
were drowsing in that iridescent haze which I have
seen nearer home than at Chambéry. But the vegetation, assuredly, had an all but Transalpine twist and
curl, and the classic wayside tangle of corn and vines
left nothing to be desired in the line of careless grace.
Chambéry as a town, however, affords little premonition

of Italy. There is shabbiness and shabbiness, the discriminating tourist will tell you ; and that of the ancient capital of Savoy lacks color. I found a better pastime, however, than strolling through the dark, dull streets in quest of "effects" that were not forthcoming. The first urchin you meet will tell you the way to Les Charmettes and the Maison Jean-Jacques. A very pleasant way it becomes as soon as it leaves the town, — a winding, climbing by-road, bordered with such a tall and sturdy hedge as to give it the air of an English lane, — if you can fancy an English lane introducing you to the haunts of a Madame de Warens! The house which formerly sheltered this lady's singular ménage stands on a hillside above the road, which a rapid path connects with the little grass-grown terrace before it. It is a small, shabby, homely dwelling, with a certain reputable solidity, however, and more of internal spaciousness than of outside promise. The place is shown by an elderly Frenchwoman, who points out the very few surviving objects which you may touch, with the reflection — complacent in whatsoever degree suits you — that Rousseau's hand has often lain there. It was presumably a meagrely appointed house, and I wondered that on these scanty features so much expression should linger. But the edifice has an ancient ponderosity of structure, and the dust of the eighteenth century seems to lie on its worm-eaten floors, to cling to the faded old *papiers à ramages* on the walls, and to lodge in the crevices of the brown wooden ceilings. Madame de Warens's bed remains, with Rousseau's own narrow couch, his little warped and cracked yellow spinet, and

a battered, turnip-shaped silver timepiece, engraved
with its master's name, — its primitive tick as extinct
as his heart-beats. It cost me, I confess, a somewhat
pitying acceleration of my own to see this intimately
personal relic of the *genius loci* — for it had dwelt in
his waistcoat-pocket, than which there is hardly a material point in space nearer to a man's consciousness,
— tossed so irreverently upon the table on which you
deposited your fee, beside the dog's-eared visitors'
record — the *livre de cuisine* recently denounced by
Madame Sand. In fact, the place generally, in so far
as some faint ghostly presence of its famous inmates
seems to linger there, is by no means exhilarating.
Coppet and Ferney tell, if not of pure happiness, at least
of prosperity and honor, wealth and success. But Les
Charmettes is haunted by ghosts unclean and forlorn.
The place tells of poverty, trouble, and impurity. A
good deal of clever modern talent in France has been
employed in touching up the episode of which it was
the scene, and tricking it out in idyllic love-knots.
But as I stood on the charming terrace I have mentioned, — a little jewel of a terrace, with grassy flags
and a mossy parapet, and an admirable view of great
swelling violet hills, — stood there reminded how much
sweeter Nature is than man, the story looked rather
wan and unlovely beneath these literary decorations,
and I could muster no keener relish for it than is implied in perfect pity. Hero and heroine were first-rate
subjects for psychology, but hardly for poetry. But,
not to moralize too sternly for a tourist between trains,
I should add that, as an illustration, to be inserted men-

4

tally in the text of the "Confessions," a glimpse of Les
Charmettes is pleasant enough. It completes the rare
charm of good autobiography to behold with one's eyes
the faded and battered background of the story ; and
Rousseau's narrative is so incomparably vivid and forcible, that the sordid little house at Chambéry seems of
a hardly deeper shade of reality than the images you
contemplate in his pages.

If I spent an hour at Les Charmettes, fumbling thus
helplessly with the past, I frankly recognized on the
morrow that the Mont Cenis Tunnel savors strongly of
the future. As I passed along the St. Gothard, a couple
of months since, I perceived, half-way up the Swiss
ascent, a group of navvies at work in a gorge beneath
the road. They had laid bare a broad surface of granite, and had punched in the centre of it a round, black
cavity, of about the dimensions, as it seemed to me, of
a soup-plate. This was the embryonic form of the dark
mid-channel of the St. Gothard Railway, which is to
attain its perfect development some eight years hence.
The Mont Cenis, therefore, may be held to have set a
fashion which will be followed till the highest Him-
alaya is but the ornamental apex or snow-capped gable-
tip of some resounding fuliginous corridor. The tunnel differs but in length from other tunnels ; you spend
half an hour in it. But you come whizzing out of it
into Transalpine Italy, and, as you look back, may
fancy it shrugging its mighty shoulders over the track —
a spasmodic protest of immobility against speed. The
tunnel is certainly not a poetic object, but there is no
perfection without its beauty ; and as you measure the

long rugged outline of the pyramid of which it forms
the base, you must admit that it is the perfection of a
short cut. Twenty-four hours from Paris to Turin is
speed for the times — speed which may content us, at
any rate, until expansive Berlin has succeeded in placing itself at thirty-six from Milan. I entered Turin
of a lovely August afternoon, and found a city of arcades, of pink and yellow stucco, of innumerable cafés,
blue-legged officers, and ladies draped in the Spanish
veil. An old friend of Italy, coming back to her, finds
an easy waking for sleeping memories. Every object
is a reminder. Half an hour after my arrival, as I
stood at my window, looking out on the great square,
it seemed to me that the scene within and without was
a rough epitome of every pleasure and every impression
I had formerly gathered from Italy ; the balcony and
the Venetian-blind, the cool floor of speckled concrete,
the lavish delusions of frescoed wall and ceiling, the
broad divan framed for the noonday siesta, the massive
mediæval Castello in mid-square, with its shabby rear
and its pompous Palladian front, the brick campaniles
beyond, the milder, yellower light, the brighter colors
and softer sounds. Later, beneath the arcades, I found
many an old acquaintance, beautiful officers, resplen-
dent, slow-strolling, contemplative of female beauty ;
civil and peaceful dandies, hardly less gorgeous, with
that religious faith in their mustaches and shirt-fronts
which distinguishes the *belle jeunesse* of Italy ; ladies
most artfully veiled in lace mantillas, but with too little
art — or too much nature, at least — in the region of
the boddice ; well-conditioned young *abbati*, with neatly

drawn stockings. These, indeed, are not objects of
first-rate interest, and with such Turin is rather meagrely furnished. It has no architecture, no churches,
no monuments, nor especially picturesque street-scen-
ery. It has, indeed, the great votive temple of the Superga, which stands on a high hilltop above the city,
gazing across at Monte Rosa, and lifting its own fine
dome against the sky with no contemptible art. But
when you have seen the Superga from the quay beside
the Po, as shrivelled and yellow in August as some
classic Spanish stream, and said to yourself that in
architecture position is half the battle, you have nothing left to visit but the Museum of pictures. The
Turin Gallery, which is large and well arranged, is the
fortunate owner of three or four masterpieces ; a couple
of magnificent Vandycks and a couple of Paul Veroneses ; the latter a Queen of Sheba and a Feast at the
House of Levi, — the usual splendid combination of
brocades, grandees, and marble colonnades dividing
skies *de turquoise malade*, as Théophile Gautier says.
The Veroneses are fine, but with Venice in prospect
the traveller feels at liberty to keep his best attention
in reserve. If, however, he has the proper relish for
Vandyck, let him linger long and fondly here ; for that
admiration will never be more potently stirred than by
the delicious picture of the three little royal highnesses,
the sons and the daughter of Charles I. All the purity
of childhood is here, and all its soft solidity of structure, rounded tenderly beneath the spangled satin, and
contrasted charmingly with its pompous rigidity. Clad
respectively in crimson, white, and blue, the royal ba-

bies stand up in their ruffs and fardingales in dimpled serenity, squaring their infantine stomachers at the spectator with an innocence, a dignity, a delightful grotesqueness, which make the picture as real as it is elegant. You might kiss their hands, but you certainly would think twice before pinching their cheeks, — provocative as they are of this tribute of admiration, — and would altogether lack presumption to lift them off the ground, — the royal dais on which they stand so sturdily planted by right of birth. There is something inimitable in the paternal gallantry with which the painter has touched off the young lady. She was a princess, yet she was a baby, and he has contrived, we may fancy, to work into his picture an intimation that she was a creature whom in her teens, the lucklessly smitten — even as he was prematurely — must vainly sigh for. Although the work is a masterpiece of execution, its merits under this head may be emulated — at a distance. The lovely modulations of color in the three contrasted and harmonized little satin petticoats — the solidity of the little heads, in spite of all their prettiness — the happy, unexaggerated squareness and maturity of *pose* — are, severally, points to study, to imitate, and to reproduce with profit. But the taste of the picture is its great secret as well as its great merit — a taste which seems one of the lost instincts of mankind. Go and enjoy this supreme expression of Vandyck's fine sense, and admit that never was a politer work.

Milan is an older, richer, more historic city than Turin ; but its general aspect is no more distinctly

Italian. The long Austrian occupation, perhaps, did something to Germanize its physiognomy; though, indeed, this is an indifferent explanation when one remembers how well, picturesquely, Italy held her own in Venetia. Far be it from me, moreover, to accuse Milan of a want of picturesqueness. I mean simply that at certain points it seems rather like the last of the Northern capitals than the first of the Southern. The cathedral is before all things picturesque; it is not interesting, it is not logical, it is not even, to some minds, commandingly beautiful; but it is grandly curious, superbly rich. I hope, for my own part, that I shall never grow too fastidious to enjoy it. If it had no other beauty it would have that of impressive, immeasurable achievement. As I strolled beside its vast indented base one evening, and felt it above me, massing its gray mysteries in the starlight, while the restless human tide on which I floated rose no higher than the first few layers of street-soiled marble, I was tempted to believe that beauty in great architecture is almost a secondary merit, and that the main point is mass — such mass as may make it a supreme embodiment of sustained effort. Viewed in this way, a great building is the greatest conceivable work of art. More than any other it represents difficulties annulled, resources combined, labor, courage, and patience. And there are people who tell us that art has nothing to do with morality! Little enough, doubtless, when it is concerned, ever so little, in painting the roof of Milan Cathedral within to represent carved stone-work. Of this famous roof every one has heard, — how good it is, how bad, how perfect a delusion, how transparent an artifice. It is the first thing your cicerone shows you on entering the church. The discriminating tourist may accept it philosophically, I think ; for the interior, though admirably effective, has no very recondite beauties. It is splendidly vast and dim ; the altar-lamps twinkle afar through the incense-thickened air like fog-lights at sea, and the great columns rise straight to the roof, which hardly curves to meet them, with the girth and altitude of oaks of a thousand years ; but there is little refinement of design — few of those felicities of proportion which the eye caresses, when it finds them, very much as the memory retains and repeats some happy line of poetry or some delightful musical phrase. But picturesque, I repeat, is the whole vast scene, and nothing more so than a certain exhibition which I privately enjoyed of the relics of St. Charles Borromeus. This holy man lies at his eternal rest in a small but gorgeous sepulchral chapel, beneath the pavement of the church, before the high altar ; and for the modest· sum of five francs you may have his shrivelled mortality unveiled, and gaze at it in all the dreadful double scepticism of a Protestant and a tourist. The Catholic Church, I believe, has some doctrine that its ends justify at need any means whatsoever ; *a fortiori*, therefore, nothing it does can be ridiculous. The performance in question, of which the good San Carlo paid the cost, was impressive, certainly, but as great grotesqueness is impressive. The little sacristan, having secured his audience, whipped on a white tunic over his frock, lighted a couple of extra candles, and proceeded to re-

move from above the altar, by means of a crank, a sort
of sliding shutter, just as you may see a shop-boy do
of a morning at his master's window. In this case, too,
a large sheet of plate-glass was uncovered, and, to form
an idea of the *étalage*, you must imagine that a jeweller,
for reasons of his own, has struck an unnatural partner-
ship with an undertaker. The black, mummified corpse
of the saint is stretched out in a glass coffin, clad in his
mouldering canonicals, mitred, crosiered, and gloved,
and glittering with votive jewels. It is an extraordinary mixture of death and life; the desiccated · clay,
the ashen rags, the hideous little black mask and skull,
and the living, glowing, twinkling splendor of diamonds,
emeralds, and sapphires. The collection is really fine,
and various great historic names are attached to the
different offerings. Whatever may be the better opinion as to whether the Church is in a decline, I cannot
help thinking that she will make a tolerable figure in
the world so long as she retains this great capital of
bric-à-brac, scintillating throughout Christendom at
effectively scattered points. You see, I am forced to
agree after all, in spite of the sliding shutter and the
profane exhibitory arts of the sacristan, that the majesty
of the Church saved the situation, or made it, at least,
sublimely ridiculous. Yet it was from a natural desire
to breathe a sweeter air that I immediately afterwards
undertook the interminable climb to the roof of the
cathedral. This is a great spectacle, and one of the
best known; for every square inch of wall on the winding stairways is bescribbled with a traveller's name.
There is a great glare from the far-stretching slopes of

marble, a confusion (like the masts of a navy or the spears of an army) of image-capped pinnacles, biting the impalpable blue, and, better than either, a delicious view of level Lombardy, sleeping in its rich Transalpine light, and looking, with its white-walled dwellings, and the spires on its horizon, like a vast green sea spotted with ships. After two months of Switzerland, the Lombard plain is a delicious rest to the eye, and the yellow, liquid, free-flowing light (as if on favored Italy the vessels of heaven were more widely opened) had for mine a charm which made me think of a great opaque mountain as a blasphemous invasion of the atmospheric spaces.

I have mentioned the cathedral first, but the prime treasure of Milan at the present hour is the beautiful, tragical Leonardo. The cathedral is good for another thousand years, but I doubt whether our children will find in the most majestic and most luckless of frescos much more than the shadow of a shadow. Its fame for many years now has been that, as one may say, of an illustrious invalid whom people visit to see how he lasts, with death-bed speeches. The picture needs not another scar or stain, now, to be the saddest work of art in the world; and battered, defaced, ruined as it is, it remains one of the greatest. It is really not amiss to compare its decay to the slow extinction of a human organism. The creation of the picture was a breath from the infinite, and the painter's conception not immeasurably less complex than that implied, say, by his own composition. There has been much talk lately about the irony of fate, but I suspect that fate was

never more ironical than when she led this most deeply
calculating of artists to spend fifteen long years in
building his goodly house upon the sand. And yet,
after all, can I fancy this apparent irony but a deeper
wisdom, for if the picture enjoyed the immortal health
and bloom of a first-rate Titian we should have lost
one of the most pertinent lessons in the history of art.
We know it as hearsay, but here is the plain proof, that
there is no limit to the amount of substance an artist
may put into his work. Every painter ought once in
his life to stand before the Cenacolo and decipher its
moral. Pour everything you mentally possess into your
picture, lest perchance your " prepared surface " should
play you a trick ! Raphael was a happier genius ; you
cannot look at his lovely Marriage of the Virgin at the
Brera, beautiful as some first deep smile of conscious
inspiration, without feeling that he foresaw no complaint against fate, and that he looked at the world
with the vision of a graceful optimist. But I have left
no space to speak of the Brera, nor of that paradise of
bookworms with an eye for the picturesque — if such
creatures exist — the Ambrosian Library ; nor of that
solid old basilica of St. Ambrose, with its spacious
atrium and its crudely solemn mosaics, in which it is
surely your own fault if you do not forget Dr. Strauss
and M. Renan and worship as simply as a Christian of
the ninth century.

It is part of the sordid prose of the Mont Cenis
road that, unlike those fine, old unimproved passes, the
Simplon, the Splügen, and — yet awhile longer — the
St. Gothard, it denies you a glimpse of that paradise

adorned by the four lakes, as that of uncommented Scripture by the rivers of Eden. I made, however, an excursion to the Lake of Como, which, though brief, lasted long enough to make me feel as if I too were a hero of romance, with leisure for a love-affair, and not a hurrying tourist, with a Bradshaw in his pocket. The Lake of Como has figured largely in novels with a tendency to immorality — being commonly the spot to which inflammatory young gentlemen invite the wives of other gentlemen to fly with them and ignore the restrictions of public opinion. But here is a chance for the stern moralist to rejoice; the Lake of Como, too, has been improved, and can boast of a public opinion. I should pay a poor compliment, at least, to the swarming inmates of the hotels which now alternate, attractively, by the water-side, with villas old and new, to think that it could not. But if it is lost to wicked novels, the unsophisticated American tourist may still do a little private romancing there. The pretty hotel at Cadenabbia offers him, for instance, the romance of what we call at home summer board. It is all so unreal, so fictitious, so elegant and idle, so framed to undermine a rigid sense of the chief end of man not being to float forever in an ornamental boat, beneath an awning tasselled like a circus-horse, impelled by an affable Giovanni or Antonio from one stately stretch of lake-laved villa steps to another, that departure seems as harsh and unnatural as the dream-dispelling note of some punctual voice at your bedside on a dusky winter morning. Yet I wondered, for my own part, where I had seen it all before — the pink-

walled villas gleaming through their shrubberies of
orange and oleander, the mountains shimmering in the
hazy light like so many breasts of doves, the constant
presence of the melodious Italian voice. Where, indeed, but at the Opera, when the manager has been
more than usually regardless of expense? Here, in
the foreground, was the palace of the nefarious barytone, with its banqueting-hall opening as freely on the
stage as a railway buffet on the platform; beyond, the
delightful back scene, with its operatic gamut of coloring; in the middle, the scarlet-sashed *barcaiuoli*, grouped
like a chorus, hat in hand, awaiting the conductor's signal. It was better even than being in a novel, — this
being in a libretto.

FROM VENICE TO STRASBURG.

THERE would be much to say about that golden chain of historic cities which stretches from Milan to Venice, in which the very names — Brescia, Verona, Mantua, Padua — are an ornament to one's phrase; but I should have to draw upon recollections now three years old, and to make my short story a long one. Of Verona and Venice only have I recent impressions, and even to these I must do hasty justice. I came into Venice, just as I had done before, toward the end of a summer's day, when the shadows begin to lengthen, and the light to glow, and found that the attendant sensations bore repetition remarkably well. There was the same last intolerable delay at Mestre, just before your first glimpse of the lagoon confirms the already distinct sea-smell which has added speed to the precursive flight of your imagination; then the liquid level, edged far off by its band of undiscriminated domes and spires, soon distinguished and proclaimed, however, as excited and contentious heads multiply at the windows of the train; then your long rumble on the immense white railway bridge, which, in spite of the invidious contrast drawn (very properly) by Mr. Ruskin, between

the old and the new approach to Venice, does truly, in
a manner, shine across the green lap of the lagoon like
a mighty causeway of marble; then the plunge into the
station, which would be exactly similar to every other
plunge, save for one little fact, — that the key-note of
the great medley of voices borne back from the exit is
not " Cab, sir ! " but " Barca, signore ! " I do not mean,
however, to follow the traveller through every phase
of his initiation, at the risk of stamping poor Venice
beyond repair as the supreme bugbear of literature;
though, for my own part, I hold that, to a fine, healthy
appetite for the picturesque, the subject cannot be too
diffusely treated. Meeting on the Piazza, on the evening of my arrival, a young American painter, who told
me that he had been spending the summer at Venice,
I could have assaulted him, for very envy. He was
painting, forsooth, the interior of St. Marks ! To be
a young American painter, unperplexed by the mocking,
elusive soul of things, and satisfied with their wholesome, light-bathed surface and shape; keen of eye;
fond of color, of sea and sky, and anything that may
chance between them ; of old lace, and old brocade, and
old furniture (even when made to order); of time-mel-
lowed harmonies on nameless canvases, and happy contours in cheap old engravings ; to spend one's mornings
in still, productive analysis of the clustered shadows
of the Basilica, one's afternoons anywhere, in church
or campo, on canal or lagoon, and one's evenings in
starlight gossip at Florian's, feeling the sea-breeze throb
languidly between the two great pillars of the Piaz-
zetta and over the low, black domes of the church, —

this, I consider, is to be as happy as one may safely be.

The mere use of one's eyes, in Venice, is happiness enough, and generous observers find it hard to keep an account of their profits in this line. Everything the eye rests on is effective, pictorial, harmonious — thanks to some inscrutable flattery of the atmosphere. Your brown-skinned, white-shirted gondolier, twisting himself in the light, seems to you, as you lie staring beneath your awning, a perpetual symbol of Venetian "effect." The light here is, in fact, a mighty magician, and, with all respect to Titian, Veronese, and Tintoret, the greatest artist of them all. You should see, in places, the material on which it works — slimy brick, marble battered and befouled, rags, dirt, decay. Sea and sky seem to meet half-way, to blend their tones into a kind of soft iridescence, a lustrous compound of wave and cloud, and a hundred nameless local reflections, and then to fling the clear tissue against every object of vision. You may see these elements at work everywhere, but to see them in their intensity you should choose the finest day in the month, and have yourself rowed far away across the lagoon to Torcello. Without making this excursion, you can hardly pretend to know Venice, or to sympathize with that longing for pure radiance which animated her great colorists. It is a perfect bath of light, and I could not get rid of a fancy that we were cleaving the upper atmosphere on some hurrying cloud-skiff. At Torcello there is nothing but the light to see — nothing, at least, but a sort of blooming sand-bar, intersected by a single

narrow creek which does duty as a canal, and occupied
by a meagre cluster of huts,, the dwellings, apparently,
of market-gardeners and fishermen, and by a ruinous
church of the eleventh century. It is impossible to
imagine a more poignant embodiment of unheeded
decease. Torcello was the mother-city of Venice, and
it lies there now, a mere mouldering vestige, like a
group of weather-bleached parental bones left impiously
unburied. I stopped my gondola at the mouth of the
shallow inlet, and walked along the grass beside a
hedge to the low-browed, crumbling cathedral. The
charm of certain vacant grassy spaces, in Italy, over-
frowned by masses of brickwork honeycombed by the
suns of centuries, is something that I hereby renounce,
once for all, the attempt to express ; but you may be
sure, whenever I mention such a spot, that it is something delicious. A delicious stillness covered the little
campo at Torcello; I remember none so *audible* save
that of the Roman Campagna. There was no life there
but the visible tremor of the brilliant air and the cries
of half a dozen young children, who dogged our steps
and clamored for coppers. These children, by the way,
were the handsomest little brats in the world, and each
was furnished with a pair of eyes which seemed a sort
of protest of nature against the stinginess of fortune.
They were very nearly as naked as savages, and their
little bellies protruded like those of infant Abyssinians
in the illustrations of books of travel; but as they
scampered and sprawled in the soft, thick grass, grin-
ning like suddenly translated cherubs, and showing
their hungry little teeth, they suggested forcibly that

the best assurance of happiness in this world is to be found in the maximum of innocence and the minimum of wealth. One small urchin — framed, if ever a child was, to be the joy of an aristocratic mamma — was the most expressively beautiful little mortal I ever looked upon. He had a smile to make Correggio sigh in his grave ; and yet here he was, running wild among these sea-stunted bushes, on the lonely margin of a decaying world, in prelude to how blank, or to how dark, a destiny ? Verily, nature is still at odds with fortune ; though, indeed, if they ever really pull together, I am afraid nature will lose her picturesqueness. An infant citizen of our own republic, straight-haired, pale-eyed, and freckled, duly darned and catechised, marching into a New England school-house, is an object often seen and soon forgotten ; but I think I shall always remember, with infinite tender conjecture, as the years roll by, this little unlettered Eros of the Adriatic strand. Yet all youthful things at Torcello were not cheerful, for the poor lad who brought us the key of the cathedral was shaking with an ague, and his melancholy presence seemed to point the moral of forsaken nave and choir. The church is admirably primitive and curious, and reminded me of the two or three oldest churches of Rome — St. Clement and St. Agnes. The interior is rich in grimly mystical mosaics of the twelfth century, and the patchwork of precious fragments in the pavement is not inferior to that of St. Mark's. But the terribly distinct Apostles are ranged against their dead gold backgrounds as stiffly as grenadiers presenting arms — intensely personal sentinels of a personal De-

ity. Their stony stare seems to wait forever vainly for
some visible revival of primitive orthodoxy, and one
may well wonder whether it finds much beguilement
in idly gazing troops of Western heretics — passionless
even in their heresy.

I had been curious to see whether, in the galleries
and churches of Venice, I should be disposed to trans-
pose my old estimates — to burn what I had adored,
and to adore what I had burned. It is a sad truth that
one can stand in the Ducal Palace for the first time
but once, with the deliciously ponderous sense of that
particular half-hour being an era in one's mental history ; but I had the satisfaction of finding at least — a
great comfort in a short stay — that none of my early
memories were likely to change places, and that I could
take up my admirations where I had left them. I still
found Carpaccio delightful, Veronese magnificent, Titian
supremely beautiful, and Tintoret altogether unqualifi-
able. I repaired immediately to the little church of
San Cassano, which contains the smaller of Tintoret's
two great Crucifixions ; and when I had looked at it
awhile, I drew a long breath, and felt that I could contemplate any other picture in Venice with proper self-
possession. It seemed to me that I had advanced to
the uttermost limit of painting ; that beyond this another art — inspired poetry — begins, and that Bellini,
Veronese, Giorgione, and Titian, all joining hands and
straining every muscle of their genius, reach forward
not so far but that they leave a visible space in which
Tintoret alone is master. I well remember the excite-
ment into which he plunged me, when I first learned

to know him; but the glow of that comparatively youthful amazement is dead, and with it, I fear, that confident vivacity of phrase, of which, in trying to utter my impressions, I felt less the magniloquence than the impotence. In his power there are many weak spots, mysterious lapses, and fitful intermissions; but, when the list of his faults is complete, he still seems to me to remain the most *interesting* of painters. His reputation rests chiefly on a more superficial sort of merit — his energy, his unsurpassed productivity, his being, as Théophile Gautier says, *le roi des fougueux.* These qualities are immense, but the great source of his impressiveness is that his indefatigable hand never drew a line that was not, as one may say, a moral line. No painter ever had such breadth and such depth; and even Titian, beside him, has often seemed to me but a great decorative artist. Mr. Ruskin, whose eloquence, in dealing with the great Venetians, sometimes outruns his discretion, is fond of speaking even of Veronese as a painter of deep spiritual intentions. This, it seems to me, is pushing matters too far, and the author of the " Rape of Europa " is, pictorially speaking, no greater casuist than any other genius of supreme good taste. Titian was, assuredly, a mighty poet, but Tintoret — Tintoret was almost a prophet. Before his greatest works you are conscious of a sudden evaporation of old doubts and dilemmas, and the eternal problem of the conflict between idealism and realism dies the most natural of deaths. In Tintoret, the problem is practically solved, and the alternatives so harmoniously interfused that I defy the keenest critic to say where one

begins and the other ends. The homeliest prose melts
into the most ethereal poetry, and the literal and imaginative fairly confound their identity. This, however,
is vague praise. Tintoret's great merit, to my mind,
was his unequalled distinctness of vision. When once
he had conceived the germ of a scene, it defined itself
to his imagination with an intensity, an amplitude, an
individuality of expression, which make one's observation of his pictures seem less an operation of the mind
than a kind of supplementary experience of life. Veronese and Titian are content with a much looser speci-
fication, as their treatment of any subject which Tintoret has also treated abundantly proves. There are few
more suggestive contrasts than that between the absence of a total character at all commensurate with its
scattered variety and brilliancy, in Veronese's "Marriage of Cana," in the Louvre, and the poignant, almost
startling, completeness of Tintoret's illustration of the
theme at the Salute Church. To compare his "Presentation of the Virgin," at the Madonna dell' Orto, with
Titian's at the Academy, or his "Annunciation" with
Titian's, close at hand, is to measure the essential difference between observation and imagination. One has
certainly not said all that there is to say for Titian
when one has called him an observer. *Il y mettait du
sien,* as the French say, and I use the term to designate
roughly the artist whose apprehension, infinitely deep
and strong when applied to the single figure or to
easily balanced groups, spends itself vainly on great dramatic combinations — or, rather, leaves them ungauged.
It was the whole scene that Tintoret seemed to have

beheld, in a flash of inspiration intense enough to stamp it ineffaceably on his perception; and it was the whole scene, complete, peculiar, individual, unprecedented, which he committed to canvas with all the vehemence of his talent. Compare his " Last Supper," at San Giorgio, — its long, diagonally placed table, its dusky spaciousness, its scattered lamp-light and halo-light, its startled, gesticulating figures, its richly realistic foreground, — with the usual formal, almost mathematical, rendering of the subject, in which impressiveness seems to have been sought in elimination rather than comprehension. You get from Tintoret's work the impression that he *felt*, pictorially, the great, beautiful, terrible spectacle of human life very much as Shakespeare felt it poetically — with a heart that never ceased to beat a passionate accompaniment to every stroke of his brush. Thanks to this fact, his works are signally grave, and their almost universal and rapidly increasing decay does not relieve their gloom. Nothing, indeed, can well be sadder than the ' great collection of Tintorets at San Rocco. Incurable blackness is settling fast upon all of them, and they frown at you across the sombre splendor of their great chambers like gaunt, twilight phantoms of pictures. To our children's children, Tintoret, as things are going, can be hardly more than a name; and such of them as shall miss the tragic beauty, already so dimmed and stained, of the great " Bearing of the Cross," at San Rocco, will live and die without knowing the largest eloquence of art. If you wish to add the last touch of solemnity to the place, recall, as vividly as possible,

while you linger at San Rocco, the painter's singularly
interesting portrait of himself, at the Louvre. The old
man looks out of the canvas from beneath a brow as
sad as a sunless twilight, with just such a stoical hope-
lessness as you might fancy him to wear, if he stood at
your side gazing at his rotting canvases. It was not
whimsical to fancy it the face of a man who felt that
he had given the world more than the world was likely
to repay. Indeed, before every picture of Tintoret, you
may remember this tremendous portrait with profit.
On one side, the power, the passion, the illusion of his
art ; on the other, the mortal fatigue of his spirit. The
world's knowledge of Tintoret is so small that the
portrait throws a doubly precious light on his personality ; and when we wonder vainly what manner of
man he was, and what were his purpose, his faith, and
his method, we may find forcible assurance there that
they were, at any rate, his life — and a very intense
one.

Verona, which was my last Italian stopping-place,
is, under any circumstances, a delightfully interesting
city ; but the kindness of my own memory of it is
deepened by a subsequent ten days' experience of Germany. I rose one morning at Verona, and went to bed
at night at Botzen ! The statement needs no comment,
and the two places, though but fifty miles apart, are as
painfully dissimilar as their names. I had prepared
myself for your delectation with a copious tirade on
German manners, German scenery, German art, and the
German stage — on the lights and shadows of Inns-
brück, Munich, Nüremberg, and Heidelberg ; but just

as I was about to put pen to paper, I glanced into a
little volume on these very topics, lately published by
that famous novelist and moralist, M. Ernest Feydeau, the fruit of a summer's observation at Homburg.
This work produced a reaction; and if I chose to follow
M. Feydeau's own example when he wishes to qualify
his approbation, I might call his treatise by any vile
name known to the speech of man, but I content myself with pronouncing it — superficial. I then reflect
that my own opportunities for seeing and judging were
extremely limited, and I suppress my tirade, lest some
more enlightened critic should come and pronounce *me*
superficial. Its sum and substance was to have been
that — superficially — Germany is ugly; that Munich
is a nightmare, Heidelberg a disappointment (in spite
of its charming castle) and even Nuremberg not a joy
forever. But comparisons are odious; and if Munich
is ugly, Verona is beautiful enough. You may laugh
at my logic, but you will probably assent to my meaning. I carried away from Verona a certain mental picture upon which I cast an introspective glance whenever between Botzen and Strasburg the oppression of
external circumstance became painful. It was a lovely
August afternoon in the Roman arena — a ruin in
which repair and restoration have been so gradually
and discreetly practised that it seems all of one harmonious antiquity. The vast stony oval rose high against
the sky in a single, clear, continuous line, broken here
and there only by strolling and reclining loungers.
The massive tiers inclined in solid monotony to the
central circle, in which a small open-air theatre was in
active operation. A small section of the great slope of

masonry facing the stage was roped off into an auditorium, in which the narrow level space between the foot-lights and the lowest step figured as the pit. Footlights are a figure of speech, for the performance was going on in the broad glow of the afternoon, with a delightful, and apparently by no means misplaced, confidence in the good-will of the spectators. What the piece was that was deemed so superbly able to shift for itself I know not — very possibly the same drama that I remember seeing advertised during my former visit to Verona ; nothing less than *La Tremenda Giustizia di Dio.* If titles are worth anything, this product of the melodramatist's art might surely stand upon its own legs. Along the tiers above the little group of regular spectators was gathered a sort of free-list of unauthorized observers, who, although beyond ear-shot, must have been enabled by the generous breadth of Italian gesture to follow the tangled thread of the piece. It was all deliciously Italian — the mixture of old life and new, the mountebank's booth (it was hardly more) grafted upon the antique circus, the dominant presence of a mighty architecture, the loungers and idlers beneath the kindly sky, upon the sun-warmed stones. I never felt more keenly the difference between the background to life in the Old World and the New. There are other things in Verona to make it a liberal education to be born there, though that it is one for the contemporary Veronese I do not pretend to say. The Tombs of the Scaligers, with their soaring pinnacles, their high-poised canopies, their exquisite refinement and concentration of the Gothic idea, I cannot profess, even after much worshipful gazing, to have fully comprehended and enjoyed. They seemed to me full of deep architectural meanings, such as must drop gently into the mind one by one, after infinite tranquil contemplation. But even to the hurried and preoccupied traveller the solemn little chapel-yard in the city's heart, in which they stand girdled by their great swaying curtain of linked and twisted iron, is one of the most impressive spots in Italy. Nowhere else is such a wealth of artistic achievement crowded into so narrow a space; nowhere else are the daily comings and goings of men blessed by the presence of *manlier* art. Verona is rich, furthermore, in beautiful churches — several with beautiful names: San Fermo, Santa Anastasia, San Zenone. This last is a structure of high antiquity, and of the most impressive loveliness. The nave terminates in a double choir, that is, a sub-choir or crypt, into which you descend, and wander among primitive columns whose variously grotesque capitals rise hardly higher than your head, and an upper choral level into which you mount by broad stairways of the most picturesque effect. I shall never forget the impression of majestic chastity that I received from the great nave of the building on my former visit. I decided to my satisfaction then that every church is from the devotional point of view a solecism, that has not something of a similar absolute felicity of proportion; for strictly formal beauty seems best to express our conception of spiritual beauty. The nobly serious effect of San Zenone is deepened by its single picture — a masterpiece of the most serious of painters, the severe and exquisite Mantegna.

THE PARISIAN STAGE.

Paris, December, 1872.

IT is impossible to spend many weeks in Paris without observing that the theatre plays a very important part in French civilization; and it is impossible to go much to the theatre without finding it a copious source of instruction as to French ideas, manners, and philosophy. I supposed that I had a certain acquaintance with these complex phenomena, but during the last couple of months I have occupied a great many orchestra chairs, and in the merciless glare of the footlights I have read a great many of my old convictions with a new distinctness. I have had at the same time one of the greatest attainable pleasures; for, surely, among the pleasures that one deliberately seeks and pays for, none beguiles the heavy human consciousness so totally as a first-rate evening at the Théâtre Français or the Gymnase. It was the poet Gray, I believe, who said that his idea of heaven was to lie all day on a sofa and read novels. He, poor man, spoke while "Clarissa Harlowe" was still the fashion, and a novel was synonymous with an eternity. A much better heaven, I think, would be to sit all night in a fauteuil (if they were only a little better stuffed) listening to Delaunay, watching Got, or falling in love with Mademoiselle Desclée. An acted play is a novel intensified; it realizes what the novel suggests, and, by paying a liberal tribute to the senses, anticipates your possible complaint that your entertainment is of the meagre sort styled "intellectual." The stage throws into relief the best gifts of the French mind, and the Théâtre Français is not only the most amiable but the most characteristic of French institutions. I often think of the inevitable first sensations there of the "cultivated foreigner," let him be as stuffed with hostile prejudice as you please. He leaves the theatre an ardent Gallomaniac. This, he cries, is the civilized nation *par excellence.* Such art, such finish, such grace, such taste, such a marvellous exhibition of applied science, are the mark of a chosen people, and these delightful talents imply the existence of every virtue. His enthusiasm may be short and make few converts; but certainly during his stay in Paris, whatever may be his mind in the intervals, he never listens to the traditional *toc — toc — toc* which sounds up the curtain in the Rue Richelieu, without murmuring, as he squares himself in his chair and grasps his lorgnette, that, after all, the French are prodigiously great!

I shall never forget a certain evening in the early summer when, after a busy, dusty, weary day in the streets, staring at charred ruins and finding in all things a vague aftertaste of gunpowder, I went to the Théâtre Français to listen to "Le Village Forcé" and Alfred de Musset's Barbier

The entertainment

what a perfumed bath is to one's weary limbs, and I
sat in a sort of languid ecstasy of contemplation and
wonder — wonder that the tender flower of poetry and
art should bloom again so bravely over blood-stained
pavements and fresh-made graves. Molière is played
at the Théâtre Français as he deserves to be — one can
hardly say more — with the most ungrudging breadth,
exuberance, and *entrain*, and yet with a kind of aca-
demic harmony and solemnity. Molière, if he ever
drops a kindly glance on MM. Got and Coquelin, must
be the happiest of the immortals. To be read two
hundred years after your death is something; but to be
acted is better, at least when your name does not happen to be Shakespeare and your interpreter the great
American (or, indeed, the great British) tragedian. Such
powerful, natural, wholesome comedy as that of the
creator of Sganarelle certainly never was conceived,
and the actors I have just named give it its utmost
force. I have often wondered that, in the keen and
lucid atmosphere which Molière casts about him, some
of the effusions of his modern successors should live
for an hour. Alfred de Musset, however, need fear no
neighborhood, and his "Il ne Faut Jurer," after Molière's
tremendous farce, was like fine sherry after strong ale.
Got plays in it a small part, which he makes a great
one, and Delaunay, the silver-tongued, the ever-young,
and that plain robust person and admirable artist, Madame Nathalie, and that divinely ingenuous ingénue,
Mademoiselle Reichemberg. It would be a poor compliment to the performance to say that it might have
been mistaken for real life. If real life were a tithe as

charming it would be a merry world. De Musset's plays, which, in general, were not written for the stage, are of so ethereal a quality that they lose more than they gain by the interpretation, refined and sympathetic as it is, which they receive at the Théâtre Français. The most artistic acting is coarser than the poet's intention.

The play in question, however, is an exception and keeps its silvery tone even in the glare of the foot-lights. The second act, at the rising of the curtain, represents a drawing-room in the country; a stout, eccentric baronne sits with her tapestry, making distracted small talk while she counts her points with a deliciously rustic abbé; on the other side, her daughter, in white muslin and blue ribbons, is primly taking her dancing-lesson from a venerable choregraphic pedagogue in a wig and tights. The exquisite art with which, for the following ten minutes, the tone of random accidental conversation is preserved, while the baronne loses her glasses and miscounts her stitches, and the daughter recommences her step for the thirtieth time, must simply, as the saying is, be seen to be appreciated. The acting is full of charming detail — detail of a kind we not only do not find, but do not even look for, on the English stage. The way in which, in a subsequent scene, the young girl, listening at evening in the park to the passionate whisperings of the hero, drops her arms half awkwardly along her sides in fascinated self-surrender, is a touch quite foreign to English invention. Unhappily for us as actors, we are not a gesticulating people. Mademoiselle Reichemberg's movement here

is an intonation in gesture as eloquent as if she had
spoken it. The incomparable Got has but a dozen
short speeches to make, but he distils them with magical neatness. He sits down to piquet with the baronne.
"You risk nothing, M. l'Abbé?" she soon demands. The
concentrated timorous prudence of the abbé's "Oh!
non!" is a master-stroke; it depicts a lifetime. Where
Delaunay plays, however, it is hard not to call him the
first. To say that he *satisfies* may at first seem small
praise; but it may content us when we remember what
a very loose fit in the poet's vision is the usual *jeune
premier* of the sentimental drama. He has at best a
vast deal of fustian to utter, and he has a perilous balance to preserve between the degree of romantic expression expected in a gentleman whose trade is love-making
and the degree tolerated in a gentleman who wears a
better or worse made black coat and carries the hat of
the period. Delaunay is fifty years old, and his person
and physiognomy are meagre; but his taste is so unerring, his touch so light and true, his careless grace so
free and so elegant, that in his hands the *jeune premier*
becomes a creation as fresh and natural as the unfolding
rose. He has a voice of extraordinary sweetness and
flexibility, and a delivery which makes the commonest
phrases musical; and when as Valentin, as Perdican, or
as Fortunio, he embarks on one of De Musset's melodious tirades, and his utterance melts and swells in
trembling cadence and ringing emphasis, there is really
little to choose between the performance, as a mere
vocal exhibition, and an aria by a first-rate tenor.

An actor equally noted for his elegance, now attested

by forty years of triumphs, is Bressant, whose name, with old Parisians, is a synonyme for *la distinction.* "Distingué comme Bressant" is an accepted formula of praise. A few years ago comedians were denied Christian burial; such are the revenges of history. Bressant's gentility is certainly a remarkable piece of art, but he always seems to me too conscious that an immense supply of the cómmodity is expected from him. Nevertheless, the Théâtre Français offers nothing more effective and suggestive than certain little comedies (the "Post Scriptum," for instance, by Emile Augier), in which he receives the *réplique* from that venerable *grande coquette,* Madame Plessy, the direct successor, in certain parts, of Mademoiselle Mars. I find these illustrious veterans, on such occasions, more interesting even than they aspire to be, and the really picturesque figures are not the Comte nor the Marquise, but the grim and battered old comedians, with a life's length of foot-lights making strange shadows on their impenetrable masks. As a really august exhibition of experience, I recommend a tête-à-tête between these artists. The orchestra of the Théâtre Français is haunted by a number of old gentlemen, classic play-goers, who look as if they took snuff from boxes adorned with portraits of the fashionable beauty of 1820. I caught an echo of my impressions from one of them the other evening, when, as the curtain fell on Bressant and Plessy, he murmured ecstatically to his neighbor, " Quelle connaissance de la scène . . . et de la vie ! "

The audience at the Parisian theatres is indeed often as interesting to me as the play. It is, of course, com-

posed of heterogeneous elements. There are a great
many ladies with red wigs in the boxes, and a great
many bald young gentlemen staring at them from the
orchestra. But *les honnêtes gens* of every class are
largely represented, and it is clear that even people of
serious tastes look upon the theatre, not as one of the
" extras," but as one of the necessities of life; a periodical necessity hardly less frequent and urgent than
their evening paper and their *demi-tasse*. I am always
struck with the number of elderly men, decorated, grizzled, and grave, for whom the stage has kept its mysteries. You may see them at the Palais Royal, listening
complacently to the carnival of lewdness nightly enacted
there, and at the Variétiés, levelling their glasses pater-
nally at the lightly clad heroines of Offenbach. The
truth is, that in the theatre the French mind *se recon-
nait*, according to its own idiom, more vividly than
elsewhere. Its supreme faculty, the art of form, of
arrangement and presentation, is pre-eminently effective
on the stage, and I suppose many a good citizen has
before this consoled himself for his country's woes by
reflecting that if the Germans *have* a Gravelotte in their
records, they have not a " Rabagas," and if they possess
a Bismarck and a Moltke, they have neither a Dumas
nor a Schneider. A good French play is an admirable
work of art, of which it behooves patrons of the contemporary English drama, at any rate, to speak with
respect. It serves its purpose to perfection, and French
dramatists, as far as I can see, have no more secrets to
learn. The first half-dozen a foreign spectator listens
to seem to him among the choicest productions of the

an mind, and it is only little by little that he
mes conscious of the extraordinary meagreness of
: material. The substance of the plays I have
y seen seems to me, when I think them over,
thing really amazing, and it is what I had chiefly
ind in speaking just now of the stage as an index
cial character. Prime material was evidently long
xhausted, and the best that can be done now is to
ange old situations with a kind of desperate inge-
:. The field looks terribly narrow, but it is still
rly worked. " An old theme, — but with a differ-
" the workman claims; and he makes the most of
ifference — for laughter, if he is an *amuseur* pure
imple ; for tears, if he is a moralist.
 not for a moment imagine that moralists are
ing. Alexandre Dumas is one — he is a dozen,
d, in his single self. M. Pailleron (whose " Hé-
' is the last novelty at the Théâtre Français) is
er; and I am not sure that, since " Rabagas," M.
u is not a third. The great dogma of M. Dumas
at if your wife is persistently unfaithful to you,
must kill her. He leaves you, I suppose, the
e of weapons; but that the thing must somehow
ne, he has written a famous pamphlet, now reach-
ts fortieth edition, to prove. M. Pailleron holds,
e other hand, that if it was before your marriage,
before she had ever heard of you, and with her
n, when she was a child and knew no better, you
 — after terrific vituperation, indeed, and imminent
de on the lady's part — press her relentingly to
bosom. M. Pailleron enforces this moral in cap-

5 *

itally turned verse, and with Delaunay's magical aid;
but as I sat through his piece the other evening, I
racked my brain to discover what heinous offence Delicacy has ever committed that she should have to do
such cruel penance. I am afraid that she has worse
things in store for her, for the event of the winter (if a
coup d'état does not carry off the honors) is to be the
new play of Dumas, "La Femme de Claude." Whatever becomes of the state, I shall go early to see the
play, for it is to have the services of the first actress in
the world. I have not the smallest hesitation in so
qualifying Mademoiselle Desclée. She has just been
sustaining by her sole strength the weight of a ponderous drama called "La Gueule du Loup," in which her
acting seemed to me a revelation of the capacity of the
art. I have never seen nature grasped so in its essence,
and rendered with a more amazing mastery of the fine
shades of expression. Just as the light drama in France
is a tissue of fantastic indecencies, the serious drama is
an agglomeration of horrors. I had supped so full of
these that, before seeing the "Gueule du Loup," I had
quite made up my mind to regard as an offence against
civilization every new piece, whether light or serious,
of which the main idea should not be *pleasing*. To do
anything so pleasant as to please is the last thing that
M. Dumas and his school think of. But Mademoiselle
Desclée renders the chief situation of M. Laya's drama
— that of a woman who has fancied herself not as other
women are, coming to her senses at the bottom of a
moral abyss, and measuring the length of her fall —
with a verity so penetrating that I could not but ask

myself whether, to become a wholesome and grateful
spectacle, even the ugliest possibilities of life need anything more than rigorous exactness of presentation.
Mademoiselle Desclée, at any rate, was for half an hour
the most powerful of moralists. M. Laya, her author,
on the other hand, is an atrocious one. His trivial
dénouement, treading on the heels of the sombre episode
I have mentioned, is an insult to the spectator's sympathies. Even Mademoiselle Desclée's acting fails to
give it dignity. Here, as everywhere, an inexpressible
want of moral intelligence is the striking point. Novel
and drama alike betray an incredibly superficial perception of the moral side of life. It is not only that
adultery is their only theme, but that the treatment of
it is so singularly vicious and arid. It has been used
now for so many years as a mere pigment, a source of
dramatic color, a *ficelle*, as they say, that it has ceased
to have any apparent moral bearings. It is turned
inside out by hungering poetasters in search of a new
"effect" as freely as an old glove by some thrifty dame
intent on placing a prudent stitch. I might cite some
striking examples, if I had space; some are too detest-
able. I do not know that I have found anything more
suggestive than the revival, at the Gymnase, of that
too familiar drama of the younger (the then very youthful) Dumas, the "Dame aux Camélias." Mademoiselle
Pierson plays the heroine — Mademoiselle Pierson, the
history of whose *embonpoint* is one of the topics of the
day. She was formerly almost corpulent — fatally so
for that beauty which even her rivals admitted to be
greater than her talent. She devoted herself bravely

to a diet of raw meat and other delicacies recommended by Banting, and she has recently emerged from the ordeal as superbly spare as a racing filly. This result, I believe, "draws" powerfully, though it seemed to me, I confess, that even raw meat had not made Mademoiselle Pierson an actress. I went to the play because I had read in the weekly feuilleton of that very sound and sensible critic, M. Francisque Sarcey, that even in its old age it bore itself like a masterpiece, and produced an immense effect. If I could speak with the authority of Dr. Johnson, I should be tempted to qualify it with that vigorous brevity which he sometimes used so well. In the entr'actes I took refuge in the street to laugh at my ease over its colossal flimsiness. But I should be sorry to linger on the sombre side of the question, and my intention, indeed, was to make a note of none but pleasant impressions. I have, after all, received so many of these in Paris play-houses that my strictures seem gracelessly cynical. I bear the actors, at least, no grudge; they are better than the authors. Molière and De Musset, moreover, have not yet lost favor, and Corneille's "Cid" was recently revived with splendor and success. Here is a store of imperishable examples. What I shall think of regretfully when I have parted with the opportunity is, not the *tragédies bourgeoises* of MM. Dumas, Feuillet, and Pailleron, but the inimitable Got strutting about as the podestà in the "Caprices de Marianne," and twitching his magisterial train from the nerveless grasp of that delicious idiot, his valet; and Delaunay murmuring his love-notes like a summer breeze in the ear of the blond Cécile; and Coquelin as

ascarille, looking like an old Venetian print, and
aying as if the author of the "Etourdi" were in the
ulisse, prompting him; and M. Mounet Sully (the
dent young débutant of the "Cid") shouting with the
ost picturesque fury possible the famous sortie, —

"Paraissez Navarrins, Maures et Castillans!"

an ingenuous American the Théâtre Français may
t offer an æsthetic education.

A ROMAN HOLIDAY.

Rome, February, 1873.

IT is certainly sweet to be merry at the right moment; but the right moment hardly seems to me to be the ten days of the Roman Carnival. It was a rather cynical suspicion of mine, perhaps, that they would not keep to my imagination the brilliant promise of tradition; but I have been justified by the event, and have been decidedly less conscious of the festal influences of the season than of the inalienable gravity of the place. There was a time when the Carnival was a serious matter, — that is, a heartily joyous one; but in the striding march of progress which Italy has recently witnessed, the fashion of public revelry has fallen wofully out of step. The state of mind and manners under which the Carnival was kept in generous good faith, I doubt if an American can very exactly conceive: he can only say to himself that, for a month in the year, it must have been comfortable to *forget !* But now that Italy is made, the Carnival is unmade; and we are not especially tempted to envy the attitude of a population who have lost their relish for play, and not yet acquired, to any striking extent, an enthusiasm for work. The spectacle on the Corso has seemed to me, on the whole, a sort of measure of that great breach with the past of which Catholic Christendom felt the somewhat muffled shock in September, 1870. A traveller who had seen old Rome, coming back any time during the past winter, must have immediately perceived that something momentous had happened, — something hostile to picturesqueness. My first warning was that, ten minutes after my arrival, I found myself face to face with a newspaper-stand. The impossibility in the other days of having anything in the journalistic line but the *Osservatore Romano* and the *Voce della Verità* used to seem to me to have much to do with the extraordinary leisure of thought and stillness of mind to which Rome admitted you. But now the slender piping of the Voice of Truth is stifled by the raucous note of eventide venders of the *Capitale,* the *Libertà,* and the *Fanfulla;* and Rome reading unexpurgated news is another Rome indeed. For every subscriber to the *Libertà,* I incline to think there is an antique masker and reveller less. As striking a sign of the new régime seemed to me the extraordinary increase of population. The Corso was always a well-filled street: now it 's a perpetual crush. I never cease to wonder where the new-comers are lodged, and how such spotless flowers of fashion as the gentlemen who stare at the carriages can bloom in the atmosphere of those *camere mobiliate* of which I have had glimpses. This, however, is their own question; bravely they resolve it. They seemed to proclaim, as I say, that by force of numbers Rome had been secularized. An Italian dandy is a very fine fellow; but I confess these goodly throngs of them are to my sense an insufficient compensation for the absent monsignori, treading the streets in their purple stockings, and followed by their solemn servants, returning on their behalf the bows of the meaner sort; for the mourning gear of the cardinals' coaches that formerly glittered with scarlet, and swung with the weight of the footmen clinging behind; for the certainty that you 'll not, by the best of traveller's luck, meet the Pope sitting deep in the shadow of his great chariot with uplifted fingers, like some inaccessible idol in his shrine. You may meet the king, indeed, who is as ugly, as imposingly ugly, as some idols, though not as inaccessible. The other day, as I was passing the Quirinal, he drove up in a low carriage, with a single attendant; and a group of men and women, who had been waiting near the gate, rushed at him with a number of folded papers. The carriage slackened pace, and he pocketed their offerings with a business-like air — that of a good-natured man accepting hand-bills at a street-corner. Here was a monarch at his palace gate receiving petitions from his subjects — being adjured to right their wrongs. The scene ought to have been picturesque, but, somehow, it had no more color than a woodcut in an illustrated newspaper. Comfortable I should call it at most; admirably so, certainly, for there were lately few sovereigns standing, I believe, with whom their people enjoyed these filial hand-to-hand relations. The king this year, however, has had as little to do with the Carnival as the Pope, and the innkeepers and Americans have marked it for their own.

It was advertised to begin at half past two o'clock of a certain Saturday; and punctually, at the stroke of the hour, from my room across a wide court, I heard a sudden multiplication of sounds and confusion of tongues in the Corso. I was writing to a friend for whom I cared more than for a Roman holiday; but as the minutes elapsed and the hubbub deepened, curiosity got the better of affection, and I remembered that I was really within eye-shot of a spectacle whose reputation had ministered to the day-dreams of my infancy. I used to have a scrap-book with a colored print of the starting of the bedizened wild horses, and the use of a library rich in keepsakes and annuals whose frontispiece was commonly a masked lady in a balcony — the heroine of a delightful tale further on. Agitated by these tender memories, I descended into the street; but I confess that I looked in vain for a masked lady who might serve as a frontispiece, or any object whatever that might adorn a tale. Masked and muffled ladies there were in abundance; but their masks were of ugly wire, and perfectly resembled the little covers placed upon strong cheese in German hotels, and their drapery was a shabby water-proof, with the hoods pulled over their chignons. They were armed with great tin scoops or funnels, with which they were solemnly shovelling lime and flour out of bushel baskets down upon the heads of the people in the street. They were packed into balconies all the way down the long vista of the Corso, in which their calcareous shower maintained a dense, gritty, unpalatable fog. The crowd was compact in the street, and the Ameri-

H

cans in it were tossing back confetti out of great satch-
els hung around their necks. It was quite the "you 're
another" sort of repartee, and less flavored than I had
hoped with the airy mockery which tradition associates
with this festival. The scene was striking, certainly;
but, somehow, not as I had dreamed of its being. I
stood contemplating it, I suppose, with a peculiarly
tempting blankness of visage, for in a moment I received half a bushel of flour on my too-philosophic
head. Decidedly it was an ignoble form of humor. I
shook my ears like an emergent diver, and had a sudden vision of how still and sunny and solemn, how
peculiarly and undisturbedly themselves, how secure
from any intrusion less sympathetic than one's own,
certain outlying parts of Rome must just now be. The
Carnival had received its death-blow, in my imagination; and it has been ever since but a thin and dusky
ghost of pleasure that has flitted at intervals in and
out of my consciousness. I turned my back on the
Corso and wandered away, and found the grass-grown
quarters delightfully free even from the possibility of a
fellow-countryman! And so, having set myself an example, I have been keeping Carnival by strolling perversely along the silent circumference of Rome. I have
no doubt I have lost a great deal. The Princess Margaret has occupied a balcony opposite the open space
which leads into the Via Condotti, and, I believe, like
the discreet princess that she is, has dealt in no missiles but bonbons, bouquets, and white doves. I would
have waited half an hour any day to see the Princess
Margaret holding a dove on her forefinger; but I never

chanced to notice any preparations for this delightful spectacle. And yet, do what you will, you cannot really elude the Carnival. As the days elapse, it filters down, as it were, into the manners of the common people, and before the week is over the very beggars at the church-doors seem to have gone to the expense of a domino. When you meet these specimens of dingy drollery capering about in dusky back streets at all hours of the day and night, and flitting out of black doorways between those greasy groups which cluster about Roman thresholds, you feel that once upon a time the seeds of merriment must have been implanted in the Roman temperament with a vigorous hand. An unsophisticated American cannot but be struck with the immense number of persons, of every age and various conditions, to whom it costs nothing in the nature of an ingenuous blush to walk up and down the streets in the costume of a theatrical supernumerary. Fathers of families do it at the head of an admiring progeniture; aunts and uncles and grandmothers do it; all the family does it, with varying splendor, but the same good conscience. "A pack of babies!" the philosophic American pronounces it for its pains, and tries to imagine himself strutting along Broadway in a battered tin helmet and a pair of yellow tights. Our vices are certainly different; it takes those of the innocent sort to be ridiculous! Roman childishness seems to me so intimately connected with Roman amenity, urbanity, and general gracefulness, that, for myself, I should be sorry to lay a tax on it, lest these other commodities should also cease to come to market.

I was rewarded, when I had turned away with my
ears full of flour, by a glimpse of an intenser sort of
life than the dingy foolery of the Corso. I walked
down by the back streets to the steps which ascend
to the Capitol — that long inclined plane, rather, broken
at every two paces, which is the unfailing disappointment, I believe, of tourists primed for retrospective
raptures. Certainly the Capitol, seen from this side,
is not commanding. The hill is so low, the ascent so
narrow, Michael Angelo's architecture in the quadrangle at the top so meagre, the whole place, somehow, so
much more of a mole-hill than a mountain, that for the
first ten minutes of your standing there Roman history
seems suddenly to have sunk through a trap-door. It
emerges, however, on the other side, in the Forum ; and
here, meanwhile, if you get no sense of the sublime,
you get gradually a delightful sense of the picturesque.
Nowhere in Rome is there more color, more charm,
more sport for the eye. The gentle slope, during the
winter months, is always covered with lounging sun-
seekers, and especially with those more constantly obvious members of the Roman population — beggars,
soldiers, monks, and tourists. The beggars and peasants lie kicking their heels along that grandest of
loafing-places, the great steps of the Ara Cœli. The
dwarfish look of the Capitol is greatly increased, I
think, by the neighborhood of this huge blank staircase, mouldering away in disuse, with the weeds in its
crevices, and climbing to the rudely solemn façade of
the church. The sunshine glares on this great unfinished wall only to light up its featureless despair, its

expression of conscious, irremediable incompleteness. Sometimes, massing its rusty screen against the deep blue sky, with the little cross and the sculptured porch casting a clear-cut shadow on the bricks, it seems to have an even more than Roman desolation, and confusedly suggests Spain and Africa — lands with absolutely nothing but a past. The legendary wolf of Rome has lately been accommodated with a little artificial grotto, among the cacti and the palms, in the fantastic triangular garden squeezed between the steps of the church and the ascent to the Capitol, where she holds a perpetual levee, and "draws," apparently, as powerfully as the Pope himself. Above, in the little piazza before the stuccoed palace which rises so jauntily on a basement of thrice its magnitude, are more loungers and knitters in the sun, seated round the massively inscribed base of the statue of Marcus Aurelius. Hawthorne has perfectly expressed the attitude of this admirable figure in saying that it extends its arm with "a command which is in itself a benediction." I doubt if any statue of king or captain in the public places of the world has more to commend it to the popular heart. Irrecoverable simplicity has no sturdier representative. Here is an impression that the sculptors of the last three hundred years have been laboriously trying to reproduce; but contrasted with this mild old monarch, their prancing horsemen seem like a company of riding-masters, taking out a young ladies' boarding-school. The admirably human character of the figure survives the rusty decomposition of the bronze and the archaic angularity of the design; and one may call it singular that in the capital of Christendom the portrait most suggestive of a Christian will is that of a pagan emperor.

You recover in some degree your stifled hopes of sublimity as you pass beyond the palace, and take your choice of two curving slopes, to descend into the Forum. Then you see that the little stuccoed edifice is but a modern excrescence upon the mighty cliff of a primitive construction whose great squares of porous tufa, as they descend, seem to resolve themselves back into the colossal cohesion of unhewn rock. There is a prodigious picturesqueness in the union of this airy, fresh-faced superstructure and these deep-plunging, hoary foundations; and few things in Rome are more entertaining to the eye than to measure the long plumb-line which drops from the inhabited windows of the palace, with their little overpeeping balconies, their muslin curtains, and their bird-cages, down to the rugged handiwork of the Republic. In the Forum proper the sublime is eclipsed again, though the late extension of the excavations gives a chance for it.

Nothing in Rome helps your fancy to a more vigorous backward flight than to lounge on a sunny day over the railing which guards the great central researches. It gives one the oddest feeling to see the past, the ancient world, as one stands there, bodily turned up with the spade, and transformed from an immaterial, inaccessible fact of time into a matter of soils and surfaces. The pleasure is the same — in kind — as what you enjoy at Pompeii, and the pain the same. It was not here, however, that I found my compensation for forfeiting the

spectacle on the Corso, but in a little church at the end
of the narrow byway which diverges up the Palatine
from just beside the Arch of Titus. This byway leads
you between high walls, then takes a bend and intro-
duces you to a long row of rusty, dusty little pictures
of the stations of the cross. Beyond these stands a
small church with a façade so modest that you hardly
recognize it until you see the leather curtain. I never
see a leather curtain without lifting it; it is sure to
cover a picture of some sort — good, bad, or indifferent.
The picture this time was poor — whitewash and tar-
nished candlesticks and mouldy muslin flowers being
its principal features. I should not have remained if
I had not been struck with the attitude of the single
worshipper — a young priest kneeling before one of the
side-altars, who, as I entered, lifted his head and gave
me a sidelong look — so charged with the languor of
devotion that he immediately became an object of interest. He was visiting each of the altars in turn, and
kissing the balustrade beneath them. He was alone in
the church, and, indeed, in the whole neighborhood.
There were no beggars, even, at the door; they were
plying their trade on the skirts of the Carnival. In
the whole deserted place he alone knelt there for religion, and, as I sat respectfully by, it seemed to me
that I could hear in the perfect silence the far-away
uproar of the maskers. It was my late impression of
these frivolous people, I suppose, joined with the extraordinary gravity of the young priest's face — his
pious fatigue, his devout prayer, his pale consolation —
which gave me just then and there an impression

of the religious passion — its privations and resigna-
tions and exhaustions, and its terribly small share of
amusement. He was young and strong and evidently
of not too refined a fibre to enjoy the Carnival; but
planted there with his face pale with fasting and his
knees stiff with praying, he seemed so stern a satire on
it and on the crazy thousands who were preferring it
to *his* way, that I half expected to see some heavenly
portent out of a monastic legend come down and confirm his choice. But, I confess, though I was not
enamored of the Carnival myself, that his seemed a
grim preference, and this forswearing of the world a
terrible game — a gaining one only if your zeal never
falters; a hard fight when it does! In such an hour,
to a stout young fellow like the hero of my anecdote,
the smell of incense must seem horribly stale, and the
muslin flowers and gilt candlesticks a very meagre
piece of splendor. And it would not have helped him
much to think that not so very far away, just beyond
the Forum, in the Corso, there was sport for the million, for nothing. I doubt whether my young priest
had thought of this. He had made himself a temple
out of the very substance of his innocence, and his
prayers followed each other too fast for the tempter to
slip in a whisper. And so, as I say, I found a solider
fact of human nature than the love of *coriandoli!*

One never passes the Coliseum, of course, without
paying it one's respects — without going in under one
of the hundred portals and crossing the long oval and
sitting down awhile, generally at the foot of the cross
in the centre. I always feel, as I do so, as if I were

sitting in the depths of some Alpine valley. The upper portions of the side toward the Esquiline seem as remote and lonely as an Alpine ridge, and you look up at their rugged sky-line, drinking in the sun and silvered by the blue air, with much the same feeling with which you would look at a gray cliff on which an eagle might lodge. This roughly mountainous quality of the great ruin is its chief interest; beauty of detail has pretty well vanished, especially since the high-growing wild-flowers have been plucked away by the new government, whose functionaries, surely, at certain points of their task, must have felt as if they shared the dreadful trade of those who gather samphire. Even if you are on your way to the Lateran, you will not grudge the twenty minutes it will take you, on leaving the Coliseum, to turn away under the Arch of Constantine, whose noble, battered bas-reliefs, with the chain of tragic statues — fettered, drooping barbarians — round its summit, I assume you to have profoundly admired, to the little piazza before the church of San Giovanni e Paolo, on the slope of the Cælian. There is no more charmingly picturesque spot in Rome. The ancient brick apse of the church peeps down into the trees of the little wooded walk before the neighboring church of San Gregorio, intensely venerable beneath its excessive modernization; and a series of heavy brick buttresses, flying across to an opposite wall, overarches the short, steep, paved passage which leads you into the piazza. This is bordered on one side by the long mediæval portico of the church of the two saints, sustained by eight time-blackened columns of granite and mar-

6

ble; on another by the great scantily windowed walls
of a Passionist convent; on a third by the gate of a
charming villa, whose tall porter, with his cockade and
silver-topped staff, standing sublime behind his grating,
seems a kind of mundane St. Peter, I suppose, to the
beggars who sit at the church-door or lie in the sun
along the farther slope which leads to the gate of the
convent. The place always seems to me the perfection
of an out-of-the-way corner — a place you would think
twice before telling people about, lest you should find
them there the next time you were to go. It is such a
group of objects, singly and in their happy combination, as one must come to Rome to find at one's villa
door; but what makes it peculiarly a picture is the
beautiful dark red campanile of the church, standing
embedded in the mass of the convent. It begins, as so
many things in Rome begin, with a stout foundation
of antique travertine, and rises high, in delicately
quaint mediæval brickwork — little stories and aper-
tures, sustained on miniature columns and adorned
with little cracked slabs of green and yellow marble,
inserted almost at random. When there are three or
four brown-breasted contadini sleeping in the sun before the convent doors, and a departing monk leading
his shadow down over them, I think you will not find
anything in Rome more *sketchable*.

If you stop, however, to observe everything worthy
of your water-colors, you will never reach the Lateran.
My business was much less with the interior of St.
John Lateran, which I have never found peculiarly
interesting, than with certain charming features of its

surrounding precinct — the crooked old court beside
it, which admits you to the Baptistery and to a delightful rear-view of the queer architectural odds and
ends which in Rome may compose a florid ecclesiastical
façade. There are more of these, a stranger jumble of
chance detail, of lurking recesses and wanton projec-
tions and inexplicable windows, than I have memory
or phrases for; but the gem of the collection is the
oddly perched peaked turret, with its yellow travertine welded upon the rusty brickwork, which was not
meant to be suspected, and the brickwork retreating
beneath and leaving it in the odd position of a tower
under which you may see the sky. As to the great
front of the church overlooking the Porta San Giovanni, you are not admitted behind the scenes; the
phrase is quite in keeping, for the architecture has
a vastly theatrical air. It is extremely imposing —
that of St. Peter's alone is more so; and when from far
off on the Campagna you see the colossal images of the
mitred saints along the top standing distinct against
the sky, you forget their coarse construction and their
breezy draperies. The view from the great space which
stretches from the church-steps to the city wall is the
very prince of views. Just beside you, beyond the
great alcove of mosaic, is the Scala Santa, the marble
staircase which (says the legend) Christ descended
under the weight of Pilate's judgment, and which all
Christians must forever ascend on their knees; before
you is the city gate which opens upon the Via Appia
Nuova, the long gaunt file of arches of the Claudian
aqueduct, their jagged ridge stretching away like the

vertebral column of some monstrous, mouldering skeleton, and upon the blooming brown and purple flats and
dells of the Campagna and the glowing blue of the
Alban Mountains, spotted with their white, high-nes-
tling towns; and to your left is the great grassy space
lined with dwarfish mulberry-trees, which stretches
across to the damp little sister-basilica of Santa Croce
in Gerusalemme. During a former visit to Rome I
lost my heart to this idle tract, and wasted much time
in sitting on the steps of the church and watching certain white-cowled friars who were sure to be passing
there for the delight of my eyes. There are fewer friars
now, and there are a great many of the king's recruits
who inhabit the ex-conventual barracks adjoining Santa
Croce, and are led forward to .practise their goose-step
on the sunny turf. Here, too, the poor old cardinals,
who are no longer to be seen on the Pincio, descend
from their mourning-coaches and relax their venerable
knees. These members alone still testify to the traditional splendor of the princes of the Church; for as
they advance, the lifted black petticoat reveals a flash
of scarlet stockings, and makes you groan at the victory
of civilization over color.

If St. John Lateran disappoints you internally, you
have an easy compensation in traversing the long lane
which connects it with Santa Maria Maggiore and
entering the singularly perfect nave of that most delightful of churches. The first day of my stay in
Rome, under the old dispensation, I spent in wandering
at random through the city, with accident for my valet
de place. It served me to perfection and introduced me

to the best things; among others to Santa Maria Maggiore. First impressions, memorable impressions, are generally irrecoverable; they often leave one the wiser, but they rarely return in the same form. I remember of my coming uninformed and unprepared into Santa Maria Maggiore, only that I sat for half an hour on the edge of the base of one of the marble columns of the beautiful nave and enjoyed a perfect feast of fancy. The place seemed to me so endlessly suggestive that perception became a sort of throbbing confusion of images, and I departed with a sense of knowing a good deal that is not set down in Murray. I have sat down more than once at the base of the same column again; but you live your life but once, the parts as well as the whole. The obvious charm of the church is the elegant grandeur of the nave — its perfect shapeliness and its rich simplicity, its long double row of white marble columns and its high flat roof, embossed with intricate gildings and mouldings. It opens into a choir of an extraordinary splendor of effect, which I recommend you to visit of a fine afternoon. At such a time, the glowing western light, entering the high windows of the tribune, kindles the scattered masses of color into sombre brightness, scintillates on the great solemn mosaic of the vault, touches the porphyry columns of the superb baldachino with ruby lights, and buries its shining shafts in the deep-toned shadows which cluster over frescos and sculptures and mouldings. The deeper charm to me, however, is the social atmosphere of the church, as I must call it for want of a better term — the sense it gives you, in common with most of the

Roman churches, and more than any of them, of having been prayed in for several centuries by a singularly complicated and picturesque society. It takes no great shrewdness to perceive that the social *rôle* of the Church in Italy is terribly shrunken nowadays; but also as little, perhaps, to feel that, as they stand, these deserted temples were produced by a society leavened through and through by ecclesiastical manners, and that they formed for ages the constant background of the human drama. They are, as one may say, the *churchiest* churches in Europe — the fullest of gathered detail and clustering association. There is not a figure that I have read of in old-world social history that I cannot imagine in its proper place kneeling before the lamp-decked Confession beneath the altar of Santa Maria Maggiore. One sees after all, however, even among the most palpable realities, very much what one's capricious intellect projects there; and I present my remarks simply as a reminder that one's constant excursions into churches are not the least interesting episodes of one's walks in Rome.

I had meant to give a simple specimen of these daily strolls; but I have given it at such a length that I have scanty space left to touch upon the innumerable topics which occur to the pen that begins to scribble about Rome. It is by the aimless *flânerie* which leaves you free to follow capriciously every hint of entertainment, that you get to know Rome. The greater part of Roman life goes on in the streets; and to a traveller fresh from a country in which town scenery is rather wanting in variety, it is full of picturesque and curious incident. If at times you find it rather unsavory, you may turn aside into the company of shining statues, ranged in long vistas, into the duskily splendid galleries of the Doria and Colonna Palaces, into the sun-checkered boskages of antique villas, or into ever-empty churches, thankful even for a tourist's tribute of interest. The squalor of Rome is certainly a stubborn fact, and there is no denying that it is a dirty place. "Don't talk to me of liking Rome," an old sojourner lately said to me ; "you don't really like it till you like the dirt." This statement was a shock to my nascent passion ; but — I blush to write it — I am growing to think there is something in it. The nameless uncleanness with which all Roman things are oversmeared seems to one at first a damning token of moral vileness. It fills you with more even of contempt than pity for Roman poverty, and you look with inexpressible irritation at the grovelling creatures who complacently vegetate in the midst of it. Soon after his arrival here, an intimate friend of mine had an illness which depressed his spirits and made him unable to see the universal "joke" of things. I found him one evening in his arm-chair, gazing grimly at his half-packed trunk. On my asking him what he intended : " This horrible place," he cried, " is an insufferable weight on my soul, and it seems to me monstrous to come here and feast on human misery. You 're very happy to be able to take things easily ; you 've either much more philosophy than I, or much less. The squalor, the shabbiness, the provincialism, the barbarism, of Rome are too much for me. I must go somewhere and drink deep of modern civilization.

This morning, as I came up the Scalianta, I felt as if
I could strangle every one of those filthy models that
loaf there in their shameless degradation and sit staring
at you with all the ignorance, and none of the innocence, of childhood. Is n't it an abomination that our
enjoyment here directly implies their wretchedness;
their knowing neither how to read nor to write, their
draping themselves in mouldy rags, their doing never a
stroke of honest work, their wearing those mummy-
swathings round their legs from one year's end to
another? So they 're kept, that Rome may be picturesque, and the forestieri abound, and a lot of profligate
artists may paint wretchedly poor pictures of them.
What should I stay for? I know the Vatican by
heart; and, except St. Peter's and the Pantheon, there's
not a fine building in Rome. I 'm sick of the Italian
face — of black eyes and blue chins and lying vowel
sounds. I want to see people who look as if they
knew how to read and write, and care for something
else than flocking to the Pincio to suck the knobs on
their canes and stare at fine ladies they 'll never by
any hazard speak to. The Duke of Sermoneta has just
been elected to — something or other — by a proper
majority. But what do you think of their mustering
but a hundred voters? I like the picturesque, but
I like the march of mind as well, and I long to see a
newspaper a little bigger than a play-bill. I shall leave
by the first train in the morning, and if you value your
immortal soul you will come with me!"

My friend's accent was moving, and for some moments I was inclined to follow his example; but deep

in my heart I felt the stir of certain gathered pledges of future enjoyment, and after a rapid struggle I bade him a respectful farewell. He travelled due north, and has been having a delightful winter at Munich, where the march of mind advances to the accompaniment of Wagner's music. Since his departure, to prove to him that I have rather more than less philosophy, I have written to him that the love of Rome is, in its last analysis, simply that perfectly honorable and legitimate instinct, the love of the *status quo* — the preference of contemplative and slow-moving-minds for the visible, palpable, measurable present — touched here and there with the warm lights and shadows of the past. "What you call dirt," an excellent authority has affirmed, "I call color"; and it is certain that, if cleanliness is next to godliness, it is a very distant neighbor to chiaroscuro. That I have come to relish dirt as dirt, I hesitate yet awhile to affirm; but I admit that, as I walk about the streets and glance under black archways into dim old courts and up mouldering palace façades at the colored rags that flap over the twisted balustrades of balconies, I find I very much enjoy their "tone"; and I remain vaguely conscious that it would require a strong stomach to resolve this tone into its component elements. I do not know that my immortal soul permanently suffers; it simply retires for a moment to give place to that of a hankering water-color sketcher. As for the models on the Spanish Steps, I have lately been going somewhat to the studios, and the sight of the copies has filled me with compassionate tenderness for the originals. I regard them as an

abused and persecuted race, and I freely forgive them
their decomposing gaiters and their dusky intellects.

I owe the reader amends for writing either of Roman
churches or of Roman walks, without an allusion to St.
Peter's. I go there often on rainy days, with prosaic
intentions of "exercise," and carry them out, body and
mind. As a mere promenade, St. Peter's is unequalled.
It is better than the Boulevards, than Piccadilly or
Broadway, and if it were not the most beautiful place
in the world, it would be the most entertaining. Few
great works of art last longer to one's curiosity. You
think you have taken its measure; but it expands
again, and leaves your vision shrunken. I never let
the ponderous leather curtain bang down behind me,
without feeling as if all former visits were but a vague
prevision, and this the first crossing of the threshold.
Tourists will never cease to be asked, I suppose, if they
have not been disappointed in the size of St. Peter's;
but a few modest spirits, here and there, I hope, will
never cease to say, No. It seemed to me from the first
the hugest thing conceivable — a real exaltation of
one's idea of space; so that one's entrance, even from
the great empty square, glaring beneath the deep blue
sky, or cool in the far-cast shadow of the immense
façade, seems not so much a going in somewhere as a
going out. I should confidently recommend a first
glimpse of the interior to a man of pleasure in quest
of new sensations, as one of the strongest the world
affords. There are days when the vast nave looks
vaster than at others, and the gorgeous baldachino a
longer journey beyond the far-spreading tessellated

plain of the pavement, when the light has a quality
which lets things look their largest, and the scattered
figures mark happily the scale of certain details. Then
you have only to stroll and stroll, and gaze and gaze,
and watch the baldachino lift its bronze architecture,
like a temple within a temple, and feel yourself, at the
bottom of the abysmal shaft of the dome, dwindle to a
crawling dot. Much of the beauty of St. Peter's resides, I think, in the fact, that it is all general beauty,
that you are appealed to by no specific details, that the
details indeed, when you observe them, are often poor
and sometimes ridiculous. The sculptures, with the
sole exception of Michael Angelo's admirable Pietà,
which lurks obscurely in a dusky chapel, are either bad
or indifferent; and the universal incrustation of marble, though sumptuous enough, has a less brilliant effect than much later work of the same sort — that, for
instance, of St. Paul's without the Walls. The supreme
beauty of the church is its magnificently sustained simplicity. It seems — as it is — a realization of the happiest mood of a colossal imagination. The happiest
mood, I say, because this is the only one of Michael
Angelo's works in the presence of which you venture
to be cheerful. You may smile in St. Peter's without
a sense of sacrilege, which you can hardly do, if you
have a tender conscience, in Westminster Abbey or
Notre Dame. The abundance of enclosed light has
much to do with your smile. There are no shadows, to
speak of, no marked effects of shade; but effects of
light innumerable — points at which the light seems
to mass itself in airy density, and scatter itself in

enchanting gradations and cadences. It performs the office of shadow in Gothic churches ; hangs like a roll-. ing mist along the gilded vault of the nave, melts into bright interfusion the mosaic scintillations of the dome, clings and clusters and lingers and vivifies the whole vast atmosphere. A good Catholic, I suppose, is a Catholic anywhere, in the grandest as well as in the humblest churches; but to a traveller not especially pledged to be devout, St. Peter's speaks more of contentment than of aspiration. The mind seems to expand there immensely, but on its own level, as we may say. It marvels at the reach of the human imagination and the vastness of our earthly means. This is heaven enough, we say: what it lacks in beauty it makes up in certainty. And yet if one's half-hours at St. Peter's are not actually spent on one's knees, the mind reverts to its tremendous presence with an ardor deeply akin to a passionate effusion of faith. When you are weary of the swarming democracy of your fellow-tourists, of the unremunerative aspects of human nature on the Corso and Pincio, of the oppressively frequent combination of coronets on carriage panels and stupid faces in carriages, of addled brains and lacquered boots, of ruin and dirt and decay, of priests and beggars and the myriad tokens of a halting civilization, the image of the great temple depresses the balance of your doubts and seems to refute the invasive vulgarity of things and assure you that nothing great is impossible. It is a comfort, in other words, to feel that there is at the worst nothing but a cab-fare between your discontent and one of the greatest of human achievements.

This might serve as a Lenten peroration to these remarks of mine which have strayed so wofully from their jovial text, but that I ought fairly to confess that my last impression of the Carnival was altogether Carnivalesque. The merry-making on Shrove Tuesday had an air of native vigor, and the dead letter of tradition seemed at moments to be informed with a living spirit. I pocketed my scepticism and spent a long afternoon on the Corso. Almost every one was a masker, but I had no need to conform; the pelting rain of confetti effectually disguised me. I cannot say I found it all very exhilarating; but here and there I noticed a brighter episode — a capering clown inflamed with contagious jollity, some finer humorist, forming a circle every thirty yards to crow at his indefatigable sallies. One clever performer especially pleased me, and I should have been glad to catch a glimpse of the natural man. I had a fancy that he was taking a prodigious intellectual holiday, and that his gayety was in inverse ratio to his daily mood. He was dressed like a needy scholar, in an ancient evening-coat, with a rusty black hat and gloves fantastically patched, and he carried a little volume carefully under his arm. His humors were in excellent taste, his whole manner the perfection of genteel comedy. The crowd seemed to relish him vastly, and he immediately commanded a gleefully attentive audience. Many of his sallies I lost; those I caught were excellent. His trick was often to begin by taking some one urbanely and caressingly by the chin and complimenting him on the *intelligenza della sua fisionomia.* I kept near him as long as I could;

for he seemed to me an artist, cherishing a disinterested
passion for the grotesque.   But I should have liked to
see him the next morning, or when he unmasked that
night, over his hard-earned supper, in a smoky trattoria!
As the evening went on, the crowd thickened and became a motley press of shouting, pushing, scrambling
— everything but squabbling — revellers.   The rain
of missiles ceased at dusk; but the universal deposit
of chalk and flour was trampled into a cloud, made
lurid by the flaring pyramids of gas-lamps, replacing
for the occasion the stingy Roman luminaries.   Early
in the evening came off the classic exhibition of the
moccoletti, which I but half saw, like a languid reporter
resigned beforehand to be cashiered for want of enterprise.   From the mouth of a side-street, over a thousand
heads, I beheld a huge, slow-moving illuminated car,
from which blue-lights and rockets and Roman candles
were being discharged, and meeting in a dim fuliginous
glare far above the house-tops.   It was like a glimpse
of some public orgy in ancient Babylon.   In the small
hours of the morning, walking homeward from a private
entertainment, I found Ash-Wednesday still kept at
bay.   The Corso was flaring with light, and smelt like
a circus.   Every one was taking friendly liberties with
every one else, and using up the dregs of his festive
energy in convulsive hootings and gymnastics.   Here
and there certain indefatigable spirits, clad all in red,
as devils, were leaping furiously about with torches, and
being supposed to startle you.   But they shared the
universal geniality, and bequeathed me no midnight
fears as a pretext for keeping Lent — the *carnevale dei*

preti, as I read in that profanely radical sheet, the Capitale. Of this, too, I have been having glimpses. Going lately into Santa Francesca Romana, the picturesque church near the Temple of Peace, I found a feast for the eyes — a dim, crimson-toned light through curtained windows, a great festoon of tapers round the altar, a bulging girdle of lamps before the sunken shrine beneath, and a dozen white-robed Dominicans scattered in the happiest composition on the pavement. It was better than the moccoletti.

ROMAN RIDES.

Rome, last of April, 1873.

I SHALL always remember the first I took: out of
the Porta del Popolo, to where the Ponte Molle,
whose single arch sustains a weight of historic tradition,
compels the sallow Tiber to flow between its four great-
mannered ecclesiastical statues, over the crest of the
hill, and along the old posting-road to Florence. It
was mild midwinter, the season, peculiarly, of color on
the Roman Campagna; and the light was full of that
mellow purple glow, that tempered intensity, which
haunts the after-visions of those who have known
Rome like the memory of some supremely irresponsible
pleasure. An hour away, I pulled up, and stood for
some time at the edge of a meadow, gazing away into
remoter distances. Then and there, it seemed to me, I
measured the deep delight of knowing the Campagna.
But I saw more things in it than it is easy to repeat.
The country rolled away around me into slopes and
dells of enchanting contour, checkered with purple and
blue and blooming brown. The lights and shadows
were at play on the Sabine Mountains — an alternation
of tones so exquisite that you can indicate them only
by some fantastic comparison to sapphire and amber.

In the foreground a contadino, in his cloak and peaked hat, was jogging solitary on his ass; and here and there in the distance, among blue undulations, some white village, some gray tower, helped deliciously to make the scene the typical " Italian landscape " of old-fashioned art. It was so bright and yet so sad, so still and yet so charged, to the supersensuous ear, with the murmur of an extinguished life, that you could only say it was intensely and deliciously strange, and that the Roman Campagna is the most suggestive place in the world. To ride once, under these circumstances, is of course to ride again, and to allot to the Campagna a generous share of the time one spends in Rome.

It is a pleasure that doubles one's horizon, and one can scarcely say whether it enlarges or limits one's impression of the city proper. It certainly makes St. Peter's seem a trifle smaller, and blunts the edge of one's curiosity in the Forum. If you have ridden much, to think of Rome afterwards will be, I imagine, to think still respectfully and regretfully enough of the Vatican and the Pincio, the streets and the duskily picturesque street-life; but it will be even more to wonder, with an irrepressible contraction of the heart, when again you shall feel yourself bounding over the flower-smothered turf, or pass from one framed picture to another beside the open arches of the crumbling aqueducts. You look at Rome so often from some grassy hill-top — hugely compact within its walls, with St. Peter's overtopping all things and yet seeming small, and the vast girdle of marsh and meadow receding on all sides to the mountains and the sea — that you come to remember it at

last as hardly more than a large detail in an impressive
landscape. And within the walls you think of your
intended ride as a sort of romantic possibility; of
the Campagna generally as an illimitable experience.
One's rides certainly make Rome a richer place to live
in than most others. To dwell in a city which, much
as you grumble at it, is, after all, very fairly a modern
city; with crowds, and shops, and theatres, and *cafés*,
and balls, and receptions, and dinner-parties, and all
the modern confusion of social pleasures and pains; to
have at your door the good and evil of it all; and yet
to be able in half an hour to gallop away and leave it
a hundred miles, a hundred years, behind, and to look
at the tufted broom glowing on a lonely tower-top in
the still blue air, and the pale pink asphodels trembling
none the less for the stillness, and the shaggy-legged
shepherds leaning on their sticks in motionless brotherhood with the heaps of ruin, and the scrambling goats
and staggering little kids treading out wild desert
smells from the top of hollow-sounding mounds; and
then to come back through one of the great gates, and,
a couple of hours later, find yourself in the "world,"
dressed, introduced, entertained, inquiring, talking
about Middlemarch to a young English lady, or listening to Neapolitan songs from a gentleman in a very
low-cut shirt — all this is to lead a sort of double life,
and to gather from the hurrying hours more impressions
than a mind of modest capacity quite knows how to
dispose of. I touched lately upon this theme with a
friend who, I fancied, would understand me, and who
immediately assured me that he had just spent a day

which this mingled diversity of sensation made to the days one spends elsewhere what an uncommonly good novel is to a newspaper. "There was an air of idleness about it, if you will," he said, "and it was certainly pleasant enough to have been wrong. Perhaps, being, after all, unused to long stretches of dissipation, this was why I had a half-feeling that I was reading an odd chapter in the history of a person very much more of a *héros de roman* than myself." Then he proceeded to relate how he had taken a long ride with a lady whom he extremely admired. "We turned off from the Tor di Quinto Road to that castellated farm-house you know of — once a Ghibelline fortress — whither Claude Lorraine used to come to paint pictures of which the surrounding landscape is still artistically suggestive. We went into the inner court, a cloister almost, with the carven capitals of its loggia columns, and looked at a handsome child swinging shyly against the half-opened door of a room whose impenetrable shadow, behind her, made her, as it were, a sketch in bituminous water-colors. We talked with the farmer, a handsome, pale, fever-tainted fellow, with a well-to-do air, who did n't in the least prevent his affability taking a turn which resulted in his acceptance of small coin; and then we galloped away and away over the meadows which stretch with hardly a break to Veii. The day was strangely delicious, with a cool gray sky and just a touch of moisture in the air, stirred by our rapid motion. The Campagna, in the colorless, even light, was more solemn and romantic than ever; and a ragged shepherd, driving a meagre, straggling flock, whom we stopped to. ask our way of, was a perfect type of pastoral, weather-beaten misery. He was precisely the shepherd for the foreground of a scratchy etching. There were faint odors of spring in the air, and the grass here and there was streaked with great patches of daisies; but it was spring with a foreknowledge of autumn — a day to be enjoyed with a sober smile — a day somehow to make one feel as if one had seen and felt a great deal — quite, as I say, like a *héros de roman.* Apropos of such people, it was the illustrious Pelham, I think, who, on being asked if he rode, replied that he left those violent exercises to the ladies. But under such a sky, in such an air, over acres of daisied turf, a long, long gallop is certainly the gentlest, the most refined of pleasures. The elastic bound of your horse is the poetry of motion; and if you are so happy as to add to it — not the prose of companionship, riding comes to seem to you really as an intellectual pursuit. My gallop, at any rate," said my friend, "threw me into a mood which gave an extraordinary zest to the rest of the day." He was to go to a dinner-party at a villa on the edge of Rome, and Madame X——, who was also going, called for him in her carriage. "It was a long drive," he went on, "through the Forum, past the Coliseum. She told me a long story about a most interesting person. Toward the end I saw through the carriage window a slab of rugged sculptures. We were passing under the Arch of Constantine. In the hall pavement of the villa is a rare antique mosaic — one of the largest and most perfect; the ladies, on their way to the drawing-room, trail over it the flounces of Worth. We drove home late, and there 's my day."

On your exit from most of the gates of Rome you have generally half an hour's riding through winding lanes, many of which are hardly less charming than the open meadows. On foot, the walls and high hedges would vex you and spoil your walk; but in the saddle you generally overtop them and see treasures of picturesqueness. Yet a Roman wall in the springtime is, for that matter, as picturesque as anything it conceals. Crumbling grain by grain, colored and mottled to a hundred tones by sun and storm, with its rugged structure of brick extruding through its coarse complexion of peeling stucco, its creeping lace-work of wandering ivy starred with miniature violets, and its wild fringe of stouter flowers against the sky — it is as little as possible a blank partition; it is almost a piece of landscape. At this moment, in mid-April, all the ledges and cornices are wreathed with flaming poppies, nodding there as if they knew so well what faded grays and yellows were an offset to their scarlet. But the best point in a dilapidated wall of vineyard or villa is of course the gateway, lifting its great arch of cheap rococo scroll-work, its balls and shields and mossy dish-covers (as they always seem to me) and flanked with its dusky cypresses. I never pass one without taking out my mental sketch-book and jotting it down as a vignette in the insubstantial record of my ride. They always look to me intensely sad and dreary, as if they led to the moated grange where Mariana waited in desperation for something to happen; and I fancy the

usual inscription over the porch to be a recommendation to those who enter to renounce all hope of anything but a glass of more or less agreeably acrid *vino
romano*. For what you chiefly see over the walls and
at the end of the straight, short avenue of rusty cypresses are the appurtenances of a *vigna* — a couple of
acres of little upright sticks, blackening in the sun, and
a vast, sallow-faced, scantily windowed mansion, whose
expression denotes little intellectual life beyond what
goes to the driving of a hard bargain over the tasted
hogsheads. If Mariana is there, she certainly has no
pile of old magazines to beguile her leisure. Intellectual life, if the term is not too pompous, seems to the
contemplative tourist as he wanders about Rome, to
exist only as a kind of thin deposit of the past. Within
the rococo gateway, which itself has a vague literary
suggestiveness, at the end of the cypress walk, you will
probably see a mythological group in rusty marble —
a Cupid and Psyche, a Venus and Paris, an Apollo and
Daphne — the relic of an age when a Roman proprietor
thought it fine to patronize the arts. But I imagine
you are safe in thinking that it constitutes the only
literary allusion that has been made on the premises
for three or four generations.

There is a franker cheerfulness — though certainly a
proper amount of that forlornness which lurks about
every object to which the Campagna forms a background — in the primitive little taverns where, on the
homeward stretch, in the waning light, you are often
glad to rein up and demand a bottle of their best.
But their best and their worst are the same, though

with a shifting price, and plain *vino bianco* or *vino
rosso* (rarely both) is the sole article of refreshment in
which they deal. There is a ragged bush over the
door, and within, under a dusky vault, on crooked
cobble-stones, sit half a dozen contadini in their indigo
jackets and goatskin breeches, with their elbows on the
table. There is generally a rabble of infantile beggars
at the door, pretty enough in their dusty rags, with
their fine eyes and intense Italian smile, to make you
forget your private vow of doing your individual best
to make these people, whom you like so much, unlearn
their old vices. Was Porta Pia bombarded three years
ago that Peppino should still grow up to whine for a
copper? But the Italian shells had no direct message
for Peppino's stomach — and you are going to a dinner-
party at a villa. So Peppino " points " an instant for
the copper in the dust and grows up a Roman beggar.
The whole little place is the most primitive form of
hostelry ; but along any of the roads leading out of the
city you may find establishments of a higher type, with
Garibaldi, superbly mounted and foreshortened, painted
on the wall, or a lady in a low-necked dress opening a
fictive lattice with irresistible hospitality, and a yard
with the classic pine-wreathed arbor casting thin shadows upon benches and tables draped and cushioned with
the white dust from which the highways from the gates
borrow most of their local color. But, as a rider, I
say, you avoid the high-roads, and, if you are a person
of taste, don't grumble at the occasional need of following the walls of the city. City walls, to a properly
constituted American, can never be an object of in-

difference ; and there is certainly a fine solemnity in pacing in the shadow of this massive cincture of Rome. I have found myself, as I skirted its base, talking of trivial things, but never without a sudden reflection on the deplorable impermanence of first impressions. A twelvemonth ago the raw plank fences of a Boston suburb, inscribed with the virtues of healing drugs, bristled along my horizon : now I glance with idle eyes at this compacted antiquity, in which a more learned sense may read portentous dates and signs — Servius, Aurelian, Honorius. But even to idle eyes the walls of Rome abound in picturesque episodes. In some places, where the huge brickwork is black with time, and certain strange square towers look down at you with still blue eyes — the Roman sky peering through lidless loopholes — and there is nothing but white dust in the road and solitude in the air, I feel like a wandering Tartar touching on the confines of the Celestial Empire. The wall of China must have very much such a gaunt robustness. The color of the Roman ramparts is everywhere fine, and their rugged patchwork has been subdued by time and weather into the mellow harmony which painters love. On the northern side of the city, behind the Vatican, St. Peter's, and the Trastevere, I have seen them glowing in the late afternoon with the tones of ancient bronze and rusty gold. Here, at various points, they are embossed with the Papal insignia — the tiara with its flying bands and crossed keys— for which the sentimental tourist has possibly a greater kindness than of yore. With the dome of St. Peter's resting on their cornice and the hugely clustered archi-

tecture of the Vatican rising from them as from a terrace, they seem indeed the valid bulwark of an ecclesiastical city. Vain bulwark, alas! sighs the sentimental
tourist, fresh from the meagre entertainment of this latter
Holy Week. But he may find picturesque consolation
in this neighborhood at a source where, as I pass, I never
fail to apply for it. At half an hour's walk beyond
the Porta San Pancrazio, beneath the wall of the Villa
Doria, is a delightfully pompous ecclesiastical gateway
of the seventeenth century, erected by Paul V. to commemorate his restoration of the aqueducts through
which the stream bearing his name flows towards that
fine, florid portico which covers its clear-sheeted out-
gush on the crest of the Janiculan. It arches across
the road in the most ornamental manner of the period,
and one can hardly pause before it without seeming to
assist at a ten minutes' revival of old Italy — without
feeling as if one were in a cocked hat and sword, and
were coming up to Rome in another mood than Lu-
ther's, with a letter of recommendation to the mistress
of a Cardinal.

The Campagna differs greatly on the two sides of the
Tiber; and it is hard to say which, for the rider, has
the greater charm. The half-dozen rides you may take
from the Porta San Giovanni possess the perfection of
traditional Roman interest, and lead you through a far-
strewn wilderness of ruins — a scattered maze of tombs
and towers and nameless fragments of antique masonry.
The landscape here has two great features; close before
you on one side is the long, gentle swell of the Alban
Mountains, deeply, fantastically blue in most weathers,

7   J

and marbled with the vague white masses of their
scattered towns and villas. It is hard to fancy a softer
curve than that with which the mountain sweeps down
from Albano to the plain; it is a perfect example of the
classic beauty of line in the Italian landscape — that
beauty which, when it fills the background of a picture,
makes us look in the foreground for a broken column
couched upon flowers, and a shepherd piping to dan-
cing nymphs. At your side, constantly, you have the
broken line of the Claudian Aqueduct, carrying its
broad arches far away into the plain. The meadows
along which it lies are not the smoothest in the world
for a gallop, but there is no pleasure greater than to
wander over it. It stands knee-deep in the flower-
strewn grass, and its rugged piers are hung with ivy, as
the columns of a church are draped for a festa. Every
archway is a picture, massively framed, of the distance
beyond — of the snow-tipped Sabines and lonely Soracte. As the spring advances, the whole Campagna
smiles and waves with flowers; but I think they are
nowhere more rank and lovely than in the shifting
shadow of the aqueducts, where they muffle the feet
of the columns and smother the half-dozen brooks
which wander in and out like silver meshes between
the legs of a file of giants. They make a niche for
themselves, too, in every crevice and tremble on the
vault of the empty conduits. The ivy hereabouts, in
the springtime, is peculiarly brilliant and delicate; and
though it cloaks and muffles these Roman fragments far
less closely than the castles and abbeys of England, it
hangs with the light elegance of all Italian vegetation.

It is partly, doubtless, because their mighty outlines
are still unsoftened that the aqueducts are so impressive. They seem the very source of the solitude in
which they stand ; they look like architectural spectres,
and loom through the light mists of their grassy desert,
as you recede along the line, with the same insubstantial
vastness as if they rose out of Egyptian sands. It is
a great neighborhood of ruins, many of which, it must
be confessed, you have applauded in many an album.
But station a peasant with sheepskin coat and ban-
daged legs in the shadow of the tomb or tower best
known to drawing-room art, and scatter a dozen goats
on the mound above him, and the picture has a charm
which has not yet been sketched away.

The other side of the Campagna has wider fields and
smoother turf and perhaps a greater number of delightful rides ; the earth is sounder, and there are fewer
pitfalls and ditches. The land for the most part lies
higher and catches more breezes, and the grass, here
and there, is for great stretches as smooth and level as
a carpet. You have no Alban Mountains before you,
but you have in the distance the waving ridge of the
nearer Apennines, and west of them, along the course
of the Tiber, the long seaward level of deep-colored
fields, deepening as they recede to the blue and purple
of the sea itself. Beyond them, of a very clear day, you
may see the glitter of the Mediterranean. These are
the rides, perhaps, to remember most fondly, for they
lead you to enchanting nooks, and the landscape has
details of supreme picturesqueness. Indeed, when my
sense reverts to the lingering impressions of these

blessed days, it seems a fool's errand to have attempted
to express them, and a waste of words to do more than
recommend the reader to go citywards at twilight, at
the end of March, toward the Porta Cavalleggieri, and
note what he sees. At this hour the Campagna seems
peculiarly its melancholy self, and I remember roadside
"effects" of the most poignant suggestiveness. Certain
mean, mouldering villas behind grass-grown courts
have an indefinably sinister look; there was one in
especial, of which it was impossible not to fancy that
a despairing creature had once committed suicide there,
behind bolted door and barred window, and that no one
has since had the pluck to go in and see why he never
came out. But, to my sense, every slight wayside detail in the country about Rome has a penetrating eloquence, and I may possibly exaggerate the charms of
very common things. This is the more likely, because
the charms I touch on are so many notes in the scale
of melancholy. To delight in the evidence of meagre
lives might seem to be a heartless pastime, and the
pleasure, I confess, is a pensive one. Melancholy is as
common an influence from Southern things as gayety,
I think; it rarely fails to strike a Northern observer
when he misses what he calls comfort. Beauty is no
compensation for the loss; it only makes it more poignant. Enough beauty of climate hangs over these Roman cottages and farm-houses — beauty of light, of
atmosphere, and of vegetation; but their charm for
seekers of the picturesque is the way in which the lustrous air seems to illuminate their intimate desolation.
Man lives more with Nature in Italy than in New

England; she does more work for him and gives him more holidays than in our short-summered clime; and his home is therefore much more bare of devices for helping him to do without her, forget her and forgive her. These reflections are, perhaps, the source of the entertainment you find in a moss-coated stone stairway climbing outside of a wall; in a queer inner court, befouled with rubbish and drearily bare of convenience; in an ancient, quaintly carven well, worked with infinite labor from an overhanging window; in an arbor of time-twisted vines, under which you may sit with your feet in the dirt, and remember as a dim fable that there are races for which the type of domestic allurement is the parlor hearth-rug. For reasons apparent or otherwise, these things amuse me beyond expression, and I am never weary of staring into gateways, of lingering by dreary, shabby, half-barbaric farm-yards, of feasting a foolish gaze on sun-cracked plaster and unctuous indoor shadows.

I must not forget, however, that it is not for wayside effects that one rides away behind St. Peter's, but for the enchanting sense of wandering over boundless space, of seeing great classic lines of landscape, of watching them dispose themselves into pictures so full of "style" that you can think of no painter who deserves to have you admit that they suggest him — hardly knowing whether it is better pleasure to gallop far and drink deep of air and grassy distance and the whole delicious opportunity, or to walk and pause and linger, and try and grasp some ineffaceable memory of sky and color and outline. Your pace can hardly help

falling into a contemplative measure at the time, everywhere so wonderful, but in Rome so persuasively divine, when the winter begins palpably to soften and to
quicken into spring.   Far out on the Campagna, early
in February, you feel the first vague, earthy emanations,
which in a few weeks come wandering into the heart of
the city and throbbing through the close, dark streets.   —
Springtime in Rome is an immensely poetic affair; but
you must stand often in the meadows, between grass
and sky, to measure its deep, full, steadily accelerated
rhythm.   The winter has an incontestable beauty, and is
pre-eminently the time of color—the time when it is no
affectation, but homely verity, to talk about the " purple " tone of the atmosphere.   As February comes and
goes your purple is streaked with green, and the rich,
dark bloom of the distance begins to lose its intensity.
But your loss is made up by other gains; none more
precious than that inestimable gain to the ear — the
disembodied voice of the lark.   It comes with the early
flowers, the white narcissus and the cyclamen, the half-
buried violets and the pale anemones, and makes the
whole atmosphere ring, like a vault of tinkling glass.
You never see the bird himself, and are utterly unable
to localize his note, which seems to come from everywhere at once, to be some hundred-throated voice of
the air.   Sometimes you fancy you just distinguish
him, a mere vague spot against the blue, an intenser
throb in the universal pulsation of light.   As the
weeks go on, the flowers multiply and the deep blues
and purples of the hills turn to azure and violet, and
creep higher toward the narrowing snow-line of the

Sabines. The first hour of your ride becomes rather
warm for comfort, but you beguile it with brushing the
hawthorn-blossoms as you pass along the hedges, and
catching at the wild rose and honeysuckle; and when
you get into the meadows, there is stir enough in the
air to lighten the dead weight of the sun. The Roman
air, however, is not a tonic medicine, and it seldom
allows your rides to be absolutely exhilarating. It has
always seemed to me, indeed, part of their picturesqueness that your keenest enjoyment is haunted with a
vague languor. Occasionally, when the sirocco blows,
this amounts to a sensation really worth having on
moral and intellectual grounds. Then, under the gray
sky, toward the veiled distances which the sirocco generally brings with it, you seem to ride forth into a
world from which all hope has departed, and in which,
in spite of the flowers that make your horse's footfalls
soundless, nothing is left save a possibility of calamity
which your imagination is unable to measure, but from
which it hardly shrinks. An occasional sense of de-
pression from this source may almost amount to exhila-
ration; but a season of sirocco would be an overdose
of morbid pleasure. I almost think that you may best
feel the peculiar beauty of the Campagna on those mild
days of winter when the brilliant air alone suffices to
make the whole landscape smile, and you may pause
on the brown grass in the sunny stillness, and, by listening long enough, almost fancy you hear the shrill
of the midsummer cricket. It is detail and ornament
that vary from month to month, from week to week
even, and make your rides over familiar fields a con-

stant feast of unexpectedness ; but the great essential
lines and masses of the Campagna preserve throughout
the year the same impressive serenity. Soracte, in
January and April, rises from its blue horizon like an
island from the sea, with an elegance of contour which
no mood of the year can deepen or diminish. You
know it well; you have seen it often in the mellow
backgrounds of Claude ; and it has such an irresistibly
classical, academical air that, while you look at it, your
saddle begins to feel like a faded old arm-chair in a
palace gallery. A month's riding on the Campagna,
indeed, will show you a dozen prime Claudes. After I
had seen them all, I went piously to the Doria gallery
to refresh my memory of its two famous specimens,
and I vastly enjoyed their delightful air of reference to
something which had become a part of my personal
experience. Delightful it certainly is to feel the common element in one's own impressions and those of a
genius whom it has helped to do great things. Claude
must have wandered much on the Campagna, and interfused its divine undulations with his exquisite conception of the picturesque. He was familiar with a
landscape in which there was not a single uncompromising line. I saw, a few days later, a small finished
sketch from his hand, in the possession of an American
artist, which was almost startling in its clear reflection of forms unaltered by the two centuries which
have dimmed and cracked the paint and canvas.

This unbroken continuity of impressions which I
have tried to indicate is an excellent example of the
intellectual background of all enjoyment in Rome. It

effectually prevents pleasure from becoming vulgar, for your sensation rarely begins and ends with itself; it reverberates ; it recalls, commemorates, resuscitates something else. At least half the merit of everything you enjoy must be that it suits you absolutely ; but the larger half, here, is generally that it has suited some one else, and that you can never flatter yourself you have discovered it. It is historic, literary, suggestive ; it has played some other part than it is just then playing to your eyes. It was an admission of this truth that my discriminating friend who showed me the Claudes found it impossible to designate a certain delightful region which you enter at the end of an hour's riding from Porta Cavalleggieri as anything but Arcadia. The exquisite correspondence of the term in this case altogether revived its faded bloom ; here veritably the oaten pipe must have stirred the windless air, and the satyrs have laughed among the brookside reeds. Three or four long grassy dells stretch away in a chain between low hills over which slender trees are so discreetly scattered that each one is a resting-place for a shepherd. The elements of the scene are simple enough, but the composition has extraordinary refinement. By one of those happy chances which keep observation, in Italy, always in her best humor, a shepherd had thrown himself down under one of the trees in the very attitude of Meliboeus. He had been washing his feet, I suppose, in the neighboring brook, and had found it pleasant afterwards to roll his short breeches well up on his thighs. Lying thus in the shade, on his elbow, with his naked legs stretched out

7 *

on the turf, and his soft peaked hat over his long hair
crushed back like the veritable bonnet of Arcady, he
was exactly the figure of the background of this happy
valley. The poor fellow, lying there in rustic weariness
and ignorance, little fancied that he was a symbol of
old-world meanings to new-world eyes.   Such eyes
may find as great a store of picturesque meanings in
the cork-woods of Monte Mario, tenderly loved of all
equestrians.   These are less severely pastoral than our
Arcadia, and you might more properly lodge there a
damosel of Ariosto than a nymph of Theocritus.
Among them is strewn a lovely wilderness of flowers
and shrubs, and the whole place has such a charming
woodland air, that, casting about me the other day for
a compliment, I declared that it reminded me of New
Hampshire.   My compliment had a double edge, and I
had no sooner uttered it than I smiled — or sighed —
to perceive in all the undiscriminated botany about me
the wealth of detail, the idle elegance and grace of
Italy alone — the natural stamp of the land which has
the singular privilege of making one love her unsancti-
fied beauty all but as well as those features of one's
own country toward which nature's small allowance
doubles that of one's own affection.   In this matter
of suggestiveness, no rides are more profitable than
those you take in the Villa Doria or the Villa Borghese ; or do not take, possibly, if you prefer to reserve
these particular regions (the latter in especial) for your
walking hours. People do ride, however, in both villas, which deserve honorable mention in this regard.
The Villa Doria, with its noble site, its lovely views,

its great groups of stone-pines, so clustered and yet so
individual, its lawns and flowers and fountains, its
altogether princely disposition, is a place where one
may pace, well mounted, of a brilliant day, with an
agreeable sense of its being a rather more elegant pastime to balance in one's stirrups than to trudge on even
the smoothest gravel. But at the Villa Borghese the
walkers have the best of it ; for they are free of those
delicious, outlying corners and bosky by-ways which the
rumble of barouches never reaches. Early in March it
becomes a perfect epitome of the spring. You cease to
care much for the melancholy greenness of the disfeatured statues which has been your chief winter's intimation of verdure ; and before you are quite conscious
of the tender streaks and patches in the great, quaint,
grassy arena round which the Propaganda students, in
their long skirts, wander slowly, like dusky seraphs
revolving the gossip of Paradise, you spy the brave
little violets uncapping their azure brows beneath the
high-stemmed pines. One's walks, here, would take us
too far, and one's pauses detain us too long, when, in
the quiet parts, under the wall, one comes across a
group of certain charming little scholars in full-dress
suits and white cravats, shouting over their play in
clear Italian, while a grave young priest, under a tree,
watches them over the top of his book. I have wished
only to say a word for one's Rides — to suggest that
they give one, not only exercise but memories.

ROMAN NEIGHBORHOODS.

I MADE a note after my first stroll at Albano to the effect that I had been talking of the picturesque all my life, but that now for a change I beheld it. I had been looking all winter across the Campagna at the free-flowing outline of the Alban Mount, with its half-dozen towns shining on its purple side, like vague sun-spots in the shadow of a cloud, and thinking it simply an agreeable incident in the varied background of Rome. But now that during the last few days I have been treating it is a foreground, and suffering St. Peter's to play the part of a small mountain on the horizon, with the Campagna swimming mistily in a thousand ambiguous lights and shadows in the interval, I find as good entertainment as any in the Roman streets. The walk I speak of was just out of the village, to the south, toward the neighboring town of Ariccia,— neighboring these twenty years, since the Pope (the late Pope, I was on the point of calling him) threw his superb viaduct across the deep ravine which divides it from Albano. At the risk of being thought fan-tastic, I confess that the Pope's having built the via-duct — in this very recent antiquity — made me linger

there in a pensive posture and marvel at the march of
history and at Pius the Ninth's beginning already to
profit by the sentimental allowances we make to vanished powers. An ardent *nero* then would have had
his own way with me, and obtained an easy admission
that the Pope was indeed a father to his people. Far
down into the charming valley which slopes out the
ancestral woods of the Chigis into the level Campagna
winds the steep, stone-paved road, at the bottom of
which, in the good old days, tourists in no great hurry
saw the mules and oxen tackled to their carriage for
the opposite ascent. And, indeed, even an impatient
tourist might have been content to lounge back in his
jolting chaise and look out at the mouldy foundations
of the little city, plunging into the verdurous flank of
the gorge. If I were asked what is the most delectable piece of oddity hereabouts, I should certainly say
the way in which the crumbling black houses of these
ponderous villages plant their weary feet on the flowery edges of all the steepest chasms. Before you enter
one of them you invariably find yourself lingering outside of its pretentious old gateway, to see it clutched
and stitched, as it were, to the stony hillside, by this
rank embroidery of wild weeds and flowers. Just at
this moment nothing is prettier than the contrast between their dusky ruggedness and this tender fringe of
yellow and pink and violet. All this you may observe
from the viaduct at Ariccia ; but you must wander
below to feel the full force of the eloquence of our
imaginary *papalino*. The pillars and arches of pale
gray peperino arise in huge tiers, with a magnificent

spring and solidity. The older Romans built no better ; and the work has a deceptive air of being one of
their sturdy bequests, which helps one to drop a sigh
over Italy's long, long yesterday. In Ariccia I found a
little square with a couple of mossy fountains, occupied
on one side by a vast, dusky-faced Palazzo Chigi, and
on the other by a goodly church with an imposing
dome. The dome, within, covers the whole edifice, and
is adorned with some extremely elegant stucco-work of
the seventeenth century. It gave a great value to this
fine old decoration, that preparations were going forward for a local festival, and that the village carpenter
was hanging certain mouldy strips of crimson damask
against the piers of the vaults. The damask might
have been of the seventeenth century, too, and a group
of peasant-women were seeing it unfurled with evident
awe. I regarded it myself with interest ; it seemed to
me to be the tattered remnant of a fashion that had
gone out. I thought again of the poor, disinherited
Pope, and wondered whether, when that venerable frip-
pery will no longer bear the carpenter's nails, any more
will be provided. It was hard to fancy anything but
shreds and patches in that musty tabernacle. Wherever you go in Italy, you receive some such intimation
as this of the shrunken proportions of Catholicism, and
every church I have glanced into on my walks hereabouts has given me an almost pitying sense of it.
One finds one's self at last (without fatuity, I hope)
feeling sorry for the loneliness of the remaining faithful. The churches seem to have been made so for the
world, in its social sense, and the world seems so irrevo-

cably away from them. They are in size out of all
modern proportion to the local needs, and the only
thing that seems really to occupy their melancholy
vacancy is the smell of stale incense. There are pictures on all the altars by respectable third-rate painters ; pictures which I suppose once were ordered and
paid for and criticised by worshippers who united taste
with piety. At Genzano, beyond Ariccia, rises on the
gray village street a pompous Renaissance temple,
whose imposing nave and aisles would contain the
population of a metropolis. But where is the *taste* of
Ariccia and Genzano ? Where are the choice spirits
for whom Antonio Raggi modelled the garlands of his
dome, and a hundred clever craftsmen imitated Guido
and Caravaggio ? Here and there, from the pavement,
as you pass, a dusky crone interlards her devotions
with more profane importunities ; or a grizzled peasant
on rusty-jointed knees, tilted forward with his elbows
on a bench, reveals the dimensions of the patch in his
blue breeches. But where is the connecting link between Guido and Caravaggio and those poor souls for
whom an undoubted original is only a something behind a row of candlesticks, of no very clear meaning
save that you must bow to it ? You find a vague
memory of it at best in the useless grandeurs about
you, and you seem to be looking at a structure of which
the stubborn earth-scented foundations alone remain,
with the carved and painted shell that bends above
them, while the central substance has utterly crumbled
away.

I shall seem to have adopted a more meditative pace

than befits a brisk constitutional, if I say that I also
fell a thinking before the shabby façade of the old
Chigi Palace.　But it seemed somehow, in its gray forlornness, to respond to the sadly superannuated expression of the opposite church ; and indeed, under any
circumstances, what contemplative mind can forbear to
do a little romancing in the shadow of a provincial
palazzo ?　On the face of the matter, I know, there is
often no very salient peg to hang a romance on.　A sort
of dusky blankness invests the establishment, which
has often a rather imbecile old age.　But a hundred
brooding secrets lurk in this inexpressive mask, and the
Chigi Palace seemed to me in the suggestive twilight a
very pretty specimen of a haunted house.　Its basement walls sloped outward like the beginning of a pyramid, and its lower windows were covered with massive iron cages.　Within the doorway, across the court,
I saw the pale glimmer of flowers on a terrace, and on
the roof I beheld a great covered loggia, or belvedere,
with a dozen window-panes missing, or mended with
paper.　Nothing gives one a stronger impression of old
manners than an ancestral palace towering in this
haughty fashion over a shabby little town ; you hardly
stretch a point when you call it an impression of feu-
dalism.　The scene may pass for feudal to American
eyes, for which a hundred windows on a façade mean
nothing more exclusive than a hotel kept (at the worst)
on the European plan.　The mouldy gray houses on
the steep, crooked street, with their black, cavernous
archways filled with evil smells, with the braying of
asses, and with human intonations hardly more musical,

the haggard and tattered peasantry staring at you with hungry-heavy eyes, the brutish-looking monks (there are still enough to be effective), the soldiers, the mounted constables, the dirt, the dreariness, the misery, and the dark, overgrown palace frowning over it all from barred window and guarded gateway — what more than all this do we dimly descry in a mental image of the dark ages ? With the strongest desire to content himself with the picturesqueness of things, the tourist can hardly help wondering whether the picture is not half spoiled for pleasure by all that it suggests of the hardness of human life. At Genzano, out of the very midst of the village squalor, rises the Palazzo Cesarini, separated from its gardens by a dirty lane. Between peasant and prince the contact is unbroken, and one would say that Italian good-nature must be sorely taxed by their mutual allowances; that the prince in especial must be trained not to take things too hard. There are no comfortable townsfolk about him to remind him of the blessings of a happy mediocrity of fortune. When he looks out of his window he sees a battered old peasant against a sunny wall, sawing off his dinner from a hunch of black bread.

I must confess, however, that " feudal " as it amused me to find the little piazza of Ariccia, it displayed no especial symptoms of a *jacquerie*. On the contrary, the afternoon being cool, many of the villagers were contentedly muffled in those ancient cloaks, lined with green baize, which, when tossed over the shoulder and surmounted with a peaked hat, form one of the few lingering remnants of " costume " in Italy ; others were tossing wooden balls, light-heartedly enough, on the grass outside the town. The egress, on this side, is under a great stone archway, thrown out from the palace and surmounted with the family arms. Nothing could better confirm your fancy that the townsfolk are groaning serfs. The road leads away through the woods, like many of the roads hereabouts, among trees less remarkable for their size than for their picturesque contortions and posturings. The woods, at the moment at which I write, are full of the raw green light of early spring, and I find it vastly becoming to the various complexions of the wild flowers which cover the waysides. I have never seen these untended parterres in such lovely exuberance ; the sturdiest pedestrian becomes a lingering idler if he allows them to catch his eye. The pale purple cyclamen, with its hood thrown back, stands up in masses as dense as tulip-beds ; and here and there, in the duskier places, great sheets of forget-me-not seem to exhale a faint blue mist. These are the commonest plants ; there are dozens more I know no name for — a rich profusion, in especial, of a beautiful, five-petalled flower with its white texture pencilled with hair-strokes which certain fair copyists I know of would have to hold their breath to imitate. An Italian oak has neither the girth nor the height of its Anglo-Saxon brothers, but it contrives, in proportion, to be perhaps even more effective. It crooks its back and twists its arms and clinches its hundred fists with the most fantastic extravagance, and wrinkles its bark into strange rugosities from which its first scattered sprouts of yellow green seem to break out like a

morbid fungus. But the tree which has the greatest
charm to Northern eyes is the cold, gray-green ilex,
whose clear, crepuscular shade is a delicious provision
against a Southern sun. The ilex has even less color
than the cypress, but it is much less funereal, and a
landscape full of ilexes may still be said to smile —
soberly. It abounds in old Italian gardens, where the
boughs are trimmed and interlocked into vaulted corridors, in which, from point to point, as in the niches
of some dimly frescoed hall, you encounter mildewed
busts, staring at you with a solemnity which the even
gray light makes strangely intense. A humbler relative of the ilex, though it does better things than help
broken-nosed emperors to look dignified, is the olive,
which covers many of the neighboring hillsides with
its little smoky puffs of foliage. A piece of picturesqueness I never weary of is the sight of the long
blue stretch of the Campagna, making a high horizon,
and resting on this vaporous base of olive-tops. A
tourist intent upon a metaphor might liken it to the
ocean seen above the smoke of watch-fires kindled on
the strand.

To do perfect justice to the wood-walk away from
Ariccia, I ought to touch upon the birds that were
singing vespers as I passed. But the reader would
find my rhapsody as poor entertainment as the programme of a concert he had been unable to attend. I
have no more learning about bird-music than would
help me to guess that a dull, dissyllabic refrain in the
heart of the wood came from the cuckoo; and when at
moments I heard a twitter of fuller tone, with a more

suggestive modulation, I could only *hope* it was the nightingale. I have listened for the nightingale more than once, in places so charming that his song would have seemed but the articulate expression of their beauty; but I have never heard anything but a provoking snatch or two — a prelude that came to nothing. But in spite of a natural grudge, I generously believe him a great artist, or at least a great genius — a creature who despises any prompting short of absolute inspiration. For the rich, the multitudinous melody around me seemed but the offering to my ear of the prodigal spirit of picturesqueness. The wood was ringing with sound, because it was twilight, spring, and Italy. It was also because of these good things and various others beside, that I relished so keenly my visit to the Capuchin convent, upon which I emerged after half an hour in the wood. It stands above the town, on the slope of the Alban Mount, and its wild garden climbs away behind it and extends its melancholy influence. Before it is a stiff little avenue of trimmed ilexes which conducts you to a grotesque little shrine beneath the staircase ascending to the church. Just here, if you are apt to grow timorous at twilight, you may take a very pretty fright; for as you draw near you behold, behind the grating of the shrine, the startling semblance of a gaunt and livid monk. A sickly lamplight plays down upon his face, and he stares at you from cavernous eyes with a dreadful air of death in life. Horror of horrors, you murmur; is this a Capuchin penance? You discover of course in a moment that it is only a Capuchin joke, that the monk is

a pious dummy, and his spectral visage a matter of the
paint-brush. You resent his intrusion on the surrounding loveliness; and as you proceed to demand entertainment at their convent, you declare that the Capu-
chins are very vulgar fellows. This declaration, as I
made it, was supported by the conduct of the simple
brother who opened the door of the cloister in obedi-
ence to my knock, and, on learning my errand, demurred
about admitting me at so late an hour. If I would return on the morrow morning, he would be most happy.
He broke into a blank grin when I assured him that this
was the very hour of my desire, and that the garish
morning light would do no justice to the view. These
were mysteries beyond his ken, and it was only his
good-nature (of which he had plenty) and not his
imagination that was moved. So that when, passing
through the narrow cloister and out upon the grassy
terrace, I saw another cowled brother standing with
folded hands profiled against the sky, in admirable harmony with the scene, I ventured to doubt that he knew
he was picturesque amid picturesqueness. This, however, was surely too much to ask of him, and it was
cause enough for gratitude that, though he was there
before me, he was not a fellow-tourist with an opera-
glass slung over his shoulder. There was reason in my
fancy for seeing the convent in the expiring light, for
the scene was supremely enchanting. Directly below
the terrace lay the deep-set circle of the Alban, Lake,
shining softly through the light mists of evening. This
beautiful pool — it is hardly more — occupies the crater
of a prehistoric volcano — a perfect cup, moulded and

smelted by furnace-fires. The rim of the cup rises high and densely wooded around the placid, stone-blue water, with a sort of natural artificiality. The sweep and contour of the long circle are admirable; never was a lake so charmingly lodged. It is said to be of extraordinary depth; and though stone-blue water seems at first a very innocent substitute for boiling lava, it has a sinister look which betrays its dangerous antecedents. The winds never reach it, and its surface is never ruffled; but its deep-bosomed placidity seems to cover guilty secrets, and you fancy it in communication with the capricious and treacherous forces of nature. Its very color has a kind of joyless beauty — a blue as cold and opaque as a solidified sheet of lava. Streaked and wrinkled by a mysterious motion of its own, it seemed the very type of a legendary pool, and I could easily have believed that I had only to sit long enough into the evening to see the ghosts of classic nymphs and naiads cleave its sullen flood and beckon to me with irresistible arms. Is it because its shores are haunted with these vague Pagan influences, that two convents have risen there to purge the atmosphere? From the Capuchin terrace you look across at the gray Franciscan monastery of Palazzuola, which is not less picturesque certainly than the most obstinate myth it may have exorcised. The Capuchin garden is a wild tangle of great trees and shrubs and clinging, trembling vines which, in these hard days, are left to take care of themselves; a weedy garden, if there ever was one, but none the less charming for that, in the deepening dusk, with its steep, grassy vistas struggling away into

impenetrable shadow. I braved the shadow for the
sake of climbing upon certain little flat-roofed, crumbling pavilions, which rise from the corners of the farther wall, and give you a wider and lovelier view of
the lake and hills and sky.

I have perhaps justified to the reader the declaration
with which I started, and helped him to fancy — and
possibly to remember — that one's walks at Albano are
entertaining. They may be various, too, and have little
in common but the merit of keeping in the shade.
"Galleries" the roads are prettily called, and with a
great deal of justice; for they are vaulted and draped
overhead and hung with an immense succession of pictures. As you follow the long road from Genzano to
Frascati, you have perpetual views of the Campagna,
framed by clusters of trees, and its vast, iridescent expanse completes the charm and comfort of your verdurous dusk. I compared it just now to the sea, and
with a good deal of truth, for it has the same fantastic
lights and shades, the same confusion of glitter and
gloom. But I have seen it at moments — chiefly in
the misty twilight — when it seemed less like the
positive ocean than like something more portentous —
the land in a state of dissolution. I could fancy that
the fields were dimly surging and tossing, and melting away into quicksands, and that the last "effect"
was being presented to the eyes of imaginative tourists.
A view, however, which has the merit of being really
as interesting as it seems, is that of the Lake of Nemi,
which the enterprising traveller hastens to compare
with its sister sheet of Albano. Comparison in this

case is particularly odious; for in order to prefer one lake to the other, you have to discover faults where there are none. Nemi is a smaller circle, but she lies in a deeper cup; and if she has no gray Franciscan convent to guard her woody shores, she has, in quite the same position, the little, high-perched, black town to which she gives her name, and which looks across at Genzano on the opposite shore, as Palazzuola contemplates Castel Gandolfo. The walk from Ariccia to Genzano is charming, most of all when it reaches a certain grassy piazza from which three public avenues stretch away under a double row of stunted and twisted elms. The Duke Cesarini has a villa at Genzano — I mentioned it just now — whose gardens overhang the lake; but he has also a porter, in a faded, rakish-looking livery, who shakes his head at your proffered franc, unless you can reinforce it with a permit countersigned at Rome. For this annoying complication of dignities he is justly to be denounced; but I forgive him for the sake of that ancestor who in the seventeeth century planted this shady walk. Never was a prettier approach to a town than by these low-roofed, light-checkered corridors. Their only defect is that they prepare you for a town with a little more rustic coquetry than Genzano possesses. It seemed to me to have more than the usual portion of mouldering disrepair; to look dismally as if its best families had all fallen into penury together and lost the means of keeping anything better than donkeys in their great, dark, vaulted basements, and mending their broken window-panes. It was à propos of this drear Genzano that I

had a difference of opinion with a friend, who maintained that there was nothing in the same line so pretty in Europe as a pretty New England village.   The
proposition, to a sentimental tourist, seemed at first
inacceptable; but, calmly considered, it has a measure of truth.   I am not fond of white clapboards, certainly; I vastly prefer the dusky tones of ancient
stucco and peperino; but I confess I am sensible of
the charms of a vine-shaded porch, of tulips and dahlias glowing in the shade of high-arching elms, of
heavy-scented lilacs bending over a white paling to
brush your cheek.

"I prefer Siena to Lowell," said my friend; "but I
prefer Northampton to Genzano."   In fact, an Italian
village is simply a miniature Italian city, and its various parts imply a town of fifty times the size.   At
Genzano there are neither dahlias nor lilacs, and no
odors but foul ones.   Flowers and perfumes are all
confined to the high-walled precincts of Duke Cesarini,
to which you must obtain admission twenty miles
away.   The houses, on the other hand, would generally
lodge a New England cottage, porch and garden and
high-arching elms included, in one of their cavernous
basements.   These vast gray dwellings are all of a fashion denoting more generous social needs than any they
serve nowadays.   They seem to speak of better days,
and of a fabulous time when Italy was not shabby.
For what follies are they doing penance?   Through
what melancholy are they their fortunes ebbed?
You ask these questions the shady side
of the long blank an glaring

upon the dust-colored walls and pausing before the fetid gloom of open doors.

I should like to spare a word for mouldy little Nemi, perched upon a cliff high above the lake, on the opposite side ; but after all, when I had climbed up into it from the water-side, and passed beneath a great arch which, I suppose, once topped a gateway, and counted its twenty or thirty apparent inhabitants peeping at me from black doorways, and looked at the old round tower at whose base the village clusters, and declared that it was all queer, queer, desperately queer, I had said all that is worth saying about it. Nemi has a much better appreciation of its lovely position than Genzano, where your only view of the lake is from a dunghill behind one of the houses. At the foot of the round tower is an overhanging terrace, from which you may feast your eyes on the only freshness they find in these dusky human hives — the blooming seam, as one may call it, of strong wild-flowers which binds the crumbling walls to the face of the cliff. Of Rocca di Papa I must say as little. It kept generally what I had fancied the picturesque promise of its name ; but the only object I made a note of as I passed through it on my way to Monte Cavo, which rises directly above it, was a little black house with a tablet in its face setting forth that Massimo d'Azeglio had dwelt there. The story of his sojourn is not the least entertaining episode in his delightful Memoirs. From the summit of Monte Cavo is a prodigious view, which you may enjoy with whatever good-nature is left you by the reflection that the modern Passionist convent which occupies this admirable

site was erected by the Cardinal of York (grandson of
James II.) on the demolished ruins of an immemorial
temple of Jupiter: the last foolish act of a foolish
race. For me, I confess, this folly spoiled the convent,
and the convent all but spoiled the view; for I kept
thinking how fine it would have been to emerge upon
the old pillars and sculptures from the lava pavement
of the Via Triumphalis, which wanders grass-grown
and untrodden through the woods. A convent, however, which nothing spoils is that of Palazzuola, to
which I paid my respects on this same occasion. It
rises on a lower spur of Monte Cavo, on the edge of the
Alban Lake, and though it occupies a classic site —
that of early Alba Longa — it displaced nothing more
precious than memories and legends so dim that the
antiquarians are still quarrelling about them. It has a
meagre little church and the usual impossible Perugino
with a couple of tinsel crowns for the Madonna and the
Infant inserted into the canvas; and it has also a
musty old room hung about with faded portraits and
charts and queer ecclesiastical knick-knacks, which
borrowed a mysterious interest from the sudden assurance of the simple Franciscan brother who accompanied me, that it was the room of the Son of the King
of Portugal! But my peculiar pleasure was the little
thick-shaded garden which adjoins the convent and
commands from its massive artificial foundations an
enchanting view of the lake. Part of it is laid out in
cabbages and lettuce, over which a rubicund brother,
with his frock tucked up, was bending with a solicitude
which he interrupted to remove his skull-cap and greet

me with the unsophisticated, sweet-humored smile which every now and then in Italy does so much to make you forget the uncleanness of monachism. The rest is occupied by cypresses and other funereal umbrage, making a dank circle round an old cracked fountain, black with water-moss. The parapet of the terrace is furnished with good stone seats, where you may lean on your elbows and gaze away a sunny half-hour, and, feeling the general charm of the scene, declare that the best mission of Italy in the world has been to produce this sort of thing. If I wished a single word for the whole place and its suggestions, I should talk of their exquisite *mildness*. Mild it all seemed to me as a dream, as resignation, as one's thoughts of another life. I could have fancied that my lingering there was not an experience of the irritable flesh, but a deep revery on a summer's day over a passage in a poem by a man of genius.

From Albano you may take your way through several ancient little cities to Frascati, a rival centre of *villeggiatura*, the road following the hillside for a long morning's walk and passing through alternations of denser and clearer shade — the dark, vaulted alleys of ilex and the brilliant corridors of fresh-sprouting oak. The Campagna lies beneath you continually, with the sea beyond Ostia receiving the silver arrows of the sun upon its chased and burnished shield, and mighty Rome, to the north, lying at no great length in the idle immensity around it. The highway passes below Castel Gandolfo, which stands perched on an eminence behind a couple of gateways surmounted with the Papal tiara and twisted cordon; and I confess that I have more than once chosen the roundabout road for the sake of passing beneath these pompous insignia. Castel Gandolfo is indeed an ecclesiastical village and under the peculiar protection of the Popes, whose huge summer-palace rises in the midst of it like a sort of rural Vatican. In speaking of the road to Frascati, I necessarily revert to my first impressions, gathered on the occasion of the feast of the Annunziata, which falls on the 25th of March, and is celebrated by a peasants' fair. As Murray strongly recommends you to visit this spectacle, at which you are promised a brilliant exhibition of all the costumes of modern Latium, I took an early train to Frascati and measured, in company with a prodigious stream of humble pedestrians, the half-hour's interval to Grotta Ferrata, where the fair is held. The road winds along the hillside, among the silver-sprinkled olives, and through a charming wood where the ivy seemed tacked upon the oaks by woman's fingers and the birds were singing to the late anemones. It was covered with a very jolly crowd of vulgar pleasure-takers, and the only creatures who were not in a state of manifest hilarity were the pitiful little overladen, over-beaten donkeys (who surely deserve a chapter to themselves in any description of these neighborhoods) and the horrible beggars who were thrusting their sores and stumps at you from under every tree. Every one was shouting, singing, scrambling, making light of dust and distance, and filling the air with that childlike jollity which the blessed Italian temperament never goes roundabout to conceal. There is no crowd, surely,

at once so jovial and so gentle as an Italian crowd, and
I doubt if in any other country the tightly packed
third-class car in which I went out from Rome would
introduced me to so much smiling and so little swearing.   Grotta Ferrata is a very dirty little village, with
a number of raw new houses baking on the hot hillside, and nothing to charm the tourist but its situation and its old fortified abbey.   After pushing about
among the shabby little booths and declining a number
of fabulous bargains in tinware, shoes, and pork, I was
glad to retire to a comparatively uninvaded corner of
the abbey and divert myself with the view.   This gray
ecclesiastical citadel is a very picturesque affair, hanging over the hillside on plunging foundations which
bury themselves among the olive-trees.   It has massive
round towers at the corners, and a grass-grown moat,
enclosing a church and monastery.   The outer court,
within the abbatial gateway, now serves as the public
square of the village, and in fair-time, of course, witnessed the best of the fun.   The best of the fun was to
be found in certain great vaults and cellars of the
abbey, where wine was being freely dispensed from
gigantic hogsheads.   At the exit of these trickling
grottos, shady trellises of bamboo and gathered twigs
had been improvised, under which a prodigious guz-
zling went forward.   All this was very curious, and I
was roughly reminded of the wedding-feast of Gamacho.
The banquet was far less substantial, of course, but it
had an air of old-world revelry which could not fail to
suggest romantic analogies to an ascetic American.
There was a feast of reason close at hand, however,

and I was careful to visit the famous frescos of Domenichino in the adjoining church. It sounds rather brutal perhaps to say that, when I came back into the clamorous little piazza, I found the peasants swilling down their sour wine more picturesque than the masterpieces (Murray calls them so) of the famous Bolognese. It amounts, after all, to saying that I prefer Teniers to Domenichino; which I am willing to let pass for the truth. The scene under the rickety trellises was the more suggestive of Teniers that there were no costumes to make it too Italian. Murray's attractive statement on this point was, like many of his statements, much truer twenty years ago than to-day. Costume is gone or fast going; I saw among the women not a single crimson bodice and not a couple of classic head-cloths. The poorer sort are dressed in vulgar rags of no fashion and color, and the smarter ones adorned with calico gowns and printed shawls of the vilest modern fabric, with their dusky tresses garnished with nothing more pictorial than the lustrous pomatum. The men are still in jackets and breeches, and, with their slouched and pointed hats and open-breasted shirts and rattling leather leggings, may remind one sufficiently of the Italian peasant as he figured in the woodcuts familiar to our infancy. After coming out of the church I found a delightful nook — a queer little terrace before a more retired and tranquil drinking-shop — where I called for a bottle of wine to help me to guess why I liked Domenichino no better.

This little terrace was a capricious excrescence at the end of the piazza, which was itself simply a great ter-

race ; and one reached it, picturesquely, by ascending
a short inclined plane of grass-grown cobble-stones and
passing across a little dusky kitchen, through whose
narrow windows the light of the mighty landscape beyond was twinkling on old earthen pots. The terrace
was oblong, and so narrow that it held but a single
small table, placed lengthwise ; but nothing could be
pleasanter than to place one's bottle on the polished
parapet. Here, by the time you had emptied it, you
seemed to be swinging forward into immensity —
hanging poised above the Campagna. A beautiful
gorge with a twinkling . stream wandered down the
hill far below you, beyond which Marino and Castel
Gandolfo peeped above the trees. In front you could
count the towers of Rome and the tombs of the Appian
Way. I don't know that I came to any very distinct
conclusion about Domenichino; but it was perhaps
because the view was perfection, that he seemed to
me more than ever to be mediocrity. And yet I don't
think it was my bottle of wine, either, that made me
feel half sentimental about him ; it was the sense of
there being something cruelly feeble in his tenure of
fame, something derisive in his exaggerated honors.
It is surely an unkind stroke of fate for him to have
Murray assuring ten thousand Britons every winter in
the most emphatic manner that his Communion of
St. Jerome is the "second finest picture in the world."
If this were so, I should certainly, here in Rome, where
such institutions are convenient, retire into the very
nearest convent; with such a world I should have a
standing quarrel. And yet Domenichino is an inter-

esting painter, and I would take a moderate walk, in most moods, to see one of his pictures. He is so supremely good an example of effort detached from inspiration, and school-merit divorced from spontaneity, that one of his fine, frigid performances ought to hang in a conspicuous place in every academy of design. Few pictures contain more urgent lessons or point a more precious moral; and I would have the head master in the drawing-school take each ingenuous pupil by the hand and lead him up to the Triumph of David or the Chase of Diana or the red-nosed Persian Sibyl, and make him some such little speech as this: "This great picture, my son, was hung here to show you how you must *never* paint; to give you a perfect specimen of what in its boundless generosity the providence of nature created for our fuller knowledge — an artist whose development was a negation. The great thing in art is charm, and the great thing in charm is spontaneity. Domenichino had great talent, and here and there he is an excellent model; he was devoted, conscientious, observant, industrious; but now that we've seen pretty well what can simply be learned do its best, these things help him little with us, because his imagination was cold. It loved nothing, it lost itself in nothing, its efforts never gave it the heart-ache. It went about trying this and that, concocting cold pictures after cold receipts, dealing in the second-hand and the ready-made, and putting into its performances a little of everything but itself. When you see so many things in a picture, you might fancy that among them all charm might be born, but they are really but the hundred mouths through which you may hear the picture murmur, ' I 'm dead!' It 's in the simplest thing it has that a picture lives — in its temper! Look at all the great talents, at Domenichino as well as at Titian; but think less of dogma than of plain nature, and I can almost promise you that yours will remain true." This is very little to what the æsthetic sage I have imagined *might* say; and after all we are all unwilling to let our last verdict be an unkind one upon any great bequest of human effort. The faded frescos in the chapel at Grotta Ferrata leave one a memory the more of what man has done for man, and mingle harmoniously enough with one's multifold impressions of Italy. It was, perhaps, an ungracious thing to be critical, among all the appealing old Italianisms round me, and to treat poor exploded Domenichino more harshly than, when I walked back to Frascati, I treated the charming old water-works of the Villa Aldobrandini. I should like to confound these various products of antiquated art in a genial absolution; and I should like especially to tell how fine it was to watch this prodigious fountain come tumbling down its channel of mouldy rockwork, through its magnificent vista of ilex, to the fantastic old hemicycle where a dozen tritons and naiads sit posturing to receive it. The sky above the ilexes was incredibly blue, and the ilexes themselves incredibly black; and to see the young white moon peeping above the trees, you could easily have fancied it was midnight. I should like, furthermore, to expatiate on the Villa Mondragone, the most grandly impressive of Italian villas. The great Casino is as big as the

Vatican, which it strikingly resembles, and it stands perched on a terrace as vast as the parvise of St. Peter's, looking straight away over black cypress-tops into the shining vastness of the Campagna. Everything, somehow, seemed immense and solemn; there was nothing small, but certain little nestling blue shadows on the Sabine Mountains, to which the terrace seems to carry you wonderfully near. The place has been for some time lost to private uses, for it figures fantastically in a novel of Madame Sand (*La Daniella*) and now — in quite another way — as a Jesuit college for boys. The afternoon was perfect, and, as it waned, it filled the dark alleys with a wonderful golden haze. Into this came leaping and shouting a herd of little collegians, with a couple of long-skirted Jesuits striding at their heels. We all know the monstrous practices of these people; yet as I watched the group I verily believe I declared that if I had a little son he should go to Mondragone and receive their crooked teachings, for the sake of the other memories — the avenues of cypress and ilex, the view of the Campagna, the atmosphere of antiquity. But, doubtless, when a sense of the picturesque has brought one to this, it is time one should pause.

THE AFTER-SEASON IN ROME.

Rome, May 20, 1873.

ONE may say without injustice to anybody that the state of mind of a great many foreigners in Rome is one of intense impatience for the moment when all other foreigners shall have departed. One may confess to this state of mind, and be no misanthrope. Rome has passed so completely for the winter months into the hands of the barbarians, that that estimable character, the " quiet observer," finds it constantly harder to concentrate his attention. He has an irritating sense of his impressions being perverted and adulterated ; the venerable visage of Rome betrays an unbecoming eagerness to see itself mirrored in English, American, German eyes. It is not simply that you are never first or never alone at the classic or historic spots where you have dreamt of persuading the shy *genius loci* into confidential utterance; it is not simply that St. Peter's, the Vatican, the Palatine, are forever ringing with English voices: it is the general oppressive feeling that the city of the soul has become for the time a monstrous mixture of the watering-place and the curiosity-shop, and that its most ardent life is that of the tourists who haggle over false intaglios, and

yawn through palaces and temples. But you are told
of a happy time when these abuses begin to pass away,
when Rome becomes Rome again, and you may have it
all to yourself. "You may like Rome more or less
now," I was told during the height of the season ; "but
you must wait till the month of May to love it. Then
the foreigners, or the excess of them, are gone; the galleries and ruins are empty, and the place," said my
informant, who was a Frenchman, " renait à elle-même."
Indeed, I was haunted all winter by an irresistible
prevision of what Rome *must* be in spring. Certain
charming places seemed to murmur : " Ah, this is nothing ! Come back in May, and see the sky above us
almost black with its excess of blue, and the new grass
already deep, but still vivid, and the white roses tumbling in odorous spray over the walls, and the warm
radiant air dropping gold into all our coloring."

A month ago I spent a week in the country, and on
my return, the first time I went into the Corso, I became conscious of a change. Something very pleasant
had happened, but at first I was at a loss to define it.
Then suddenly I comprehended : there were but half
as many people, and these were chiefly good Italians.
There had been a great exodus, and now, physically,
morally, æsthetically, there was elbow-room. In the
afternoon I went to the Pincio, and the Pincio was
almost dull. The band was playing to a dozen ladies,
as they lay in their landaus, poising their lace-fringed
parasols ; but they had only one light-gloved dandy
apiece hanging over their carriage-doors. By the parapet of the great terrace which sweeps the city stood

three or four quiet observers looking at the sunset,
with their Baedekers peeping out of their pockets
— the sunsets not being down with their tariff in
these precious volumes. I good-naturedly hoped
that, like myself, they were committing the harmless
folly of taking mental possession of the scene before
them.

It is the same good-nature that leads me to violate
the instinct of monopoly, and proclaim that Rome in
May is worth waiting for. I have just been so gratified
at finding myself in undisturbed possession for a couple
of hours of the Museum of the Lateran that I can
afford to be magnanimous. And yet I keep within the
bounds of reason when I say that it would be hard as
a traveller or student to pass pleasanter days than
these. The weather for a month has been perfect, the
sky magnificently blue, the air lively enough, the nights
cool, too cool, and the whole gray old city illumined
with the most irresistible smile. Rome, which in some
moods, especially to new-comers, seems a terribly
gloomy place, gives on the whole, and as one knows it
better, an indefinable impression of gayety. This contagious influence lurks in all its darkness and dirt and
decay — a something more careless and hopeless than
our thrifty Northern cheerfulness, and yet more genial,
more urbane, than mere indifference. The Roman temper is a healthy and happy one, and you feel it abroad
in the streets even when the sirocco blows, and the
goal of man's life assumes a horrible identity with the
mouth of a furnace. But who can analyze even the
simplest Roman impression ? It is compounded of so

many things, it says so much, it suggests so much, it so quickens the intellect and so flatters the heart, that before we are fairly conscious of it the imagination has marked it for her own, and exposed us to a perilous likelihood of talking nonsense about it.

The smile of Rome, as I have called it, and its intense suggestiveness to those who are willing to ramble irresponsibly and take things as they come, is ushered in with the first breath of spring, and it grows and grows with the advancing season, till it wraps the whole place in its tenfold charm. As the process goes on, you can do few better things than go often to the Villa Borghese, and sit on the grass (on a stout bit of drapery) and watch its exquisite stages. It is a more magical spring than ours, even when ours has left off its damnable faces and begun. Nature surrenders herself to it with a frankness which outstrips your most unutterable longings, and leaves you, as I say, nothing to do but to lay your head among the anemones at the base of a high-stemmed pine, and gaze up crestward and skyward along its slanting silvery column. You may look at the spring in Rome from a dozen of these choice standpoints, and have a different villa for your observations every day in the week. The Doria, the Ludovisi, the Medici, the Albani, the Wolkonski, the Chigi, the Mellini, the Massimo — there are more of them, with all their sights, and sounds, and odors, and memories, than you have senses for. But I prefer none of them to the Borghese, which is free to all the world at all times, and yet never crowded; for when the whirl of carriages is great in the middle regions, you may find a hundred untrodden spots and silent corners, tenanted at the worst by a group of those long-skirted young Propagandists who stalk about with solemn angularity, each with a book under his arm, like silhouettes from a mediæval missal, and "compose" so extremely well with the picturesqueness of cypresses, and of stretches of golden-russet wall overtopped by the intense blue sky. And yet if the Borghese is good, the Medici is strangely charming; and you may stand in the little belvedere which rises with such surpassing oddity out of the dusky heart of the Boschetto at the latter establishment — a miniature presentation of the wood of the Sleeping Beauty — and look across at the Ludovisi pines lifting their crooked parasols into a sky of what a painter would call the most morbid blue, and declare that the place where *they* grow is the most delightful in the world. The Villa Ludovisi has been all winter the residence of the lady familiarly known in Roman society as "Rosina," the king's morganatic wife. But this, apparently, is the only familiarity which she allows, for the grounds of the villa have been rigidly closed, to the inconsolable regret of old Roman sojourners. But just as the nightingales began to sing, the august *padrona* departed, and the public, with certain restrictions, have been admitted to hear them. It is a really princely place, and there could be no better example of the expansive tendencies of ancient privilege than the fact of its whole vast extent falling within the city walls. It has in this respect very much the same sort of impressiveness as the great intramural demesne of Magdalen College at Oxford. The stern old ramparts of Rome form the outer enclosure of the villa, and hence a series of picturesque effects which it would be unscrupulous flattery to say you can imagine. The grounds are laid out in the formal last-century manner; but nowhere do the straight black cypresses lead off the gaze into vistas of a more fictive sort of melancholy; nowhere are there grander, smoother walls of laurel and myrtle.

I recently spent an afternoon hour at the little Protestant cemetery close to St. Paul's Gate, where the ancient and the modern world are most impressively contrasted. They make between them one of the solemn places of Rome — although, indeed, when funereal things are so interfused with picturesqueness, it seems ungrateful to call them sad. Here is a mixture of tears and smiles, of stones and flowers, of mourning cypresses and radiant sky, which almost tempts one to fancy one is looking back at death from the brighter side of the grave. The cemetery nestles in an angle of the city wall, and the older graves are sheltered by a mass of ancient brickwork, through whose narrow loopholes you may peep at the purple landscape of the Campagna. Shelley's grave is here, buried in roses — a happy grave every way for a poet who was personally poetic. It is impossible to imagine anything more impenetrably tranquil than this little corner in the bend of the protecting rampart. You seem to see a cluster of modern ashes held tenderly in the rugged hand of the Past. The past is tremendously embodied in the hoary pyramid of Caius Cestius, which rises hard by, half within the wall and half without, cutting solidly into the solid blue of the sky, and casting its pagan shadow upon the grass of English graves — that of Keats, among others — with a certain poetic justice. It is a wonderful confusion of mortality and a grim enough admonition of our helpless promiscuity in the crucible of time. But to my sense, the most touching thing there is the look of the pious English inscriptions among all these Roman memories. There is something extremely appealing in their universal expression of that worst of trouble — trouble in a foreign land; but something that stirs the heart even more deeply is the fine Scriptural language in which everything is recorded. The echoes of massive Latinity with which the atmosphere is charged suggest nothing more majestic and monumental. I may seem unduly sentimental; but I confess that the charge to the reader in the monument to Miss Bathurst, who was drowned in the Tiber in 1824: "If thou art young and lovely, build not thereon, for she who lies beneath thy feet in death was the loveliest flower ever cropt in its bloom" — seemed to me irresistibly a case for tears. The whole elaborate inscription, indeed, was curiously suggestive. The English have the reputation of being the most reticent people in the world, and, as there is no smoke without fire, I suppose they have done something to deserve it; but for my own part, I am forever meeting the most startling examples of the insular faculty to "gush." In this instance the mother of the deceased takes the public into her confidence with surprising frankness, omits no detail, and embraces the opportunity to mention by the way that she had already lost her husband by a most mysterious death. Yet the whole elaborate record is profoundly touching. It has an air of old-fashioned gentility which makes its frankness tragic. You seem to hear the garrulity of passionate grief.

To be choosing this well-worn picturesqueness for a theme, when there are matters of modern moment going on in Rome, may seem to demand some apology. But I can make no claim to your special correspondent's faculty for getting an " inside view " of things, and I have hardly more than a picturesque impression of the Pope's illness and of the discussion of the Law of the Convents. Indeed, I am afraid to speak of the Pope's illness at all, lest I should say something egregiously heartless about it, and recall too forcibly that unnatural husband who was heard to wish that his wife would get well or — something! He had his reasons, and Roman tourists have theirs in the shape of a vague longing for something spectacular at St. Peter's. If it takes a funeral to produce it, a funeral let it be. Meanwhile, we have been having a glimpse of the spectacular side of the Religious Corporations Bill. Hearing one morning a great hubbub in the Corso, I stepped forth upon my balcony. A couple of hundred men were strolling slowly down the street with their hands in their pockets, shouting in unison, " Abbasso il ministero! " and huzzaing in chorus. Just beneath my window they stopped and began to murmur, " Al Quirinale, al Quirinale! " The crowd surged a moment gently, and then drifted to the Quirinal, where it scuffled harmlessly with half a dozen of the king's soldiers. It ought to have been impressive, for what was it, essentially, but the seeds of revolution? But its carriage was too gentle and its cries too musical to send the most timorous tourist to packing his trunk. As I began with saying: in Rome, in May, everything has an amiable side, even *émeutes!*

FROM A ROMAN NOTE-BOOK.

DECEMBER 28, 1872. — In Rome again for the
last three days — that second visit, which, if the
first is not followed by a fatal illness in Florence, the
story goes that one is doomed to pay. I did n't drink
of the Fountain of Trevi when I was here before; but
I feel as if I had drunk of the Tiber itself. Nevertheless, as I drove from the station in the evening, I wondered what I should think of Rome at this first glimpse
if I did n't know it. All manner of evil, I am afraid.
Paris, as I passed along the Boulevards three evenings
before, to take the train, was swarming and glittering
as befits a great capital. Here, in the black, narrow,
crooked, empty streets, I saw nothing for a city to build
an eternity upon. But there were new gas-lamps round
the spouting Triton in the Piazza Barberini and a newspaper stall on the corner of the Condotti and the Corso
— salient signs that Rome *had* become a capital. An
hour later I walked up to the Via Gregoriana by the
Piazza di Spagna. It was all silent and deserted, and
the great flight of steps looked surprisingly small.
Everything seemed meagre, dusky, provincial. Could
Rome, after all, be such an entertaining place! That

queer old rococo garden gateway at the top of the Gregoriana stirred an old memory; it awoke into a consciousness of the delicious mildness of the air, and very soon, in a little crimson drawing-room, I concluded that Rome was pleasant enough. . . . . Everything is dear (in the way of lodgings) but it hardly matters, as everything is taken and some one else is paying for it. I must make up my mind to be but half comfortable. But it seems a shame here to care for one's comfort or to be perplexed by the economical side of life. The intellectual side is so intense that you feel as if you ought to live on the mere atmosphere — the historic whisperings, the nameless romantic intimations. Literally, what an atmosphere it is! The weather is perfect, the sky as blue as the most exploded tradition fames it, the whole air glowing and throbbing with lovely color. . . . . Paris glitters with gaslight! And oh, the monotonous miles of rain-washed asphalte!

December 30*th.* — I have had nothing to do with the "ceremonies." In fact, I believe there have hardly been any — no midnight mass at the Sistine chapel, no silver trumpets at St. Peter's. Everything is remorselessly clipped and curtailed — the Vatican in mourning. But I saw it in its superbest scarlet in '69. . . . . I went yesterday with L. to the Colonna gardens — an adventure which would have reconverted me to Rome if the thing were not already done. It 's a rare old place — rising in mouldy, bosky terraces, and mossy stairways, and winding walks, from the back of the palace to the top of the Quirinal. It 's the grand style of gardening, and resembles the present natural manner as a chapter of

Johnsonian rhetoric resembles a piece of clever contemporary prose. But it's a better style in horticulture
than in literature; I prefer one of the long-drawn blue-
green Colonna vistas, with a maimed and mossy-coated
garden goddess at the end, to the finest possible quotation from a last-century classic. Perhaps the best thing
there is the old orangery with its trees in fantastic terra-
cotta tubs. The late afternoon light was gilding the
monstrous jars and suspending golden checkers among
the golden-fruited leaves. Or perhaps the best thing
is the broad terrace with its mossy balustrade, and its
benches, and its ruin of the great naked Torre di Nerone
(I think) which might look stupid if its rosy brickwork did n't take such a color in the blue air. It's a
very good thing, at any rate, to stroll and talk there in
the afternoon sunshine.

January 2d, 1873. — Two or three drives with A.
To St. Paul's out of the Walls and back by a couple
of old churches on the Aventine. I was freshly struck
with the rare (picturesqueness of the little Protestant
cemetery at the gate, lying in the shadow of the black,
sepulchral Pyramid and the thick-growing black cypresses. Bathed in the clear Roman light, the place
seems intensely funereal. I don't know whether it
should make one in love with death to lie there; it
certainly makes death seem terribly irrevocable. The
weight of a tremendous past appears to press upon the
flowery sod, and the sleeper's mortality feels the contact of all the mortality with which the brilliant air is
tainted. . . . The restored Basilica is incredibly splendid.
It seems a last pompous effort of formal Catholicism,

and there are few more striking emblems of later Rome
— the Rome foredoomed to see Victor Emanuel in the
Quirinal, the Rome of abortive councils and unheeded
anathemas. It rises there, gorgeous and useless, on its
miasmatic site, with an air of conscious bravado, like
a florid advertisement of the superabundance of faith.
Within, it is magnificent, and its magnificence has no
shabby spots — a rare thing in Rome. Marble and
mosaic, alabaster and malachite, lapis and porphyry, in-
crust it from pavement to cornice, and flash back their
polished lights at each other with such a splendor of
effect that you seem to stand at the heart of some immense prismatic crystal. One has to come to Italy to
know marbles and love them. I remember the fascination of the first great show of them I saw at Venice —
at the Scalzi and Gesuiti. Color has in no other form
so cool and unfading a purity and lustre. Softness of
tone and hardness of substance — is not that the sum
of the artist's desire? G., with his beautiful, caressing,
open-lipped Roman utterance, which is so easy to understand, and, to my ear, so finely suggestive of Latin,
urged upon us the charms of a return by the Aventine,
to see a couple of old churches. The best is Santa
Sabina, a very fine old structure of the fifth century,
mouldering in its dusky solitude and consuming its own
antiquity. What a massive heritage Christianity and
Catholicism are leaving here ! What a substantial fact,
in all its decay, is this memorial Christian temple, out-
living its uses among the sunny gardens and vineyards !
It has a noble nave, filled with a stale smell which (like
that of the onion) brought tears to my eyes, and bor-

dered with twenty-four fluted marble columns of Pagan
origin. The crudely primitive little mosaics along the
entablature are extremely curious. A Dominican monk,
still young, who showed us the church, seemed a creature generated from its musty shadows and odors. His
physiognomy was wonderfully *de l'emploi*, and his voice,
which was most agreeable, had the strangest jaded
humility. His lugubrious salute and sanctimonious
impersonal appropriation of my departing franc would
have been a master-touch on the stage. While we were
still in the church a bell rang which he had to go and
answer, and as he came back and approached us along
the nave, he made with his white gown and hood and
his cadaverous face, against the dark church background,
one of those pictures which, thank the Muses, have not
yet been reformed out of Italy. It was strangely like
the mental pictures suggested in reading certain plays
and poems. We got back into the carriage and talked
of profane things, and went home to dinner — drifting
recklessly, it seemed to me, from æsthetic luxury to
social.

On the 31st we went to the musical vesper-service
at the Gesù — hitherto done so splendidly before the
Pope and the cardinals. The manner of it was eloquent
of change — no Pope, no cardinals, and indifferent
music; but a great picturesqueness, nevertheless. The
church is gorgeous; late Renaissance, of great proportions, and full, like so many others, but in a pre-eminent
degree, of seventeenth and eighteenth century Romanism.
It does not impress the imagination, but it keenly irritates the curiosity: suggests no legends, but innumera-

ble anecdotes, à la Stendhal. There is a vast dome,
filled with a florid concave fresco of tumbling, foreshortened angels, and all over the ceilings and cornices there
is a wonderful outlay of dusky gildings and mouldings.
There are various Bernini saints and seraphs in stucco-
sculpture, astride of the tablets and door-tops, backing
against their rusty machinery of coppery *nimbi* and
egg-shaped cloudlets. Marble, damask, and tapers in
gorgeous profusion. The high altar a great screen of
twinkling chandeliers. The choir perched in a little
loft high up in the right transept, like a balcony in a
side-scene at the opera, and indulging in surprising
roulades and flourishes. . . . . Near me sat a handsome,
opulent-looking nun — possibly an abbess or prioress
of noble lineage. Can a gentle prioress listen to a fine
operatic barytone in such a sumptuous temple, and receive none but ascetic impressions ? What a cross-fire
of influences does Catholicism provide !

January 4th. — A drive with A. out of the Porta
San Giovanni, along the Via Appia Nuova. More and
more beautiful as you get well away from the walls, and
the great view opens out before you — the rolling green-
brown dells and flats of the Campagna, the long, disjointed arcade of the aqueducts, the deep-shadowed
blue of the Alban Mountains, touched into pale lights
by their scattered towns. We stopped at the ruined
basilica of San Stefano, an affair of the fifth century,
rather meaningless without a learned companion. But
the perfect little sepulchral chambers of the Pancratii,
disinterred beneath the church, tell their own tale — in
their hardly dimmed frescos, their beautiful sculptured

coffin, and great sepulchral slab. Better still is the tomb of the Valerii adjoining it, — a single chamber with an arched roof, covered with stucco mouldings, perfectly intact, exquisite figures and arabesques, as sharp and delicate as if the plasterer's scaffold had just been taken from under them. Strange enough to think of these things — so many of them as there are — surviving their long earthly obscuration in this perfect shape, and coming up like long-lost divers from the sea of time.

16th. — A delightful walk last Sunday with Z. to Monte Mario. We drove to the Porta Angelica, the little gate hidden behind the right wing of Bernini's colonnade, and strolled thence up the winding road to the Villa Mellini, where one of the greasy peasants huddled under the wall in the sun admits you for half a franc into the finest old ilex-walk in Italy. (As fine there may be, but not a finer.) It is all vaulted gray-green shade, with blue Campagna stretches in the interstices. The day was perfect. The still sunshine, as we sat at the twisted base of the old trees, seemed to have the drowsy hum of midsummer. The charm of Italian vegetation is something indefinable. In a certain cheapness and thinness of substance (as compared with the English) it reminds me of our own, and it is relatively dry enough and pale enough to explain the contempt of many unimaginative Britons. But it has a kind of idle abundance and wantonness, a romantic shabbiness and dishevelment which appeals to one's tenderest perceptions. At the Villa Mellini is the famous lonely pine which "tells" so in the landscape from other points, bought off from destruction by (I believe) Lord Beaumont. He, at least, was not an unimaginative Briton. As you stand under it, its far-away, shallow dome, supported on a single column almost white enough to be marble, seems to dwell in the dizziest depths of the blue. Its pale gray-blue boughs and its silvery stem make a wonderful harmony with the ambient air. The Villa Mellini is full of the elder Italy of one's imagination — the Italy of Boccaccio. There are twenty places where his story-tellers might have sat round on the grass. Outside the villa walls, beneath the overcrowding orange-boughs, straggled old Italy as well, but not in Boccaccio's velvet — a row of ragged and livid contadini ; some simply stupid in their squalor, but some good square brigands of romance (or of reality) with matted locks and terribly sullen eyes.

A couple of days later I walked for old acquaintance' sake over to San Onofrio. The approach is one of the dirtiest adventures in Rome, and though the view is fine from the little terrace, the church and convent are of a meagre and musty pattern. Yet here — almost like pearls in a dunghill — are hidden mementos of two of the most exquisite of Italian minds. Torquato Tasso spent the last months of his life here, and I saw his room and various warped and faded relics. The most interesting is a cast of his face, taken after death — looking, like all such casts, very gallant and distinguished. But who should look so if not he ? In a little shabby, chilly corridor adjoining is a fresco of Leonardo, a Virgin and Child, with the *donatorio*. It is very small, simple, and faded, but it has all the

artist's magic.   It has that mocking, illusive refinement, that hint of a vague *arrière-pensée*, which marks
every stroke of Leonardo's brush.   Is it the perfection
of irony òr the perfection of tenderness ?   What does
he mean, what does he affirm, what does he deny ?
Magic would not be magic if we could explain it.   As
I glanced from the picture to the poor, stupid little
red-faced brother at my side, I fancied it might pass
for an elegant epigram on monasticism.   Certainly, at
any rate, there is more *mind* in it than under all the
monkish tonsures it has seen coming and going these
three hundred years.

21*st*. — The last three or four days I have regularly
spent a couple of hours from noon baking myself in
the sun, on the Pincio, to get rid of a cold.   The
weather perfect and the crowd (especially to-day) amazing.   Such a staring, lounging, dandified, amiable crowd!
Who does the vulgar, stay-at-home work of Rome ?
All the grandees and half the foreigners are there in
their carriages ; the *bourgeoisie* on foot, staring at them,
and the beggars lining all the approaches.   The great
difference between public places in America and Europe is in the number of unoccupied people, of every
age and condition, sitting about, early and late, on
benches, and gazing at you, from your hat to your
boots, as you pass.   Europe is certainly the continent
of *staring*.   The ladies on the Pincio have to run the
gantlet ; but they seem to do so complacently enough.
The European woman is brought up to the sense of
having a definite part (in the way of manners) to play
in public.   To lie back in a barouche alone, balancing

a parasol, and seeming to ignore the extremely imme-
diate gaze of two serried ranks of male creatures on
each side of her path, save here and there to recognize
one of them with an imperceptible nod, is one of her
daily duties. The number of young men here who lead
a purely contemplative life is enormous. They muster
in especial force on the Pincio, but the Corso all day
is thronged with them. They are well dressed, good-
humored, good-looking, polite ; but they seem never to
do a harder stroke of work than to stroll from the
Piazza Colonna to the Hôtel de Rome, or *vice versa.*
Some of them don't even stroll, but stand leaning by
the hour against the doorways, sucking the knobs of
their canes, feeling their back hair, and settling their
shirt-cuffs. At my café in the morning several stroll
in, already (at nine o'clock) in light gloves. But they
order nothing, turn on their heels, glance at the mirrors,
and stroll out again. When it rains they herd under
the *portes-cochères* and in the smaller cafés. . . . . Yesterday Prince Humbert's little *primogenito* was on the
Pincio in an open landau, with his governess. He is a
sturdy, blond little fellow, and the image of the King.
They had stopped to listen to the music, and the crowd
was planted about the carriage-wheels, staring and crit-
icising under the child's snub little nose. It seemed to
be bold, cynical curiosity, without the slightest man-
ifestation of "loyalty," and it gave me a singular sense
of the vulgarization of Rome under the new régime.
When the Pope drove abroad it was a solemn spectacle ;
even if you neither kneeled nor uncovered, you were
irresistibly impressed. But the Pope never stopped to

listen to opera tunes, and he had no little popelings, under the charge of superior nurse-maids, whom you might take liberties with. The family at the Quirinal make something of a merit, I believe, of their modest and inexpensive way of life. The merit is great ; but, picturesquely, what a change for the worse from a dispensation which proclaimed stateliness as a part of its essence ! The divinity that doth hedge a king is pretty well on the wane apparently. But how many more fine old traditions will the extremely sentimental traveller miss in the Italians over whom that little jostled prince in the landau will have come into his kinghood ? . . . . The Pincio has a great charm ; it is a great resource. I am forever being reminded of the " æsthetic luxury," as I called it above, of living in Rome. To be able to choose of an afternoon for a lounge (respectfully speaking) between St. Peter's and the Pincio (counting nothing else) is a proof that if in Rome you may suffer from ennui, at least your ennui has a throbbing soul in it. It is something to say for the Pincio that you don't always choose St. Peter's. Sometimes I lose patience with its air of eternal idleness ; but at others this very idleness is balm to one's conscience. Life on just these terms seems so easy, so monotonously sweet, that you feel as if it would be unwise, really unsafe, to change. The Roman atmosphere is distinctly demoralizing.

26th. — With X. to the Villa Medici — perhaps on the whole the most enchanting place in Rome. The part of the garden called the Boschetto has a kind of incredible, impossible charm : an upper terrace, behind locked gates, covered with a little dusky forest of evergreen oaks. Such a deliciously dim light — such a soft suffusion of tender, gray-green tones — such a company of gnarled and twisted little miniature trunks — dwarfs playing with each other at being giants — and such a shower of golden sparkles playing in from the glowing west! At the end of the wood is a steep, circular mound, up which the little trees scramble amain, with a long, mossy staircase climbing up to a belvedere. This staircase, rising suddenly out of the leafy dusk, to you don't see where, is delightfully fantastic. You expect to see an old woman in a crimson petticoat, with a distaff, come hobbling down and turn into a fairy, and offer you three wishes. I should wish one was not obliged to be a Frenchman to come and live and dream and work at the Académie de France. Can there be for a while a happier destiny than that of a young artist, conscious of talent, with no errand but to educate, polish, and perfect it, transplanted to these sacred shades? One has fancied Plato's Academy — his gleaming colonnades, his blooming gardens and Athenian sky; but was it as good as this one, where Monsieur —— does the Platonic? The blessing in Rome is not that this or that or the other isolated object is so very unsurpassable; but that the general atmosphere is so pictorial, so prolific of impressions which you long to make a note of. And from the general atmosphere the Villa Medici has distilled an essence of its own — walled it in and made it delightfully private. The great façade on the gardens is like an enormous rococo clock-face, all incrusted with images and arabesques and tablets. What mornings and afternoons one might spend there, brush in hand, unpreoccupied, untormented, pensioned, satisfied, resolving golden lights and silver shadows into imaginative masterpieces !

At a later date — middle of March. — A ride with X. out of the Porta Pia to the meadows beyond the Ponte Nomentana — close to the site of Phaon's villa where Nero, in hiding, had himself stabbed. It was deeply delightful — more so than *now* one can really know or say. For these are predestined memories and the stuff that regrets are made of; the mild divine efflorescence of spring, the wonderful landscape, the talk suspended for another gallop. . . . . Returning, we dismounted at the gate of the Villa Medici and walked through the twilight of the vaguely perfumed, bird-haunted alleys to H.'s studio, hidden in the wood like a cottage in a fairy tale. I spent there a charming half-hour in the fading light, looking at the pictures while X. discoursed of her errand. The studio is small and more like a little *salon;* the painting refined, imaginative, somewhat morbid, full of consummate French ability. A portrait, idealized and etherealized, but a likeness of Mme. de —— (from last year's *Salon*) in white satin, quantities of lace, a coronet, diamonds, and pearls — a wonderful combination of brilliant silvery tones. A "Femme Sauvage," a naked dusky girl in a wood with a wonderfully clever pair of shy, passionate eyes. . . . . H. is different enough from the American artists. They may be producers, but he is a product as well — a product of influences that do not touch us.

9 *

One of them is his spending his days, his years, working away in that unprofessional-looking little studio,
with his enchanted wood on one side and the plunging
wall of Rome on the other.

January 30th. — A drive the other day with X. to
the Villa Madama, on the side of Monte Mario; a place
like a page out of Browning, wonderful in its haunt-
ing melancholy. What a grim commentary such a
place is on history — what an irony of the past! The
road up to it through the outer enclosure is almost
impassable with mud and stones. At the end, on a
terrace, rises the once elegant Casino, with hardly a
whole pane of glass in its façade, gloomy with its sallow stucco and degraded ornaments. The front away
from Rome has in the basement a great loggia, now
walled in from the weather, preceded by a grassy, be-
littered platform, with an immense sweeping view of
the Campagna; the sad-looking — more than sad-looking, evil-looking — Tiber beneath (the color of gold, the
sentimentalists say; the color of mustard, the realists);
a great vague stretch beyond, of various complexions
and uses; and on the horizon the ' lovely iridescent
mountains. The place is turned into a very shabby
farm-house, with muddy water in the old *pièces d'eau*
and dunghills on the old parterres. The "feature" is
the contents of the loggia: a vaulted roof and walls
decorated by Giulio Romano; exquisite stucco-work
and still brilliant frescos; arabesques and *figurines;*
nymphs and fauns, animals and flowers — gracefully
lavish designs of every sort. Much of the color —
especially the blues — is still almost vivid, and all the

work is wonderfully ingenious, elegant, and charming. Apartments so decorated can have been meant only for the recreation of great people — people for whom life was impudent ease and success. Margaret Farnese was the lady of the house, but where she trailed her cloth of gold the chickens now scamper between your legs over rotten straw. It is all inexpressibly dreary. A stupid peasant scratching his head, a couple of critical Americans picking their steps, the walls tattered and befouled breast-high, dampness and decay striking in on your heart, and the scene overbowed by these heavenly frescos, mouldering there in their airy artistry! It 's poignant; it provokes tears; it tells so of the waste of effort. Something human seems to pant beneath the gray pall of time and to implore you to rescue it, to pity it, to stand by it, somehow. But you leave it to its lingering death without compunction, almost with pleasure; for the place seems vaguely crime-haunted — paying at least the penalty of some hard immorality. The end of a Renaissance casino! The didactic observer may take it as a symbol of the eventual destiny of the House of Pleasure.

February 12th. — Yesterday to the Villa Albani. Over-formal and (as my companion says) too much like a tea-garden; but with beautiful stairs and splendid geometrical lines of immense box-hedge, intersected with long pedestals supporting little antique busts. The light to-day was magnificent; the Alban Mountains of an intenser broken purple than I have ever seen them — their white towns blooming upon it like vague projected lights. It was like a piece of very

modern painting, and a good example of how Nature
has at times a sort of mannerism which ought to make
us careful how we condemn out of hand the more refined and affected artists. The collection of marbles in
the Casino (Winckelmann's) admirable, and to be seen
again. The famous Antinous crowned with lotus, a
strangely beautiful and impressive thing. One sees
something every now and then which makes one declare that the Greek manner, even for purely romantic
and imaginative effects, surpasses any that has since
been invented. If there is not imagination in the baleful beauty of that perfect young profile, there is none
in Hamlet or in Lycidas. There is five hundred times
as much as in the "Transfiguration." At any rate,
with this to point to, it is not for sculpture to confess
to an inability to produce any emotion that painting
can. There are numbers of small and delicate fragments of bas-reliefs of exquisite beauty, and a huge
piece (two combatants — one, on horseback, beating
down another — murder made eternal and beautiful)
attributed to the Parthenon, and certainly as grandly
impressive as anything in the Elgin marbles. X. suggested again the Roman villas as a "subject." Excellent, if one could find a feast of facts, à la Stendhal. A
lot of vague picturesque talk would not at all pay.
There's been too much already. Enough facts are recorded, I suppose; one should discover them and soak
in them for a twelvemonth. And yet a Roman villa,
in spite of statues, ideas, and atmosphere, seems to me
to have less of human and social suggestiveness, a
shorter, lighter reverberation, than an old English

country-house, round which experience seems piled so thick. But this perhaps is hair-splitting.

March 9th. — The Vatican is still deadly cold; a couple of hours there yesterday with Mr. E. Yet he, enviable man, fresh from the East, had no overcoat and wanted none. Perfect bliss, I think, would be to live in Rome without thinking of overcoats. The Vatican seems very familiar, but strangely smaller than of old. I never lost the sense before of confusing vastness. *Sancta simplicitas!* But all my old friends stand there in undimmed radiance, keeping, most of them, their old pledges. I am perhaps more struck now with the enormous amount of padding, — the number of third and fourth rate statues which weary the eye that would fain approach freshly the twenty and thirty best. In spite of the padding, there are dozens of things that one passes regretfully; but the impression of the whole place is the great thing — the feeling that through these solemn vistas flows the source of an incalculable part of our present conception of Beauty.

April 10th. — I went last night, in the rain, to Valle, to see a comedy of Goldoni, in Venetian dialect — " I Quattro Rustighi." I could not half follow it; enough, however, to suspect that, with all its fun, it was not so good as Molière. The acting was capital — broad, free, and natural; the dialogue more conversational even than life itself; but, like all the Italian acting I have seen, it was wanting in *finesse* and culture. I contrasted the affair with the evening in December last that I walked over (also in the rain) to the Odéon and saw the " Plaideurs " and the " Malade Imaginaire."

There, too, was hardly more than a handful of spectators ; but what rich, ripe, picturesque, *intellectual* comedy ! and what polished, educated playing ! These
Italians, however, have a marvellous *entrain* of their
own ; they seem even less than the French to recite.
Some of the women — ugly, with red hands and shabby dresses — have an extraordinary faculty of natural
utterance — of seeming to invent joyously as they go.

Later. — Last evening in ——'s box at the Apollo
to hear Ernesto Rossi in Othello. He shares su-
premacy with Salvini in Italian tragedy. Beautiful
great theatre, with boxes you can walk about in ; brilliant audience. The Princess Margaret was there, (I
have never been to the theatre that she was not), and
a number of other princesses in neighboring boxes.
—— came in and instructed us that they were the
M., the L., the P., etc. Rossi is both very bad and
very good ; bad where anything like taste and discretion is required, but quite tremendous in violent passion. The last act was really moving — as it could
not well help being. The interesting thing to me was
to observe the Italian conception of the part — to see
how crude it was, how little it expressed the hero's
moral side, his depth, his dignity — anything more
than his being a creature capable of being terrible in
a rage. The great point was his seizing Iago's head
and whacking it half a dozen times on the floor, and
then flinging him twenty yards away. It was wonderfully done, but in the doing of it and in the evident
relish for it in the house there seemed to me something
unappreciative, irreflective.

April 27*th.* — A morning with I., at the Villa Ludovisi, which we agreed that we should not soon forget.
The villa now belongs to the King, who has lodged
his morganatic wife there. There is surely nothing
better in Rome; nothing perhaps exactly so good.
The grounds and gardens are immense, and the great
rusty-red city wall stretches away behind them, and
makes Rome seem vast without making them seem
small. There is everything — dusky avenues, trimmed
by the clippings of centuries, groves and dells, and
glades and glowing pastures, and reedy fountains and
great flowering meadows, studded with enormous slanting pines. The day was delicious, the trees were all
one melody, the whole place seemed a revelation of
what Italy and hereditary grandeur can do together.
Nothing could well be more picturesque than this
garden view of the city ramparts, lifting their fantastic
battlements above the trees and flowers. They are all
tapestried with vines, and made to serve as sunny
fruit-walls — grim old defence as they once were; now
giving nothing but a kind of magnificent privacy. The
sculptures in the little Casino are few, but there are
two great ones — the beautiful sitting Mars and the
head of the great Juno, thrust into a corner behind a
shutter. These things it is almost impossible to praise;
we can only mark them well and be the wiser. . . . .
If I don't praise Guercino's Aurora in the greater
Casino, it is for another reason; it is certainly a very
muddy masterpiece. It figures on the ceiling of a
small low hall; the painting is coarse, and the ceiling
too near. Besides, it is unfair to pass straight from

the Athenian mythology to the Bolognese. We were left to roam at will through the house; the custode shut us in, and went to walk in the park. The apartments were all open, and I had an opportunity to reconstruct, from its *milieu* at least, the character of a morganatic queen. I saw nothing to indicate that it was not amiable; but I should have thought more highly of the lady's discrimination if she had had the Juno removed from behind her shutter. In such a house, girdled about with such a park, methinks I could be amiable — and perhaps discriminating, too. The Ludovisi Casino is small, but it seems to me that the perfection of a life of leisure might be led there. In an English house you are subject to the many small needs and observances — to say nothing of a red-faced butler, dropping his *h*'s. You are oppressed with comfort. Here, the billiard-table is old-fashioned — perhaps a trifle crooked; but you have Guercino above your head, and Guercino, after all, is almost as good as Guido. The rooms, I noticed, all please by their shape, by a lovely proportion, by a mass of delicate ornamentation on the high concave ceilings. It seems as if one might live over again here some gently hospitable life of a forgotten type. If I had fifty thousand. dollars, I should certainly buy, for mere fancy's sake, an Italian villa (I am told there are very good ones still to be had) with graceful old rooms, and immensely thick walls, and a winding stone staircase, and a view from the loggia on the top, as nearly as possible like that from the Villa Ludovisi — a view with twisted parasol-pines balanced high above a wooded horizon against a sky of faded sapphire.

May 17*th.* — It was wonderful yesterday at St. John Lateran. The spring now has turned to perfect summer.; there are cascades of verdure over all the walls; the early flowers are a fading memory, and the new grass is knee-deep in the Villa Borghese. The winter aspect of the region about the Lateran is one of the best things in Rome; the sunshine seems nowhere so yellow, and the lean shadows look nowhere so purple as on the long grassy walk to Santa Croce. But yesterday I seemed to see nothing but green and blue. The expanse before Santa Croce was vivid green; the Campagna rolled away in great green billows, which seemed to break high about the gaunt aqueducts; and the Alban Hills, which in January and February keep shifting and melting along the whole scale of azure, were almost monotonously green, and had lost some of the fine drawing of their contours. But the sky was superbly blue; everything was radiant with light and warmth — warmth which a soft, steady breeze kept from being fierce. I strolled some time about the church, which has a grand air enough, though I don't seize the point of view of Miss ——, who told me the other day that she thought it vastly finer than St. Peter's. But on Miss ——'s lips this seemed a very pretty paradox. The choir and transepts have a certain sombre splendor, and I like the old vaulted passage with its slabs and monuments behind the choir. The charm of charms at St. John Lateran is the admirable twelfth-century cloister, which was never more charming than yesterday. The shrubs and flowers around the ancient well were blooming away in the dazzling

N

light, and the twisted pillars and chiselled capitals of
the perfect little colonnade seemed to enclose them like
the sculptured rim of a precious vase. Standing out
among the flowers, you may look up and see a section
of the summit of the great façade of the church. The
robed and mitred apostles, bleached and rain-washed by
the ages, rose into the blue air like huge snow figures.
I spent some time afterward at the museum of the
Lateran, pleasantly enough, and had it quite to myself.
It is rather scantily stocked, but the great cool halls
open out impressively, one after the other, and the wide
spaces between the statues seem to suggest, at first, that
each is a masterpiece. I was in the loving mood of
one's last days in Rome, and when I had nothing else
to admire I admired the magnificent thickness of the
embrasures of the doors and windows. If there were
no statues at all in the Lateran, the palace would be
worth walking through every now and then, to keep up
one's ideal of solid architecture. I went over to the
Scala Santa, where there was no one but a very shabby
priest, sitting like a ticket-taker at the door. But he
let me pass, and I ascended one of the profane lateral
stairways, and treated myself to a glimpse of the Sancta
Sanctorum. Its threshold is crossed but once or twice
a year, I believe, by three or four of the most exalted
divines, but you may look into it freely enough through
a couple of gilded lattices. It is very sombre and
splendid, and looks indeed like a very holy place.
And yet, somehow, it suggested irreverent thoughts; it
had, to my fancy — perhaps on account of the lattice
— a kind of Oriental, of Mahometan air. I expected

every moment to see a sultana come in, in a silver veil, and sit down in her silken trousers on the crimson carpet.

Farewells, packing, etc. . . . . One would like, after five months in Rome, to be able to make some general statement of one's experience, one's gains. It is not easy. One has the sense of a kind of passion for the place, and of a large number of gathered impressions. Many of these have been intense, momentous, but one has trodden on the other, and one can hardly say what has become of them. They store themselves noiselessly away, I suppose, in the dim but safe places of memory, and we live in an insistent faith that they will emerge into vivid relief if life or art should demand them. As for the *passion*, we need n't trouble ourselves about that. Sooner or later it will be sure to bring us back !

A CHAIN OF CITIES.

ONE day in midwinter, some years since, during a
transit from Rome to Florence too rapid to admit
of much wayside dalliance with the picturesque, I waited
for the train at Narni. There was time to stroll far
enough from the station to have a look at the famous
old bridge of Augustus, broken short in mid-Tiber.
While I stood observing, the measure of enjoyment was
filled up by the unbargained spectacle of a white-cowled
monk trudging up a road which wound into the gate of
the town. The little town stood on a hill, a good space
away, boxed in behind its perfect gray wall, and the
monk crept slowly along and disappeared within the
aperture. Everything was distinct in the clear air, and
the view was like a bit of background in a Perugino.
The winter is bare and brown enough in Southern
Italy, and the earth has even a shabbier aspect than
with ourselves, with whom the dark side of the year
has a robust self-assurance which enables one to regard
it very much as a fine nude statue. But the winter
atmosphere in these regions has often an extraordinary
charm; it seems to smile with a tender sense of being
sole heir to the duty of cheering man's heart. It gave

such a charm to the broken bridge, the little walled town, and the trudging friar, that I turned away with an impatient vow that in some blessed springtime of the future I would take the journey again and pause to my heart's content at Narni, at Spoleto, at Assisi, at Perugia, at Cortona, at Arezzo. But we have generally to clip our vows a little when we come to fulfil them ; and so it befell that when my blessed springtime arrived, I had to begin resignedly at Assisi.

I suppose enjoyment would have a simple zest which it often lacks, if we always did things when we want to ; for we can answer too little for future moods. Winter, at least, seemed to me to have put something into these mediæval cities which the May sun had melted away — a certain delectable depth of local color, an excess of duskiness and decay. Assisi, in the January twilight, looked like a vignette out of some brown old missal. But you 'll have to be a fearless explorer now to find of a fine spring day a quaint Italian town which does not primarily seem simply the submissive correlative of Mr. Baedeker's polyglot word-pictures. This great man was at Assisi in force, and a brand-new inn for his accommodation has just been opened cheek by jowl with the church of Saint Francis. I don't know that even its dire discomfort makes it seem less impertinent ; but I confess I stayed there, and the great view seemed hardly less beautiful from my window than from the gallery of the convent. It embraces the whole wide plain of Umbria, which, as twilight deepens, becomes an enchanting counterfeit of the misty sea. The traveller's first errand is with the church ; and it is fair, furthermore, to admit that when he has crossed the threshold, the position and the quality of his inn cease for the time to be matters of moment. This double temple of Saint Francis is one of the very sacred places of Italy, and it is hard to fancy a church with an intenser look of sanctity. It seems especially solemn if you have just come from Rome, where everything ecclesiastical is, in aspect, so very much of this world — so florid, so elegant, so full of profane suggestiveness. Its position is superb, and they were brave builders who laid its foundation-stones. It rises straight from a steep mountain-side and plunges forward on its great substructure of arches, like a headland frowning over the sea. Before it stretches a long, grassy piazza, at the end of which you look along a little gray street, and see it climb a little way the rest of the hill, and then pause and leave a broad green slope, crowned, high in the air, with a ruined castle. When I say before it, I mean before the upper church; for by way of doing something supremely handsome and impressive, the sturdy architects of the thirteenth century piled temple upon temple, and bequeathed a double version of their idea. One may fancy them to have intended perhaps an architectural image of the relation between human heart and head. Entering the lower church at the bottom of the great flight of steps which leads from the upper door, you seem to penetrate at last into the very heart of Catholicism. For the first few minutes after leaving the hot daylight, you see nothing but a vista of low, black columns, closed by the great fantastic cage which surrounds the altar; the place looks like a sort of gor-

geous cavern. With time you distinguish details, and
become accustomed to the penetrating chill, and even
manage to make out a few frescos ; but the general
effect remains magnificently sombre and subterranean.
The vaulted roof is very low and the pillars dwarfish,
though immense in girth — as befits pillars with a
small cathedral on top of them. The tone of the place
is superb — the richest harmony of lurking shadows
and dusky corners, relieved by scattered images and
scintillations. There was little light but what came
through the windows of the choir, over which the red
curtains had been dropped and were beginning to glow
with the declining sun. The choir was guarded by a
screen, behind which half a dozen venerable voices were
droning vespers ; but over the top of the screen came
the heavy radiance, and played among the ornaments
of the high fence around the shrine, and cast the shadow
of the whole elaborate mass forward into the dusky
nave. The gloom of the vault and the side-chapels is
overwrought with vague frescos, most of them of Giotto
and his school, out of which the terribly distinct little
faces which these artists loved to draw stare at you with
a solemn formalism. Some of them are faded and in-
jured, and many so ill-lighted and ill-placed that you
can only glance at them with reverential conjecture ; the
great group, however — four paintings by Giotto on the
ceiling above the altar — may be examined with some
success. Like everything of Giotto's, they deserve examination ; but I hesitate to say that they repay it by
raising one's spirits. He was an admirably expressive
genius, and in the art of making an attitude unmistaka-

ble I think he has hardly been surpassed ; it is perhaps this rigid exactness of posture that gives his personages their formidable grimness.   Meagre, primitive, undeveloped as he is, he seems immeasurably strong, and suggests that if he had lived a hundred and fifty years later, Michael Angelo might have found a rival.   Not that Giotto is fond of imaginative contortions.   The something strange that troubles and haunts in his works dwells in their intense reality.

It is part of the wealth of the lower church that it contains an admirable primitive fresco by an artist of genius rarely encountered — a certain Pietro Cavallini, pupil of Giotto.   It represents the Crucifixion ; the three crosses rising into a sky spotted with the winged heads of angels, with a dense crowd pressing below. I have never seen anything more direfully lugubrious ; it comes near being as impressive as Tintoretto's great renderings of the scene in Venice.   The abject anguish of the crucified, and the straddling authority and brutality of the mounted guards in the foreground, are contrasted in a fashion worthy of a great dramatist. But the most poignant touch is the tragic grimaces of the little angelic heads, as they fall like hailstones through the dark air.   It is genuine, realistic weeping that the painter has depicted, and the effect is a singular mixture of the grotesque and the pitiful.   There are a great many more frescos beside ; all the chapels on one side are lined with them ; but they are chiefly interesting in their general effect — as they people the dim recesses with startling shadows and dwarfish phantoms.   Before leaving the church, I lingered a long

time near the door, for it seemed to me I should not
soon again enjoy such a feast of chiaroscuro. The
opposite end glowed with subdued color; the middle
portion was vague and brown, with two or three scattered worshippers looming through the dusk; and all
the way down, the polished pavement with its uneven
slabs, glittering dimly in the obstructed light, seemed
to me the most fascinating thing in the world. It is
certainly desirable, if one takes the lower church of
Saint Francis to represent the human heart, that one
should find a few bright places in it. But if the general effect is gloomy, is the symbol less valid? For
the contracted, passionate, prejudiced heart let it stand!

One thing, at all events, I can say: that I would
give a great deal to possess as capacious, symmetrical
and well-ordered a head as the upper sanctuary.
Thanks to these merits, in spite of a great array of
frescos of Giotto which have the advantage of being
easily seen, it lacks the picturesqueness of its coun-
terpart. The frescos, which are admirable, represent
certain leading events in the life of Saint Francis, and
suddenly remind you, by one of those anomalies which
abound amid the picturesqueness of Catholicism, that
the apostle of beggary — the saint whose only tenement
in life was the ragged robe which barely covered him
— is the hero of this massive structure. Church upon
church, — nothing less will adequately shroud his consecrated clay. The great reality of Giotto's designs
increases the helpless wonderment with which we look
at the passionate pluck of Saint Francis — the sense
of being separated from it by an impassable gulf — the

10

reflection on all that has come and gone to make us forgive ourselves for not being capable of such high-strung virtue. An observant friend, who has lived long in Italy, lately declared to me that she detested the name of Saint Francis — she deemed him the chief. propagator of that Italian vice which is most trying to those who have a kindness for the Italian character — the want of personal self-respect. There is a solidarity in cleanliness, and every cringing beggar, idler, liar, and pilferer seemed to her to flourish under the shadow of this great man's unwashed sanctity. She was possibly right; at Rome, at Naples, at least, I would have admitted that she was right; but at Assisi, face to face with Giotto's vivid chronicle, it is impossible to refuse to the painter's ascetic hero that compassionate respect which we feel for all men whose idea and life have been identical, whose doctrine was an unflinching personal example.

I should find it hard to give a very definite account of my subsequent adventures at Assisi; for there is incontestably such a thing as being too good-humored to discriminate, too genial to be critical. One need not be ashamed to confess that the ultimate result of one's meditations at the shrine of Saint Francis was a great charity. My charity led me slowly up and down for a couple of hours through the steep little streets, and finally stretched itself on the grass beside me in the shadow of the great ruined castle which decorates so magnificently the eminence above the town. I remember edging along against the sunless side of the mouldy little houses, and pausing very often to look at nothing

very particular. It was all very hot, very still, very
drearily antique. A wheeled vehicle at Assisi is a
rarity, and the foreigner's interrogative tread in the
blank sonorous lanes has the privilege of bringing the
inhabitants to their doorways. Some of the better
houses, however, have an air of sombre stillness which
seems a protest against all curiosity as to what may
happen in the nineteenth century. You may wonder,
as you pass, what lingering old-world social types are
vegetating there, but you will not find out. Yet in
one very silent little street I had a glimpse of an open
door which I have not forgotten. A long-haired pedler, with a tray of mass-books and rosaries, was offering his wares to a stout old priest. The priest had
opened the door rather stingily, and seemed to be half-
heartedly dismissing him. But the pedler held up
something which I could not see; the priest wavered,
with an air of timorous concession to profane curiosity,
and then furtively pulled the pedler into the house.
I should have liked to go in with the pedler. I saw
later some gentlemen of Assisi who also seemed bored
enough to have found entertainment in a pedler's tray.
They were at the door of the café on the Piazza, and
were so thankful to me for asking them the way to the
cathedral that they all answered in chorus, and smiled
as if I had done them a favor. The Piazza has a fine
old portico of an ancient Temple of Minerva — six
fluted columns and a pediment, of beautiful proportions,
but sadly battered and decayed. Goethe, I believe,
found it much more interesting than the mighty mediæval church, and Goethe, as a cicerone, doubtless could

have persuaded you that it was so; but in the humble
society of Murray we shall most of us find deeper
meanings in the church. I found some very quaint ones
in the dark yellow façade of the small cathedral, as I
sat on a stone bench beside the oblong green which lies
before it. It is a very pretty piece of Italian Gothic,
and, like several of its companions at Assisi, it has an
elegant wheel window and a number of grotesque little
sculptures of creatures human and bestial. If, with
Goethe, I inclined to balance something against the
attractions of the great church, I should choose the
ruined castle on the hill above the town. I had been
having glimpses of it all the afternoon at the end of
steep street vistas, and promising myself half an hour
beside its gray walls at sunset. The sun was very long
setting, and my half-hour became a long lounge in the
lee of an abutment which arrested the gentle uproar of
the wind. The castle is a magnificent piece of ruin,
perched upon the summit of the mountain to whose
slope Assisi clings, and dropping a pair of stony arms
to enclose the little town in its embrace. The city-
wall, in other words, straggles up the steep green slope
and meets the crumbling skeleton of the castle. On
the side away from the town the mountain plunges
into a deep ravine, on the other side of which rises
the powerful undraped shoulder of Monte Subasio — a
fierce reflector of the sun. Gorge and mountain are
wild enough, but their frown expires in the teeming
softness of the great vale of Umbria. To lie aloft there
on the grass, with a silver-gray castle at one's back and
the warm rushing wind in one's ears, and watch the

beautiful plain mellowing into the tones of twilight, was as exquisite a form of repose as ever fell to a tired tourist's lot.

At Perugia is an ancient castle; but unhappily one must speak of it in earnest as that unconscious humorist, the classic American traveller, is found invariably to speak of the Coliseum: it will be a very handsome building when it is finished. Even Perugia is going the way of all Italy — straightening out her streets, repairing her ruins, laying her venerable ghosts. The castle is being completely *remis à neuf* — a Massachusetts school-house could not suggest a briefer yesterday. There are shops in the basement and fresh putty on all the windows. The only thing proper to a castle that it has kept is its magnificent position and view, which you may enjoy from the broad platform where the Perugini assemble at eventide. Perugia is chiefly known to fame as the city of Raphael's master; but it has an even higher claim to renown, and ought to be set down in one's sentimental gazetteer as the City with the Views. The little dusky, crooked town is full of picturesqueness; but the view, somehow, is ever present, even when your back is turned to it, or fifty house-walls conceal it, and you are forever rushing up by-streets and peeping round corners in the hope of catching another glimpse of it. As it stretches away before you in all its lovely immensity, it is altogether too vast and too fair to be described. You can only say, and rest upon it, that you prefer it to any other in the world. For it is such a wondrous mixture of blooming plain and gleaming river and waving multitudinous mountain, vaguely dotted with pale gray cities, that, placed as you are, roughly speaking, in the centre of Italy, your glance seems to compass the lovely land from sea to sea. Up the long vista of the Tiber you look — almost to Rome; past Assisi, Spello, Foligno, Spoleto, all perched on their respective mountains and shining through the blue haze. To the north, to the east, to the west, you see a hundred variations of the prospect, of which I have kept no record. Two notes only I have made : one (I have made it over and over again) on the exquisite elegance of mountain forms and lines in Italy; — it is exactly as if there were a sex in mountains, and their contours and curves and complexions were here all of the feminine gender: second, on the possession of such an outlook on the world really going far to make a modest little city like Perugia a kind of æsthetic metropolis. It must deepen the civic consciousness and take off the edge of ennui. It performs this kindly office, at any rate, for the traveller who is overstaying his curiosity as to Perugino and the Etruscan relics. It continually solicits his eyes and his imagination, and doubles his entertainment. I spent a week in the place, and when it was gone, I had had enough of Perugino, but I had not had enough of the view.

I should, perhaps, do the reader a service by telling him just how a week at Perugia may be spent. His first care must be not to be in a hurry — to walk everywhere, very slowly and very much at random, and gaze good-naturedly at anything his eye may happen to encounter. Almost everything that meets the eye has an ancient oddity which ekes out the general picturesqueness. He must look a great deal at the huge Palazzo Pubblico, which indeed is very well worth looking at. It masses itself gloomily above the narrow street to an immense elevation, and leads up the eye along a cliff-like sur-face of rugged wall, mottled with old scars and new repairs, to the loggia dizzily perched upon its cornice. He must repeat his visit to the Etruscan Gate, whose extreme antiquity he will need more than one visit to take the measure of. He must uncap to the pictu-resque statue of Pope Julius III., before the cathedral, remembering that Hawthorne fabled his Miriam to have given rendezvous to Kenyon at its base. Its material is a vivid green bronze, and the mantle and tiara are covered with a delicate embroidery worthy of a silver-smith. He must bestow on Perugino's frescos in the Exchange, and his pictures in the University, all the placid contemplation they deserve. He must go to the theatre every evening in an orchestra chair at twenty-two soldi, and enjoy the curious didacticism of *Amore senza Stima, Severità e Debolezza, La Società Equivoca,* and other popular specimens of contemporaneous Italian comedy. I shall be very much surprised if, at the end of a week of this varied entertainment, he does not confess to a sentimental attachment to Perugia. His strolls will abound in small picturesque chances, of which a dozen pencil-strokes would be a better memento than this vague word-sketching. From the hill on which the town is planted radiate a dozen ra-vines, down whose sides the houses slide and scramble with an alarming indifference to the cohesion of their

little rugged blocks of flinty red stone. You cannot
ramble far without emerging upon some little court or
terrace from which you may look across a gulf of
tangled gardens or vineyards at a cluster of serried
black dwellings, which seem to be hollowing in their
backs to keep their balance on its opposite edge. On
archways and street-staircases and dark alleys boring
through a chain of massive basements, and curving and
climbing and plunging as they go, on the soundest
mediæval principles, you may feast your fill. These
are the architectural commonplaces of Perugia. Some
of the little streets in out-of-the-way corners always
suggested to me a singular image. They were so
rugged, so brown, so silent, that you would have fancied
them passages long since hewn by the pickaxe in some
deserted stone-quarry. The battered brown houses
looked like sections of natural rock — none the less
so when, across some narrow gap, I saw the glittering
azure of the great surrounding landscape.

But I ought not to talk of mouldy alleys or even of
azure landscapes as if they were the chief delight of
the eyes in this accomplished little city. In the Sala
del Cambio, where in ancient days the money-changers
rattled their sculptured florins and figured up their profits, you may enjoy one of the serenest artistic pleasures
which the golden age of art has bequeathed to us.
Bank parlors, I believe, are always luxuriously furnished, but I doubt whether even those of Messrs.
Rothschild are decorated in as fine a taste as this little
counting-house of a bygone fashion. Perugino was
the artist chosen, and he did his best. He covered the

four low walls and ceiling with Scriptural and mythological figures of extraordinary beauty. They are ranged
in artless attitudes around the upper half of the room
— the sibyls, the prophets, the philosophers, the Greek
and Roman heroes — looking down with broad, serene
faces, with their small mild eyes, their small sweet
mouths, at the incongruous proceedings of a Board of
Brokers. Had finance a very high tone in those days,
or was genius simply very convenient, as the Irish
say? The great charm of the Sala del Cambio is that
it seems to murmur a *yes* to both these questions.
There was a rigid probity, it seems to say; there was
an abundant inspiration. . . . . About the artist there
would be much to say — more than I can attempt; for
he was not, I think, to an attentive observer, the very
simple genius that he seems. He has that about him
which leads one to say to one's self that, after all, he
plays a proper part enough here as the patron of the
money-changers. He is the delight of a million of
young ladies; but I suspect that if his works could be
exactly analyzed, we should find in them a trifle more
of manner than of conviction — of skill than of senti-
ment. His portrait, painted on the wall of the Sala
(you may see it also at Rome and Florence) might
serve for the likeness of Mr. Worldly-Wiseman, in
Bunyan's allegory. He was fond of his glass, I believe,
and he made his art lucrative. This tradition is not
refuted by his portrait, and after some experience of
his pictures, you may find an echo of it in their monotonous grace, their somewhat conscious purity. But
I confess that Perugino, so interpreted, seems to me

10 *   o

hardly less interesting. If he was the inventor of
what the French call *la facture*, he applied his system
with masterly skill; he was the forerunner of a mighty
race. After you have seen a certain number of his
pictures, you have taken his measure. They are all
unerring reproductions of a single primary type which
had the good fortune to be adorably fair — to look as
if it had freshly dawned upon a vision unsullied by
the shadows of earth. As painter and draughtsman
Perugino is delightful; one takes a singular pleasure
in being able to count confidently on his unswerv-
ing beauty of line, and untroubled harmony of color.
Scepticism much more highly developed than Perugino's would be easy to forgive, if it were as careful to
replace one conscience by another. The spiritual conscience — the conscience of Giotto and Fra Angelico —
must have lurked in a corner of his genius even after
the trick of the trade had been mastered. In the sacristy of the charming church of San Pietro — a museum
of pictures and carvings — is a row of small heads of
saints which formerly ornamented the frame of the
artist's Ascension, carried off by the French. It is
almost miniature work, and as candidly devout in
expression as it is delicious in touch. Two of the holy
men are reading their breviaries, but with an air of
infantine innocence which makes you feel sure that
they are holding the book upside down.

Between Perugia and Cortona lies Lake Thrasymene,
where Hannibal treated the Romans to an unwonted
taste of disaster. The reflections it suggests are a
proper preparation for Cortona itself, which is one of

the most sturdily ancient of Italian towns. It must indeed have been a hoary old city when Hannibal and Flaminius came to the shock of battle, and have looked down afar from its gray ramparts, on the contending swarm, with something of the philosophic composure befitting a survivor of Pelasgian and Etruscan revolutions. These gray ramparts are in great part still visible, and form the chief attraction of Cortona. It is perched on the very pinnacle of a mountain, and I wound and doubled interminably over the face of the great hill, and still the jumbled roofs and towers of the arrogant little city seemed nearer to the sky than to the railway station. " Rather rough," Murray pronounces the local hotel; and rough indeed it was; it fairly bristled with discomfort. But the landlord was the best fellow in the world, and took me up into a rickety old loggia on the summit of his establishment and played showman to the wonderful panorama. I don't know whether my loss or my gain was greater that I saw Cortona through the medium of a festa. On the one hand the museum was closed (and in a certain sense the smaller and obscurer the town, the more I like the museum), the churches were impenetrably crowded, and there was not an empty stool nor the edge of a table at the café. On the other I saw — but this is what I saw. A part of the mountain-top is occupied by the church of Saint Margaret, and this was Saint Margaret's Day. The houses pause and leave a grassy slope, planted here and there with lean black cypresses. The peasantry of the place and of the neighboring country had congregated in force, and were

crowding into the church or winding up the slope.
When I arrived, they were all kneeling or uncovered;
a bedizened procession, with banners and censers, bearing abroad, I believe, the relics of the saint, was re-
entering the church.   It was vastly picturesque.   The
day was superb, and the sky blazing overhead like a
vault of deepest sapphire.   The brown contadini, in no
great costume, but decked in various small fineries of
scarlet and yellow, made a mass of motley color in the
high wind-stirred light.   The procession chanted in the
pious hush, and the boundless prospect melted away
beneath us in tones of azure hardly less brilliant than
the sky.   Behind the church was an empty, crumbling
citadel, with half a dozen old women keeping the gate
for coppers.   Here were views and breezes and sun
and shade and grassy corners, to one's heart's content.
I chose a spot which fairly combined all these advantages, and spent a good part of my day at Cortona,
lying there at my length and observing the situation
over the top of a novel of Balzac.   In the afternoon, I
came down and hustled awhile through the crowded
little streets, and then strolled forth under a scorching
sun, and made the outer circuit of the walls.   I saw
some tremendous uncemented blocks; they were glaring and twinkling in the powerful light, and I had to
put on a blue eye-glass, to throw the vague Etruscan
past into its proper perspective.

I spent the next day at Arezzo, in very much the
same uninvestigating fashion.   At Arezzo, you are far
from Rome, you are well within genial Tuscany, and
you encounter Romance in a milder form.   The ruined

castle on the hill, for instance (like Assisi and Cortona, Arezzo is furnished with this agreeable feature), has been converted into a blooming market-garden. But I lounged away the hot hours there, under a charm as potent as fancy could have foreshadowed it. I had seen Santa Maria della Pieve and its campanile of quaint colonnades, the stately, dusky cathedral and John of Pisa's elaborate marble shrine, the museum and its Etruscan vases and majolica platters. The old pacified citadel was more delicious. There were lovely hills all around it, cypresses casting straight shadows on the grassy bastions at its angles, and in the middle, a wondrous Italian tangle of growing wheat and corn, vines and figs, peaches and cabbages.

THE ST. GOTHARD.

LEAVES FROM A NOTE-BOOK.

BERNE, *September 25th*, 1873.—In Berne again, some eleven weeks after having left it in July. I have never been in Switzerland so late, and I came hither innocently supposing that the last Cook's tourist would have paid out his last coupon and departed. But I was lucky, it seems, to discover an empty cot in an attic and a very tight place at a table d'hôte. People are all flocking out of Switzerland, as in July they were flocking in, and the main channels of egress are terribly choked. I have been here several days, watching them come and go; it is like the march-past of an army. It gives one a lively impression of the quantity of luxury now diffused through the world. Here is little Switzerland disgorging its tens of thousands of honest folks, chiefly English, and rarely, to judge by their faces and talk, children of light, in any eminent degree; for whom snow-peaks, and glaciers, and passes, and lakes, and chalets, and sunsets, and a *café complet*, "including honey," as the coupon says, have become prime necessities for six weeks every year. It's not so long ago that lords and nabobs monopolized these pleasures; but nowadays a month's tour in Switzerland is no more a *jeu de prince* than a Sunday excursion. To watch this huge Anglo-Saxon wave ebbing through Berne makes one fancy that the common lot of mankind is after all not so very hard, and that the masses have reached a rather high standard of comfort. The view of the Oberland chain, as you see it from the garden of the hotel, really butters one's bread very handsomely; and here are I don't know how many hundred Cook's tourists a day, looking at it through the smoke of their pipes. Is it really the "masses" I see every day at the table d'hôte? They have rather too few h's to the dozen, as one may say, but their good-nature is great. Some people complain that they "vulgarize" Switzerland; but as far as I am concerned, I freely give it up to them, and take a peculiar satisfaction in seeing them here. Switzerland is a "show country" — I think so more and more every time I come here; and its use in the world is to reassure persons of a benevolent imagination when they begin to wish the mass of mankind had only a little more elevating amusement. Here is amusement for a thousand years, and as elevating, certainly, as mountains five miles high can make it. I expect to live to see the summit of Monte Rosa heated by steam-tubes and adorned with a hotel setting three tables d'hôte a day.

I have been walking about the arcades, which used to bestow a grateful shade in July, but which seem rather dusky and chilly in these shortening autumn days. I am struck with the way the English always speak of them — with a shudder, as gloomy, as dirty, as evil-smelling, as suffocating, as freezing (as it may be) — as anything and everything but admirably picturesque. I believe we Americans are the only people who, in travelling, judge things on the first impulse — when we do judge them at all — not from the standpoint of simple comfort. Most Americans, strolling forth into these bustling cloisters, are, I imagine, too much amused, too much diverted from their sense of an inalienable right to be comfortable, to be conscious of heat or cold, of thick air, or even of the universal smell of strong *charcuterie*. If the picturesque were banished from the face of the earth, I think the idea would survive in some typical American heart. . . . . I have perhaps spent too many days here to call Berne interesting, but the sturdy little town has certainly a powerful individuality. I ought before this to have made a few memoranda.

It stands on a high promontory, with the swift, green Aar girding it about and making it almost an island. The sides plunge down to the banks of the river, in some places steeply terraced (those, for instance, overlooked by the goodly houses of the grave old Junkerngasse) — gardens which brown, skinny old women are always raking and scraping and watering, nosing and fumbling among the cabbages like goats on the edge of a precipice; in others, as beneath the cathedral terrace, cemented by an immense precipice of buttressed masonry. Within, it is homely, ugly, almost grotesque, but full of character. Indeed, I do not know why it should have so much when there are cities which have played twice the part in the world which wear a much less striking costume. The town is almost all in length, and lies chiefly along a single street, stretching away, under various names, from the old city gate, with its deserted grassy bear-pit, where little chamois now are kept — tender little chamois, which must create an appetite, one would think, in the lurking ursine ghosts, if they still haunt the place — to the great single-arched bridge over the Aar and the new bear-pit, where tourists hang over the rail and fling turnips to the shaggy monsters. This street, like most of its neighbors, is 'built on arcades — great, massive, low-browed, straddling arcades — in the manner of Chester and Bologna (but far more solidly). The houses are gray and uneven, and mostly capped with great pent-house red roofs, surmounted with quaint little knobs and steeples and turrets. They have flower-pots in the windows and red cushions on the sills, on which, toward evening, there are generally planted a pair of solid Bernese elbows. If the elbows belong to a man, he is smoking a big-bowled pipe; if they belong to one of the softer sex, the color in her cheeks is generally a fair match to the red in the cushion. The arcades are wonderful in their huge, awkward solidity; there is superfluous stone and mortar enough stowed away in the piers to build a good-sized city on the American plan. Some of these are of really fabulous thickness; I should think those in the Theater-Platz measured laterally, from edge to edge, some ten feet. The little shops in the arcades are very dusky and unventilated; few of them can

have known a good fresh air-current these twenty
years. There is always a sort of public extension
of the household life on the deep green benches which
occupy the depths of the piers. Here the women sit
nursing their babies and patching their husbands'
breeches. One, who is young and most exceptionally
pretty, sits all day plying her sewing-machine, with
her head on one side and an upward glance at observant passers — a something that one may call the
coquetry of industry. Another, a perfect mountain
of a woman, is brought forth every morning, lowered,
with the proper precautions, into her bench, and left
there till night. She is always knitting a stocking;
I have an idea that she is the *fournisseuse* of the whole
little Swiss army; or she ought to wear one of those
castellated crowns which form the coiffure of ladies
on monuments, and sit there before all men's eyes as
the embodied genius of the city — the patroness of
Berne. Like the piers of the arcades, she has a most
fantastic thickness, and her superfluous fleshly substance could certainly furnish forth a dozen women
on the American plan. I suppose she is forty years
old, but her tremendous bulk is surmounted by a face
of the most infantine freshness and naïveté. She is
evidently not a fool; on the contrary, she looks very
sensible and amiable; but her immense circumference
has kept experience at bay, and she is perfectly innocent because nothing has ever happened to her. This
wonderful woman is only a larger specimen of the
general Bernese type — the heaviest, grossest, stolid-
est, certainly, that I have ever seen. Every one here

is ugly (except the little woman with the sewing-machine); every one is awkward, dogged, boorish, and bearish. Mr. B—— called my attention to the shape of the men; it is precisely the shape of the bears in the pit when they stand up on their hind paws to beg for turnips — the short, thick neck, the big, sturdy trunk, the flat, meagre hips — the total absence of hips, in fact — the shrunken legs and long flat feet. Since making this discovery I see the bear element humanly and socially at every turn, and begin to regard it as a kind of bearish cynicism that the townsfolk should hug the likeness as they do, and thrust the ugly monsters at you, in the flesh or in effigy — carved on gate-posts and emblazoned on shields — wherever you glance.

All down the middle of the long gray street are posted antique fountains — sculptured and emblazoned columns rising out of a great stone trough, and supporting some grotesque symbolic figure. These figures are frankly ugly, like the people and the architecture, but they have a rude humor which seems to have passed out of the local manners. If you make a joke, your interlocutor stares at you as if you were a placard in a foreign tongue. Doubtless the joke is not broad enough; the joke of one of the fountains is to show you an ogre gobbling down a handful of little children. . . . . There are broad jokes made, I imagine, at the *abbayes* or headquarters of the old guilds, of which some half a dozen present a wide antique façade to the main street, ornamented with some immense heraldic device, hung out like an inn sign. They serve, in a measure, the purpose of inns, though whether they entertain persons not members of their respective crafts, I am unable to say. All crafts at any rate are represented, — the *marchands*, the *maréchaux*, the *tisserands*, the *charpentiers*; there is even an *abbaye des gentils-hommes*, with a great genteel device of plumes and crossed swords. They all look as if they had a deal of heavy plate on their sideboards — as if a great many schoppen were emptied by the smokers in the deep red-cushioned window-seats. The landlord of the Faucon showed me a quantity of ancient silver in his keeping, which figures at those copious civic banquets at which the burghers of Berne warm themselves up, not infrequently, I believe, during their long winters. It was very handsome and picturesque, and seemed to tell of a great deal of savory in-door abundance behind the thick walls of the gray houses.

The cathedral, indeed, indicates an opulent city, and is a building of some consequence. It is fifteenth-century Gothic, of a rather artificial and, as Mr. Ruskin would say, insincere kind: a long nave, without transepts; a truncated tower, capped with a little wooden coiffure which decidedly increases its picturesqueness, especially as I see it from my window at sunrise, when it lifts its odd silhouette against the faintly flushing sky, like some fantastic cluster of spires in a drawing of Doré's; a number of short flying buttresses — jumping buttresses, they might be called, as they perform the feat rather clumsily; a great many crocketed pinnacles, and a wealth of beautiful balustrade-work around the roof of the nave and aisles. The great doorway is covered with quaint theological sculptures

— the wise and foolish virgins, the former with a good deal of awkward millinery in the shape of celestial crowns, and the usual bas-relief of the blessed ascending to heaven, and the damned tumbling into the pit. But in the middle of the portal, dividing the two doors, stands a tall, slim figure of a lady with a sword and scales, so light and elegant and graceful that she casts the angular sisterhood about her into ignominious shadow. This seraphic Justitia, and the running lace-work of stone I have just mentioned, around the high parts of the church, seem to me to contain all the elegance that is to be found in Berne. This, however, sounds like an unthankful speech when I remember that every evening, in this very cathedral, one may hear some very fine music. The organ is famous, like those of Fribourg and Lucerne, and people adjourn from the table d'hôte to listen to it, at a franc a head. The church is lighted only by a few glimmering tapers, and as I have never been into it but at this hour, I know nothing of its interior aspect. I believe that, thanks to Swiss Protestantism, though of fine proportions, it is as bare and bleak as a Methodist conventicle. While the organ plays, however, it is filled with a presence which affects the imagination in very much the same way as gorgeous colors and vistas receding through mists of incense. The tremendous tones of the instrument resound in the darkness with an energy and variety which even an unmusical man — reclining irreverently in the impenetrable gloom of the deep choir — may greatly enjoy. The organist, I believe, is rather unskilled, and addicted, according to his light, to musical clap-trap. I don't know whether his wonderful performances on the *vox humana* stops are clap-tráp; to my poor ear they seem the perfect romance of harmony. He gives you a thunder-storm complete, with shattering bolts and wind and rain; then a lull and a sound of dripping water and sobbing trees; and then, softly, a wonderful solemn choir of rejoicing voices. The voices are intensely real, but the charm of the thing is their strangely unlocalized whereabouts. From a myriad miles away they seem to come; from elysian spaces to which no Cook's coupon will help to convey us.

The terrace beside the cathedral was the bishop's garden, I believe, in the Catholic days, and a stately many-windowed house (which must have been a good deal modernized a hundred and fifty years ago) was the bishop's palace. Now the terrace is planted with a dense cool shade of clipped horse-chestnut trees, with a capacious wooden bench under each; and you may sit there of a fine day as if you were in the balcony of a theatre, and look off at the great spectacle — the view of the Oberland Alps. The foundations of the terrace plunge down to the bank of the Aar, a prodigious distance below, and the swift green river sends up a constant uproar as it shoots foaming over its dam. Across the river lie blooming slopes and woods and hills; never was a city more in the fields than Berne. No shabby suburbs, no dusty walks between walls; the cornfields ripen at its gates; the smell of the mown grass, when I was here before, came wandering across into the streets. It is a place of three

elements — the straddling black arcades, the rapid green
river, flung in a loop, as it were, around its base, the
goodly green country at five minutes' walk. Of the
Oberland chain, on the two or three days out of the
seven when it glitters its brightest, what is one to say?
During the clear hot days that I spent here in July it
was constantly visible, and yet somehow I never came
quite to accept it as a natural ornament of the horizon.
It seemed, in its fantastic beauty, a kind of spasmodic
effort of Nature toward something in a higher key than
her common performances, an attempt to please herself,
— not man with his meagre fancy. Man is certainly
pleased, though, as he sits at his ease forty miles off,
and caresses with idle eyes the glittering bosom of
the Jungfrau and the hoary forehead of the Monk.
Hour after hour the vision lingers — a mosaic of marble on a groundwork of lapis. Here at Berne we have
the vision; nearer, in the clouds, on the ice, on the
edge of a chasm, with a rope round your waist and
twenty pounds of nails in your shoes, you may have
the reality. Every summer a couple of thousand Englishmen and others find the supreme beauty in that.
There are plenty of delightful walks hereabouts, for
which you need neither rope nor nails. All the main
roads leading from the town are bordered with great
trees, rising from grassy margins and meeting overhead;
and sooner or later these verdurous vistas conduct you,
in any direction, to a genuine Alpine fir forest. Beside
the road the grain-bearing fields stretch away without
hedge or ditch or wall. In July the crops were yel-
lowing under a great sun; but now there is nothing

but stubble, with enormous ravens jumping about in it. The way the fields lie side by side for miles, without any prosaic property-marks, makes them seem a part of some landscape of picture or fable ; they seem all to belong to the Marquis of Carabas. I have heard painters complain of the want of color — of certain colors at least — in the Swiss summer landscape ; of the greens all being blue, the browns all being cold. Perhaps they are right ; autumn has fairly begun, but the foliage simply shrivels and rusts, and promises none of our October yellows and crimsons. But there is an indefinable, poignant charm in any autumn, under a long avenue of great trees, where you walk kicking the fallen leaves and looking at an old peasant-woman in the hazy distance, as she trudges under her fagot.

Lucerne, September 29th. — Berne, I find, has been filling with tourists at the expense of Lucerne, which I have been having almost to myself. There are six people at the table d'hôte ; the excellent dinner denotes, on the part of the *chef*, the easy leisure in which true artists love to work. The waiters have nothing to do but lounge about the hall and chink in their pockets the fees of the past season. The day has been most lovely in itself, and pervaded, to my sense, by the gentle glow of a natural satisfaction at finding myself on the threshold of Italy again. I am lodged *en prince*, in a room with a balcony hanging over the lake — a balcony on which I spent a long time this morning at dawn, thanking the mountain-tops, from the depths of a tourist's heart, for their promise of superbly fair weather. There were a great many mountain-tops to thank, for the crags and peaks and pinnacles tumbled away through the morning mist, in an endless confusion of grandeur. I have been all day in better humor with Lucerne than ever before — a forecast reflection of Italian moods. If Switzerland, as I wrote the other day, is a show-place, Lucerne is certainly one of the biggest booths at the fair. The little quay, under the trees, squeezed in between the decks of the steamboats and the doors of the hotels, is a terrible medley of Saxon dialects — a jumble of pilgrims in all the phases of devotion, equipped with book and staff — alpenstock and Baedeker. There are so many hotels and trinket-shops, so many omnibuses and steamers, so many St. Gothard veturini, so many ragged urchins thrusting photographs, minerals, and Lucernese English at you, that you feel as if lake and mountains themselves, in all their loveliness, were but a part of the "enterprise" of landlords and pedlers, and half expect to see the Righi, and Pilatus, and the fine weather figure as items on your hotel-bill, between the *bougie* and the *siphon.* Nature herself assists you in this fancy; for there is something extremely operatic and suggestive of foot-lights and scene-shifters in the view on which Lucerne looks out. You are one of five thousand — fifty thousand — " accommodated " spectators; you have taken your season-ticket, and there is a responsible impresario somewhere behind the scenes. There is such a luxury of beauty in the prospect — such a redundancy of composition and effect — so many more peaks and pinnacles than are needed to make one heart happy or regale the vision of one quiet observer, that you finally accept the

little Babel on the quay and the looming masses in the
clouds as equal parts of a perfect system, and feel as if
the mountains had been waiting so many ages for the
hotels to come and balance the colossal group, that they
have a right, after all, to have them big and numerous.
The scene-shifters have been at work all day long, com-
posing and discomposing the beautiful background of
the prospect — massing the clouds and scattering the
light, effacing and reviving, making play with their
wonderful machinery of mist and haze. The mountains
rise one behind the other, in an enchanting gradation of
distances and of melting blues and grays; you think
each successive tone the loveliest and haziest possible, till you see another looming dimly behind it. I
could n't enjoy even the Swiss Times, over my breakfast, until I had marched forth to the office of the St.
Gothard diligences and demanded the banquette for to-
morrow. The one place at the disposal of the office
was taken, but I might possibly *m'entendre* with the
conductor for his own seat — the conductor being generally visible, in the intervals of business, at the post-
office. To the post-office, after breakfast, I repaired,
over the fine new bridge which now spans the green
Reuss, and gives such a woful air of country-cousin-
ship to the crooked old wooden causeway which did sole
service when I was here four years ago. The old bridge
is covered with a running hood of shingles, and adorned
with a series of very quaint and vivid little paintings
of the Dance of Death, quite in the Holbein manner;
the new bridge sends up a painful glare from its white
limestone, and is ornamented with candelabra in a mer-

etricious imitation of platinum. As a pure-minded
tourist, I ought to have chosen to return at least by the
dark and narrow way; but mark how luxury unmans
us! I was already demoralized. I crossed the threshold of the timbered portal, took a few steps, and re-
treated. It *smelt badly!* So I marched back, counting
the lamps in their mendacious platinum. But it smelt
very badly indeed; and no good American is without
a fund of accumulated sensibility to the odor of stale
timber.

Meanwhile I had spent an hour in the great yard of
the post-office, waiting for my conductor to turn up,
and watching the yellow malles-postes being pushed to
and fro. At last, being told my man was at my service,
I was brought to speech of a huge, jovial, bearded, delightful Italian, clad in the blue coat and waistcoat,
with close, round silver buttons, which are a heritage
of the old postilions. No, it was not he; it was a
friend of his; and finally the friend was produced, *en
costume de ville*, but equally jovial, and Italian enough
— a brave Lucernese, who had spent half of his life
between Bellinzona and Camerlata. For ten francs
this worthy man's perch behind the luggage was made
mine as far as Bellinzona, and we separated with recip-
rocal wishes for good weather on the morrow. To-
morrow is so manifestly determined to be as fine as any
other 30th of September since the weather became, on
this planet, a topic of conversation, that I have had
nothing to do but stroll about Lucerne, staring, loafing,
and vaguely intent upon regarding the fact that, whatever happens, my place is paid to Milan, as the most

comfortable fact in this uncertain world. I loafed into the immense new Hôtel National, and read the New York Tribune on a blue satin divan, and was rather surprised, on coming out, to find myself staring at a green Swiss lake, and not at the Broadway omnibuses. The Hôtel National is adorned with a perfectly appointed Broadway bar — one of the " prohibited " ones, seeking hospitality in foreign lands, like an old-fashioned French or Italian refugee.

Milan, October 4th. — My journey hither was such a pleasant piece of traveller's luck that it seems almost indelicate to take it to pieces to see what it was made of. But do what we will, there remains in all deeply agreeable impressions a charming something we cannot analyze. I found it agreeable even, under the circumstances, to turn out of bed, at Lucerne, at four o'clock, into the chilly autumn darkness. The thick-starred sky was cloudless, and there was as yet no flush of dawn ; but the lake was wrapped in a ghostly white mist, which crept half-way up the mountains, and made them look as if they too had been lying down for the night, and were casting away the vaporous tissues of their bedclothes. Into this fantastic fog the little steamer went creaking away, and I hung about the deck with the two or three travellers who had known better than to believe it would save them francs or midnight sighs — over those debts you " pay with your person " — to go and wait for the diligence at the Poste at Flüelen, or yet at the Guillaume Tell. The dawn came sailing up over the mountain-tops, flushed but unperturbed, and blew out the little stars and then the

big ones, as a thrifty matron, after a party, blows out
her candles and lamps; the mist went melting and
wandering away into the duskier hollows and recesses·
of the mountains, and the summits defined their pro-
files against the cool, soft light.

At Flüelen, before the landing, the big yellow coaches
were actively making themselves bigger, and piling up
boxes and bags on their roofs in a way to make nervous people think of the short turns on the downward
zigzags of the St. Gothard. I climbed into my own
banquette, and stood eating peaches (half a dozen women were hawking them about under the horses' legs)
with an air of security which might have been offensive
to the people scrambling and protesting below between
coupé and intérieur. They were all English, and they
all had false alarms about some one else being in their
places — the places which they produced their tickets
and proclaimed in three or four different languages that
British gold had given them a sacred right to. They
were all serenely confuted by the stout, purple-faced,
many-buttoned conductors, patted on the backs, assured
that their bath-tubs had every advantage of position
on the top, and stowed away according to their dues.
When once one has fairly started on a journey and has
but to go and go, by the impetus received, it is surprising what entertainment one finds in very small things.
The traveller's humor falls upon us, and surely it is not
the unwisest the heart knows. I do not envy people, at
any rate, who have outlived or outworn the simple entertainment of feeling settled to go somewhere, with bag
and umbrella. If we are settled on the top of a coach,

and the " somewhere" contains an element of the new and strange, the case is at its best. In this matter wise people are content to become children again. We don't turn about on our knees to look out of the omnibus-window, but we indulge in very much the same round-eyed contemplation of accessible objects. Responsi-bility is left at home, or, at the worst, packed away in the valise, in quite another part of the diligence, with the clean shirts and the writing-case. I imbibed the traveller's humor, for this occasion, with the somewhat acrid juice of my indifferent peaches; it made me think them very good. This was the first of a series of kindly services it rendered me. It made me agree next, as we started, that the gentleman at the booking-office at Lucerne had played but a harmless joke when he told me the regular seat in the banquette was taken. No one appeared to claim it; so the conductor and I reversed positions, and I found him quite as profitable a neighbor as the usual Anglo-Saxon. He was trolling snatches of melody, and showing his great yellow teeth in a jovial grin all the way to Bellinzona — and this in the face of the sombre fact that the St. Gothard tun-nel is scraping away into the mountain, all the while, under his nose, and numbering the days of the many-buttoned brotherhood. But he hopes, for long service' sake, to be taken into the employ of the railway; he has no æsthetic prejudices. I found the railway com-ing on, however, in a manner very shocking to mine. About one hour short of Andermatt they have pierced a huge black cavity in the mountain, and around this dusky aperture there has grown up a swarming, dig-

ging, hammering, smoke-compelling colony. There are
great barracks, with tall chimneys, down in the romantic gorge, and a wonderful increase of wine-shops in
the little village of Göschenen above. Along the breast
of the mountain, beside the road, come wandering several miles of very handsome iron pipes, of a stupendous
girth — a conduit for the water-power with which
some of the machinery is worked. It lies at its mighty
length among the rocks like an immense black serpent,
and serves, as a mere detail, to give one the measure of
the central enterprise. When at the end of our long
day's journey, well down in warm Italy, we came upon
the other aperture of the tunnel, I felt really like uncapping, with a kind of reverence. Truly, Nature is
great, but she seems to me to stand in very much the
same shoes as my poor friend the conductor. She is
being superseded at her strongest points, successively,
and nothing remains but for her to take humble service
with her master. If she can hear herself think, amid
that din of blasting and hammering, she must be reck-
oning up the years which may elapse before the clev-
erest of Ober-Ingénieurs decides that mountains are
altogether superfluous, and has the Jungfrau melted
down and the residuum carried away in balloons and
dumped upon another planet.

The Devil's Bridge, apparently, has the same failing
as the good Homer. It was decidedly nodding. The
volume of water in the torrent was shrunken, and
there was none of that thunderous uproar and far-
leaping spray which have kept up a miniature tempest
in the neighborhood when I have passed before. It

suddenly occurs to me that the fault is not in the good Homer's inspiration, but simply in the big black pipes I just mentioned. They dip into the rushing stream higher up, apparently, and pervert its fine frenzy to their prosaic uses. There could hardly be a more vivid reminder of the standing quarrel between use and beauty, and the hard time poor beauty is having. I looked wistfully, as we rattled into dreary Andermatt, at the great white zigzags of the Oberalp road climbing away to the left. Even on one's way to Italy one may spare a pulsation of desire for that beautiful journey through the castled Grisons. I shall always remember my day's drive last summer through that long blue avenue of mountains, to queer little mouldering Ilanz, visited before supper in the ghostly dusk, as an episode with color in it. At Andermatt a sign over a little black doorway, flanked by two dunghills, seemed to me tolerably comical : *Minéraux, Quadrupèdes, Oiseaux, Œufs, Tableaux Antiques.* We bundled in to dinner, and the American gentleman in the banquette made the acquaintance of the Irish lady in the coupé, who talked of the weather as *foine,* and wore a Persian scarf twisted about her head. At the other end of the table sat an Englishman out of the intérieur, who bore a most extraordinary resemblance to the portraits of Edward VI.'s and Mary's reigns. He was a walking Holbein. It was fascinating, and he must have wondered why I stared at him. It was not him I was staring at, but some handsome Seymour, or Dudley, or Digby, with a ruff and a round cap and plume. From Andermatt, through its high, cold, sunny valley, into

rugged little Hospenthal, and then up the last stages
of the ascent. From here the road was all new to me.
Among the summits of the various Alpine passes there
is little to choose. You wind and double slowly into
keener cold and deeper stillness; you put on your
overcoat and turn up the collar; you count the nestling
snow-patches, and then you cease to count them; you
pause, as you trudge before the lumbering coach, and
listen to the last-heard cow-bell tinkling away below
you, in kindlier herbage. The sky was tremendously
blue, and the little stunted bushes, on the snow-
streaked slopes, were all dyed with autumnal purples
and crimsons. It was a great piece of color. Purple
and crimson, too, though not so fine, were the faces
thrust out at us from the greasy little double casements
of a barrack beside the road, where the horses paused
before the last pull. There was one little girl in particular, beginning to *lisser* her hair, as civilization approached, in a manner not to be described, with her
poor little blue-black hands. At the summit there are
the two usual grim little stone taverns, the steel-blue
tarn, the snow-white peaks, the pause in the cold sunshine. Then we began to rattle down, with two horses.
In five minutes we were swinging along the famous
zigzags. Engineer, driver, horses — it's very handsomely done by all of them. The road curves and
curls, and twists and plunges, like the tail of a kite;
sitting perched in the banquette, you see it making below you, in mid-air, certain bold gyrations, which bring
you as near as possible, short of the actual experience,
to the philosophy of that immortal Irishman who

11 *

wished that his fall from the house-top would only last.
But the zigzags last no more than Paddy's fall, and in
due time we were all coming to our senses over café au
lait in the little inn at Faido. After Faido, the valley,
plunging deeper, began to take thick afternoon shadows
from the hills, and at Airolo we were fairly in the twilight. But the pink and yellow houses shimmered
through the gentle gloom, and Italy began in broken
syllables to whisper that she was at hand. For the
rest of the way to Bellinzona her voice was muffled in
the gray of evening, and I was half vexed to lose the
charming sight of the changing vegetation. But only
half vexed, for the moon was climbing all the while
nearer the edge of the crags which overshadowed us,
and a thin, magical light came trickling down into the
winding, murmuring gorges. It was a most enchanting
ride. The chestnut-trees loomed up with double their
daylight stature; the vines began to swing their low
festoons like nets to trip up the fairies. At last the
ruined towers of Bellinzona stood gleaming in the
moonshine, and we rattled into the great post-yard. It
was eleven o'clock, and I had risen at four; moonshine
apart, I was not sorry.

All that was very well; but the drive next day from
Bellinzona to Como is to my mind what gives its
supréme beauty to the St. Gothard road. One cannot
describe the beauty of the Italian lakes, nor would one
try, if one could; the floweriest rhetoric can recall it
only as a picture on a fireboard recalls a Claude. But
it lay spread before me for a whole perfect day — in
the long gleam of Lago Maggiore, from whose head the

diligence swerves away, and begins to climb the bosky hills which divide it from Lugano; in the shimmering, melting azure of the Italian Alps; in the luxurious tangle of nature and the familiar picturesqueness of man; in the lawn-like slopes, where the great grouped chestnuts make so cool a shadow in so warm a light; in the rusty vineyards, the littered cornfields, and the tawdry wayside shrines. But most of all, it is the deep yellow light which enchants you and tells you where you are. See it come filtering down through a vine-covered trellis on the red handkerchief with which a ragged contadina has bound her hair; and all the magic of Italy, to the eye, seems to make an aureole about the poor girl's head. Look at a brown-breasted reaper eating his chunk of black bread under a spreading chestnut; nowhere is shadow so charming, nowhere is color so charged, nowhere is accident so picturesque. The whole drive to Lugano was one long loveliness, and the town itself is admirably Italian. There was a great unlading of the coach, during which I wandered under certain brown old arcades, and bought for six sous, from a young woman in a gold necklace, a hatful of peaches and figs. When I came back, I found the young man holding open the door of the second diligence, which had lately come up, and beckoning to me with a despairing smile. The young man, I must note, was the most amiable of Ticinese; though he wore no buttons, he was attached to the diligence in some amateurish capacity, and had an eye to the mail-bags and other valuables in the boot. I grumbled, at Berne, over the want of soft curves in the Swiss temperament; but the children of

the tangled Tessin are cast in the Italian mould. My
friend had as many quips and cranks as a Neapolitan;
we walked together for an hour under the chestnuts,
while the coach was plodding up from Bellinzona, and
he never stopped singing till we reached a little wine-
house, where he got his mouth full of bread and cheese.
. . . . I looked into the open door and saw the young
woman sitting rigid and grim, staring over his head,
with a great pile of bread and butter in her lap. He
had only informed her, most politely, that she was to
be transferred to another diligence, and must do him
the favor to descend; but she evidently thought there
was but one way for a respectable British young woman, dropping her h's, to receive the politeness of a
foreign young man with a moustache and much latent
pleasantry in his eye. Heaven only knew what he was
saying! I told her, and she gathered up her parcels
and emerged. A part of the day's great pleasure, perhaps, was my grave sense of being an instrument in the
hands of Providence toward the safe consignment of
this young woman and her boxes. When once you
have taken a baby into your arms, you are in for it;
you can't drop it — you have to hold it till some one
comes. My rigid Abigail was a neophyte in foreign
travel, though doubtless cunning enough at her trade,
which I inferred to be that of making up those prodigious chignons which English ladies wear. Her mistress had gone on a mule over the mountains to Cadennabbia, and she was coming up with her wardrobe, in
two big boxes and a bath-tub. I had played my part,
under Providence, at Bellinzona, and had interposed

between the poor girl's frightened English and the
dreadful Ticinese French of the functionaries in the
post-yard. At the custom-house, on the Italian frontier,
I was of peculiar service; there was a kind of fateful
fascination in it. The wardrobe was voluminous; I
exchanged a paternal glance with my charge as the
douanier plunged his brown fists into it. Who was the
lady at Cadennabbia? What was she to me or I to
her? She would n't know, when she rustled down to
dinner next day, that it was *I* who had guided the frail
skiff of her decorative fortunes to port. So, unseen,
but not unfelt, do we cross each other's orbits. The
skiff, however, may have foundered that evening, in
sight of land. I disengaged the young woman from
among her fellow-travellers, and placed her boxes on a
hand-cart, in the picturesque streets of Como, within a
stone's throw of that lovely cathedral, with its façade
of cameo medallions. I could only make the *facchino*
swear to take her to the steamboat. He too was a
jovial dog, and I hope he was polite — but not too
polite.

SIENA.

Siena, October, 1873.

FLORENCE being oppressively hot and delivered over to the mosquitoes, the occasion seemed excellent to pay that visit to Siena which I had more than once planned and missed. I arrived late in the evening, by the light of a magnificent moon; and while a couple of benignantly mumbling old crones were making up my bed at the inn, I strolled forth in quest of a first impression. Five minutes brought me to where I might gather it unhindered, as it bloomed in the white moonshine. The great Piazza in Siena is famous, and though in this day of photographs none of the world's wonders can pretend, like Wordsworth's phantom of delight, really "to startle and waylay," yet as I suddenly stepped into this Piazza from under a dark archway, it seemed a vivid enough revelation of the picturesque. It is in the shape of a shallow horseshoe, the untravelled reader who has turned over his travelled friend's portfolio will remember; or, better, of a bow, in which the high façade of the Palazzo Pubblico forms the chord and everything else the arc. It was void of any human presence which could recall me to the current year, and, the moonshine assisting, I had half an hour's fantastic vision of mediæval Italy. The Piazza being

built on the side of a hill — or rather, as I believe
science affirms, in the cup of a volcanic crater — the
vast pavement converges downward in slanting radia-
tions of stone, like the spokes of a great wheel, to a
point directly in front of the Palazzo, which may figure
the hub, though it is nothing more ornamental than
the mouth of a drain. The Palazzo stands on the lower
side and might seem, in spite of its goodly mass and
its embattled cornice, to be rather defiantly out-coun-
tenanced by the huge private dwellings which occupy
the opposite eminence. This *might* be — if it were not
that the Palazzo asserts itself with an architectural
gesture, as one may say, of extraordinary dignity.

On the firm edge of the edifice, from bracketed base
to gray-capped summit against the sky, there grows a
slender tower, which soars and soars till it has given
notice of the city's greatness over the blue mountains
which define the horizon. It rises straight and slim as
a pennoned lance, planted on the steel-shod ·toe of a
mounted knight, and retains unperturbed in the blue
air, far above the changing fashions of the market-
place, an indefinable expression of mediæval rectitude
and chivalric honor. This beautiful tower is the finest
thing in Siena, and, in its rigid fashion, one of the
finest in the world. As it stood silvered by the moonlight during my traveller's revery, it seemed to say
with peculiar distinctness that it survived from an order
of things which the march of history had trampled out,
but which had had an epoch of intense vitality. The
gigantic houses enclosing the rest of the Piazza took up
the tale, and seemed to murmur, " We are very old and

a trifle weary, but we were built strong and piled high, and we shall last for many a year. The present is cold and heedless, but we keep ourselves in heart by brooding over our treasure of memories and traditions. We are haunted houses, in every creaking timber and crumbling stone." In the moonshine, one may fancy a group of Sienese *palazzi* dropping a few dusky hints, in this manner, to a well-disposed American traveller.

Since that night I have been having a week's daylight knowledge of this ancient city, and I don't know that I can present it as anything more than a deeper impression than ever that Italy is the land for the artist. Siena has kept, to the eye, her historic physiognomy most unchanged. Other places, perhaps, may treat you to as drowsy a perfume of antiquity, but few of them exhale it from so large a surface. Lying massed within her walls upon a dozen clustered hilltops, Siena still looks like a place which once lived in a large way; and if much of her old life is extinct, her smouldering ashes form a very goodly pile. This general impression of the past is the main thing that she has to offer the casual observer. The casual observer is generally not very learned nor much of an historical specialist; his impression is necessarily vague, and many of the chords of his imagination respond with a rather muffled sound. But such as it is, his impression keeps him faithful company and reminds him from time to time that even the lore of German doctors is but the shadow of satisfied curiosity. I have been living at the inn and walking about the streets; these are the simple terms of my experience.

But inns and streets in Italy are the vehicles of half
one's knowledge; if one has no fancy for their lessons, one may burn one's note-book. In Siena everything is Sienese. The inn has an English sign over
the door — a little battered plate with a rusty representation of the lion and the unicorn; but advance
hopefully into the mouldy stone alley which serves as
vestibule, and you will find local color enough. The
landlord, I was told, had been servant in an English
family, and I was curious to see how he met the frown
of the casual Anglo-Saxon after the latter's first twelve
hours in his establishment. As he failed to appear, I
asked the waiter if he was not at home. " O," said
the latter, " he's a *piccolo vecchiotto grasso* who does n't
like to move." I'm afraid this little fat old man has
simply a bad conscience. It's no small burden for
one who likes the Italians — as who does n't, under
this restriction? — to have this matter of the neglected,
the proscribed scrubbing-brush to dispose of. What
is the real philosophy of dirty habits, and are foul surfaces merely superficial? If unclean manners have in
truth the moral meaning which I suspect in them, we
must love Italy better than consistency. This a number of us are prepared to do, but while we are making
the sacrifice it is as well we should know it.

We may plead, moreover, for these impecunious
heirs of the past, that even if it were easy to be clean
in the midst of their mouldering heritage, it would be
difficult to appear so. At the risk of seeming a shame-
fully sordid Yankee, I feel tempted to say that the
prime result of my contemplative strolls in the dusky

Q

alleys of Siena is an ineffable sense of *disrepair.*
Everything is cracking, peeling, fading, crumbling,
rotting. No young Sienese eyes rest upon anything
youthful; they open into a world battered and befouled
with long use. Everything has passed its meridian
except the brilliant façade of the cathedral, which is
being diligently retouched and restored, and a few
private palaces whose broad fronts seem to have been
lately furbished and polished. Siena was long ago
mellowed to the pictorial tone; the operation of time,
now, is to deposit shabbiness upon shabbiness. But it
is for the most part a patient, sturdy, sympathetic
shabbiness, which soothes rather than irritates the
nerves, and has in most cases, doubtless, as long a
career to run as most of our brittle new-world freshness. It projects at all events a deeper shadow into
the constant twilight of the narrow streets — that
vague, historic dusk, as I may call it, in which one
walks and wonders. These streets are hardly more
than sinuous flagged alleys, into which the huge black
houses, between their almost meeting cornices, suffer a
meagre light to filter down over rough-hewn stone, past
windows often of graceful Gothic form, and great pendent iron rings and twisted sockets for torches. Scattered over their many-headed hill, they are often quite
grotesquely steep, and so impracticable for carriages
that the sound of wheels is only a trifle less anomalous
than it would be in Venice. But all day long there
comes up to my window an incessant shuffling of feet
and clangor of voices. The weather is very warm for
the season, all the world is out of doors, and the Tus-

can tongue (which in Siena is reputed to have a classic purity) is wagging in every imaginable key. It does not rest even at night, and I am often an uninvited guest at concerts and *conversazioni* at two o'clock in the morning. The concerts are sometimes charming. I not only do not curse my wakefulness, but I go to my window to listen. Three men come carolling by, trolling and quavering with voices of delightful sweetness, or a lonely troubadour in his shirt-sleeves draws such artful love-notes from his clear, fresh tenor, that I seem for the moment to be behind the scenes at the opera, watching some Rubini or Mario go " on," and waiting for the round of applause. In the intervals, a couple of friends or enemies stop — Italians always make their points in conversation by stopping, letting you walk on a few paces, to turn and find them standing with finger on nose, and engaging your interrogative eye — they pause, by a happy instinct, directly under my window, and dispute their point or tell their story or make their confidence. I can hardly tell which it is, everything has such an explosive promptness, such a redundancy of inflection and action. Whatever it is, it 's a story, compared with our meagre Anglo-Saxon colloquies, or rather it 's a drama, improvised, mimicked, shaped and rounded, carried bravely to its *dénouement*. The speaker seems actually to establish his stage and face his foot-lights, to create by a gesture a little scenic circumscription about him ; he rushes to and fro and shouts and stamps and postures and ranges through every phase of his inspiration. I observed the other evening a striking instance of the spontaneity of

Italian gesture, in the person of a little Sienese of I hardly know what exact age — the age of inarticulate sounds and the experimental use of a spoon. It was a Sunday evening, and this little man had accompanied his parents to the café. The Caffè Greco at Siena is a most delightful institution ; you get a capital *demi-tasse* for three sous, and an excellent ice for eight, and while you consume these easy luxuries you may buy from a little hunchback the local weekly periodical, the Vita Nuova, for three centimes (the two centimes left from your sou, if you are under the spell of this magical frugality, will do to give the waiter). My young friend was sitting on his father's knee, and helping himself to the half of a strawberry-ice with which his mamma had presented him. He had so many misadventures with his spoon that this lady at length confiscated it, there being nothing left of his ice but a little crimson liquid which he might dispose of as other little boys had done before him. But he was no friend, it appeared, to such irregular methods ; he was a perfect little gentleman, and he resented the imputation of indelicacy. He protested, therefore, and it was the manner of his protest that struck me. He did not cry audibly, though he made a very wry face. It was no stupid squall, and yet he was too young to speak. It was a penetrating concord of inarticulably pleading, accusing sounds, accompanied with the most exquisitely modulated gestures. The gestures were perfectly mature ; he did everything that a man of forty would have done if he had been pouring out a flood of sonorous eloquence. He shrugged his shoulders and wrinkled his eyebrows, tossed out his hands and folded his arms, obtruded his chin and bobbed about his head — and at last, I am happy to say, recovered his spoon. If I had had a solid little silver one I would have presented it to him as a testimonial to a perfect, though as yet unconscious, artist.

My artistic infant, however, has diverted me from what I had in mind — a much weightier matter — the great private palaces which are so powerful a feature in the physiognomy of the city. They are extraordinarily spacious and numerous, and one wonders what part they can play in the meagre economy of the Siena of to-day. The Siena of to-day is a mere shrunken semblance of the vigorous little republic which in the thirteenth century waged triumphant war with Florence, cultivated the arts with splendor, planned a cathedral (though it had ultimately to curtail the design) of proportions almost unequalled, and contained a population of two hundred thousand souls. Many of these dusky piles still bear the names of the old mediæval magnates, whose descendants occupy them in a much more irresponsible fashion. Half a dozen of them are as high as the Strozzi and Riccardi palaces in Florence; they could n't well be higher. There is to an American something richly artificial and scenic, as it were, in the way these colossal dwellings are packed together in their steep streets, in the depths of their little enclosed, agglomerated city. When we, in our day and country, raise a structure of half the mass and stateliness, we leave a great space about it in the manner of a pause after an effective piece of talking. But

when a Sienese countess, as things are here, is doing
her hair near the window, she is a wonderfully near
neighbor to the cavalier opposite, who is being shaved
by his valet. Possibly the countess does not object to
a certain chosen publicity at her toilet: an Italian gentleman tells me the aristocracy are very "corrupt."
Some of the palaces are shown, but only when the
occupants are at home, and now they are in *villeggiatura*. Their villeggiatura lasts eight months of the
year, the waiter at the inn informs me, and they spend
little more than the carnival in the city. The gossip
of an inn-waiter ought, perhaps, to be beneath the
dignity of even such meagre history as this; but I confess that when I have come in from my strolls with a
kind of irritated sense of the dumbness of stones and
mortar, I have listened with a certain avidity, over my
dinner, to the proffered confidences of the worthy man
who stands by with a napkin. His talk is really very
fine, and he prides himself greatly on his cultivated
tone. He called my attention to it. He has very little good to say about the Sienese nobility. They are
"proprio d'origine egoista" — whatever that may be —
and there are many who can't write their names. This
may be calumny; but I doubt whether the biggest coronet of them all could have spoken more delicately of
a lady of peculiar personal appearance, who had been
dining near me. "She's too fat," I said grossly, when
she had left the room, The waiter shook his head,
with a little sniff: "È troppo materiale." This lady
and her companion were the party whom, thinking I
would relish a little company (I had been dining alone

for a week), he gleefully announced to me as newly
arrived Americans. They were Americans, I found,
who wore black lace veils pinned on their heads, con-
veyed their beans to their mouths with a knife, and
spoke a strange, raucous Spanish. They were from
Montevideo. The genius of old Siena, however, would
be certainly rather amused at the stress I lay on the
distinction; for one American is about as much in
order as another, as he stands before the great loggia
of the Casino dei Nobili. The nobility, which is very
numerous and very rich, is still, said the Italian gentleman whom I just now quoted, perfectly feudal. Morally, intellectually, behind the walls of its palaces,
you 'll find the fourteenth century. There is no bourgeoisie to speak of; immediately after the aristocracy
come the poor people, who are very poor indeed. My
friend's account of this domiciliary mediævalism made
me wish more than ever, as an amateur of the picturesque, that your really appreciative tourist was not
reduced to simply staring at black stones and peeping up
stately staircases; but that when he has examined the
façade of the palace, Murray in hand, he might march
up to the great drawing-room, make his bow to the master and mistress, the old abbé and the young count, and
invite them to favor him with a little sketch of their
social philosophy, or a few first-rate family anecdotes.

The dusky labyrinth of the streets of Siena is interrupted by two great sunny spaces: the fan-shaped
Piazza, of which I just now said a word, and the little
square in which the cathedral erects its shining walls
of marble. Of course since paying the great Piazza

my compliments by moonlight, I have strolled through
it often both at sunnier and shadier hours. The market is held there, and where Italians are buying and
selling you may count upon lively entertainment. It
has been held there, I suppose, for the last five hundred years, and during that time the cost of eggs and
earthen pots has been gradually but inexorably increasing. The buyers, nevertheless, wrestle over their pur-
chases as lustily as if they were fourteenth-century
burghers suddenly waking up in horror to current
prices. You have but to walk aside, however, into the
Palazzo Pubblico, to feel yourself very much like a
thrifty old mediævalist. The state affairs of the republic were formerly transacted here, but it now gives
shelter to modern law-courts and other prosy business.
I was marched through a number of vaulted halls and
chambers, which, in the intervals of the administrative
sessions held in them, are peopled only with the presence of the great, mouldering, archaic frescos on the
walls and ceilings. The chief painters of the Sienese
school lent a hand in decorating them, and you may
complete here the connoisseurship in which, possibly,
you embarked at the Academy. I say "possibly," in
order to be very judicial, for my own observation has
led me no great length. I have been taking an idle
satisfaction in the thought that the Sienese school has
suffered my enthusiasm peacefully to slumber, and
benignantly abstained from adding to my intellectual
responsibilities. "A formidable rival to the Florentine," says some book — I forget which — into which I
recently glanced. Not a bit of it, say I; the Floren-

tines may rest on their laurels, all along the line. The early painters of the two groups have indeed much in common; but the Florentines had the good fortune of seeing their efforts gathered up and applied by a few pre-eminent spirits, such as never came to the rescue of the groping Sienese. Fra Angelico and Ghirlandaio said all their feebler *confrères* dreamt of, and a great deal more beside, but the inspiration of Simone Memmi and Ambrogio Lorenzetti and Sano di Pietro has a painful air of never efflorescing into a maximum. Sodoma and Beccafumi are to my taste a rather abortive maximum. But one should speak of them all gently — and I do, from my soul; for their earnest labors have wrought a truly picturesque heritage of color and rich, figure-peopled shadow for the echoing chambers of their old civic fortress. The faded frescos cover the walls like quaintly storied tapestries; in one way or another, they please. If one owes a large debt of pleasure to painting, one gets to think of the whole history of art tenderly, as the conscious experience of a single mysterious spirit, and one shrinks from saying rude things about any particular phase of it, just as one would from touching brusquely upon an erratic episode in the life of a person one esteemed. You don't care to remind a grizzled veteran of his defeats, and why should we linger in Siena to talk about Beccafumi? I by no means go so far as to say, with an amateur with whom I have just been discussing the matter, that "Sodoma is a precious poor painter, and Beccafumi no painter at all"; but opportunity being limited, I am willing to let the remark about Beccafumi pass for true. With regard to Sodoma, I remember seeing four years ago in the choir of the Cathedral of Pisa a certain little dusky specimen of the painter — an Abraham and Isaac, if I'm not mistaken — which was full of a kind of gloomy grace. One rarely meets him in general collections, and I had never done so till the other day. He was not prolific, apparently; he had elegance, and his rarity is a part of it.

Here in Siena are a couple of dozen scattered frescos, and three or four canvases; his masterpiece, among others, a very impressive Descent from the Cross. I would not give a fig for the equilibrium of the figures or the ladders; but while it lasts the scene is all intensely solemn and graceful and sweet — too sweet for so bitter a subject. Sodoma's women are strangely sweet; an imaginative sense of morbid, appealing attitude seems to me the author's finest accomplishment. His frescos have all the same vague softness, and a kind of mild melancholy, which I am inclined to think the sincerest part of them, for it strikes me as being simply the artist's depressed suspicion of his own want of force. Once he determined, however, that if he could not be strong, he would make capital of his weakness, and painted the Christ bound to the Column, of the Academy. It is resolutely pathetic, and I have no doubt the painter mixed his colors with his tears; but I cannot describe it better than by saying that it is, pictorially, the first of the modern Christs. Unfortunately, it is not the last.

The main strength of Sienese art went, possibly, into the erection of the cathedral, and yet even here the strength is not of the greatest strain. If, however, there are more interesting churches in Italy, there are few more richly and variously picturesque; the comparative meagreness of the architectural idea is overlaid by a marvellous wealth of ingenious detail. Opposite the church — with the dull old archbishop's palace on one side and a dismantled residence of the late Grand Duke of Tuscany on the other — is an ancient hospital with a big stone bench running all along its front. Here I have sat awhile every morning for a week, like a philosophic convalescent, watching the florid façade of the cathedral glitter against the deep blue sky. It has been lavishly restored of late years, and the fresh white marble of the densely clustered pinnacles and statues and beasts and flowers seems to flash in the sunshine like a mosaic of jewels. There is more of this goldsmith's work in stone than I can remember or describe; it is piled up over three great doors with immense margins of exquisite decorative sculpture — still in the ancient cream-colored marble — and beneath three sharp pediments embossed with images relieved against red marble and tipped with golden mosaics. It is in the highest degree fantastic and luxuriant, and, on the whole, very lovely. As an affair of color it prepares you for the interior, which is supremely rich in mellow tones and clustering shadows. The greater part of its surface is wrought in alternate courses of black and white marble; but as the latter has been dimmed by the centuries to a fine mild brown, the place seems all a rich harmony of grave colors. Except certain charming frescos by Pinturicchio in the sacristy,

there are no pictures to speak of; but the pavement
is covered with many elaborate designs in black and
white mosaic, after cartoons by Beccafumi. The patient
skill of these compositions makes them a really superb
piece of decoration ; but even here the friend whom I
lately quoted refused to relish this over-ripe fruit of
the Sienese school. The designs are nonsensical, he
declares, and all his admiration is for the cunning arti-
sans who have imitated the hatchings and shadings
and hair-strokes of the pencil by the finest curves of
inserted black stone. But the true romance of handiwork at Siena is to be seen in the superb stalls of the
choir, under the colored light of the great wheel-
window. Wood-carving is an historic specialty of the
city, and the best masters of the art during the fifteenth
century bestowed their skill on this exquisite enterprise. It is like the frost-work on one's window-panes
interpreted in polished oak. I have rarely seen a more
vivid and touching embodiment of the peculiar patience
of mediæval craftsmanship. Into such artistry as this
the author seems to put more of his personal substance
than into any other; he has not only to wrestle with his
subject, but with his material. He is richly fortunate
when his subject is charming — when his devices, inventions, and fantasies spring lightly to his hand; for
in the material itself, when age and use have ripened
and polished and darkened it to the richness of ebony
and to a greater warmth, there is something surpass-
ingly delectable and venerable. Wander behind the
altar at Siena when the chanting is over and the incense has faded, and look at the stalls of the Barili.

THE AUTUMN IN FLORENCE.

Florence, November 15, 1873.

FLORENCE, too, has its " season " as well as Rome, and I have been taking some satisfaction, for the past six weeks, in the thought that it has not yet begun. Coming here in the first days of October, I found the summer lingering on in almost untempered force, and ever since, until within a day or two, it has been dying a very gradual death. Properly enough, as the city of flowers, Florence is delightful in the spring — during those blossoming weeks of March and April, when a six months' steady shivering has not shaken New York and Boston free of the grip of winter. But something in the mood of autumn seems to suit peculiarly the mood in which an appreciative tourist strolls through these many-memoried streets and galleries and churches. Old things, old places, old people (or, at least, old races) have always seemed to me to tell their secrets more freely in such moist, gray, melancholy days as have formed the complexion of the past October. With Christmas comes the winter, the opera (the good opera), the gayeties, American and other. Meanwhile, it is pleasant enough, for persons fond of the Florentine flavor, that the opera is

indifferent, that the Americans have not all arrived,
and that the weather has a monotonous, overcast softness, extremely favorable to contemplative habits.
There is no crush on the Cascine, as on the sunny
days of winter, and the Arno, wandering away toward
the mountains in the haze, seems as shy of being
looked at as a good picture in a bad light. No light
could be better to my eyes; it seems the faded light
of that varied past on which an observer here spends
so many glances. There are people, I know, who freely
intimate that the Florentine flavor I speak of is dead
and buried, and that it is an immense misfortune not
to have tasted it in the Grand Duke's time. Some
of these friends of mine have been living here ever
since, and have seen the little historic city expanding
in the hands of its "enterprising" syndic into its
shining girdle of boulevards and *beaux quartiers*, such
as M. Haussmann set the fashion of — like some precious little page of antique text swallowed up in a
marginal commentary. I am not sure of the real
wisdom of regretting the change — apart from its being
always good sense to prefer a larger city to a smaller
one. For Florence, in its palmy days, was peculiarly
a city of change — of shifting régimes, and policies,
and humors; and the Florentine character, as we have
it to-day, is a character which takes all things easily
for having seen so many come and go. It saw the
national capital arrive, and took no further thought
than sufficed for the day; it saw it depart, and whis-
tled it cheerfully on its way to Rome. The new boulevards of the Sindaco Peruzzi come, it may be said, but

they don't go; but after all, from the æsthetic point
of view, it is not strictly necessary they should. It
seems to me part of the essential amiability of Florence — of her genius for making you take to your favor
on easy terms everything that in any way belongs to
her — that she has already flung a sort of *reflet* of
her charm over all their undried mortar and plaster.
Nothing could be prettier, in a modern way, than the
Piazza d'Azeglio, or the Avenue of the Princess Margaret; nothing pleasanter than to stroll across them,
and enjoy the afternoon lights through their liberal
vistas. They carry you close to the charming hills
which look down into Florence on all sides, and if, in
the foreground, your sense is a trifle perplexed by the
white pavements, dotted here and there with a police-
man or a nurse-maid, you have only to look just beyond
to see Fiesole on its mountain-side glowing purple
from the opposite sunset.

Turning back into Florence proper, you have local
color enough and to spare — which you enjoy the more,
doubtless, from standing off to get your light and your
point of view. The elder streets, abutting on all this
newness, go boring away into the heart of the city in
narrow, dusky vistas of a fascinating picturesqueness.
Pausing to look down them, sometimes, and to penetrate the deepening shadows through which they recede, they seem to me little corridors leading out from
the past, as mystical as the ladder in Jacob's dream;
and when I see a single figure coming up toward me
I am half afraid to wait till it arrives; it seems too
much like a ghost — a messenger from an under-world.

Florence, paved with its great mosaics of slabs, and
lined with its massive Tuscan palaces, which, in their
large dependence on pure symmetry for beauty of
effect, reproduce more than other modern styles the
simple nobleness of Greek architecture, must have
always been a stately city, and not especially rich in
that ragged picturesqueness — the picturesqueness of
poverty — on which we feast our idle eyes at Rome
and Naples. Except in the unfinished fronts of the
churches, which, however, unfortunately, are mere prosaic ugliness, one finds here less romantic shabbiness
than in most Italian cities. But at two or three points
it exists in perfection — in just such perfection as
proves that often what is literally hideous may be
constructively delightful. On the north side of the
Arno, between the Ponte Vecchio and the Ponte Santa
Trinità, is an ancient row of houses, backing on the
river, in whose yellow flood they bathe their aching
old feet. Anything more battered and befouled, more
cracked and disjointed, dirtier, drearier, shabbier, it
would be impossible to conceive. They look as if,
fifty years ago, the muddy river had risen over their
chimneys, and then subsided again and left them
coated forever with its unsightly slime. And yet,
forsooth, because the river is yellow, and the light is
yellow, and here and there, elsewhere, some mellow,
mouldering surface, some hint of color, some accident
of atmosphere, takes up the foolish tale and repeats
the note — because, in short, it is Florence, it is Italy,
and you are a magnanimous Yankee, bred amid the
micaceous sparkle of brown-stone fronts and lavish of

enthusiasm, these miserable dwellings, instead of simply suggesting mental invocations to an enterprising board of health, bloom and glow all along the line in the perfect felicity of picturesqueness. Lately, during the misty autumn nights, the moon has been shining on them faintly, and refining away their shabbiness into something ineffably strange and spectral. The yellow river sweeps along without a sound, and the pale tenements hang above it like a vague miasmatic exhalation. The dimmest back-scene at the opera, when the tenor is singing his sweetest, seems hardly to belong to a more dreamily fictitious world.

What it is that infuses so rich an interest into the charm of Florence is difficult to say in a few words; yet as one wanders hither and thither in quest of a picture or a bas-relief, it seems no marvel that the place should be interesting. Two industrious English ladies have lately published a couple of volumes of "Walks" through the Florentine streets, and their work is a long enumeration of great artistic deeds. These things remain for the most part in sound preservation, and, as the weeks go by and you spend a constant portion of your days among them, you seem really to be living in the magical time. It was not long; it lasted, in its splendor, for less than a century; but it has stored away in the palaces and churches of Florence a heritage of beauty which these three enjoying centuries since have not yet come to the end of. This forms a distinct intellectual atmosphere, into which you may turn aside from the modern world and fill your lungs with the breath of a forgotten creed.

The memorials of the past in Florence have the advantage of being somehow more cheerful and exhilarating than in other cities which have had a great æsthetic period. Venice, with her old palaces cracking with the weight of their treasures, is, in its influence, insupportably sad; Athens, with her maimed marbles and dishonored memories, transmutes the consciousness of sensitive observers, I am told, into a chronic heartache. But in one's impression of old Florence there is something very sound and sweet and wholesome — something which would make it a growing pleasure to live here long. In Athens and Venice, surely, a long residence would be a pain. The reason of this is partly the peculiarly lovable, gentle character of Florentine art in general — partly the tenderness of time, in its lapse, which, save in a few cases, has been as sparing of injury as if it knew that when it had dimmed and corroded these charming things, it would have nothing so sweet again for its tooth to feed on. If the beautiful Ghirlandaios and Lippis are fading, this generation will never know it. The large Fra Angelico in the Academy is as clear and keen as if the good old monk were standing there wiping his brushes; the colors seem to *sing*, as it were, like new-fledged birds in June. Nothing is more characteristic of early Tuscan art than the bas-reliefs of Luca della Robbia; yet, save for their innocence, there is not one of them that might not have been modelled yesterday. The color is mild but not faded, the forms are simple but not archaic. But perhaps the best image of the absence of stale melancholy in Florentine antiquity is the bell-tower of Giotto beside the Cathedral. No traveller has forgotten how it stands there, straight and slender, plated with colored marbles, seeming so strangely rich in the common street. It is not even simple in design, and I never cease to wonder that the painter of so many grimly archaic little frescos should have fashioned a building which, in the way of elaborate elegance, leaves the finest modern culture nothing to suggest. Nothing can be imagined at once more lightly and more richly fanciful; it might have been a present, ready-made, to the city by some Oriental genie. Yet, with its Eastern look, it seems of no particular time; it is not gray and hoary like a Gothic spire, nor cracked and despoiled like a Greek temple; its marbles shine so little less freshly than when they were laid together, and the sunset lights up its embroidered cornice with such a friendly radiance, that you come to regard it at last as simply the graceful, indestructible soul of the city made visible. The Cathedral, externally, in spite of its solemn hugeness, strikes the same light, cheerful note; it has grandeur, of course, but such a pleasant, agreeable, ingenuous grandeur. It has seen so much, and outlived so much, and served so many sad purposes, and yet remains in aspect so true to the gentle epicureanism that conceived it. Its vast, many-colored marble walls are one of the sweetest entertainments of Florence; there is an endless fascination in walking past them, and feeling them lift their great acres of mosaic higher in the air than you care to look. You greet them as you do the side of ·a mountain when you are walking in the valley; you don't twist back your head to look at the top, but content yourself with some little nestling hollow — some especial combination of the marble dominos.

Florence is richer in pictures than one really knows until one has begun to look for them in outlying corners. Then, here and there, one comes upon treasures which it almost seems as if one might pilfer for the New York Museum without their being missed. The Pitti Palace, of course, is a collection of masterpieces; they jostle each other in their splendor, and they rather weary your admiration. The Uffizi is almost as fine a show, and together with that long serpentine artery which crosses the Arno and connects them, they form the great central treasure-chamber of the city. But I have been neglecting them of late for the sake of the Academy, where there are fewer copyists and tourists, fewer of the brilliant things you do not care for. I observed here, a day or two since, lurking obscurely in one of the smaller rooms, a most enchanting Sandro Botticelli. It had a mean black frame, and it was hung where no one would have looked for a masterpiece; but a good glass brought out its merits. It represented the walk of Tobias with the Angel, and there are parts of it really that an angel might have painted. Placed as it is, I doubt whether it is noticed by half a dozen persons a year. What a pity that it should not become the property of an institution which would give it a brave gilded frame and a strong American light! Then it might shed its wonderful beauty with all the force of rare example. Botticelli is, in a certain way, the most inter-

esting of the Florentine painters — the only one, save
Leonardo and Michael Angelo, who had a really in-
ventive fancy. His imagination has a complex turn
which gives him at first a strangely modern, familiar
air, but we soon discóver that what we know of him is
what our contemporary Pre-Raphaelites have borrowed.
When we read Mr. William Morris's poetry, when we
look at Mr. Rossetti's pictures, we are enjoying, among
other things, a certain amount of diluted Botticelli. He
endeavored much more than the other early Florentines
to make his faces express a mood, a consciousness, and
it is the beautiful preoccupied type of face which we
find in his pictures that our modern Pre-Raphaelites
reproduce, with their own modifications. Fra Angelico,
Filippo Lippi, Ghirlandaio, were not imaginative; but
who was ever more devotedly observant, more richly,
genially graphic ? If there should ever be a great weed-
ing out of the world's possessions, I should pray that
the best works of the early Florentine school be counted
among the flowers. With the ripest performances of
the Venetians, they seem to me the most valuable things
in the history of art. Heaven forbid that we should be
narrowed down to a cruel choice; but if it came to a
question of keeping or losing between half a dozen
Raphaels and half a dozen things I could select at the
Academy, I am afraid that, for myself, the memory
of the " Transfiguration " would not save the Raphaels.
And yet this was not the opinion of a patient artist
whom I saw the other day copying the finest of Ghirlandaios — a beautiful " Adoration of the Kings " at
the Hospital of the Innocenti. This is another speci-

men of the buried art-wealth of Florence. It hangs in a dusky chapel, far aloft, behind an altar, and, though now and then a stray tourist wanders in and puzzles awhile over the vaguely glowing forms, the picture is never really seen and enjoyed. I found an aged Frenchman of modest mien perched on the little platform beneath it, behind a great hedge of altar candlesticks, with an admirable copy almost completed. The difficulties of his task had been almost insuperable, and his performance seemed to me a real feat of magic. He could scarcely see or move, and he could only find room for his canvas by rolling it together and painting a small piece at a time, so that he never enjoyed a view of his work as a whole. The original is gorgeous with color and bewildering with ornamental detail, but not a gleam of the painter's crimson was wanting, not a curl in his gold arabesques. It seemed to me that if I had copied a Ghirlandaio under such circumstances, I would at least maintain, for my credit, that he was the first painter in the world. "Very good of its kind," said the weary old man, with a shrug, in reply to my raptures; "but O, how far short of Raphael!" However that may be, if the reader ever observes this brilliant copy in the Museum of Copies in Paris, let him stop before it with a certain reverence; it is one of the patient things of art. Seeing it wrought there, in its dusky chapel, in such scanty convenience, seemed to remind me that the old art-life of Florence was not yet extinct. The old painters are dead, but their influence is living.

FLORENTINE NOTES.

February – April, 1874.

I.

YESTERDAY that languid organism known as the Florentine Carnival put on a momentary semblance of vigor, and decreed a general *corso* through the town. The spectacle was not brilliant, but it suggested some natural reflections. I encountered the line of carriages in the square before Santa Croce, of which they were making the circuit. They rolled solemnly by, with their inmates frowning forth at each other in apparent wrath at not finding each other more amusing. There were no masks, no costumes, no decorations, no throwing of flowers or sweetmeats. It was as if each carriageful had privately resolved to be inexpensive, and was rather discomfited at finding that it was getting no better entertainment than it gave. The middle of the piazza was filled with little tables, with shouting mountebanks, mostly disguised in battered bonnets and crinolines, offering chances in raffles for plucked fowls and kerosene lamps. I have never thought the huge marble statue of Dante, which overlooks the scene, a work of the last refinement; but, as it stood there on its high pedestal, chin in hand, frowning down on all this cheap foolery, it seemed to have a great moral intention. The carriages followed a prescribed course — through the Via Ghibellina, the Proconsolo, past the Badia and the Bargello, beneath the great tessellated cliffs of the Cathedral, through the Tornabuoni, and out into ten minutes' sunshine beside the Arno. Much of all this is the gravest and stateliest part of Florence; and there was an almost ludicrous incongruity in seeing Pleasure leading her train through these dusky historic streets. It was most uncomfortably cold, and, in the absence of masks, many a fair nose was fantastically tipped with purple. But, as the carriages crept solemnly along, they seemed to me to be keeping a funeral march — to be following an antique custom, an exploded faith, to its tomb. The Carnival is dead, and these good people who had come abroad to make merry were to an observant sense no better than funeral mutes and grave-diggers. Last winter in Rome it seemed to me to have but a galvanized life; but, compared with this humble exhibition, it was quite operatic. At Rome, indeed, it was too operatic. The knights on horseback were a bevy of circus-riders, and I 'm sure that half the mad revellers repaired every night to the Capitol for their twelve sous a day.

I have just been reading over the letters of the President de Brosses. A hundred years ago, in Venice, the Carnival lasted six months; and at Rome for many weeks each year one was free to perpetrate the most fantastic follies, and cultivate the most remunerative vices under cover of a mask. It 's very well to read the President's anecdotes, which are capitally told; but I do not see, certainly, why we should expect the Italians to perpetuate a style of manners which we ourselves, if we had any responsibilities in the matter, should find intolerable. At any rate, the Florentines spend no more money nor faith on the carnivalesque. And yet this is not strictly true ; for what struck me in the whole spectacle yesterday, and prompted these observations, was not at all the more or less of costume of the people in the carriages, but the obstinate survival of the merrymaking instinct in the Florentine population. There could be no better example of it than that so dim a shadow of entertainment should keep all Florence standing and strolling, densely packed, for hours in the cold streets. There was nothing to see that might not be seen on the Cascine any fine day in the year — nothing but a name, a tradition, a pretext for sweet, staring idleness. The faculty of making much of common things and converting small occasions into great pleasures is to an American traveller the most salient characteristic of the so-called Latin civilizations. It charms him and vexes him, according to his mood ; and for the most part it seems to represent a moral gulf between his own national temperament and that of Frenchmen and Italians, far wider than the watery leagues which a steamer may annihilate. But I think his mood is wisest when he accepts it as the sign of an unconscious philosophy of life, instilled by the experience of centuries — the philosophy of people who have lived long and much, who have discovered no short cuts to happiness and no effective circumvention of effort, and so have come to regard the average lot as a ponderous fact, which may be lightened by a liberal infusion of sensuous diversion. All Florence yesterday was taking its holiday in a natural, placid fashion, which seemed to make its own temper an affair quite independent of the splendor of the compensation decreed on a higher line to the weariness of its legs. That the *corso* was stupid or lively was its own glory or shame. Common Florence, on the narrow footways, pressed against the houses, obeyed a natural need in looking about complacently, patiently, gently, and never pushing, nor trampling, nor swearing, nor staggering. This liberal margin for festivals in Italy gives the masses a sort of man-of-the-world urbanity in taking their pleasure.

Meanwhile it occurs to me that by a remote New England fireside an unsophisticated young person of either sex is reading in an old volume of travels or an old romantic tale an account of that glittering festival called the Carnival, celebrated in old Catholic lands. Across the page swims a vision of sculptured palace fronts, draped in crimson and gold and shining in a southern sun; of a motley train of maskers, sweeping on in voluptuous confusion and pelting each other with nosegays and love-letters. Into the quiet room, quenching the rhythm of the Yankee pendulum, there floats an uproar of delighted voices, a medley of stirring foreign sounds, an echo of far-heard music of a strangely alien cadence. But the dusk is falling, and the unsophisticated young person closes the book wearily and wanders to the window. The dusk is falling on the beaten snow. Down the road is a white wooden

meeting-house, looking gray among the drifts. The
young person surveys the prospect awhile, and then
wanders back and stares at the fire. The Carnival of
Venice, of Florence, of Rome ; color and costume, romance and rapture ! The young person gazes in the
firelight at the flickering chiaroscuro of the future, dis-
cerns at last the glowing phantasm of opportunity, and
determines, with a heart-beat, to go and see it all —
twenty years hence !

II.

A COUPLE of days since, driving to Fiesole, we came
back by the castle of Vincigliata. The afternoon was
lovely ; and, though there is as yet (February 10) no
visible revival of vegetation, the air was full of a vague
vernal perfume, and the warm colors of the hills and
the yellow western sunlight flooding the plain seemed
to contain the promise of Nature's return to grace. It
is true that above the distant pale blue gorge of Vallom-
brosa the mountain-line was tipped with snow ; but the
liberated soul of Spring was abroad, nevertheless. The
view from Fiesole seems vaster and richer with each
visit. The hollow in which Florence lies, and which
from below seems deep and contracted, opens out into
an immense and generous valley and leads away the
eye into a hundred gradations of distance. Florence
lay amid her checkered fields and gardens, with as
many towers and spires as a chess-board half cleared.
The domes and towers were washed over with a faint
blue mist. The scattered columns of smoke, interfused

with the sinking sunlight, hung over them like streamers and pennons of silver gauze; and the Arno, twisting and curling and glittering here and there, looked like a serpent, cross-striped with silver.

Vincigliata is a product of the millions, the leisure, and the eccentricity, I suppose people say, of an English gentleman — Mr. Temple Leader. His name should be commemorated. You reach the castle from Fiesole by a narrow road, returning toward Florence by a romantic detour through the hills, and passing nothing on its way save thin plantations of cypress and cedar. Upward of twenty years ago, I believe, this gentleman took a fancy to the crumbling shell of a mediæval fortress on a breezy hill-top overlooking the Val d'Arno, and forthwith bought it and began to "restore" it. I do not know what the original ruin cost; but in the dusky courts and chambers of the present elaborate structure this valiant archæologist must have buried a fortune. He has, however, the compensation of feeling that he has erected a monument which, if it is never to stand a feudal siege, may challenge, at least, the keenest modern criticism. It is a disinterested work of art and really a triumph of æsthetic culture. The author has reproduced with minute accuracy a sturdy home-fortress of the fourteenth century, and has kept throughout such rigid terms with his model that the place is literally uninhabitable to degenerate moderns. It is simply a massive fac-simile, an elegant museum of domestic architecture, perched on a spur of the Apennines. The place is most politely shown. There is a charming cloister, painted with extremely clever archaic frescos, celebrating the deeds of the founders of the castle — most picturesque and characteristic and mediæval, but desperately frigid and unavailable. There is a beautiful castle court, with the embattled tower climbing into the blue, far above it; and a spacious loggia, with rugged medallions and mild-hued Luca della Robbias fastened unevenly into the walls. But the apartments are the great success, and each of them is as good a " reconstruction" as a tale of Walter Scott; or, to speak frankly, a much better one. They are all low-beamed and vaulted, stone-paved, decorated in grave colors, and lighted from narrow, deeply recessed windows, through small, leaden-ringed plates of opaque glass.

The details are most ingenious and picturesque, and the in-door atmosphere of mediævalism most forcibly revived. It was a terribly cold and dusky atmosphere, apparently, and helps to account for many of the peculiarities of mediæval manners. There are oaken benches round the room, of about six inches in depth; and grim fauteuils of wrought leather, illustrating the suppressed transitions which, as George Eliot says, unite all contrasts — offering a visible link between the modern conceptions of torture and of luxury. There are no fireplaces anywhere but in the kitchen, where a couple of sentry-boxes are inserted on either side of the great hooded chimney-piece, into which people might creep and take their turn at being toasted and smoked. I doubt whether this scarcity of fireplaces was general in feudal castles; but it is a happy stroke in the representation of an Italian dwelling of any period. It proves that the graceful fiction that Italy

is a winterless clime flourished for some time before
being refuted by grumbling tourists. And yet amid
this cold comfort you feel the incongruous presence of
a constant intuitive regard for beauty. The shapely
spring of the vaulted ceilings; the richly figured walls,
coarse and hard in substance as they are; the charming
shapes of the great platters and flagons in the deep
recesses of the quaintly carved black dressers; the
wandering hand of ornament, as it were, playing here
and there for its own diversion in unlighted corners —
these things prove that the unlettered gentlefolk of the
Dark Ages had finer needs than the mere need for
blows and beef and beer.

And yet, somehow, with what dim, unillumined vision one fancies them passing their heavy eyes over
such slender household beguilements! These crepuscular chambers at Vincigliata are a mystery and a
challenge; they seem the mere propounding of a riddle. You long, as you wander through them, turning
up your coat-collar and wondering whether ghosts can
catch bronchitis, to answer it with some positive
vision of what people did there, how they looked and
talked and carried themselves, how they took their
pains and pleasures, how they counted off the hours.
Deadly ennui seems to ooze out of the stones and hang
in clouds in the brown corners. No wonder men relished a fight and panted for a fray. "Skull-smashers"
were sweet, ears ringing with pain and ribs cracking in
a tussle were soothing music, compared with the cruel
quietude of the dim-windowed castle. When they
came back, I am sure they slept a good deal and eased

their dislocated bones on those meagre oaken ledges. Then they woke up and turned about to the table and ate their portion of roasted sheep. They shouted at each other across the board, and flung the wooden plates at the serving-men. They jostled and hustled and hooted and bragged; and then, after gorging and boozing and easing their doublets, they squared their elbows one by one on the greasy table, and buried their scarred foreheads and dreamed of a good gallop after flying foes. And the women? They must have been strangely simple — simpler far than any moral archæ-ologist can show us in a learned restoration. Of course, their simplicity had its graces and devices; but one thinks with a sigh that, as the poor things turned away with patient looks from the viewless windows to the same, same looming figures on the dusky walls, they had not even the consolation of knowing that just this attitude and movement, set off by their peaked coifs, their falling sleeves, their heavy twisted trains, would be pronounced "picturesque" by an appreciative future.

There are moods in which one feels the impulse to enter a tacit protest against too generous a patronage of pure æsthetics, in this starving and sinning world. One turns half away, musingly, from certain beautiful useless things. But the healthier state of mind, surely, is to lay no tax on any really intelligent manifesta-tion of the curious and exquisite. Intelligence hangs together essentially, all along the line; it only needs time to make, as it were, its connections. This elaborate piece of imitation has no superficial use; but, even if it were less complete, less successful, less brilliant, I should feel a reflective kindness for it. So handsome a piece of work is its own justification; it belongs to the heroics of culture.

III.

I SHOULD call the collection of pictures at the Pitti Palace splendid, rather than interesting. After walking through it once or twice, you catch the key in which it is pitched — you know what you are likely to find on closer examination. You feel that you will find none of the works of the uncompromising period, as one may say; nothing from the half-groping geniuses of the early time, whose coloring was sometimes harsh and their outlines sometimes angular. I am ignorant of the principle on which the pictures were originally gathered and of the æsthetic creed of the princes who chiefly selected them. A princely creed I should roughly call it — the creed of people who believed in things presenting a fine face to society; who esteemed brilliant results, rather than curious processes, and would have hardly cared more to admit into their collection a work by one of the laborious precursors of the full efflorescence than to see a bucket and broom left standing in a state saloon. The gallery contains in literal fact some eight or ten paintings of the early Tuscan School — notably two admirable specimens of Filippo Lippi and one of the frequent circular pictures of the great Botticelli — a Madonna, chilled with tragic prescience, laying a pale cheek against that of a blighted Infant. Such a melancholy mother as this of

Botticelli would have strangled her baby in its cradle to rescue it from the future. But of Botticelli there is much to say. One of the Filippo Lippis is perhaps his masterpiece — a Madonna in a small rose-garden (such a "flowery close" as Mr. William Morris writes of), leaning over an Infant, who kicks his little human heels on the grass, while half a dozen little curly-pated angels gather about him, looking back over their shoulders with the naïveté of children in tableaux vivants, and one of them drops an armful of gathered roses one by one upon the baby. The delightful earthly innocence of these winged youngsters is quite inexpressible. Their heads are twisted about toward the spectator, as if they were playing at leap-frog and were expecting a companion to come and take a jump. Never did intellectual simplicity attempt with greater success to depict simplicity. But these three fine works are hung over the tops of doors, in a dark back room — the bucket and broom are thrust behind a curtain. It seems to me, nevertheless, that a fine Filippo Lippi is good enough company for an Allori or a Cigoli, and that that too deeply sentient Virgin of Botticelli might happily balance the flower-like irresponsibility of Raphael's Madonna of the Chair.

Taking the Pitti collection, however, simply for what it pretends to be, how impressive it is, how sumptuous, how truly grand-ducal! It is chiefly official art, as one may say; but it presents the fine side of the type — the brilliancy, the facility, the amplitude, the sovereignty of good taste. I agree, on the whole, with X——, and with what he recently said about his own humor

on these matters; that, having been, on his first acquaintance with pictures, nothing if not critical, and
thought the lesson was incomplete and the opportunity
slighted if he left a gallery without a headache, he had
come, as he grew older, to regard them more as an entertainment and less as a solemnity, and to remind
himself that, after all, it is the privilege of art to make
us relish the human mind, and not to make us patronize it. We do, in fact, as we grow older, un-
string the critical bow a little and strike a truce with
invidious comparisons. We work off the juvenile impulse to heated partisanship, and discover that one
spontaneous producer is not different enough from
another to keep the all-knowing Fates from smiling
over our loves and our aversions. We perceive a certain human solidarity in all cultivated effort, and are
conscious of a growing urbanity in our judgments — a
sort of man-of-the-world disposition to take the joke
for what it is worth, as it passes. We have, in short,
less of a quarrel with the masters we don't delight in,
and less of an impulse to renew the oath of eternal
friendship with those in whom, in more zealous days,
we fancied that we discovered peculiar meanings.
The meanings no longer seem quite so peculiar. Since
then we have discovered a few in the depths of our
own genius which are not sensibly less valuable.

And yet it must be added that all this depends vastly
upon one's mood — as a traveller's impressions do, generally, to a degree which those who give them to the
world would do well more explicitly to declare. We
have our moods of mental expansion and contraction,

and yet while we follow the traveller's trade we go about
gazing and judging with unadjusted confidence. We
cannot suspend judgment; we must take our notes,
and the notes are florid or crabbed, as the case may be.
A short time ago I spent a week in an ancient city on
a hill-top, in the humor, for which I was not to blame,
which produces crabbed notes. I knew it at the time;
but I could not help it. I went through all the views
of liberal appreciation; I uncapped in all the churches,
and on the crumbling ramparts stared all the views
fairly out of countenance; but my imagination, which
I suppose at bottom had very good reasons of its own
and knew perfectly what it was about, refused to project into the dark old town and upon the yellow hills
that sympathetic glow which forms half the substance
of our genial impressions. So it is that in museums
and palaces we are alternate radicals and conservatives.
On some days we ask to be entertained; on others,
Ruskin-haunted, to be edified. After a long absence
from the Pitti Palace, I went back there the other
morning, and transferred myself from chair to chair in
the great golden-roofed saloons (the chairs are all gilded and covered with faded silk), in the humor to be
diverted, at any price. I need not mention the things
that diverted me. I yawn now when I think of some
of them. But an artist, for instance, to whom my
kindlier judgment has made permanent concessions is
that charming Andrea del Sarto. When I first knew
him, in my cold youth, I used to say without mincing
that I did n't like him. *Cet âge est sans pitié.* The
fine, harmonious, melancholy, pleasing painter! He

has a dozen faults, and if you insist upon your rights,
the conclusive word you use about him will be the word
weak. But if you are a generous soul you will utter it
low — low as the mild, grave tone of his own impressive
coloring. He is monotonous, narrow, incomplete; he
has but a dozen different figures, and but two or three
ways of distributing them; he seems able to utter but
half his thought, and his pictures lack, apparently, some
final working-over, which would have made them
stronger — some process which his impulse failed him
before he could bestow. And yet, in spite of these
limitations, his genius is both itself of the great pattern
and lighted by the atmosphere of a great period. Three
gifts he had largely : an instinctive, unaffected, unerring grace; an admirable color (in a limited range);
and, best of all, the look of moral agitation. Whether
he had the thing or not, or in what measure, I cannot
say; but he certainly communicates the tendency. Before his handsome, vague-browed Madonnas; the mild,
robust young saints who kneel in his foregrounds and
look round at you with a rich simplicity which seems
to say that, though in the picture, they are not of it,
but of your own sentient life of commingled love and
weariness; the stately apostles, with comely heads and
harmonious draperies, who gaze up at the high-seated
Virgin like early astronomers at a newly seen star —
there comes to you a kind of dusky reflection of the
painter's moral experience. Morality, perhaps, is too
pedantic a name for Andrea del Sarto's luxurious
gravity. I should be careful how I bestow the word,
among all these zealous votaries of the serene delight

of the eyes; but his idea seems always somehow to cast
a vague shadow, and in the shadow you feel the chill
of moral suffering. Did the Lippis suffer, father or
son ? Did Raphael suffer? Did Titian ? Did Rubens
suffer ? I doubt it. And I note that our poor second-
rate Andrea del Sarto has an element of interest absent
from a number of stronger talents.

Interspaced with him at the Pitti hang the stronger
and the weaker talents in splendid abundance. Raphael is there, strong in portraiture — easy, various, boun-
tiful genius that he was — and (strong here is not the
word, but) happy beyond the common dream in his beautiful Madonna of the Chair. The general instinct of
posterity seems to have been to treat this lovely picture
as a kind of semi-sacred, an almost miraculous, manifes-
tation. People stand in a worshipful silence before it,
as they would before a taper-studded shrine. Suspend,
in imagination, on one side of it the solid, realistic,
unidealized portrait of Leo the Tenth (which hangs in
another room), and transport to the other the fresco of
the School of Athens from the Vatican, and then reflect
that these were three diverse fancies of a single youthful, amiable genius, and you 'll admit that that genius
was one of the rarest the world has held. X—— has
a phrase that he "does n't care for Raphael"; but he
confesses, when pressed, that he was a most remarkable
young man.

Titian has a dozen portraits, of unequal interest. I
never particularly noticed till lately (it is very ill-hung)
that portentous image of the Emperor Charles the
Fifth. He was a burlier, more imposing personage

than I supposed, and in his great puffed sleeves and
gold chains and full-skirted overdress he looks like
a monarch whose tread might sometimes have been
inconveniently resonant. But the *purpose* to have his
way and work his will is there—the great stomach for
divine right, the old monarchical temperament. The
great Titian, in portraiture, however, remains that formidable young man in black, with the small, compact
head, the delicate nose, and the irascible blue eye.
Who was he ? What was he ? "*Ritratto virile*" is
all the catalogue is able to call the picture. "Virile!" I should think it was. You may weave
what romance you please about it; but a romance
your conjecture must be. Handsome, clever, defiant,
passionate, dangerous, it was not his own fault if he
had no adventures. He was a gentleman and a war-
rior, and his adventures balanced between camp and
court. I imagine him the young orphan of a noble
house, about to come into mortgaged estates. I should
not have cared to be his guardian, bound to paternal
admonitions once a month as to his precocious transac-
tions with the Jews, or his scandalous abduction from
her convent of the Contessina So-and-So.

The Pitti Gallery contains none of Titian's golden-
toned groups; but it boasts a lovely composition by
Paul Veronese, the dealer in silver hues — a Baptism
of Christ. W—— said the other day, that it was the
picture he most enjoyed, and surely painting seems
here to be frankly an interpreter and ministrant of joy.
The picture bedims and enfeebles its neighbors. I
doubt whether painting, as such, can go further. It is

simply that here at last the art stands complete. The early Tuscans, as well as Leonardo, as Raphael, as Michael, saw the great spectacle in beautiful, sharp-edged elements and parts. The great Venetians felt its indissoluble unity and perceived that form and color and earth and air were equal members of every possible subject; and beneath their magical touch the hard outlines melted together and the blank intervals bloomed with meaning. In this beautiful Paul Veronese everything is part of the charm — the atmosphere as well as the figures, the look of radiant morning in the white-streaked sky as well as the beautiful human limbs, the cloth of Venetian purple about the loins of the Christ as well as the eloquent humility of his attitude. The relation to Nature of the other Italian schools differs from that of the Venetians as courtship — even ardent courtship — differs from marriage.

Was Rubens lawfully married to Nature, or did he merely keep up the most unregulated of flirtations? Three or four of his great carnal cataracts ornament the walls of the Pitti. If the union was really solemnized it must be said that the ménage was at best a stormy one. He is a strangely irresponsible jumble of the true and the false. He paints a full flesh surface that radiates and palpitates with illusion, and into the midst of it he thrusts a mouth, a nose, an eye, which you would call your latest-born a blockhead for perpetrating. But if you want breathless vigor, hit or miss, taking your ticket at a venture as in a carnival raffle or on an English railway

IV.

I WENT the other day to the suppressed Convent of
San Marco, paid my franc at the profane little wicket
which creaks away at the door (no less than six custo-
dians, apparently, are needed to turn it, as if it had
a recusant conscience), passed along the bright, still
cloister, and went in to look at Fra Angelico's " Crucifixion," in that dusky chamber in the basement. I
looked long; one can hardly do otherwise. The fresco
deals with pathos on the grand scale, and after per-
ceiving its meaning you feel as little at liberty to
go away abruptly as you would to leave church during
the sermon. You may be as little of a formal Christian as Fra Angelico was much of one; it yet seems a
kind of intellectual duty to let so sincere a present-
ment of the Christian story work its utmost purpose
on your mind. The three crosses rise high against a
strange crimson sky, which deepens mysteriously the
tragic expression of the scene; but I confess to my
inability to determine whether this lurid background
is an intentional bit of picturesqueness) or simply a
happy corruption of the original color. In the former
case it is tragedy quite in the modern taste. Between
the crosses, in no great composition, are scattered the
most exemplary saints — kneeling, praying, weeping,
pitying, worshipping. The swoon of the Madonna is
depicted at the left; and this gives the gathered saints
a strange appearance of being historically present at
the actual scene. Everything is so real that you feel
a vague impatience, and almost ask yourself how it was

that amid the army of his consecrated servants the
Lord was permitted to suffer ?   On reflection, you see
that the painter's design, in so far as it is very definite,
has been simply to offer a great representation of Pity.
This was the emotion presumably most familiar to his
own benignant spirit, and his colors here seem dissolved
in softly-falling tears.   Of this simple yearning compassion the figures are all admirably expressive.   No
later painter learned to render with more masterly truth
than Fra Angelico a single, concentrated, spiritual emotion.   Immured in his quiet convent, he apparently
never received an intelligible impression of evil ; and
his conception of human life was a tender sense of per-
petually loving and being loved.   But how, immured
in his quiet convent, away from the streets and the
studios, did he become that genuine, finished, perfectly
professional painter ?   No one is less of a mere pietistic
amateur.   His range was broad, from this really heroic
fresco to the little trumpeting seraphs, in their opaline
robes, enamelled, as it were, on the gold margins of his
pictures.

I sat out the sermon, and departed, I hope, with the
gentle preacher's blessing.   I went into the smaller
refectory, near by, to refresh my memory of the beautiful Last Supper of Domenico Ghirlandaio.   It would
be putting things roughly to say that I felt as if I had
adjourned from a sermon to a comedy ; but one may
certainly say that Ghirlandaio's theme, as contrasted
with the blessed Angelico's, was the dramatic, spectacular side of human life.   How keenly he observed
it and how richly he rendered it, the world about him

13 *

of color and costume, of handsome heads and pictorial
groupings! In his admirable school there is no painter
one enjoys more largely and irresponsibly. Lippo
Lippi is simpler, quainter, more frankly expressive;
but one looks at him with a remnant of the sympathetic discomfort provoked by all those early masters
whose conceptions were still a trifle too large for their
means. The pictorial vision in their minds seems to
stretch and strain their undeveloped skill almost to a
sense of pain. But in Ghirlandaio the skill and the
imagination are equal, and he gives us a delightful
impression of enjoying his own resources. Of all the
painters of his time he seems to us the most modern.
He enjoyed a crimson mantle spreading and tumbling
in curious folds and embroidered with needlework of
gold, just as he enjoyed a handsome, well-rounded
head, with vigorous, dusky locks, profiled in courteous
adoration. He enjoyed, in short, the various reality of
things, and he had the good fortune to live at a time
when reality was sumptuous and picturesque. He was
not especially addicted to giving spiritual hints; and
yet how hard and meagre they seem, the professed and
finished realists of our own day, ungraced by that
spiritual candor which makes half the richness of Ghirlandaio! The Last Supper at San Marco is an excellent
example of the natural reverence of an artist of that
time with whom reverence was not, as one may say, a
specialty. The main idea with him has been the variety, the picturesqueness, the material charm of the
scene, which finds expression, with irrepressible generosity, in the accessories of the background. Instinc-

tively he imagines an opulent garden — imagines it
with a good faith which quite tides him over the reflection that Christ and his disciples were poor men
and unused to sit at meat in palaces. Great full-
fruited orange-trees peep over the wall before which
the table is spread, strange birds fly through the air,
and a peacock perches on the edge of the partition and
looks down on the sacred repast. It is striking that,
without any at all intense religious purpose, the figures,
in their varied naturalness, have a dignity and sweetness of attitude which admits of numberless reverential
constructions. I should call all this the happy tact of
an unperturbed faith.

On the staircase which leads up to the little
painted cells of the Beato Angelico I suddenly faltered
and paused. Somehow I had grown averse to the
intenser zeal of the Monk of Fiesole. I wanted no
more of him that day. I wanted no more macerated
friars and spear-gashed sides. Ghirlandaio's elegant
way of telling his story had put me in the humor for
something more largely intelligent, more profanely
beautiful. I departed, walked across the square, and
found it in the Academy, standing in a certain spot
and looking up at a certain high-hung picture. It is
difficult to speak adequately, perhaps even intelligibly,
of Sandro Botticelli. An accomplished critic (Mr. Pater,
in his "Studies on the History of the Renaissance")
has lately done so, on the whole more eloquently than
conclusively. He was a most peculiar genius, and of all
the multitudinous masters of his group incomparably
the most interesting, the one who detains and perplexes

and fascinates you most.   Putting aside whatever
seems too recondite in Mr. Pater's interpretation, it is
evidence of the painter's power that he has furnished
so fastidious a critic so inspiring a theme.   A rigidly
sufficient account of his genius is that his own imagination was active, that his fancy was audacious and
adventurous.   Alone among the painters of his time,
he seems to me to possess *invention*.   The glow and
thrill of expanding observation — this was the feeling
that sent his comrades to their easels; but Botticelli
had a faculty which loved to play tricks with the
actual, to sport and wander and explore on its own
account.   These tricks are sometimes so ingenious and
so lovely that it would be easy to talk nonsense about
them.   I hope it is not nonsense, however, to say that
the picture to which I just alluded (the " Coronation of
the Virgin," with a group of life-sized saints below and
a garland of miniature angels above) is one of the supremely beautiful productions of the human mind.   It
is hung so high that you need a good glass to see it;
to say nothing of the unprecedented delicacy of the
work.   The lower half of the picture is of moderate
interest; but the dance of hand-clasped angels round
the heavenly couple above has a beauty newly exhaled
from the deepest sources of inspiration.   Their perfect
little hands are locked with ineffable elegance; their
blowing robes are tossed into folds of which each line
is a study; their charming feet have the relief of the
most delicate sculpture.   But, as I said before, of Botticelli there is much, too much to say.   Only add to this
illimitable grace of design that his adventurous fancy

goes a-Maying, not on wanton errands of its own, but on those of some mystic superstition which trembles forever in his heart.

V.

THE more I look at the old Florentine domestic architecture the more I like it — that of the great houses, at least; and if I ever am able to build a stately dwelling for myself, I don't see how in conscience I can build it different from these. They are sombre and frowning, and look a trifle more as if they were meant to keep people out than to let them in; but I know no buildings more expressive of domiciliary dignity and security, with less of obtrusive and insubstantial pretension. They are impressively handsome, and yet they contrive to be so with the narrowest means. I don't say at the smallest cost; that's another matter. There is money buried in the thick walls and diffused through the echoing excess of space. The merchant nobles of the fifteenth century, I suppose, had money enough, though the present bearers of their names are glad to let out their palaces in suites of apartments which are occupied by the commercial aristocracy of another republic. I have been told of fine old mouldering chambers of which I might enjoy possession for a sum not worth mentioning. I am afraid that in the depths of these stern-faced old houses there is a good deal of dusky discomfort, and I speak now simply of the stern faces themselves as you can see them from the street; see them ranged cheek to cheek in the gray historic light of the Via dei Bardi, the Via Maggio, the Via degli Albizzi. The stern expression depends on a few simple features : on the great iron-caged windows of the rough-hewn basement; on the noble stretch of space between the summit of one high, round-topped window and the bottom of that above; on the high-hung sculptured shield at the angle of the house; on the flat, far-projecting roof; and, finally, on the magnificent tallness of the whole building, which so dwarfs our modern attempts at size. The finest of these Florentine palaces are, I imagine, the tallest dwelling-houses in Europe. Some of those of M. Haussmann, in Paris, may climb very nearly as high; but there is all the difference in the world between the impressiveness of a building which takes breath, as it were, some six or seven times, from story to story, and of one which erects itself to an equal height in three long-drawn pulsations. When a house is ten windows wide and the drawing-room floor is as high as a chapel, it can afford to have but three stories. The spaciousness of some of these ancient drawing-rooms savors almost of the ludicrous. The "family circle," gathered anywhere within speaking distance, must look like a group of pilgrims encamped in the desert on a little oasis of carpet. Mrs. G——, living at the top of a house in that dusky, tortuous old Borgo Pinti, initiated me the other evening most good-naturedly, lamp in hand, into the far-spreading mysteries of her apartment. Such quarters seem a translation into space of the old-fashioned idea of leisure. Leisure and "room" have been passing out of our manners together; but here and there, being of stouter structure, the latter lingers and survives.

Here and there, indeed, in this blessed Italy, reluctantly modern in spite alike of boasts and lamentations, it seems to have been preserved for curiosity's and fancy's sake, with a vague, sweet odor of the embalmer's spices about it. I went the other morning to the Corsini Palace. The Corsinis, obviously, are great people. One of the ornaments of Rome is their great white-faced palace in the dark Trastevere, and its voluminous gallery, none the less picturesque for the pictures all being poor. Here they have a palace on the Arno, with another large, handsome, respectable, uninteresting collection. It contains three or four fine pictures by early Florentines. It was not especially for the pictures that I went, however; and certainly not for the pictures that I stayed. I was in the same humor as X—— when we walked the other day through the beautiful residental apartments of the Pitti Palace. "I suppose I care for nature," he said. "I know there have been times when I have thought that the greatest pleasure in life was to lie under a tree and gaze away at blue hills. But just now I had rather lie on that faded sea-green satin sofa and gaze down through the open door at that retreating vista of gilded, deserted, haunted chambers. In other words, I prefer a good 'interior' to a good landscape. It's a more concentrated pleasure. I like fine old rooms, that have been lived in in a large way. I like the musty upholstery, the antiquated knick-knacks, the view out of the tall, deep-embrasured windows at garden cypresses rocking against a gray sky. If you don't know why, I can't tell you." It seemed to me at the Palazzo Corsini that I did know why. In places that have been lived in so long and so much and in such a large way, as my friend said — that is, under social conditions so complex and, to an American sense, so curious — the past seems to have left a sensible deposit, an aroma, an atmosphere. This ghostly presence tells you no secrets, but it prompts you to try and guess a few. What has been done and said here through so many years, what has been ventured or suffered, what has been dreamed or despaired of? Guess the riddle if you can, or if you think it worth your ingenuity. The rooms at the Palazzo Corsini suggest none but comfortable memories. One of them, indeed, seemed to me such a tranquil perfection of a room, that I lounged there until the old custodian came shuffling back to see whether, possibly, I was trying to conceal a Caravaggio about my person — a great crimson-draped drawing-room of the amplest and yet most charming proportions, with its walls hung with large dark pictures, its great concave ceiling frescoed and moulded with dusky richness, and half a dozen south windows looking out on the Arno, whose swift yellow tide sends up the light in a sort of cheerful flicker. I believe that, in my relish for this fine combination, I uttered a monstrous folly — some momentary willingness to be maimed or crippled all my days if I might pass them in such a room as that. In fact, half the pleasure of inhabiting this spacious saloon would be that of using one's legs, of strolling

up and down past the windows, one by one, and
making desultory journeys from station to station and
corner to corner.   Near by is a colossal ball-room,
domed and pilastered like a Renaissance cathedral,
and superabundantly decorated with marble effigies,
all yellow and gray with the years.

VI.

IN the Carthusian Monastery, outside the Roman
Gate, mutilated and profaned though it is, one may
still gather a grateful sense of old Catholicism and old
Italy.   The road to it is ugly, being encumbered with
vulgar wagons and fringed with tenements, suggestive
of an Irish-American suburb.   Your interest begins as
you come in sight of the convent, perched on its little
mountain and lifting against the sky, around the bell-
tower of its gorgeous chapel, a kind of coronet of clustered cells.   You make your way into the lower gate,
through a clamoring press of deformed beggars, thrusting at you their stumps of limbs, and climb the steep
hillside, through a shabby plantation, which it is proper
to fancy was better tended in the monkish time.   The
monks are not totally abolished, the government having the grace to await the natural extinction of the·
half-dozen old brothers who remain, and who shuffle
doggedly about the cloisters, looking, with their white
robes and their pale, blank old faces, like anticipatory
ghosts of their future selves.   A prosaic, profane old
man, in a coat and trousers, serves you, however, as

T

custodian. The melancholy friars have not even the
privilege of doing you the honors, as we may say, of
their dishonor. One must imagine the pathetic effect
of their silent pointings to this and that conventual
treasure, emphasized by the feeling that such pointings
were narrowly numbered. The convent is very vast
and irregular, and full of that picturesqueness of
detail which one notes as one lingers and passes, but
which in Italy the overburdened memory learns to resolve into broadly general images. I rather deplore its
position, at the gates of a bustling city. It ought to be
lodged in some lonely fold of the Apennines. And yet
to look out from the shady porch of one of the quiet
cells upon the teeming vale of the Arno and the clustered towers of Florence must have deepened the sense
of monastic quietude.

The chapel, or rather the church, which is of great
proportions and designed by Andrea Orcagna, the
primitive painter, is admirably handsome. Its massive
cincture of black sculptured stalls, its dusky Gothic
roof, its high-hung, deep-toned pictures, and its superb
pavement of verd-antique and dark red marble, polished
into glassy lights, must throw the white-robed figures
of the gathered friars into singularly picturesque relief.
All this luxury of worship has nowhere such value as
in the chapels of monasteries, where one finds it contrasted with the ascetic ménage of the worshippers. The
paintings and gildings of their church, the gem-bright
marbles and fantastic carvings, are really but the monastic tribute to sensuous delight — an imperious need,
for which the Catholic Church has officiously opened

the door. One smiles when one thinks how largely an ardent imagination, if it makes the most of its opportunities, may gratify this need under the cover of devotion. Nothing is too base, too hard, too sordid for real humility; nothing is too elegant, too suggestive, too caressing for the exaltation of faith. The meaner the convent cell the richer the convent chapel. Out of poverty and solitude, inanition and cold, your honest friar may rise at his will into a supreme perception of luxury.

There are various dusky subterranean oratories, where a number of bad pictures contend faintly with the friendly gloom. Two or three of these funereal vaults, however, deserve mention. In one of them, side by side, sculptured by Donatello in low relief, lie the white marble effigies of three members of the Accaiuoli family, who founded the convent, in the thirteenth century. In another, on his back, on the pavement, lies a grim old bishop of the same stout race, by the same honest craftsman. Terribly grim he is, and scowling as if in his stony sleep he still dreamed of his hates and his hard ambitions. Last and best, in another low chapel, with the trodden pavement for its bed, lies a magnificent image of a later bishop — Leonardo Buonafede, who died in 1545, and owes his monument to Francesco di San Gallo. I have seen little from this artist's hand; but it was evidently a cunning one. His model here was a very sturdy old prelate, but, I should say, a very genial old man. The sculptor has respected his monumental ugliness; but he has suffused it with a singular homely charm — a look of thankful physical comfort in the privilege of paradise. All these figures have an inimitable reality, and their lifelike marble seems such an incorruptible incarnation of the genius of the place that you begin to imagine it a sort of perilous audacity in the present government to have begun to pull the establishment down, morally speaking, about their ears. They are lying quiet yet awhile; but, when the last old friar dies and the convent formally lapses, won't they rise on their stiff old legs and hobble out to the gates and thunder forth anathemas before which even a future and more enterprising régime may be disposed to pause?

Out of the great central cloister open the snug little detached dwellings of the absent fathers. When I said just now that the Certosa gives you a glimpse of old Italy, I was thinking of this great pillared quadrangle, lying half in sun and half in shade, with its tangled garden-growth in the centre, surrounding the ancient customary well, and the intense blue sky bending above it, to say nothing of the indispensable old white-robed monk poking about among the lettuce and parsley. We have seen such places before; we have visited them in that divinatory glance which strays away into space for a moment over the top of a suggestive book. I don't quite know whether it's more or less as one's fancy would have it that the monkish cells are no cells at all, but very tidy little *appartements complets*, consisting of a couple of chambers, a sitting-room, and a spacious loggia, projecting out into space from the cliff-like wall of the monastery and sweeping from pole to pole the loveliest view in the world. It's poor work, taking notes on views, and I will let this one pass. The little chambers are terribly cold and musty now. Their odor and atmosphere are such as I used, as a child, to imagine those of the school-room during Saturday and Sunday.

VII.

In the Roman streets, wherever you turn, the façade of a church, in more or less degenerate flamboyance, is the principal feature of the scene; and if, in the absence of purer motives, you are weary with æsthetic peregrination over the Roman cobble-stones, you may turn aside at your pleasure and take a reviving sniff at the pungency of incense. In Florence, one soon observes, the churches are relatively few and the dusky house-fronts more rarely interrupted by specimens of that extraordinary architecture which in Rome passes for sacred. In Florence, in other words, ecclesiasticism is not so cheap a commodity and not dispensed in the same abundance at the street-corners. Heaven forbid I should undervalue the Roman churches. The deep impressions one gathers in them become a substantial part of one's culture. It is a fact, nevertheless, that, after St. Peter's, I know but one really beautiful church in Rome — the enchanting basilica of St. Mary Major. Many have fine things, some are very curious, but as a rule they all lack the dignity of the great Florentine temples. Here, the list being immeasurably shorter and the seed less scattered, the great churches are all beautiful. And yet I went into the Annunziata the

other day and sat there for half an hour because, forsooth, the gildings and the marbles and the frescoed
dome and the great rococo shrine near the door, with
its little black jewelled fetish, reminded me so poig-
nantly of Rome.   Such is the city properly styled
eternal — since it is eternal, at least, as regards the
consciousness of the individual.   One loves its corrup-
tions better than the integrities of other places.

Coming out of the Annunziata, you look past the
bronze statue of the Grand Duke Ferdinand I. (whom
Mr. Browning's heroine used to watch for — in the
poem of "The Statue and the Bust" — from the red
palace near by), and down a street vista of enchanting
picturesqueness.   The street is narrow and dusky and
filled with misty shadows, and at its opposite end rises
the vast bright-colored side of the Cathedral.   It
stands up in very much the same mountainous fashion
as the far-shining mass of the Cathedral of Milan, of
which your first glimpse as you leave your hotel is
generally through another such dark avenue; only that,
if we talk of mountains, the white walls of Milan
must be likened to snow and ice from their base, while
those of the Florence Cathedral may be the image of
some mighty hillside enamelled with blooming flowers.
Within, this great church has a naked majesty which,
though it may fail of its effect at first, becomes after a
while extraordinarily touching.   Originally, it puzzled
me ; now, I have a positive passion for it.   Without, it
is one of the loveliest works of man's hands, and an
overwhelming proof, in the bargain, that when elegance
belittles grandeur you have simply had a bungling artist

Santa Croce within is not only the most beautiful church in Florence, but one of the most beautiful I know. "A trifle naked, if you like," said X——; "but that's what I call architecture." And indeed one is far enough away from the clustering odds and ends borrowed from every art and every province which compose the mere picturesqueneß of the finer Roman churches. The vastness, the lightness, the open spring of the arches, the beautiful shape of the high, narrow choir, the impressiveness without weight and the gravity without gloom — these are my frequent delight. It must be confessed that, between his coarsely imagined statue in the square before the church and his horrible monument inside of it, the author of the Divine Comedy is just hereabouts a rather awkward figure. "Ungrateful Florence," declaims Byron. Ungrateful, indeed! Would that she were, poor Dante might exclaim, as he prays — as he must in a general way a good deal, I should say — to be delivered from his friends.

The interesting church in Florence beyond all others is, of course, Santa Maria Novella, with its great lining of masterly frescos. One must be fair, though bronchitis does lurk in the dusky chapels beside them. Those of Ghirlandaio are beyond all praise; but what I have noted before as to the spirit of his work is only confirmed by these examples. In the choir, where the incense swings and the great chants resound, between the gorgeous colored window and the florid grand altar, it is still the world, the world, he relishes and renders — the beautiful, full-draped, personal world.

VIII.

THE Boboli Gardens are a very charming place.
Yesterday there was another *corso* of the same pattern
as the last, and I wandered away from the crowded
streets, passed in under the great Augean-looking archway of the Pitti Palace, and spent the afternoon strolling among the mouldy statues against their screens
of cypress, and looking down at the clustered towers
of Florence and their background of pale blue hills,
vaguely freckled with white villas. Nothing in the
world is so pleasant as a large, quiet garden within the
precincts of a city. And if the garden is in the Italian
manner, without flowers or forbidden lawns or paths
too neatly swept and shrubs too closely trimmed, but
yet with a certain fanciful formalism giving style to its
shabbiness, and here and there a dusky ilex-walk, and
here and there a dried-up fountain, and everywhere a
bit of mildewed sculpture staring at you from a green
alcove, and there, just in the right place, a grassy amphitheatre, curtained behind with black cypresses and
sloping downward in mossy marble steps — if, I say,
the garden possesses these attractions, and you lounge
there of a soft Sunday afternoon, when a racier spectacle in the streets has made your fellow-loungers few,
and you have nothing about you but deep stillness and
shady vistas, that lead you wonder where, and the old
quaint mixture of nature and art — under these conditions the sweetness of the place becomes strangely
suggestive. The Boboli Gardens are not large. You
wonder how compact little Florence finds room for

them within her walls. But they are scattered, with the happiest natural picturesqueness, over a group of steep undulations between the Pitti Palace and the old city-wall, and the unevenness of the ground doubles their apparent size. What I especially like in them is a kind of solemn, dusky, haunted look, as if the huge, grave palace which adjoins them had flung over them a permanent shadow, charged with its own ponderous memories and regrets. This is spinning one's fancies rather fine, perhaps. Now that I remember, I have always chanced to go to the Boboli Gardens on gray, melancholy days. And yet they contain no bright objects, no parterres, nor pagodas, nor peacocks, nor swans. They have a famous amphitheatre, with mossy steps and a circular wall of evergreens behind, in which little cracked images and vases are niched. Something was done here once — or meant to be done. What was it, dumb statues, who saw it with your blank eyes? Opposite stands the Palace, putting forward two great rectangular arms and looking immensely solemn, with its closed windows and its huge brown blocks of rugged stone. In the space between the wings is a fine old white marble fountain, which never plays. Its dusty idleness completes the general air of abandonment. Chancing upon such a cluster of objects in Italy — glancing at them in a certain light, in a certain mood — one gets a sense of *history* that takes away the breath. Half a dozen generations of Medici have stood at these closed windows, embroidered and brocaded according to their period, and held *fêtes champêtres* and floral games on the greensward, beneath the

14

mouldering hemicycle. And the **Medici** were great people! But what remains of it all now is a mere tone in the air, a vague expression in things, a hint to the questioning fancy. Call it much or little, this is the interest of old places. Time has devoured the doers and their doings; there hovers over the place a perfume of something done. We can build gardens in America, adorned with every device of horticulture; but we unfortunately cannot scatter abroad this strange historic aroma, more exquisite than the rarest roses.

TUSCAN CITIES.

Florence, April 18, 1873.

THE cities I mean are Leghorn, Pisa, Lucca, and Pistoia, among which I have been spending the last few days. The most striking fact as to Leghorn, it must be conceded at the outset, is that, being in Tuscany, it should be so scantily Tuscan. The traveller curious in local color must content himself with the deep blue expanse of the Mediterranean. The streets, away from the docks, are modern, genteel, and rectangular ; Liverpool might acknowledge them if it were not for their fresh-colored stucco. They are the offspring of the new industry which is death to the old idleness. Of picturesque architecture, fruit of the old idleness, or at least of the old leisure, Leghorn is singularly destitute. It has neither a church worth one's attention, nor a municipal palace, nor a museum, and it may claim the distinction, unique in Italy, of being the city of no pictures. In a shabby corner, near the docks, stands a statue of one of the elder grand-dukes of Tuscany, appealing to posterity on grounds now vague — chiefly that of having placed certain Moors under tribute. Four colossal negroes, in very bad bronze, are chained to the base of the monument, which forms with their assistance a suf-

ficiently fantastic group ; but to patronize the arts is
not the line of the Livornese, and, for want of the
slender annuity which would keep its precinct sacred,
this curious memorial is buried in dockyard rubbish.
I must add that, on the other hand, there is a very well-
conditioned and, in attitude and gesture, extremely
realistic statue of Cavour in one of the city squares,
and a couple of togaed effigies of recent grand-dukes in
another. Leghorn is a city of magnificent spaces, and
it was so long a journey from the sidewalk to the
pedestal of these images that I never took the time to
go and read the inscriptions. And in truth, vaguely, I
bore the originals a grudge, and wished to know as little
about them as possible ; for it seemed to me that as
patres patriæ, in their degree, they might have decreed
that the great blank, ochre-faced piazza should be a trifle
less ugly. There is a distinct amenity, however, in any
experience of Italy, and I shall probably in the future
not be above sparing a light regret to several of the
hours of which the one I speak of was composed. I
shall remember a large, cool, bourgeois villa in a garden,
in a noiseless suburb — a middle-aged villa, roomy and
stony, as an Italian villa should be. I shall remember
that, as I sat in the garden, and, looking up from my
book, saw through a gap in the shrubbery the red
house-tiles against the deep blue sky and the gray
underside of the ilex-leaves turned up by the Mediterranean breeze, I had a vague consciousness that I was
not in the Western world.

If you should also wish to have it, you must not
go to Pisa ; and indeed we are most of us forewarned

as to Pisa from an early age. Few of us can have had
a childhood so unblessed by contact with the arts as
that one of its occasional diversions should not have
been a puzzled scrutiny of some alabaster model of the
Leaning Tower, under a glass cover in a back-parlor.
Pisa and its monuments have, in other words, been
industriously vulgarized, but it is astonishing how well
they have survived the process. The charm of Pisa is,
in fact, a charm of a high order, and is but partially
foreshadowed by the famous crookedness of its campanile. I felt it irresistibly and yet almost inexpressibly
the other afternoon, as I made my way to the classic
corner of the city through the warm, drowsy air, which
nervous people come to inhale as a sedative. I was
with an invalid companion, who had had no sleep to
speak of for a fortnight. "Ah! stop the carriage," said
my friend, gaping, as I could feel, deliciously, "in the
shadow of this old slumbering palazzo, and let me sit
here and close my eyes, and taste for an hour of oblivion." Once strolling over the grass, however, out of
which the four marble monuments rise, we awaked re-
sponsively enough to the present hour. Most people
remember the happy remark of tasteful, old-fashioned
Forsyth (who touched a hundred other points in his
" Italy " hardly less happily) as to three beautiful buildings being "fortunate alike in their society and their
solitude." It must be admitted that they are more fortunate in their society than we felt ourselves to be in
ours ; for the scene presented the animated appearance
for which, on any fine spring day, all the choicest haunts
of ancient quietude in Italy are becoming yearly more

remarkable. There were clamorous beggars at all the sculptured portals, and bait for beggars, in abundance, trailing in and out of them under convoy of loquacious cicceroni. I forget just how I apportioned the responsibility of intrusion, for it was not long before fellow-tourists and fellow-countrymen became a vague, deadened, muffled presence, like the dentist's last words when he is giving you ether. They suffered a sort of mystical disintegration in the dense, bright, tranquil atmosphere of the place. The cathedral and its companions are fortunate indeed in everything — fortunate in the spacious angle of the gray old city-wall, which folds about them in their sculptured elegance like a strong protecting arm; fortunate in the broad greensward which stretches from the marble base of cathedral and cemetery to the rugged foot of the rampart; fortunate in the little vagabonds who dot the grass, plucking daisies and exchanging Italian cries; fortunate in the pale-gold tone to which time and the soft sea-damp have mellowed and darkened their marble plates; fortunate, above all, in an indescribable gracefulness of grouping (half hazard, half design) which insures them, in one's memory of things admired, very much the same isolated corner which they occupy in the charming city.

Of the smaller cathedrals of Italy, I know none that I prefer to that of Pisa; none which, on a moderate scale, produces more the impression of a great church. Indeed, it seems externally of such moderate size that one is surprised at its grandeur of effect within. An architect of genius, for all that he works with colossal blocks and cumbrous pillars, is certainly the most cunning of all artists. The façade of the cathedral of Pisa is a small pyramidal screen, covered with delicate carvings and chasings, distributed over a series of short columns upholding narrow arches. It looks like an imitation of goldsmith's work in stone, and the space covered is apparently so small that there seems a fitness in the dainty labor. How it is that on the inner side of this façade the wall should appear to rise to a splendid height, and to support one end of a ceiling as remote in its gilded grandeur, one could almost fancy, as that of St. Peter's ; how it is that the nave should stretch away in such solemn vastness, the shallow transepts carry out the grand impression, and the apse of the choir hollow itself out like a dusky cavern fretted with golden stalactites — all this must be expounded by a keener architectural analyst than I. To sit somewhere against a pillar, where the vista is large and the incidents cluster richly, and vaguely revolve these mysteries without answering them, is the best of one's usual enjoyment of a great church. It takes no great ingenuity to conjecture that a gigantic Byzantine Christ, in mosaic, on the concave roof of the choir, contributes largely to the impressiveness of the place. It has even more of stiff solemnity than is common to works of its school, and it made me wonder more than ever what the human mind could have been when such unlovely forms could satisfy its conception of holiness. There seems something truly pathetic in the fate of these huge mosaic idols, and in the change that has befallen our manner of acceptance of them. It is a singular contrast between the original sublimity of their pretensions and the way in which they flatter that audacious sense of the grotesque which the modern imagination has smuggled even into the appreciation of religious forms. They were meant to be hardly less grand than the Deity itself, but the only part they play now is to mark the further end of our progress in spiritual refinement. The two limits, on this line, are admirably represented in the choir at Pisa, by the flat gilded Christ on the roof and the beautiful specimen of the painter Sodoma on the wall. The latter, a small picture of the Sacrifice of Isaac, is one of the best examples of its exquisite author, and perhaps, as chance has it, the most perfect opposition that could be found to the spirit of the great mosaic. There are many painters more powerful than Sodoma — painters who, like the author of the mosaic, attempted and compassed grandeur; but none possess a more persuasive grace, none more than he have sifted and chastened their conception till it exhales the sweetness of a perfectly distilled perfume.

Of the patient, successive efforts of painting to arrive at the supreme refinement of Sodoma, the Campo Santo hard by offers a most interesting memorial. It presents a long, blank marble wall to the relative profaneness of the cathedral close, but within it is a perfect treasure-house of art. A long quadrangle surrounds an open court, where weeds and wild roses are tangled together, and a sunny stillness seems to rest consentingly, as if Nature had been won to consciousness of the precious relics committed to her. Something in the place reminded me of the collegiate cloisters of Oxford; but it must be confessed that this is a handsome compliment to Oxford. The open arches of the quadrangles of Magdalen and Christ Church are not of mellow Carrara marble, nor do their columns, slim and elegant, seem to frame the unglazed windows of a cathedral. To be buried in the Campo Santo of Pisa you need only be illustrious, and there is liberal allowance both as to the character and degree of your fame. The most obtrusive object in one of the long vistas is a most complicated monument to Madame Catalani, the singer, recently erected by her possibly too-appreciative heirs. The wide pavement is a mosaic of sepulchral slabs, and the walls, below the base of the paling frescos, are incrusted with inscriptions and encumbered with urns and antique sarcophagi. The place is at once a cemetery and a museum, and its especial charm is its strange mixture of the active and the passive, of art and rest, of life and death. Originally its walls were one vast continuity of closely pressed frescos; but now the great capricious scars and stains have come to outnumber the pictures, and the cemetery has grown to be a burial-place of pulverized masterpieces as well as of finished lives. The fragments of painting that remain are, however, fortunately, the best; for one is safe in believing that a host of undimmed neighbors would distract but little from the two great works of Orcagna. Most people know the "Triumph of Death" and the "Last Judgment" from descriptions and engravings; but to measure the possible good faith of imitative art, one must stand there and see the painter's howling potentates dragged into hell in all the vividness of his bright, hard coloring; see his feudal courtiers on their

14 *   U

palfreys, holding their noses at what they are so fast coming to ; see his great Christ, in judgment, refuse forgiveness with a gesture commanding enough to extinguish the idea. The charge that Michael Angelo borrowed his cursing Saviour from this great figure of Orcagna is more valid than most accusations of plagiarism ; but of the two figures, one at least could be spared. For direct, triumphant expressiveness these two superb frescos have probably never been surpassed. The painter aims at no very delicate meanings, but he drives certain gross ones home so effectively that for a parallel to his skill one must look to the stage. Some of his female figures are superb, but they look like creatures of a formidable temperament.

There are charming women, however, on the other side of the cloister — in the beautiful frescos of Benozzo Gozzoli. If Orcagna's work was elected to survive the ravages of time, it is a happy chance that it should be balanced by a group of performances of such a different temper. The contrast is the more striking that, in subject, the work of both painters is narrowly theological. But Benozzo cares, in his theology, for nothing but the story, the scene, and the drama — the chance to pile up palaces and spires in his backgrounds against pale blue skies cross-barred with pearly, fleecy clouds, and to scatter sculptured arches and shady trellises over the front, with every incident of human life going forward lightly and gracefully beneath them. Lightness and grace are the painter's great qualities ; and, if we had to characterize him briefly, we might say that he marks the hithermost limit of unconscious elegance.

His charm is natural fineness; a little more, and we should have refinement — which is a very different thing. Like all *les délicats* of this world, as M. Renan calls them, Benozzo has suffered greatly. The space on the walls he originally covered with his Old Testament stories is immense; but his exquisite handiwork has peeled off by the acre, as one may almost say, and the latter compartments of the series are swallowed up in huge white scars, out of which a helpless head or hand peeps forth, like those of creatures sinking into a quicksand. As for Pisa at large, although it is not exactly what one would call a mouldering city — for it has a certain well-aired cleanness and brightness, even in its supreme tranquillity — it affects the imagination in very much the same way as the Campo Santo. And, in truth, a city so ancient and deeply historic as Pisa is at every step but the burial-ground of a larger life than its present one. The wide, empty streets, the goodly Tuscan palaces (which look as if about all of them there were a genteel private understanding, independent of placards, that they are to be let extremely cheap), the delicious relaxing air, the full-flowing yellow river, the lounging Pisani, smelling, metaphorically, their poppy-flowers, seemed to me all so many admonitions to resignation and oblivion. And this is what I mean by saying that the charm of Pisa (apart from its cluster of monuments) is a charm of a high order. · The architecture is not especially curious; the lions are few; there are no fixed points for stopping and gaping. And yet the impression is profound; the charm is a moral charm. If I were ever to be incurably disappointed

in life ; if I had lost my health, my money, or my
friends ; if I were resigned, forevermore, to pitching
my expectations in a minor key, I think I should go
and live at Pisa. Something in the atmosphere would
assent most soothingly to my mind. Its quietude
would seem something more than a stillness — a hush.
Pisa may be a dull place to live in, but it is a capital
place to wait for death.

Nothing could be more charming than the country
between Pisa and Lucca — unless possibly it is the
country between Lucca and Pistoia. If Pisa is dead
Tuscany, Lucca is Tuscany still living and enjoying,
desiring and intending. The town is a charming mixture of antique picturesqueness and modern animation ;
and not only the town, but the country — the blooming, romantic country which you behold from the
famous promenade on the city-wall. The wall is of
superbly solid brickwork and of extraordinary breadth,
and its summit, planted with goodly trees, and swelling here and there into bastions and little open gardens,
surrounds the city with a circular lounging-place of
extreme picturesqueness. This well-kept, shady, ivy-
grown rampart reminded me of certain mossy corners
of England ; but it looks away to a prospect of more
than English loveliness — a broad, green plain, where
the summer yields a double crop of grain, and a circle
of bright blue mountains speckled with high-hung convents and profiled castles and nestling villas, and traversed by valleys of a deeper and duskier blue. In one
of the deepest and shadiest of these valleys a charming
watering-place is hidden away yet awhile longer from

railways — the baths to which Lucca has given its name. Lucca is pre-eminently a city of churches; ecclesiastical architecture being, indeed, the only one of the arts to which it seems to have given attention. There are picturesque bits of domestic architecture, but no great palaces, and no importunate frequency of pictures. The cathedral, however, is a résumé of the merits of its companions, and is a singularly noble and interesting church. Its peculiar boast is a wonderful inlaid front, on which horses and hounds and hunted beasts are lavishly figured in black marble over a white ground. What I chiefly enjoyed in the gray solemnity of the nave and transepts was the superb effect of certain second-story Gothic arches (those which rest on the pavement are Lombard). These arches are delicate and slender, like those of the cloister at Pisa, and they play their part in the dusky upper air with real sublimity.

At Pistoia there is, of course, a cathedral, and there is nothing unexpected in its being, externally at least, a very picturesque one; in its having a grand campanile at its door, a gaudy baptistery, in alternate layers of black and white marble, across the way, and a stately civic palace on either side. But even if I had the space to do otherwise, I should prefer to speak less of the particular objects of interest at Pistoia than of the pleasure I found it to lounge away in the empty streets the quiet hours of a warm afternoon. To say where I lingered longest would be to tell of a little square before the hospital, out of which you look up at the beautiful frieze in colored earthenware by the brothers Della

Robbia, which runs across the front of the building. It represents the seven orthodox offices of charity, and with its brilliant blues and yellows, and its tender expressiveness, it brightens up amazingly, to the sense and soul, this little gray corner of the mediæval city. Pistoia is still strictly mediæval. How grass-grown it seemed, how drowsy, how full of idle vistas and melancholy nooks! If nothing was supremely wonderful, everything was delicious.

RAVENNA.

Ravenna, June 8, 1874.

I WRITE these lines on a cold Swiss mountain-top,
shut in by an intense white mist from any glimpse
of the under-world of lovely Italy; but as I jotted
down the other day, in the ancient capital of Honorius
and Theodoric, the few notes of which they are composed, I let the original date stand for local color's
sake. Its mere look, as I transcribe it, emits a grateful glow in the midst of the Alpine rawness, and gives
a depressed imagination something tangible to grasp
while awaiting the return of fine weather. For Ravenna was glowing, less than a week since, as I edged
along the narrow strip of shadow binding one side of
the empty, white streets. After a long, chilly spring,
the summer this year descended upon Italy with a sudden jump and a terrible vehemence of purpose. I stole
away from Florence in the night, and even on top of
the Apennines, under the dull starlight and in the
rushing train, one could but sit and pant perspir-
ingly.

At Bologna I found a festa, or rather two festas, a
civil and a religious, going on in mutual mistrust and
disparagement. The civil one was the now legal Italian

holiday of the Statuto; the religious, a jubilee of certain local churches. The latter is observed by the Bolognese parishes in couples, and comes round for each couple but once in ten years — an arrangement by which the faithful at large insure themselves a liberal recurrence of expensive processions. It was not my business to distinguish the sheep from the goats, the prayers from the scoffers; it was enough that, melting together under the scorching sun, they made the picturesque city doubly picturesque. The combination at one point was really dramatic. While a long procession of priests and young virgins in white veils, bearing tapers, was being organized in one of the streets, a review of the King's troops was going on outside of the town. On its return, a large detachment of cavalry passed across the space where the incense was burning, the pictured banners swaying, and the litany being droned, and checked the advance of the little ecclesiastical troop. The long vista of the street, between the porticos, was festooned with garlands and scarlet and tinsel; the robes and crosses and canopies of the priests, the clouds of perfumed smoke, and the white veils of the maidens, were resolved by the hot, bright air into a gorgeous medley of color, across which the mounted soldiers went rattling and flashing like a conquering army trampling over an embassy of propitiation. It was, to tell the truth, the first time an Italian festa had worn to my eyes that warmth of coloring, that pictorial confusion, which tradition promises; and I confess that my eyes found more pleasure in it than they found an hour later in the picturesque on canvas, as one observes it in the Pinacoteca. I found myself scowling most unmercifully at Guido and Domenichino.

For Ravenna, however, I had nothing but smiles — grave, philosophic smiles, such as accord with the tranquil, melancholy interest of the place. I arrived there in the evening, before, even at drowsy Ravenna, the festa of the Statuto had altogether put itself to bed. I immediately strolled forth from the inn, and found it sitting up awhile longer on the piazza, chiefly at the café door, listening to the band of the garrison by the light of a dozen or so of feeble tapers, fastened along the front of the palace of the Government. Before long, however, it had dispersed and departed, and I was left alone with the gray illumination and with an affable citizen, whose testimony as to the manners and customs of Ravenna I had aspired to obtain. I had already observed to sufficient purpose to borrow confidence to suggest deferentially that it was not the liveliest place in the world, and my friend admitted that in fact it was a trifle sluggish. But had I seen the Corso? Without seeing the Corso it was unfair to conclude against Ravenna. The Corso of Ravenna, of a hot summer night, had an air of surprising seclusion and repose. Here and there in an upper, closed window glimmered a light; my companion's footsteps and my own were the only sounds; not a creature was within sight. The suffocating atmosphere helped me to believe for a moment that I was walking in the Italy of Boccaccio, hand-in-hand with the plague, through a city which had lost half its population by pestilence and the other half by flight. I turned back into my inn, profoundly satisfied. This, at last, was old-world dulness of a prime distillation; this, at last, was antiquity, history, repose.

This impression was largely confirmed and enriched on the following day; but it was obliged, at an early stage of my explorations, to give precedence to another — the lively realization, namely, of my imperfect acquaintance with Gibbon and other cognate authorities. At Ravenna, the waiter at the café and the coachman who drives you to the Pine-Forest allude to Galla Placidia and Justinian, as to any attractive topic of the hour; wherever you turn you encounter some peremptory challenge to your knowledge of unfamiliar periods. For myself, I could only attune my intellect vaguely to the intensely historical character of the place — I could only feel that I was breathing an atmosphere of records and relics. I conned my guide-book and looked up at the great mosaics, and then fumbled at poor Murray again for some intenser light on the court of Justinian; but I can imagine that to a visitor more intimate with the originals of the various great almond-eyed mosaic portraits in the vaults of the churches, these extremely curious works of art may have a really formidable interest. I found Ravenna looking by daylight like a vast, straggling, depopulated village. The streets with hardly an exception are grass-grown, and though I walked about all day I failed to perceive a single wheeled vehicle. I remember no shop but the little establishment of an urbane photographer, whose views of the Pine-Forest gave me an irresistible desire to transport myself thither. There was no architecture ·

to speak of; and though there are a great many large domiciles with aristocratic names, they stand cracking and baking in the sun in no very comfortable fashion. The houses for the most part have a half-rustic look; they are low and meagre and shabby and interspersed with high garden walls, over which the long arms of tangled vines hang motionless into the stagnant streets. Here and there in all this dreariness, in some particularly silent and grassy corner, rises an old brick church with a façade more or less spoiled by cheap modernization, and a strange cylindrical campanile, pierced with small arched windows and extremely suggestive of the fifth century. These churches constitute the palpable interest of Ravenna, and their own principal interest, after thirteen centuries of well-intentioned spoliation, resides in their unequalled collection of early Christian mosaics. It is in a certain sense a curiously simple interest, and it leads one's reflections along a narrow and definite channel. There are older churches in Rome, and churches which, looked at as museums, are more variously and richly entertaining; but in Rome you stumble at every step upon some curious pagan memorial, often beautiful enough to lead your thoughts wandering far from the primitive rigidities of the Christian faith.

Ravenna, on the other hand, began with the church, and all its monuments and relics are harmoniously rigid. By the middle of the first century it possessed an exemplary saint — Apollinaris, a disciple of Peter — to whom its two finest churches are dedicated. It was to one of these, jocosely entitled the "new" one, that

I first directed my steps. I lingered outside awhile and looked at the great red, barrel-shaped bell-towers, so rusty, so crumbling, so archaic, and yet so resolute to ring in another century or two, and then went in to the coolness, the shining marble columns, the queer old sculptured slabs and sarcophagi, and the long mosaics, scintillating under the roof, along the wall of the nave. San Apollinare Nuovo, like most of its companions, is a magazine of early Christian odds and ends; of fragments of yellow marble incrusted with quaint sculptured emblems of primitive dogma; great rough troughs, containing the bones of old bishops; episcopal chairs with the marble worn narrow with centuries of pressure from the solid episcopal person; slabs from the fronts of old pulpits, covered with carven hieroglyphics of an almost Egyptian abstruseness — lambs, and stags, and fishes, and beasts of theological affinities even less apparent. Upon all these strange things the strange figures in the great mosaic panorama look down, with colored cheeks and staring eyes, lifelike enough to speak to you and answer your wonderment, and tell you in bad Latin of the decadence that it was in such and such a fashion they believed and worshipped. First, on each side, near the door, are houses and ships and various old landmarks of Ravenna; then begins a long procession, on one side, of twenty-two white-robed virgins and three obsequious magi, terminating in a throne bearing the Madonna and Child, surrounded by four angels; on the other side, of an equal number of male saints (twenty-five, that is) holding crowns in their hands and leading to the Saviour, enthroned between angels of singular expressiveness. What it is these long, slim seraphs express I cannot quite say, but they have an odd, knowing, sidelong look out of the narrow ovals of their eyes which, though not without sweetness, would certainly make me feel like murmuring a defensive prayer or so if I were to find myself alone in the church toward dusk. All this work is of the latter part of the sixth century and brilliantly preserved. The gold backgrounds twinkle as if they had been inserted yesterday, and here and there a figure is executed almost too much in the modern manner to be interesting; for the charm of mosaic work is, to my sense, confined altogether to the infancy of the art. The great Christ, in the series of which I speak, is quite an elaborate picture, and yet he retains enough of the orthodox stiffness to make him impressive in the simpler, elder sense. He is clad in a purple robe, like an emperor, his hair and beard are artfully curled, his eyebrows arched, his complexion brilliant, his whole aspect such a one as the popular mind may have attributed to Honorius or Valentinian. It is all very Byzantine, and yet I found in it much of that interest which is inseparable, to a facile imagination, from all early representations of the Saviour. Practically, they are no more authentic than the more or less plausible inventions of Ary Scheffer and Holman Hunt; but they borrow a certain value, factitious perhaps but irresistible, from the mere fact that they are twelve or thirteen centuries less distant from the original. It is something that this is the way people in the sixth

century imagined Jesus to have looked ; the image is
· by so much the less complex. The great purple-robed
monarch on the wall at Ravenna is at least a very
potent and positive Christ, and the only objection I
have to make to him is that, though in this character
he must have had a full apportionment of divine foreknowledge, he betrays no apprehension of Dr. Chan-
ning and M. Renan. If one's preference lies, for distinctness' sake, between the old narrowness and the
modern complexity, one must admit that the narrowness here has a very grand outline.

I spent the rest of the morning in picturesque tran-
sition between the hot yellow streets and the cool gray
interiors of the churches. The grayness everywhere
was lighted up by the scintillation, on vault and entablature, of mosaics more or less archaic, but always
brilliant and elaborate, and everywhere, too, by the
same keen wonderment that, while centuries had worn
themselves away and empires risen and fallen, these
little cubes of colored glass had stuck in their allotted
places and kept their freshness. I have no space to
enumerate the Ravennese churches one by one, and, to
tell the truth, my memory of them has already become
a sort of hazy confusion and formless meditation.
The total aspect of the place, its sepulchral stillness,
its absorbing perfume of evanescence and decay and
mortality, confounds the distinctions and blurs the
details. The Cathedral, which is very vast and high,
has been excessively modernized, and was being still
more so by a lavish application of tinsel and cotton-
velvet in preparation for the centenary feast of St.

Apollinaris, which befalls next month. Things on this occasion are to be done handsomely, and a fair Ravennese informed me that a single family had contributed three thousand francs towards a month's vesper-music. It seemed to me hereupon that I should like in the August twilight to wander into the quiet nave of San Apollinare, and look up at the great mosaics through the resonance of some fine chanting. I remember distinctly enough, however, the tall basilica of San Vitale, of octagonal shape, like an exchange or custom-house — modelled, I believe, upon St. Sophia at Constantinople. It is very lofty, very solemn, and, as to the choir, densely pictured over on arch and apse with mosaics of the time of Justinian. These are regular pictures, full of movement, gesture, and perspective, and just enough sobered in hue by time to look historic and venerable. In the middle of the church, under the great dome, sat an artist whom I envied, making at an effective angle a picture of the choir and its broken lights, its decorated altar, and its incrusted, twinkling walls. The picture, when it is finished, will hang, I suppose, on the library wall of some person of taste ; but even if it is much better than is probable (I did n't look at it), all his taste will not tell the owner, unless he has been there, in just what a soundless, mouldering, out-of-the-way corner of old Italy it was painted. An even better place for an artist fond of dusky architectural nooks, except that here the dusk is excessive and he would hardly be able to tell his green from his red, is the extraordinary little church of the Santi Nazaro e Celso, otherwise known as the mausoleum of Galla

Placidia. This, perhaps, on the whole, is the most impressive and picturesque spot in Ravenna. It consists of a sort of narrow, low-browed cave shaped like a Latin cross, every inch of which, except the floor, is covered with dense symbolic mosaics. Before you and on each side, through the thick, brown light, loom three enormous barbaric sarcophagi, containing the remains of potentates of the Lower Empire. It is as if history had burrowed under ground to escape from research, and you had fairly run it to earth. On the right lie the ashes of the Emperor Honorius, and in the middle those of his sister, Galla Placidia, a lady who, I believe, had great adventures. On the other side rest the bones of Constantius III. The place is like a little natural grotto lined with glimmering mineral substances, and there is something quite tremendous in being shut up so closely with these three imperial ghosts. The shadow of the great Roman name seems to brood upon the huge sepulchres and abide forever within the narrow walls.

But there are other memories attached to Ravenna beside those of primitive bishops and degenerate emperors. Byron lived here and Dante died here, and the tomb of the one poet and the dwelling of the other are among the regular objects of interest. The grave of Dante, it must be said, is anything but Dantesque, and the whole precinct is disposed with that curious vulgarity of taste which distinguishes most modern Italian tributes to greatness. Dante memorialized in stucco, even in a slumbering corner of Ravenna, is not a satisfactory spectacle. Fortunately, of all poets he

least needs a monument, as he was pre-eminently an
architect in diction, and built himself his memorial in
verses more solid than Cyclopean blocks. If Dante's
tomb is not Dantesque, neither is Byron's house Byronic, being a homely, shabby, two-storied dwelling,
directly on the street, with as little as possible of isolation and mystery. In Byron's time it was an inn, and
it is rather a curious reflection that " Cain " and the
" Vision of Judgment " should have been written at a
hotel. Here is a commanding precedent as to self-
abstraction for tourists who are at once sentimental and
literary. I must declare, indeed, that my acquaintance
with Ravenna considerably increased my esteem for
Byron and helped to renew my faith in the sincerity of
his inspiration. A man so much *de son temps* as Byron was, can have spent two long years in this profoundly stagnant city only by the help of taking a
great deal of disinterested pleasure in his own genius.
He had indeed a notable pastime (the various churches,
by the way, are adorned with monuments of ancestral
Guicciolis); but it is none the less obvious that Ravenna, fifty years ago, would have been an intolerably
dull residence to a foreigner of distinction unprovided
with a real intellectual passion. The hour one spends
with Byron's memory, then, is a charitable one. After
all, one says to one's self, as one turns away from the
grandiloquent little slab in the front of his house and
looks down the deadly provincial vista of the empty,
sunny street, the author of so many superb stanzas
asked less from the world than he gave to it. One of
his diversions was to ride in the Pineta, which, begin-

ning a couple of miles from the city, extends for some twenty-five miles along the sands of the Adriatic. I drove out to it for Byron's sake, and Dante's, and Boccaccio's, all of whom have interwoven it with their fictions, and for that of a possible whiff of coolness from the sea. Between the city and the forest, in the midst of malarious rice-swamps, stands the finest of the Ravennese churches, the stately temple of San Apollinare in Classe. The Emperor Augustus constructed hereabouts a harbor for fleets, which the ages have choked up, and which survives only in the title of this ancient church. Its extreme loneliness makes it doubly impressive. They opened the great doors for me, and let a shaft of heated air go wander up the beautiful nave, between the twenty-four lustrous, pearly columns of cipollino marble, and mount the wide staircase of the choir, and spend itself beneath the mosaics of the vault. I passed a delicious half-hour sitting in this wave of tempered light, looking down the cool, gray avenue of the nave, out of the open door at the vivid green swamps, listening to the melancholy stillness. I rambled for an hour in the Pineta, between the tall, smooth, silvery stems of the pines, beside a creek which led me to the outer edge of the wood and a view of white sails, gleaming and gliding behind the sand-hills. It was infinitely picturesque; but, as the trees stand at wide intervals, and bear far aloft in the blue air but a little parasol of foliage, I suppose that, of a glaring summer day, the forest was only the more Italian for being perfectly shadeless.

THE SPLÜGEN.

I.

I AM puzzled to say just when and where my journey began; but I think I may date it from my discovery that the heat was penetrating into the interior of Milan Cathedral. Then the case seemed serious. The Italian summer was maturing, with inexorable consistency. Florence had become intolerable; the arcades of Bologna were a defence against the sun, but not against the deadly heaviness of the air; Ravenna was plunged in its summer siesta — the sultry sleep from which it never wakes; and Milan lay basking on the Lombard plain, distributing reflected heat from every glittering pinnacle of its famous church. It seemed, for a conscientious traveller, the lowest depth of demoralization to sit all day in an American rocking-chair in the court of a hotel, watching the comings and goings of English families, under the conduct of those English papas who, in sunny climes, as a tribute to an unwonted and possibly perilous sensation, wear their hats sheeted with white draperies so voluminous that they look as if they had chosen this method of carrying the family linen to the wash. But it was too hot to wander and explore; too many scorching pavements

intervened between the Corso and the Brera. So I
adjourned daily for a couple of hours to the cathedral,
and found what I supposed to be an immitigable coolness in its gorgeous, dusky vastness. The Church has
always been, spiritually, a refuge from the world, and
its virtue in this respect was here magnificently sym-
bolized. The world without was glaring, suffocating,
insupportable ; the cathedral within was all shadow
and comfort and delight. It was, I suppose, because it
was so comfortable to sit there uncovered in the cool
air and breathe at one's ease that I was shortly won to
the opinion that Milan Cathedral is, after all, a very
noble piece of Gothic architecture. Noble within I had
never exactly found it, and had indulged the innocent
paradox of saying that there were a dozen scantier
churches that had more real grandeur. But now it
seemed to me to have grandeur enough, in all conscience, and I found an endless interest in its rich picturesqueness. It is not, like St. Peter's, and even more
like the beautiful cathedral of Florence, what one may
call an intellectual church ; it does little toward leading one's musings away into the realm of ideas ; but
its splendid solidity of form, its mysterious accumula-
tions of shadow, the purple radiance of its painted windows, and the dark magnificence of the whole precinct
of the high altar and choir, make it peculiarly gratifying to the sensuous side of one's imagination. I was
struck more than ever with the extraordinary breadth
of the church from transept to transept. That of St.
Peter's may be as great, but the immense colored windows of Milan seem to lengthen the reach of these

great wings. Sitting at the base of one of the stupendous columns — as massive as they need be to sustain
the great city of statues, as one may call it, on the roof
— you may look for hours at a great spectacle, a spectacle which in truth reminds you very much of a huge
piece of scenic mechanism. There are so many odds
and ends of adornment tacked about on the pillars and
dangling from the roof, so many ropes and wires playing their parts in the complex machinery and swinging
from vaults and arches, so many pendent lamps and
tinselled draperies catching the light here and there as
they traverse the dusky upper air, that you may almost
fancy that you are behind the curtain on the stage, before the various loose ends of the scenic architecture
have been shuffled out of sight. I do not exactly know
how to speak of an immense gilded crucifix which from
time immemorial has hung high above the great altar,
at a short distance beneath the roof. The melancholy
fashion in which it caught the afternoon light made it
glitter picturesquely against the deepening shadows of
the choir, and yet seemed to bring out with tragic
force its moral significance. The crucifix in Catholic
churches is repeated with what seems to me trivial frequency. It would be better, surely, in the interest of
reverence, to present it sparingly and only on the most
impressive occasions. But something in the position
of this great high-hung cross of Milan makes it peculiarly commanding, and helps it to say effectually that,
in spite of the color and splendor, the perfumes and
draperies, the place is dedicated to a religion founded
in poverty and obscurity. I found a good deal of in-

terest of another sort in looking at the extremely handsome Milanese women who come to the Cathedral to
their devotions. If the place has a theatrical air, they
certainly might serve as the characters of a romantic
comedy. When I call them extremely handsome I
may possibly let some of them off on easy terms, for
they wear on their heads those black lace Spanish
mantillas which, if they make a beautiful woman irresistibly charming, supply even the plainest with a very
fair imitation of good looks. But, indeed, as a rule, the
ladies of Milan are extraordinarily fair, especially to an
eye accustomed to the stunted stature and meagre contours of the Tuscans ; and, after much respectful observation of them in the streets, the churches, and that long
glass gallery (the Palais Royal of Milan), which offers
to an attentive spectator a résumé of the local physiognomy, I found myself ready to declare that of all the
feminine types I had had the felicity to contemplate,
this one is, as the Italians say, the most sympathetic.
It would take too long to tell in what the sympathy
consists, and in these matters a word to the wise is
sufficient. The most grateful memory one can carry
away from a country one is fond of is an agreeable impression of its women, and I am free to confess that
these lovely Lombards gave an edge to my relish for
Italy of which in other places I had been at best but
fitfully conscious. South of the Apennines, and especially at Rome and Naples, one enters the circle of
Oriental tradition as regards female deportment. Zu-
leikas and Gulnares are very captivating in Byron and
Moore ; but in real life even those modified imitations

of them which hang in dishabille over Roman balconies or sit in toilets hardly less "advantageous," as the French say, in Florentine barouches, have a regrettable absence of what is called style. The lovely penitents of Milan, with their dusky veils and their long fans, who came rustling so far over the vast cathedral pavement to say their prayers, had style in abundance, and a style altogether their own.

My impressions at the first stage of my journey, at which they passed beyond a mood of fervid meditation on the temperature, were of sterner things than picturesque dévotes and painted windows. I lay on a grassy hillside, five thousand feet in the air, inhaling the Alpine atmosphere and gazing away at the Alpine view. There can be no better place for this delicious pastime than that beautiful series of turf-covered ridges which rise out of the chestnut woods of the Lake of Lugano and bear the charming name of Monte Generoso. Here, on a grassy plateau, within an hour's walk of the highest of these carpeted pinnacles, stands an excellent mountain inn, looking down over the dim blue plain of Lombardy and just catching on the hazy horizon the flash of the marble walls of Milan Cathedral. The place is called the Italian Righi, which is an indifferent compliment, unless one particularly emphasizes the adjective. It is lovelier far, to my sense, than its Swiss rival; and when I just now spoke of its sternness I simply meant that everything is relative, and that an Alp, even with an Italian exposure, has a different sort of charm from a pretty woman. But Alpine grandeur, as you look at it from Monte Generoso, is suffused with a wonderful

softness and sweetness, and the Italian atmosphere
tones down the view, as it takes the edge from any
importunate freshness in the breeze. Views and breezes
at Monte Generoso are the sum of one's entertainment,
and all are admirable in their kind. You behold almost
every mountain of notable importance in Switzerland
(exclusive of the Mont Blanc range), and see it melting
away in such enchanting confusions of aerial blue that
you take it at first for some fantastic formation of mist
and cloud. Betimes in the morning, before the clouds
gather, Monte Rosa is queen of the prospect — rising
white and serene above her blue zone of warm haze,
like some Venus of divine stature emerging from the
sunny sea. Monte Generoso is an ideal place for taking
a holiday that has been well earned, and that finds you
tired and languid enough to appreciate an unlimited
opportunity to lie on shady slopes and listen to cow-
bells and watch the bees thumping into the cups of
flowers, which look tall as you see them against the sky.
Shade is scarce, as on all mountain-tops ; but there are
grassy hollows and screens of rock, and the shadows
grow with the afternoon, and, as you lounge there, too
contented to rise, creep across the nestling valleys, in
which white villages have been glittering, and cover the
long slopes. Even in the sun you may be fairly comfortable, with the assistance of your umbrella and of
the agreeable lightness of the air. I noted this during
an afternoon which I spent lying at my length, with a
book, on the grassy apex of the mountain. It is rather
a dizzy perch. You must mind your steps, and if you
are subject to the baleful fascination of precipices you

will lie down for your nerves' sake. Everything around
me was so vast and silent and sublime that it took all
meaning from the clever prose with which I had provided myself; so that I closed the volume and gave
myself up to the perusal of the fine wrinkles on the
azure brow of the Lake of Lugano, ever so far beneath
me. It is hard to break the spell of silence and sublimity on such a spot by picking yourself up and jolting
back to the hotel. You have been lifted deliciously
out of the world, and the hotel seems the first stage
of a melancholy return to it. This, indeed, is the mood
that soon begins to govern your general attitude at
Monte Generoso, among the breezes, the wild-flowers,
and the cattle-bells. At first you feel exiled and cabined
and confined. You are in ill-humor with the dimensions of your room, with the bad smells on the staircase,
with the infrequency of the post and the frequency of
the Church of England service in the parlor, where you
have left the second volume of your Tauchnitz novel.
But at the end of two or three days you find a charm
in the very simplification of your life, and wish devoutly
that the post came but half as often. You desire to
know as little as possible about the horrible things that
are taking place in the world, four thousand feet below
you, and to steep yourself indefinitely in your bath of
idleness and sunny coolness and piny smells. If you
come away, as I did, after a short stay, it will probably
be in self-defence. If you have work to do, it is, of
course, bad policy to lapse into languid scepticism as
to the existence of the powers to whom you are ac-
countable for it.

15 *

II.

ONCE the charm broken, it seemed simpler and more sternly practical to leave Italy altogether, and to this end I found myself sailing in profound regretfulness along the Lake of Como. It was not for the first time, and I don't know that I made any very novel observations. The hotel at Cadennabbia looked more than ever like an artful palace at the back of the stage at the opera, and the boatmen and porters, in their crimson sashes, like robust choristers before the foot-lights. Bellagio, opposite, propounded with its usual force the query as to why a tourist in the full possession of his reason should remain there an hour, when it costs him but a franc or two to be rowed across to Cadennabbia. Apparently the race of irrational tourists is large; for the pretty villas at Bellagio are, one and all, being turned into inns. The afternoon waned and the violet lights on the mountains slowly cooled down into grays; the passengers, group by group, descended into the picturesque old hooded scows which row out from the villages to meet the little steamer; the evening came on, warm as the day; and at last I disembarked at Colico and waited for the lading of the Splügen diligence. Colico is a very raw little village, and I could have fancied myself for half an hour in some lakeside settlement of our Western world. I sat on a pile of logs by the roadside, opposite to a tavern with an unattractive bar, amid a circle of contemplative village loafers. The road was deep in dust, there was no gendarme within sight, and every one seemed about equally commissioned to "heave" the trunks and put in the horses. It was a good human, genial last impression of ancient Italy.

I shall not undertake to describe the journey across the Splügen Pass, as I enjoyed it in the banquette of the coach. With this portion of my route I was also already acquainted — intimately and in detail, as a pedestrian learns to be. My attention, indeed, during no small part of the time, was absorbed in wonderment at my ever having found it sport to do so laboriously what I was now doing so luxuriously. For my position ceased to be luxurious only when the fantastic crags above the close, dusky valleys had enticed the innocent young moon to peep below their sinister battlements and we began to climb, with a long, steady pull, into keener air. Then it became uncomfortably cold, and the temperature was not more tolerable that I sat self-convicted of a want of imagination for having declined, at fervid Colico, to equip myself with various incongruous draperies. But in the middle of June the nights are short, and while still in the very small hours and well below the top of the Pass I was treated to the spectacle of an Alpine morning twilight. It was prodigiously fine; but the poor coffee at the village of Splügen seemed to me finer still, in virtue of being tolerably hot. By the time we entered the Via Mala, however, the sun had climbed high, and I was able to do easy justice to the grandeur of things. They are certainly very grand indeed in the Via Mala, and there could not be a finer specimen of the regular "romantic scenery" of song and story. The crags tower above your head and the gorge plunges beneath your feet

as wildly and strangely as if the genius of Doré had
given them the finishing strokes. At moments you
have the perfect extravagance of the sublime ; the top
of the ravine becomes a rugged vault, streaked crookedly
with a little thread of blue, and the bottom a kind of
longitudinal caldron, in which, through a deep, black
fissure, you discover a terrific boiling of waters. All
this grandeur gathers itself up at last on each side of a
mighty portal of forest-crowned cliffs and forms a frame
for the picture of a long green valley, at the entrance
of which lies charming Thusis, upon soft slopes, among
orchards and cornfields. You rattle out into the hard
light, the cold coloring, the angular mountain forms of
veritable Switzerland.

The terminus of the Splügen road is the curious
little town of Chur, the ancient capital of the Grisons,
which is perhaps known to the general English reader
chiefly as the place in which Thackeray found the text
of the first of his Roundabout Papers — " On a Lazy,
Idle Boy." This young désœuvré was hanging over the
railing of the bridge, reading a tattered volume, which
Thackeray fondly conceives to be the " Three Musketeers " — starting from this facile postulate to deliver a
charming puff of the novelist's trade. I did not see
the boy ; but I saw the bridge and the admirable little
mountain river which it spans, and which washes the
base of the excellent Steinbock inn and forms a magnificent moat to the ancient circumference of the city.
At the end of the bridge is an old tower and archway,
under which you pass into a labyrinth of clean little
quiet streets, lined with houses whose doorways are

capped with an armorial shield with an ancient date, and
darkened by the overhanging tops of the gloomy pine-
clad hills. These lead you to another gray tower and another straddling tunnel, through which you emerge into
the Hof — the old ecclesiastical precinct of Chur. Here,
on a little scrubbed and soundless square, flanked on
one side by an old yellow episcopal palace, adorned with
those rococo mouldings in white stucco which flourished
late in the seventeenth century, rises one of the most
venerable churches in Europe. The cathedral of Chur,
however, has nothing in its favor but its thirteen centuries of duration and its little museum in the sacristy
of queer ecclesiastical bric-a-brac. It is neither spacious
nor elegant in an architectural way, and there is something almost pitiful in its awkward attempts at internal
bedizenment. You seem to see an old woman of ninety
pomaded and painted and overladen with false jewelry.
The adornments at Chur are both very florid and very
frugal; and, if there is pity in the matter, it should be
for the story they tell of the immemorial impecuniosity
of the toiling and trudging Swiss people. The old
prince-bishops of Chur were persons of much consequence, and the province of the Grisons one of the
largest and most powerful in Switzerland; but the cathedral chapter evidently never had the funds for doing
things handsomely. Late in the sixteenth century, indeed, it treated itself to a goodly work of art in the
shape of a large altar-piece in carved wood, painted
and gilded with extraordinary verisimilitude, representing the Nativity and the Magi; but the church has
the air of never having fairly recovered from the effect

of this sumptuous purchase.   It yields, however, a substantial interest in the way of glory; for, although the
work belongs to a rather charmless department of art,
it has remarkable merit.   The figures are almost uncomfortably lifelike, and one of the kings, with a knowing black eye and a singularly clever short beard, is,
I am sure, quite capable of speaking (and saying something very disagreeable) to a person of a fanciful turn
of mind who should happen to be alone in the church
at twilight.   I suppose the church has a fund of poten-
tial wealth in its rich collection of archaic brasses and
parchments.   Here is a multitude of strange crosses
and croziers and candlesticks and reliquaries, dating
from the infancy of Christian art, and which seem
somehow more intensely old and more penetrated with
the melancholy of history for having played their part
for so many centuries amid the remoteness and stillness of the steep pine forests which hang across the
windows as a dark outer curtain.   The great treasure
is a series of documents of the early Carlovingian kings
— grants of dominion to old bishops strong enough to
ask and get; and the gem of this collection is a crum-
pled shred of parchment, covered with characters slowly
and painfully formed, yet shapely and stately in their
general aspect, which is neither more nor less than a
portion of a deed of Charlemagne himself.   He is such
a shadowy and legendary monarch that this venerable
tattler reminded me of the stories told by "spiritual-
ists," in which the apparition, on retiring, deposits on
the table a flower or a ribbon, a photograph or a visit-
ing-card.

The last of the picturesque memories of my journey is that of a morning spent at Basel among the works of the great Hans Holbein. With the exception of a glance at the spacious red sandstone cathedral (cold, naked, and Lutheran within), and another at the broad yellow Rhine which sweeps beneath the windows of the hotel, this in the only æsthetic diversion to be found at Basel, the most prosaic and prosperous of all the Swiss cities. It is probably the only place in Switzerland which is wholly without pretensions to "scenery"; but no other place, on the other hand, has an art-treasure of the value of the collection of Holbeins. The great portraitist lived for many years at Basel, and the city fell heir in one way and another to a number of his drawings and to several of his pictures. I found it a different sort of art from any that has ever flourished in the lovely land I had left, but a very admirable art in its own way — firm, compact, and comfortable, sure alike of its end and of its means. The Museum of Basel contains many other specimens of the early German school, and to an observer freshly arrived from Italy they have a puzzling and an almost painful interest. Every artist of talent has somewhere lurking in his soul, I suppose, a guiding conception, an ideal of formal beauty, and even Martin Schongauer must have dimly discriminated in his scheme of things portrayable between a greater and a less degree of hideousness. This ruthless caricaturist of humanity, it is to be presumed, has bequeathed to us his most favorable view of things, and he leaves us wondering from what monstrous human types he can have drawn his inspiration.

The heart grows heavy as one reflects what art might
have come to if it had developed exclusively in northern hands. The Italian painters of the great schools
certainly often enough fall short of beauty — miss it,
overlook it, wander erringly to one side of it ; but its
name, at least, is always on their lips and its image
always at their hearts. The early Germans do not
seem to have suspected that such a thing existed, and
the painter's mission, in their eyes, is simply to appro-
priate, ready-made, the infinite variations of grotesqueness which they regard as the necessary environment
of the human lot. Even Holbein, superb genius as he
was, is never directly and essentially beautiful. Beauty,
to his sense, is verity, dignity, opulence, goodliness of
costume and circumstance ; and the thoroughly handsome look of many of his figures resides simply in the
picturesque assemblage of these qualities. Admirably
handsome some of them are ; not the least so the fascinating little drawings in pen and ink and sepia, familiar now half the world over by Messrs. Braun's photographs. Holbein had, at least, an ideal of beauty of
execution, of manipulation, of touch. Anything firmer,
finer, more suggestive of the fascination of what is
vulgarly called "niggling" with brush and.pencil it
would be difficult to conceive. The finest example of
this among the drawings is the artist's delightful portrait of himself. He ought to have believed in handsome forms, for he was himself a very handsome fellow.
Among the paintings all the portraits are admirable,
and two have an extraordinary interest. One is the
famous profile of Erasmus, with his eyes dropped on a

book, and that long, thin, delicate nose, which curves largely over the volume, as if it also were a kind of sympathetic absorbent of science. The other is a portrait of a mysterious young man, in a voluminous black cap, pulled forward over his brow, a searching dark eye, and a nose at once prominent and delicate, like that of Erasmus. Beside him is a tablet with a Latin inscription, and behind him a deep blue sky. The sky is crossed diagonally by the twig of a tree and bordered by a range of snow mountains. The painting is superb, and I call the subject mysterious because he was evidently no ordinary fellow, and the artist tells us of him but half that we would like to know. It was an untimely moment, I may say, in conclusion, for quarrelling with the German genius, for on turning my back upon Martin Schongauer, I went rattling across the Rhine.

HOMBURG REFORMED.

Homburg, July 28, 1873.

I HAVE been finding Homburg a very pleasant place,
but I have been half ashamed to confess it. People assure me on all sides that its glory is sadly dimmed,
and that it can be rightly enjoyed only to the music of
roulette and of clinking napoleons. It is known by
this time, I suppose, even in those virtuously disinterested communities where these lines may circulate, that
the day of roulette in these regions is over, and that in
the matter of rouge-et-noir United Germany has taken
a new departure. The last unhallowed gains at the
green tables were pocketed last summer, and the last
hard losses, doubtless, as imperturbably endured as if
good-natured chance had still a career to run. Chance,
I believe, at Homburg was not amazingly good-natured,
and kept her choicest favors for the bank ; but now
that the reign of Virtue has begun, I have no doubt
there are plenty of irregular characters who think that
she was much the more amiable creature of the two.
What provision has been made for this adventurous
multitude I am at loss to conceive, and how life
strikes people now for whom, at any time these twenty
years, it has been concentrated in the shifting victory

of red or black. Some of them have taken to better
courses, I suppose ; some of them, doubtless, to worse;
but I have a notion that many of them have begun to
wear away the dull remainder of existence in a kind
of melancholy, ghostly hovering around the deserted
Kursaals. I have seen many of these blighted surviv-
ors sitting about under the trees in the Kurgarten, with
the old habit of imperturbability still in their blank,
fixed faces — neat, elderly gentlemen, elderly ladies
not especially venerable, whose natural attitude seems
to be to sit with their elbows on the table and their
eyes on the game. They have all, of course, a pack of
cards in their pockets, and their only consolation must
be to play " patience " forevermore. When I remember, indeed, that I am in legendary Germany, I find it
easy to believe that in these mild summer nights, when
the stupid people who get up at six o'clock to drink the
waters are safely in bed, they assemble in some far-
away corner of the park, and make a green table of
the moonlit grass. Twice a week the old gaming-rooms
at the Kursaal are thrown open, the chandeliers are
lighted, and people go and stare at the painting and
gilding. There is an immense deal of it, all in the
elaborate rococo style in which French decorators of
late years have become so proficient, and which makes
an apartment look half like a throne-room and half like
a café ; but when you have walked about and looked
at the undressed nymphs on the ceilings and the listless crowd in the great mirrors, you have nothing to
do but to walk out again. The clever sumptuosity of
the rooms makes virtue look rather foolish and dingy,

and classes the famous M. Blanc, in the regard of pleasure-loving people, with the late Emperor of the French
and other potentates more sinned against than sinning
— martyred benefactors to that large portion of the
human race who would fain consider the whole world as
a watering-place. It is certainly hard to see what thrifty
use the old gaming-rooms can be put to ; they must
stand there always in their gorgeous emptiness, like
the painted tomb-chambers of Eastern monarchs.

There was certainly fair entertainment in watching
the play — and in playing, according to circumstances;
but even in the old days I think I should have got my
chief pleasure at the Kursaal in a spectacle which has
survived the fall of M. Blanc. As you pass in the
front door, you look straight across the breadth of the
building through another great door which opens on
the gardens. The Kursaal stands on an elevation, and
the ground plunges away behind it with a great stretch,
which spreads itself in a charming park. Beyond the
park it rises again into the gentle slopes of the Taunus
mountains, and makes a high wooded horizon. This
picture of the green hollow and the blue ridge greets
you as you come in, framed by the opposite doorway,
and I have sometimes wondered whether in the gaming
days an occasional novice with a tender conscience, on
his way to the tables, may not have seemed to see in it
the pleading face of that mild economist, Mother Nature herself. It is, doubtless, thinking too fancifully
of human nature to believe that a youth with a napo-
leon to stake, and the consciousness of no more rigid
maternal presence than this, should especially heed the

suggestion that it would be better far to take a walk in the woods. The truth is, I imagine, that nature has no absolute voice, and that she speaks to us very much according to our moods. The view from the terrace at the Kursaal has often had confusion pronounced upon it by players with empty pockets, and has been sentimentally enjoyed by players with a run of luck. We have the advantage now, at least, of finding it always the same, and always extremely pretty. Homburg, indeed, is altogether a very pretty place, and its prettiness is of that pleasing sort which steals gradually on the attention. It is one of nature's own watering-places, and has no need, like so many of the audacious sisterhood, to bully you by force of fashion into thinking it tolerable.

Your half-hour's run from Frankfort across a great sunny expanse of cornfields and crab-apple trees is indeed not particularly charming ; but the sight of the town as you approach it, with its deep-red roofs rising out of thick shade at the base of its blue hills, is a pledge of salubrious repose. Homburg stands on a gentle spur of the highest of these hills, and one of its prettiest features is your seeing the line of level plain across the foot of its long sloping main street and the line of wooded mountain across the top. The main street, which is almost all of Homburg proper, has the look of busy idleness which belongs to watering-places. There are people strolling along and looking into the shop-windows who seem to be on the point of buying something for the sake of something to do. The shops deal chiefly in the lighter luxuries, and the young ladies

who wait in them wear a great many ribbons and a
great deal of hair. All the houses take lodgers, and
every second one is a hotel, and every now and then
you hear them chanting defiance at each other to the
sound of the dinner-bell. In the middle of the street
is the long red stuccoed façade of the Kursaal — the
beating heart of the Homburg world, as one might have
called it formerly. Its heart beats much slower now,
but whatever social entertainment you may still find at
Homburg you must look for there. People assemble
there in very goodly crowds, if only to talk about the
dreadful dulness, and to commiserate each other for not
having been here before. The place is kept up by a
tax, promptly levied on all arriving strangers, and it
seems to be prosperously enough maintained. It gives
you a reading-room where you may go and practise
indifference as you see a sturdy Briton settling down
heavily over your coveted "Times," just as you might of
old when you saw the croupier raking in your stakes;
music by a very fair band twice a day; a theatre, a
café, a restaurant and a table-d'hôte, and a garden illuminated every three or four evenings in the Vauxhall
manner. People differ very much as to the satisfaction
they take in sitting about under flaring gas-lamps and
watching other people march up and down and pass
and repass them by the hour. The pastime, pushed to
extremes, tends, to my own thinking, to breed misan-
thropy — or an extra relish at least for a good book
in one's own room and the path through the woods
where one is least likely to meet any one. But if
you use the Kursaal sparingly, and reserve it for an

hour or two in the evening, it is certainly amusing enough.

·I should be very sorry to underestimate the entertainment to be found in observing the comings and goings of a multifarious European crowd, or the number of suggestions and conclusions which, with a desultory logic of its own, the process contributes to one's philosophy of life. Every one who prefers to sit in a chair and look rather than walk up and down and be looked at, may be assumed to possess this intellectual treasure. The observations of the "cultivated American" bear chiefly, I think, upon the great topic of national idiosyncrasies. He is apt to have a keener sense of them than Europeans; it matters more to his imagination that his neighbor is English, French, or German. He often seems to me to be a creature wandering aloof, but half naturalized himself. His neighbors are outlined, defined, imprisoned, if you will, by their respective national moulds, pleasing or otherwise; but his own type has not hardened yet into the old-world bronze. Superficially, no people carry more signs and tokens of what they are than Americans. I recognize them, as they advance, by the whole length of the promenade. The signs, however, are all of the negative kind, and seem to assure you, first of all, that the individual belongs to a country in which the social atmosphere, like the material, is extremely thin. American women, for the most part, in compliance with an instinct certainly not ungraceful, fill out the ideal mould with wonderful Paris dresses; but their dresses do little toward completing them, characterizing them, shelving and labelling them socially. The usual English lady, marching heavily about under the weight of her ingenious bad taste, has indescribably more the air of what one may call a social factor — the air of social responsibility, of having a part to play and a battle to fight. Sometimes, when the battle has been hard, the lady's face is very grim and unlovely, and I prefer the listless, rustling personality of my countrywomen ; at others, when the cause has been graceful and the victory easy, she has a robust amenity which is one of the most agreeable things in the world. But these are metaphysical depths, though in strictness they ought not to be out of the way as one sits among German pipes and beer. The smokers and drinkers are the solid element at the Kursaal — the dominant tone is the German tone. It comes home very forcibly to the sense of our observant American, and it pervades, naturally enough, all his impressions of Homburg. People have come to feel strongly within the last four years that they must take the German tone into account, and they will find nothing here to lighten the task. If you have not been used to it, if you don't particularly relish it, you doubtless deserve some sympathy ; but I advise you not to shirk it, to face it frankly as a superior critic should, and to call if necessary for a pipe and beer also, and build yourself into good-humor with it. It is very agreeable, in an unfamiliar country, to collect travellers' evidence on local manners and national character. You are sure to have some vague impressions to be confirmed, some ingenious theory to be illustrated, some favorite prejudice in any case to be revised and improved. Even if your opportunities for observation are of the commonest kind, you find them serving your purpose. The smallest things become significant and eloquent and demand a place in your note-book. I have learned no especial German secrets, I have penetrated into the bosom of no German families; but somehow I have received — I constantly receive — a weighty impression of Germany. It keeps me company as I walk in the woods and fields, and sits beside me — not precisely as a black care, but with an influence, as it were, which reminds one of the after-taste of those articles of diet which you eat because they are good for you and not because you like them — when at last, of an evening, I have found the end of a bench on the promenade behind the Kursaal. One's impression of Germany may or may not be agreeable, but there is very little doubt that it is what one may call highly nutritive. In detail, it would take long to say what it consists of. I think that, in general, in such matters attentive observation confirms the common fame, and that you are very likely to find a people on your travels what you found them described to be under the mysterious woodcut in some Peter Parley task-book or play-book of your childhood. The French are a light, pleasure-loving people; ten years of the Boulevards brings no essential amendment to the phrase. The Germans are heavy and fair-haired, deep drinkers and strong thinkers; a fortnight at Homburg does n't reverse the formula. The only thing to be said is that, as you grow older, French lightness and German weightiness become more complex ideas. A few weeks ago I left Italy in that really demoralized condition into which Italy

16

throws those confiding spirits who give her unlimited
leave to please them. Beauty, I had come to believe,
was an exclusively Italian possession, the human face
was not worth looking at unless redeemed by an Italian
smile, nor the human voice worth listening to unless
attuned to Italian vowels. A landscape was no landscape without vines festooned to fig-trees swaying in a
hot wind — a mountain a hideous excrescence unless
melting off into a Tuscan haze. But now that I have
absolutely exchanged vines and figs for corn and cabbages, and violet Apennines for the homely plain of
Frankfort, and liquids for gutturals, and the Italian
smile for the German grin, I am much better contented
than I could have ventured to expect. I have shifted
my standard of beauty, but it still commands a glimpse
of the divine idea.

There is something here, too, which pleases, suggests,
and satisfies. Sitting of an evening in the Kurgarten,
within ear-shot of the music, you have an almost inspiring feeling that you never have in Italy — a feeling
that the substantial influences about you are an element
of the mysterious future. They are of that varied order
which seems to indicate the large needs of large natures.
From its pavilion among the trees ring out the notes
of the loud orchestra, playing Mozart, Beethoven, and
Weber — such music as no other people has composed,
as no other people can play it. Round about in close
groups sit the sturdy, prosperous natives, with their
capacious heads, their stout necks, their deep voices,
their cigars, their beer, their intelligent applause, their
talk on all things — largely enjoying, and yet strongly

intending. Far away in the mild starlight stretch
the dusky woods whose gentle murmur, we may suppose, unfolds here and there to a fanciful German ear
some prophetic legend of a still larger success and a
still richer Fatherland. The success of the Fatherland
one sees reflected more or less vividly in all true German
faces, and the relation between the face and the success
seems demonstrated by a logic so unerring as to make
envy vain. It is not the German success I envy, but
the powerful German temperament and the comprehen-
sive German brain. With these advantages one need n't
be restless; one can afford to give a good deal of time to
sitting out under the trees over pipes and beer and discussion tinged with metaphysics. But success of course
is most forcibly embodied in the soldiers and officers
who now form so large a proportion of every German
group. You see them at all times lounging soberly
about the gardens; you look at them (I do, at least)
with a great deal of impartial deference, and you find in
them something which seems a sort of pre-established
negation of an adversary's chances. Compared with
the shabby little unripe conscripts of France and Italy,
they are indeed a solid, brilliant phalanx. They are
generally of excellent stature, and they have faces in
which the look of education has not spoiled the look of
good-natured simplicity. They are all equipped in brand-
new uniforms, and in these warm days they stroll about
in spotless white trousers. Many of them wear their
fine blond beards, and they all look like perfect soldiers
and excellent fellows. It does n't do, of course, for an
officer to seem too much like a good fellow, and the

young captains and adjutants who ornament the Kurgarten of an evening seldom err in this direction. But
they are business-like warriors to a man, and in their
dark blue uniforms and crimson facings, with their
swords depending from their unbelted waists through a
hole in their plain surtouts, they seem to suggest that
war is somehow a better economy than peace.

But with all this, I am giving you Hamlet with
Hamlet himself omitted. Though the gaming is
stopped, the wells have not dried up, and people still
drink them, and find them very good. They are indeed
a very palatable dose, and " medical advice " at Homburg flatters one's egotism so unblushingly as rather to
try the faith of people addicted to the old-fashioned
confusion between the beneficial and the disagreeable.
You have indeed to get up at half past six o'clock —
but of a fine summer morning this is no great hardship
— and you are rewarded on your arrival at the spring
by triumphant strains of music. There is an orchestra
perched hard by, which plays operatic selections while
you pace the shady walks and wait for your second
glass. All the Homburg world is there ; it's the fashionable hour ; and at first I paid the antique prejudice just mentioned the tribute of thinking it was all
too frivolous to be salutary. There are half a dozen
springs, scattered through a charming wooded park,
where you may find innumerable shady strolls and
rustic benches in bosky nooks, where it is pleasant to
lounge with a good light book. In the afternoon I
drink at a spring with whose luxurious prettiness I still
find it hard to associate a doctor's prescription. It

reminds me of a back-scene at the theatre, and I feel as
if I were drinking some fictitious draught prepared by
the property-man ; or rather, being a little white temple rising on slim columns among still green shades, it
reminds me of some spot in the antique world where
the goddess Hygeia was worshipped by thirsty pilgrims ;
and I am disappointed to find that the respectable
young woman who dips my glass is not a ministering
nymph in a tunic and sandals. Beyond this valley of
healing waters lie the great woods of fir and birch and
beech and oak which cover the soft slopes of the Taunus. They are full of pleasant paths and of the frequent benches which testify to the German love of sitting in the open air. I don't know why it is—because,
perhaps, we have all read so many Teutonic legends
and ballads — but it seems natural in Germany to be
in a wood. One need have no very rare culture, indeed,
to find a vague old-friendliness in every feature of the
landscape. The villages with their peaked roofs, covered with red scalloped shingles, and the brown beams
making figures on the plastered cottage walls, the grape-
vine on the wall, the swallows in the eaves, the Haus-
frau, sickle in hand, with her yellow hair in a top-knot
and her short blue skirt showing her black stockings
— what is it all but a background to one of Richter's
charming woodcuts ? I never see a flock of geese on
the roadside, and a little tow-pated maiden driving them
with a forked switch, without thinking of Grimm's
household tales. I look around for the old crone who
is to come and inform her she is a king's daughter. I
see nothing but the white Kaiserliche Deutsche sign-

post, telling one that this is such and such a district of the Landwehr. But with such easy magic as this I am perhaps right in not especially regretting that the late enchantress of the Kursaal should have been handed over to the police.

DARMSTADT.

Darmstadt, September 6, 1873.

SPENDING the summer just past at Homburg, I have been conscious of a sort of gentle chronic irritation of a natural sympathy with the whole race of suppressed, diminished, and mutilated sovereigns. This was fostered by my frequent visits to the great dispeopled Schloss, about whose huge and awkward bulk the red roofs of the little town, as seen from a distance, cluster with an air of feudal allegiance, and which stands there as a respectable makeweight to the hardly scantier mass of the florid, fresh-colored Kursaal. It was formerly the appointed residence of the Land-grafs of the very diminutive state of Hesse-Homburg, the compact circumference of which these modest poten-tates might have the satisfaction of viewing, any fine morning, without a telescope, from their dressing-room windows. It is something of course to be monarch of a realm which slopes away with the slope of the globe into climates which it requires an effort to believe in and are part of the regular stock of geography; but perhaps we are apt to underestimate the peculiar com-placency of a sovereign to whose possessions the blue horizon makes a liberal margin and shows him his cherished inheritance visibly safe and sound, unclipped, unmenaced, shining like a jewel on its velvet cushion. This modest pleasure the Landgrafs of Hesse-Homburg must have enjoyed in perfection ; the chronicle of their state-progresses should be put upon the same shelf as Xavier de Maistre's "Voyage autour de ma Chambre." Though small, however, this rounded particle of sovereignty was still visible to the naked eye of diplomacy, and Herr von Bismarck, in 1866, swallowed it as smoothly as a gentleman following a tonic régime disposes of his homœopathic pellet. It had been merged shortly before in the neighboring empire of Hesse-Darmstadt, but promptly after Sadowa it was " ceded " to Prussia. Whoever is the loser, it has not been a certain lounging American on hot afternoons. The gates of the Schloss are now wide open, and the great garden is public property, and much resorted to by old gentlemen who dust off the benches with bandannas before sitting down, and by sheepish soldiers with affectionate sweethearts. Picturesquely, the palace is all it should be — very huge, very bare, very ugly, with great clean courts, in which round-barrelled Mecklenburg coach-horses must often have stood waiting for their lord and master to rise from table. The gateways are adorned with hideous sculptures of about 1650, representing wigged warriors on corpulent chargers, corkscrew pilasters, and scroll-work like the " flourishes " of a country writing-master — the whole glazed over with brilliant red paint. In the middle of the larger court stands an immense isolated round tower, painted white, and seen from all the country about. The gardens have very few flowers, and the sound of the rake nowadays is seldom heard on the gravel; but there are plenty of fine trees — some really stupendous poplars, untrimmed and spreading abroad like oaks, chestnuts which would make a figure in Italy, beeches which would be called "rather good" in England; plenty of nooks and bowers and densely woven arcades, triumphs of old-fashioned gardenry; and a large dull-bosomed pond into which the unadorned castle-walls peep from above the trees. Such as it is, it is a place a small prince had rather keep than lose; and as I sat under the beeches — remembering that I was in the fatherland of ghost-stories — I used to fancy the warm twilight was pervaded by a thin spectral influence from this slender stream of empire, and that I could hear vague supernatural *Achs!* of regret among the bushes, and see the glimmer of broad-faced phantoms at the windows. One very hot Sunday the Emperor came, passed up the main street under several yards of red and white calico, and spent a couple of days at the Schloss. I don't know whether he saw any reproach-ful ghosts there, but he found, I believe, a rather scanty flesh-and-blood welcome in the town. The burgomas-ters measured off the proper number of festoons, and the innkeepers hung out their flags, but the townsfolk, who know their new master chiefly as the grim old wizard who has dried up the golden stream which used to flow so bounteously at the Kursaal, took an outing indeed, like good Germans, and stared sturdily at the show, but paid nothing for it in the way of hurrahs. The Emperor, meanwhile, rattled up and down the

street in his light barouche, wearing under his white
eyebrows and mustache the physiognomy of a personage quite competent to dispense with the approbation
of ghosts and shopkeepers. "Homburg may have
ceased to be Hessian, but evidently it is not yet Prus-
sian," I said to a friend; and he hereupon reminded me
that I was within a short distance of a more eloquent
memento of the energy of Bismarck, and that I had
better come over and take a look at the blighted Duchy
of Darmstadt. I have followed his advice, and have
been strolling about in quest of impressions. It is for
the reader to say whether my impressions were worth
a journey of an hour and a half.

I confess, to begin with, that they form no very terrible tale — that I saw none of the "prominent citizens"
confined in chains, and no particular symptoms of the
ravages of a brutal soldiery. Indeed, as you walk into
the town through the grand, dull, silent street which
leads from the railway station, you seem to perceive
that the *genius loci* has never been frighted, like Othello's
Cyprus, from its propriety. You behold this comfortable spirit embodied in heroic bronze on the top of a
huge red sandstone column, in the shape of the Grand-
Duke Louis the First, who, though a very small poten-
tate, surveys posterity from a most prodigious altitude.
He was a father to his people, and some fifty years ago
he created the *beaux quartiers* of Darmstadt, out of the
midst of which his effigy rises, looking down upon the
Trafalgar Square, the Place de la Concorde, of the lo-
cality. Behind him the fine, dull street pursues its
course and pauses in front of the florid façade of the

Schloss. This entrance into Darmstadt responds exactly to the fanciful tourist's preconceptions, and as soon as I looked up the melancholy vista, my imagination fell to rubbing its hands and to whispering that this indeed was the ghost of a little German court-city — a mouldering Modena or Ferrara of the North. I have never known a little court-city, having, by ill-luck, come v into the world a day too late; but I like to think of them, to visit them in these blank early years of their long historic sleep, and to try and guess what they must be dreaming of. They seem to murmur, as they snore everlastingly, of a very snug little social system — of gossiping whist-parties in wainscoted grand-ducal parlors, of susceptible Aulic Councillors and æsthetic canonesses, of emblazoned commanders-in-chief of five hundred warriors in periwigs, of blond young hussars, all gold-lace and billet-doux, of a miniature world of precedents, jealousies and intrigues, ceremonies and superstitions — an oppressively dull world, doubtless, to your fanciful tourist if he had been condemned to spend a month in it. But Darmstadt, obviously, was not dull to its own sense in the days before Bismarck, and doubtless the pith of its complaint of this terrible man is that he has made it so. All around Duke Louis's huge red pedestal rises a series of sober-faced palaces for the transaction of the affairs of this little empire. Before each of them is a striped red-and-white sentry-box, with a soldier in a spiked helmet mounting guard. These public offices all look highly respectable, but they have an ai o sepulchral stillness. Here and there, doubtless . he noise chambers, is to be heard the scratching of the bureaucratic quill; but I imagine that neither the home nor the foreign affairs of Hesse-Darmstadt require nowadays an army of functionaries, and that if some grizzled old clerk were to give you an account of his avocations, they would bear a family likeness to those of Charles Lamb at the India House. There are half a dozen droshkies drawn up at the base of the monument, with the drivers sitting in the sun and wondering sleepily whether any one of the three persons in sight, up and down the street, will be likely to want a carriage. They wake up as I approach and look at me very hard; but they are phlegmatic German drivers, and they neither hail me with persuasive cries nor project their vehicles forcibly upon me, as would certainly be the case at Modena or Ferrara. But I pass along and ascend the street, and find something that is really very Ferrarese. The grand-ducal Schloss rises in an immense mass out of a great crooked square, which has a very pretty likeness to an Italian piazza. Some of the houses have Gothic gables, and these have thrifty shop-fronts and a general air of paint and varnish; but there is shabbiness enough, and sun, and space, and bad smells, and old women under colored umbrellas selling cabbages and plums, and several persons loafing in a professional manner, and, in the midst of it all, the great moated palace, with soldiers hanging over the parapets of the little bridges, and the inner courts used as a public thoroughfare. On one side, behind the shabby Gothic gables, is huddled that elderly Darmstadt to which Duke Louis affixed the modern mask of which his own effigy is the most eminent feature. A mask of some sort old Darmstadt most certainly needs, and it were well if it might have been one of those glass covers which in Germany are deposited over too savory dishes. The little crooked, gabled streets presume quite too audaciously on uncleanness being an element of the picturesque. The gutters stroll along with their hands in their pockets, as it were, and pause in great pools before crossings and dark archways to embrace their tributary streams, till the odorous murmur of their confluence quite smothers the voice of legend. There is dirtiness and dirtiness. Sometimes, picturesquely, it is very much to the point; But the American traveller in Germany will generally prefer not to enjoy local color in this particular form, for it invariably reminds him of the most sordid, the most squalid prose he knows — the corner-groceries and the region of the docks in his native metropolis.

The Schloss, however, is picturesque without abatement, and it seems to me a great pity there should not. be some such monumental edifice in the middle of every town, to personify the municipal soul, as it were, to itself. If it can be beautiful, so much the better; but the Schloss at Darmstadt is ugly enough, and yet — to the eye — it amply serves its purpose. The two façades toward the square date from the middle of the last century, and are characteristically dreary and solemn, but they hide a great rambling structure of a quainter time: irregular courts, archways boring away into darkness, a queer great yellow bell-tower dating from the sixteenth century, a pile of multitudinous windows, roofs, and chimneys. Seen from the adjacent park, all this masses itself up into the semblance of a fantastic citadel. One rarely finds a citadel with a handsomer moat. The moat at Darmstadt yawns down out of the market-place into a deep verdurous gulf, with sloping banks of turf, on which tame shrubs are planted — mingled with the wild ones lodged in the stout foundations. It forms, indeed, below the level of the street, a charming little belt of grass and flowers. The Schloss possesses, moreover, as it properly should, a gallery of pictures, to which I proceeded to seek admission. I reflected, on my way, that it is of the first importance, picturesquely speaking, that the big building which, as I just intimated, should resume to its own sense the civic individuality of every substantial town, should always have a company of soldiers lounging under its portal and grouped about the guard-room. A green moat, a great archway, a guard-room opening out of its shadow, a couple of pacing sentinels, a group of loafing musketeers, a glimpse on one side of a sunny market-place, on the other of a dusky court — combine the objects as you may, they make a picture; they seem for the moment, as you pass, and pause, and glance, to transport you into legend. Of course the straddling men-at-arms who helped to render me this service were wearers of the spiked helmet. The Grand-Duke of Hesse-Darmstadt still occupies the Schloss, and enjoys a nominal authority. I believe that he holds it, for special reasons, on rather easy terms, but I do not envy the emotions of the grand-ducal breast when he sees a row of these peculiarly uncompromising little head-pieces bristling and twinkling under his windows.

It can hardly be balm to his resentment to know that they sometimes conceal the flaxen pates of his own hereditary Hessians. The spiked helmets, of course, salute rigorously when this very limited monarch passes in and out; but I sometimes think it fortunate, under these circumstances, that the average German countenance has not a turn for ironical expression. The Duke, indeed, in susceptible moods, might take an airing in his own palace without driving abroad at all. There is apparently no end to its corridors and staircases, and I found it a long journey to the picture-gallery. I spent half an hour, to begin with, in the library, waiting till the custodian was at liberty to attend to me. The half-hour, however, was not lost, as I was entertained by a very polite librarian, with a green shade over his eyes, and as I filled my lungs, moreover, with what I was in the humor to call the atmosphere of German science. It was a very warm day, but the windows were tight-closed, in the manner of the country, and had been closed, presumably, since the days of Louis the First. The air was as dry as iron filings; it smelt of old bindings, of the insides of old books; it tasted of dust and snuff. Here and there a Herr Professor, walled in with circumjacent authorities, was burying his nose in a folio; the gray light seemed to add a coating of dust to the tiers of long brown shelves. I came away with a headache, and that exalted esteem for the German brain, as a mere working organ, which invariably ensues upon my observation of the physical conditions of German life. I don't know that I received any very distinct impression from the picture-gallery beyond that of there being such and such a number of acres more of mouldering brush-work in the world. It was a good deal like the library, terribly close, and lined for room after room (it is a long series) with tiers of dusky brown canvases, on which the light of the unwashed windows seemed to turn sallow and joyless. There are a great many fine names on the frames, but they rarely correspond to anything very fine within them, though, indeed, there are several specimens of the early German school which are quite welcome (to my mind) to their assumed "originality." Early or late, German art rarely seems to me a happy adventure. Two or three of the rooms were filled with large examples of the modern German landscape school, before which I lingered, but not for the pleasure of it. I was reflecting that the burden of French philosophy just now is the dogma that the Germans are a race of *faux bonshommes;* that their transcendental æsthetics are a mere kicking up of dust to cover their picking and stealing; and that their frank-souled naïveté is no better than a sharper's "alias." I do not pretend to weigh the charge in a general sense, but I certainly think that a good French patriot, in my place, would have cried out that he had caught the hypocrites in the act. These blooming views of Switzerland and Italy seemed to me the most dishonest things in the world, and I was puzzled to understand how so very innocent an affair as a landscape in oils could be made such a vehicle of offence. These were extremely clever; the art of shuffling away trouble has rarely been brought to greater perfection. It is evidently an

elaborate system; there is a school; the pictures were
all from different hands, and the precious recipe had
been passed round the circle.

But why should I talk of bad pictures, since I
brought away from Darmstadt the memory of one of
the best in the world? It forms the sole art-treasure
of the place, and I duly went in quest of it; but I
kept it in reserve as one keeps the best things, and
meanwhile I strolled in the Herrengarten. The fondness of Germans for a garden, wherever a garden can
be conceived, is one of their most amiable characteris-
tics, and I should be curious to know how large a section of the total soil of the fatherland is laid out in
rusty lawns and gravel-paths, and adorned with beechen
groves and bowers. The garden-hours of one's life, as
I may say, are not the least agreeable, and there are
more garden-hours in German lives than in most others.
But I shall not describe my garden-hours at Darmstadt.
Part of them was spent in walking around the theatre,
which stands close beside the Schloss, with its face
upon the square and its back among the lawns and
bowers. The theatre, in the little court-city of my
regrets, is quite an affair of state, and the manager
second only in importance to the prime-minister or the
commander-in-chief. Or rather the Grand-Duke is
manager himself, and the leading actress, as a matter
of course, his morganatic wife. The present Grand-
Duke of Hesse-Darmstadt, I believe, is a zealous patron
of the drama, and maintains a troupe of comedians,
who doubtless do much to temper the dulness of his
capital. The present theatre is simply a picturesque

ruin, having been lately burned down, for all the world
like an American opera-house. But the actors have
found a provisional refuge, and I have just been presented with the programme of the opening night of the
winter season. I saw the rest of Darmstadt as I took
my way to the palace of Prince Karl. It was a very
quiet pilgrimage, and I perhaps met three people in
the long, dull, proper street through which it led me.
One of them was a sentinel with a spiked helmet
marching before the snug little palace of the Prince
Louis — the gentleman who awhile ago married the
Princess Alice of England. Another was a school-boy
in spectacles, nursing a green bag full of Greek roots, I
suppose, of whom I asked my way ; and the third was
the sturdy little musketeer who was trying to impart a
reflet of authority to the neat little white house occupied by the Prince Karl. But this frowning soldier is
no proper symbol of the kindly custom of the house.
I was admitted unconditionally, ushered into the little
drawing-room, and allowed half an hour's undisturbed
contemplation of the beautiful Holbein — the famous
picture of the Meyer family. The reader interested in
such matters may remember the discussion maintained
two years since, at the time of the general exhibition
of the younger Holbein's works in Dresden, as to the
respective merits — and I believe the presumptive pri-
ority in date — of this Darmstadt picture and the presentation of the same theme which adorns the Dresden
Gallery. I forget how the question was settled —
whether, indeed, it was settled at all, and I have never
seen the Dresden picture ; but it seems to me that if I

were to choose a Holbein, this one would content me. It represents a sort of plainly lovely Virgin holding her child, crowned with a kind of gorgeous episcopal crown, and worshipped by six kneeling figures — the worthy Goodman Meyer, his wife, and their progeniture. It is a wonderfully solid masterpiece, and so full of wholesome human substance that I should think its owner could go about his daily work the better — eat and drink and sleep and perform the various functions of life more largely and smoothly — for having it constantly before his eyes. I was not disappointed, and I may now confess that my errand at Darmstadt had been much more to see the " Holbeinische Gemälde " than to examine the trail of the serpent — the footprints of Bismarck.

IN HOLLAND.

IT would amount to positive impudence, I suppose, to introduce these few impressions of Dutch scenery by an overt allusion to the beauties of the Rhine. And yet it was by the Rhine, a few days since, that I entered Holland; and it was along an arm of the Rhine, subdued to the likeness of a homely Dutch canal, that I wandered this afternoon in drowsy Leyden. As many as thirty years ago, I believe, it was good taste to make an apology for a serious mention, of the descriptive sort, of the vineyards of Bingen or the cloister of Nonnenwerth; and if the theme had been rubbed threadbare then, it can hardly be considered presentable now. But thus much I may boldly affirm, that if my corrupt modern consciousness had not assured me that these were terribly faded charms, I should not have guessed it from the testimony of my eyes. After platitudes, as well as after battles, Nature has a way — all her own — of renewing herself; and in a decent attitude, at the bow of the boat, with my face to Nature and my back to man, I ventured to salute the castled crags as frankly as if I were making a voyage of discovery. The time seems to me to have come round again when one ought really to say a good word for them. I insist upon the merits of no particular member of the crumbling fraternity; there are many worthy men whose pockets it might be awkward to examine; and the Rhenish dungeons, from a more familiar standpoint than the deck of the steamer, may prove to be half buried in beer-bottles and lemon-peel. But they still pass their romantic watchword from echo to echo all along the line, and they "compose" as bravely between the river and the sky as if fifty years of sketching and sonneteering had done nothing to tame them. The fine thing about the Rhine is that it has that which, when applied to architecture and painting, is called style. It is in the grand manner — on the liberal scale; that is, it is on the liberal scale while it lasts. There is less of it, in time, than I had been remembering these fifteen years. The classic sites come and go within an easy four hours; and if you embark at Mayence you leave the last and most perfect of the castled crags — the Drachenfels — behind you just as your organism, physical and mental, is being thoroughly attuned to the supreme felicity of river navigation. It was a grayish day as I passed, and the Drachenfels looked as if it had been stolen from a background of Claude to do service in the Rhenish foreground. It has the ideal, romantic contour.

It stands there, however, like some last ringing word in an interrupted phrase. The vast white river sweeps along into Holland on a level with its banks, finally to die in a slush of marshes and a mesh of canals, within sound of the surge of the North Sea. I left it to its destiny, and gathered my first impressions of Holland from the window of the train. The most pertinent thing one may say of these first impressions is that they are exactly, to the letter, what one expects them to be. If you come this way, as I did, chiefly with an eye to Dutch pictures, your first acquisition is a sense, no longer an amiable inference, but a direct perception, of the undiluted accuracy of Dutch painters. You have seen it all before; it is vexatiously familiar; it was hardly worth while to have come! At Amsterdam, at Leyden, at The Hague, and in the country between them, this is half your state of mind; when you are looking at the originals, you seem to be looking at the copies; and when you are looking at the copies, you seem to be looking at the originals. Is it a canal-side in Haarlem, or is it a Van der Heyden? Is it a priceless Hobbema, or is it a meagre pastoral vista, stretching away from the railway track? The maid-servants in the streets seem to have stepped out of the frame of a Gerard Dow, and appear equally adapted for stepping back again. You have to rub your eyes to ascertain their normal situation. And so you wander about, with art and nature playing so assiduously into each other's hands that your experience of Holland becomes something singularly compact and complete in itself— striking no chords that lead elsewhere, and asking no outside help to unfold itself. This is what we mean when we say, as we do at every turn, that Holland is so *curious*. Italy is not curious, as a general thing, nor is England, in its leading features. They are simply both eminent specimens of a sort of beauty which pervades in a greater or less degree all our conceptions of the beautiful. We admire them because they stand, as it were, in the high-road of admiration, and whether we pass them at a run or at a walk our pace is part of the regular æsthetic business of life. But to enjoy the Low Countries, we have to put on a very particular pair of spectacles and bend our nose well over our task, and, beyond our consciousness that our gains are real gains, remain decidedly at loss how to classify them. This is the charming thing in Holland — the way one feels one's observation lowered to a relish of the harmonies of the minor key; persuaded to respect small things and take note of small differences; so that really a week's sojourn here, if properly used, ought to make one at the worst a more reasonable, and at the best a more kindly, person. The beauty which is no beauty; the ugliness which is not ugliness; the poetry which is prose, and the prose which is poetry; the landscape which seems to be all sky until you have taken particular pains to discover it, and turns out to be half water when you *have* discovered it; the virtues, when they are graceful (like cleanliness), exaggerated to a vice, and when they are sordid (like the getting and keeping of money), refined to a dignity; the mild gray light which produced in Rembrandt the very genius of chiaroscuro; the stretch of whole provinces on the principles of a billiard-table, which produced a school of consummate landscapists; the extraordinary. reversal of custom, in which man seems, with a few windmills and ditches, to do what he will, and Providence, holding the North Sea in the hollow of his hand, what he can — all these elements of the general spectacle in this entertaining country at least give one's regular habits of thought the stimulus of a little confusion, and make one feel that one is dealing with an original genius.

The curious fortunately excludes neither the impressive nor the agreeable; and Amsterdam, where I took my first Dutch walk, is a stately city, even though its street-vistas do look as if they were pictured on a tea-caddy or a hand-screen. They have for the most part a broad, sluggish canal in the middle, on either side of which a row of perfectly salubrious, but extremely attenuated trees grow out of a highly cultivated soil of compact yellow bricks. Cultivated I call it by a proper license, for it is periodically raked by the broom and the scrubbing-brush, and religiously manured with soap-suds. You lose no time, of course, in drawing the inevitable parallel between Amsterdam and Venice, and it is well worth drawing, as an illustration of the uses to which the same materials may be put by different minds. Sky and sea in both cases, with architecture between; winding sea-channels washing the feet of goodly houses erected with the profits of trade. And yet the Dutch city is a complete reversal of the Italian, and its founders might have carefully studied Venetian effects with the set purpose of producing exactly the opposite ones. It produces them in the moral line even more vividly than in the material. It is not that one place is all warm color and the other all cold; one all shimmer and softness and mellow interfusion of every possible phase of ruin, and the other rigidity, angularity, opacity, prosperity, in their very essence; it is more than anything that they tell of such different

lives and of such a different view of life. The outward
expression on one side is perfect poetry, and on the
other is perfect prose; and the marvel is the way in
which thrifty Amsterdam imparts the prosaic turn to
things which in Venice seem the perfect essence of
poetry. Take, for instance, the silence and quiet of the
canals; it has in the two places a difference of quality
which it is almost impossible to express. In the one
it is the stillness of order, and in the other of vacancy
— the sleep of idleness and the sleep of rest; the quiet
that comes of letting everything go by the board, and
the quiet that comes of doing things betimes and being
able to sit with folded hands and say they are well
done. In one of George Eliot's novels there is a portrait of a thrifty farmer's wife who rose so early in the
morning to do her work that by ten o'clock it was all
over, and she was at her wit's end to know what to do
with her day. This good woman seems to me an excellent image of the genius of Amsterdam as it is
reflected in the house-fronts — I penetrated no deeper.
It is impossible to imagine anything more expressive
of the numerous ideas represented by the French epi-
thet *bourgeois* than these straight façades of clean black
brick capped with a rococo gable of stone painted white,
and armed like the forehead of the unicorn with a little horizontal horn — a bracket and pulley for hauling
storable goods into the attic. The famous Dutch
cleanliness seems to me quite on a level with its reputation, and asserts itself in the most ingenious and
ludicrous ways. A rosy serving-maid, redolent of soap-
suds from her white cap to her white sabots, stands

squirting water from a queer little engine of polished copper over the majestic front of a genteel mansion whose complexion is not a visible shade less immaculate than her own. The performance suggests a dozen questions, and you can only answer them all with a laugh. What is she doing, and why is she doing it? Does she imagine the house has a speck or two which it is of consequence to remove, or is the squirt applied merely for purposes of light refreshment — of endearment, as it were? Where could the speck or two possibly have come from, unless produced by spontaneous generation? There are no specks in the road, which is a neat *parquet* of scoured and polished brick; nor on the trees, whose trunks are to all appearance carefully sponged every morning. The speck exists evidently only as a sort of mathematical point, capable of extension, in the good woman's Batavian brain, and the operation with her copper kettle is, as the metaphysicians would say, purely subjective. It is a necessity, not as regards the house, but as regards her own temperament. Of a dozen harmlessly factitious necessities of the same sort, the canal-sides at Amsterdam offer lively evidence. Nothing could be more thoroughly in keeping with the *bourgeois* spirit than the way in which you everywhere find this brilliant cleanliness and ceremonious thrift playing the part, not of a convenience, but of a restriction; not of a means, but of an end. The windows are of those huge plates of glass which offer a delectably uninterrupted field for friction; but they are masked internally by thick white blinds, invariably drawn, and the only use of their transparency to any mortal is to enable the passer-by to examine the texture of the stuff. The front doors are hedged in with little square padlocked barriers, to guard the doorsteps from the pollution of footprints, and the visitor must pocket his pride and apply at an humbler portal with the baker and the milkman. In such houses must dwell people whose nerves are proof against the irritation of minute precautions — people who cover their books with white paper and find occasion for a week's conversation in a mysterious drop of candle-grease on a tablecloth. The traveller with an eye for details will find some eloquence in the fact that, though the canals at Amsterdam and Leyden offer continually this charming pretext of trees by a water-side, there is not in their whole length a single bench for a lounge and a half-hour's æsthetic relish of the situation. The traveller in question though, shrewd fellow, will not be prevented by the absence of benches from getting it, as he looks up and down and sees the wide green barges come floating through the respectable stillness, and the quaint old scroll-work of the gables peep out through the meagre density of the trees.

At The Hague, evidently, people take life in a lighter, more irresponsible fashion. There are two or three benches by the canals and an air of mitigated devotion to compound interest. There are wide, tranquil squares, planted in the middle with shady walks and bordered with fine old abodes of moneyed leisure, where you may boldly ring at the front door. The Hague is in fact a very charming little city, and I should be at a loss to say how much I find it to my taste. It is the

model of a minor capital; small enough for convenience and compact sociability, and yet large enough to
exhibit certain metropolitan airs and graces. It is one
of the cities which please indefinably on a short acquaintance and prompt one's fretful fancy to say that
just *this*, at last, is the place where we could come and
lead the (from the worldly point of view) ideal life. It
hits the happy medium between the bustling and the
stagnant; it is Dutch enough for all sorts of comfortable virtues, and, where these intermit, it is English
and French, and, in its diplomatic character, cosmo-
politan. There must be very pleasant things done
here, and I hope, for symmetry's sake, there are pleasant people to do them worthily. I imagine there are.
But I do wrong to consume valuable space in these
fruitless speculations when I have not yet said a word
on the topic on which I had it chiefly at heart to touch.
A week in Holland is necessarily a week in the company of Rembrandt and Paul Potter, Ruysdael and
Gerard Dow. These admirable artists have had my
best attention, but I do not know that they have given
me any new impressions, or indeed that, in the literal
meaning of the word, they have given me any impressions at all. I looked for a long time, only this
morning, at the hand of Madame van Mieris in the
little picture in the Museum here, by her husband,
representing him and his wife playing with a tiny
spaniel. He is pulling the dog's ear and she is pressing it against her bosom with an arm bare to the elbow.
It seemed to me that it was worth the journey to Holland simply to see this appreciative husband's version

of his wife's hand, and that if I had seen nothing else
I should have been repaid; but beyond producing this
eminently practical reflection, the picture was not suggestive. I find in my guide-book, on the margin of
the page which dilates upon the great Van der Helst
at Amsterdam (the Banquet of the Civic Guard), the
inscription in pencil — *superb, superb, superb !* But
this simply connotes enjoyment and not criticism. Let
me however have the satisfaction of repeating, in ink
for the printer, that the picture *is* superb. To the
great treasure (after Rembrandt's Lesson of Anatomy)
of the Museum here — Paul Potter's famous Bull —
one would willingly pay some more elaborate compliment; not because it is a stronger work (on the contrary), but because it is the work of a lad of twenty-
two. The subject is the most prosaic conceivable, and
the treatment is perfectly in keeping; but if one con-
siders the magnificent success of the enterprise from
the painter's own point of view, there is certainly real
poetry in the fact of his youth. It is hardly less true
of Rembrandt than of his various smaller comrades
(unusual as the judgment may seem), that he is not
an intellectually suggestive painter. There are no
ideas in Ostade and Terburg, in Metzu and Ruysdael
(who, by the way, gives me the largest sum of tranquil
pleasure of any painter of the school); but you bear
them no grudge, for they give you no reason to expect
them. It is one of the regular traditions, however,
that Rembrandt does, and I can only say that in
this case tradition has distinctly missed her way. It
is the more singular that he should not, inasmuch as

(I should go so far as to say) he was really not, strictly speaking, a painter. He was perfectly arbitrary, and he kept on terms with observation only so long as it suited him. This may be verified by reference to any of the most delusively picturesque of his works. They are magnificent; but compare them, for simple verity, with the little Adrian van Ostade in the Van der Hoop collection, and compare them, for thought, with any fine Tintoretto.

IN BELGIUM.

Ostend, August 14, 1874.

BELGIUM, in most itineraries, is visited conjointly with Holland. This is all very well so long as Belgium is visited first; and my advice to travellers who relish a method in their emotions is in this region to reverse the plan which is generally most judicious, and proceed in all confidence from south to north. Passing from the Low Countries into Flanders, you come back into the common world again — into a picturesque phase of it, certainly, and a country rich in architectural and artistic treasures. But you miss that something, individual and exquisite, which forms the charm of Holland, and of which, during the last forty-eight hours of my stay there (it seems a part of the delicacy of all things that one calculates one's stay in the little Dutch garden by hours), my impression became singularly deep. It has become deeper still in retrospect, as such things do, and there are moments when I feel as if in coming away I had wantonly turned my back upon the abode of tranquil happiness. I keep seeing a green canal with a screen of thin-stemmed trees on one side of it, and a foot-path, not

at all sinuous, on the other. Beside the foot-path is
a red-brick wall, superstitiously clean, and if you follow
it a little while you come to a large iron gate flanked
with high posts, with balls on top. Although the
climate is damp, the ancient iron-work of the gate has
not a particle of rust, and its hinges, as you turn it,
are in perfect working order. Beyond it is a garden
planted with tulips of a hundred kinds, and in the
middle of the garden is a pond. Over the pond is
stretched, from edge to edge, a sort of trellis of tense
cord, which at first excites your surprise. In a moment,
however, you perceive the propriety of the pond's being
carefully guarded, for its contents are singularly precious. They consist of an immense number of gigantic
water-lilies, sitting motionless among their emerald
pads, and of a brilliancy and softness which make you
fancy they are modelled in wax; of a thousand little
gold-fishes, of so deep a crimson that they look as if
they were taken out every morning and neatly varnished over with a fine brush; and, lastly, of a majestic
swan, of the purest porcelain. About the swan there
is no doubt; he is of the finest Dutch delf — a substance which at a certain distance looks as well as
flossy feathers, and has the advantage that a creature
composed of it cannot circulate to the detriment of
varnished fishes and waxen lilies. I do not know how
this pond looks on paper, but in nature, if one may call
it nature, it was delicious. There was a skyful of
rolling gray clouds, with two or three little patches of
blue, and over the tulip-beds there played a little cool
breeze, with its edge just blurred by dampness. Under

the trees was just one bench, but it was strictly sufficient.

I must not linger on Dutch benches, however, with all the art-wealth of Flanders awaiting me. I have by no means in fact examined it all, and have had to pay the tourist's usual tribute to reluctant omission. In such cases, if you are travelling *con amore*, the things omitted assume to the mind's eye a kind of mocking perfection, and the dozen successes of your journey seem a small compensation for this fatal failure. There is a certain little hôtel-de-ville at Louvain and a cathedral at Tournay which make a delicious figure in the excellent hand-book of M. Du Pays; but I hasten to declare that I have not seen them, and am well aware that my observations are by so much the less valuable. I first made acquaintance with Belgium, however, through the cathedral of Antwerp, and this is a first-rate introduction. I went into it of a Sunday morning during mass, and immediately perceived that I was in a sturdily Catholic country. The immense edifice was crowded with worshippers, and their manner was much more *receuilli*, as the phrase is, than that of the faithful in Italian churches. This too in spite of the fact that the great Rubenses were unveiled in honor of the day, so that all the world might behold them gratis. To be *receuilli* in the presence of a Rubens seems to me to indicate the real devotional temperament. The crowd, the Rubenses, the atmosphere, and the presence of some hundred or so of dear fellow-tourists was rather hostile to tranquil appreciation, so that at first I saw little in the cathedral of Antwerp

17*

to justify its great reputation. But I came back in the late afternoon, at that time which a wise man will always choose for visiting (finally at least) a great church — the half-hour before it closes. The Rubenses, those monstrous flowers of art, had folded their gorgeous petals; but this I did not regret, as I had been in the interval to the Museum, where there are a dozen more, and I had drifted to a conclusion. The church was empty, or filled only with the faded light and its own immense solemnity. It is very magnificent; not duskily nor mysteriously so, but with a vast, simple harmony which, like all great things, grows and grows as you observe it. Its length is extraordinary, and it has the peculiarity, unique in my observation, of possessing no less than six aisles, besides the nave. Its height is in harmony with these splendid proportions, and it gave me altogether (I do not know the literal measurements) an almost unequalled impression of vastness. Externally, its great tower, of the most florid and flamboyant, the most embroidered and perforated Gothic, is one of the few worthy rivals of the peerless steeple of Strasburg.

The Antwerp Museum is very handsomely housed, and has an air of opulence very striking after the meagre and dusky contrivances in this line of thrifty Holland. But there is logic in both cases. You bend your nose over a Gerard Dow and use a magnifying glass; whereas, the least that can be done by the protectors of Rubens's glory is to give you a room in which you can stand twenty yards from the canvas. I may say directly that even at twenty yards Rubens gave me less pleasure than I had hoped. I say hoped rather than expected, for I was already sufficiently familiar with him to have felt the tendency of my impressions, and yet I had fancied that in the atmosphere in which he wrought, in the city of which he is the *genius loci*, they might be diverted into the channel of sympathy. But they followed their own course, and I can express them only by saying that the painter does not please me. If Rubens does not *please* you, what is left ? — for I find myself utterly unable to perceive in him a trace of that intellectual impressiveness claimed by some of his admirers. I read awhile since a charming book in which an acute French critic, M. Emile Montégut, records his impressions of Belgium and Holland, and this work was partly responsible for my supposition that I should find more in the author of the "Descent from the Cross" collectively, at Antwerp, than I had found in him, individually, at London, Paris, and Florence. M. Montégut, I say, is acute, and the number of things his acuteness finds in Rubens it would take up all my space to recount. According to him, Rubens was not only one of the greatest of mere painters, but he was the greatest genius who ever *thought*, brush in hand. The answer to this seems simple: Rubens, to my sense, absolutely did *not* think. He not only did not think greatly, but he did not think at all. M. Montégut declares that he was a great dramatist superadded to a great painter, and calls upon the people of Antwerp to erect to him in the market-place a colossal monument (the one already standing there will do, it seems to me) and inscribe upon the

pedestal his title to the glory of having carried his art
beyond its traditional limits, and produced effects generally achieved only by the highest dramatic poetry.
If the great painter of rosy brawn had had half his
commentator's *finesse,* he would have been richly en-
dowed. M. Montégut finds, among other things, unutterable meanings in the countenance of the Abys-
sinian king who is looking askance at the Virgin in
the "Adoration" of the Antwerp Museum. I remembered them so well that, in leaving the cathedral, I
hurried to commune with this masterpiece of expressiveness. I recommend him to the reader who may
next pass that way. Let him tell me, from an unbiassed
mind, how many supplementary emotions he finds
reflected in the broad concupiscence of the monarch's
black visage. I was disappointed; dramatists of the
first order are rare, and here was one the less. If
Rubens is anywhere dramatic, in the finer sense of the
term, it is in his masterpiece, the "Descent from the
Cross," of the cathedral; of all his pictures, this one
comes the nearest to being impressive. It is superbly
painted, and on the whole very noble; but it is only
a happier specimen of the artist's habitual manner —
painting by improvisation, not by reflection. Besides
the Rubenses at Antwerp, I have seen several others.
Those at Brussels, unfortunately, with most of their
companions of the Flemish school, have been now some
two years invisible. They are being restored; but one
is curious to see the effect of two years' refreshment
upon the native robustness of most Rubenses. I need
not speak of these various productions in detail; some

are better, some are worse, all are powerful, and all, on the whole, are irritating. They all tell the same story — that the artist had in a magnificent degree the painter's temperament, without having in anything like a proportionate degree the painter's mind. When one, therefore, says that he was perfectly superficial, one indicates a more fatal fault than in applying the same term to many a more delicate genius. What makes Rubens irritating is the fact that he always *might* have been more interesting. Half the conditions are there — vigor, facility, color, the prodigious impulse of genius. Nature has given them all, and he holds the other half in his own hands. But just when the others should appear and give the picture that stamp which draws from us, over and above our relish of the natural gift, a certain fine sympathy with the direction it takes, Rubens uncloses his careless grasp, and drops them utterly out of sight. He never approaches something really fine but to miss it ; he never attempts a really interesting effect but to vulgarize it. Our deepest interest, as to an artist, depends on the way he deliberates and chooses. Everything up to that point may be superb, but we care for him with a certain affection only when we feel him responsibly selecting among a number of possibilities. This sensible, intellectual pulsation often gives a charm to the works of painters to whom nature has been anything but liberal, and the great limitation of Rubens is that in him one never perceives it. He takes what comes, and if it happens to be really pictorial, he has a singular faculty of suggesting that there is no merit in his having taken it. He never waits to choose; he never pauses to deliberate; and one may say, vulgarly, he throws away his oranges when he has given them but a single squeeze. The foolish fellow does not know how sweet they are! One ends, in a manner, by disliking his real gifts. A little less facility, we call out, a shade or so less color, a figure or so the fewer tossed in, a bosom or two less glowingly touched; only something once in a while to arrest us with the thought that it has arrested you!

Almost as noteworthy as anything else in the Antwerp Museum is the title of a picture by Titian, of average Titianesque merit. It is worth transcribing for its bizarre conflict of suggestions: "John, Bastard of Sforza, Lord of Pesaro, husband, by her first marriage, of Lucretia Borgia, and then Bishop of Paphos and Admiral of the Pontifical Galleys, is presented to St. Peter by the Pope Alexander VI." Add to this that St. Peter is seated upon a fragment of antique sculpture, surrounded by a frieze representing a pagan sacrifice! Even that harshly sincere genius, Quentin Matsys, who shines hard by in a brilliantly pure piece of coloring, can hardly persuade us that we are in simple Flanders, and not in complex Italy.

It often happens in travelling that places turn out to be less curious that we had supposed, but it is a comparatively rare fortune to find them more so. And yet this was my luck with Brussels, a city of which my imagination had made so light that it hung by a hair whether I should go there or not. It is generally spoken of by its admirers as a miniature Paris, and I always viewed it with that contempt with which a properly regulated mind regards those shabby, pirated editions of the successful French books of the day which are put forth in Belgium. These ill-conditioned little volumes are miniature Victor Hugos and Michelets. But Brussels should ask to be delivered from its friends. It is not a miniature anything, but a very solid and extensive old city, with a physiognomy and character quite its own. It is very much less elegant than the Paris of the last twenty years; but it is decidedly more picturesque. Paris has nothing to compare for quaintness of interest with the Brussels Hôtel de Ville, and the queer old carved and many-windowed houses which surround the square. The Hôtel de Ville is magnificent, and its beautiful Gothic belfry gives, in quite another line, an equal companion in one's memory to the soaring campanile of the palace of the Signoria at Florence. Few cities have a cathedral in so impressive a position as St. Gudule — on a steep hill-top, with a long flight of steps at the base of its towers; and few cities, either, have so charming a public garden as the Parc. There is something peculiarly picturesque in that high-in-the-air look of the Parc as you glance from end to end of its long alleys, and see the sky beneath the arch of the immense trees meeting the bend of the path. All this part of Brussels, and the wide, windy Place Royale, handsome as the handsome was understood fifty years ago, has an extreme brightness and gayety of aspect which is yet quite distinct from the made-to-order brilliancy of the finest parts of renovated Paris. The Brussels Museum of pictures is admirably arranged ; but, unfortunately, as I have said, only half of it is now accessible. This, however, contains some gems of the Dutch school — among them a picture by Steen, representing a lad coming into a room to present a fish to a ruddy virago who sits leering at him. The young man, for reasons best known to himself, is sticking out his tongue, and these reasons, according to M. Montégut, are so numerous and recondite that I should like the downright old caricaturist himself to have heard a few of them. I wonder where *his* tongue would have gone.

Ghent I found to be an enormous, empty city, with an old Flemish gable-end peeping here and there from its rows of dull, white houses, and various tall and battered old church-towers looking down over deserted, sunny squares. In the middle of all this, in the stately church of St. Bavon, is the great local treasure, the " Adoration of the Lamb," by the brothers Van Eyck. This is not only one of the pictures of Ghent, but one of the pictures of the world. It represents a large daisied meadow shut in with a great flowering tangle of hedges, out of which emerge various saints of either sex, carrying crowns and palms. In front are two other groups of apostles and prophets, all kneeling and worshipping. In the centre is an altar, surmounted with the fleecy symbol of the Word, and surrounded with a ring of adoring angels. Behind is a high horizon of blue mountains, and the silhouettes of three separate fantastic cities, all apparently composed of church-towers. The picture is too perfect for praise ;

the coloring seems not only not to have lost, but actually to have been intensified and purified, by time. One may say the same of the precious Memlings at Bruges — and this is all I can say of that drowsy little city of grassy streets and colossal belfries and sluggish canals and mediæval memories.

THE END.

Cambridge : Electrotyped and Printed by Welch, Bigelow, & Co.

Milton Keynes UK
Ingram Content Group UK Ltd.
UKHW040925180224
437992UK00003B/64